The Well-known Troublemaker

THE WELL-KNOWN TROUBLEMAKER

TROUBLEMAKER

A Life of Charlotte Charke

FIDELIS MORGAN

WITH

CHARLOTTE CHARKE

faber and faber

LONDON · BOSTON

by the same author
A Woman of No Character

First published in 1988
by Faber and Faber Limited
3 Queen Square London WC1N 3AU

Typeset by Goodfellow & Egan Ltd, Cambridge
Printed in Great Britain by
Mackays of Chatham PLC, Chatham, Kent

Morgan, Fidelis, 1952–
The well-known troublemaker, Charlotte Charke.
1. Great Britain. Theatre. Acting. Charke.
Charlotte. Biographies
I. Title
792'.028'0924

ISBN 0–571–14743–7

FRONTISPIECE

Charlotte Charke in one of two surviving prints made of her during
her lifetime. (The other one, done in 1755 to coincide with
publication of her autobiography, shows her as a young child
dressed in her father's clothes, and appears on the jacket.)

Charlotte appears in a dress, carrying a fan, and bears no
resemblance to the swaggering, debauched transvestite drawn by
historians of all future generations.

'Finally, the promoter was the well-known troublemaker, Charlotte Charke.'

Arthur H. Scouten, *The London Stage 1729–47*

To my sisters
Marlena and Petrina

Contents

List of illustrations

Frontispiece: Charlotte Charke

Following page 221

Acknowledgements

I would like to thank: Jim Fowler of the Theatre Museum; Ms D. Dyer of Avon County Reference Library; John Rich of Crockerne Pill and District History Society; Mrs J. Voyce of Gloucester County Library; Mr Samways of Greater London Record Office; Peter Walne of Hertfordshire County Record Office; D.J.H. Smith of Gloucestershire County Council; G.L. Lloyd; the Mander and Mitcheson Collection; Delwyn Tibbott of Gwent County Record Office; David Richards of London Borough of Camden; Wiltshire Record Office; London Borough of Richmond; London Borough of Westminster; Eve Johannsen of the British Newspaper Library; Charles Kidd of *Debrett's*; the Guildhall Library; the Public Record Office; Liverpool University Library; Jill Spurrier; Frances Coady; Paddy Lyons; Renos Liondarus; Celia Imrie; and especially Laurance Rudic.

THE CIBBER FAMILY TREE

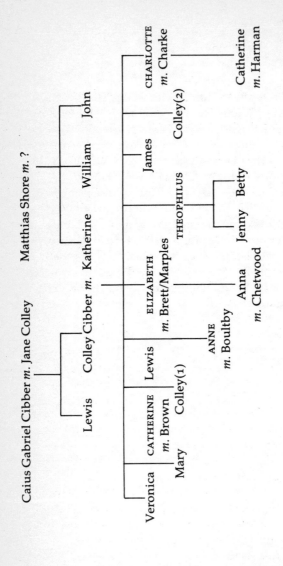

Caius Gabriel Cibber *m.* Jane Colley   Matthias Shore *m.* ?

Lewis   Colley Cibber *m.* Katherine   William   John

Veronica   Mary   CATHERINE *m.* Brown   Lewis   ELIZABETH *m.* Brett/Marples   THEOPHILUS   James   CHARLOTTE *m.* Charke

Colley(1)   ANNE *m.* Boultby   Anna *m.* Chetwood   Jenny   Betty   Colley(2)   Catherine *m.* Harman

Preface

Just as Mrs Charke breaks with tradition and places the summary of her *Narrative* at the end rather than the beginning of her book, so I intend to put what would usually be called the introduction at the end of mine.

Nine out of ten readers who read introductions prefer to leave them until the end. Some mention a schoolteacher who advised the class that it makes more sense to save the introduction until they had read the main part of the book, others found this out for themselves, through years of bitter experience.

There are editors who expect writers to include a summary of the book in the introduction. Consequently, by the time the reader has ploughed through it they feel as though there's no need to read the book itself. On top of this, introductions frequently include baffling discussions of points which are to be made in the book – and of which you as yet know nothing.

It is also difficult to clear your mind of the opinions and theories which have been thrown at you when you have only just entered the first pages of a new book. Once I read a critical work on Ibsen's play *Hedda Gabler* which suggested that Judge Brack must be a sodomite because he always entered through the back door. It then became impossible *not* to pick up many unintentional *double entendres* made by and about poor Brack, who probably only used the back door because it was more convenient.

If, despite these arguments, you wish to read the introduction now, you will find it on page 192.

Biography is a strange craft. I am infuriated when I read a biography, and shortly afterwards read the same person's autobiography only to discover that the biography is simply a poor paraphrase with a few extra dates thrown in.

The principal facts of Charlotte Charke's life are only known because she left them to us in her autobiography – *A Narrative of the Life of Mrs Charlotte Charke*. This work, complete and unexpurgated, is included within my book. I have divided it into chapters, and between these chapters have provided my own biographical notes on Mrs Charke. As the reader will discover, the charm of Mrs Charke's life lies as much in the way she tells her stories, as the stories themselves.

Mrs Charke is not a great literary writer, but her narrative provides us with as perfect an example of the conditions of life in the eighteenth century as we are likely to find anywhere. Swift, Addison, Steele, Johnson and other literary giants provide us with a witty and elegant view of the eighteenth century in all its splendour; Charlotte Charke gives us eighteenth-century life with all its *day-to-day* worries, joys and upsets.

I have used the text of the second 1755 edition of Mrs Charke's *Narrative*. I have modernized her spelling and punctuation throughout, and standardized place-names and dates in line with modern practice. In my Notes I have used the following abbreviations: Public Record Office Probate (PRO PROB); Middlesex Record Office (MRO); Lord Chamberlain (LC).

A Narrative of the Life of Mrs Charlotte Charke

THE AUTHOR TO HERSELF

MADAM, though flattery is universally known to be the spring from which dedications frequently flow, I hope I shall escape that odium so justly thrown on poetical petitioners, notwithstanding my attempt to illustrate those wonderful qualifications by which you have so eminently distinguished yourself, and gives you a just claim to the title of a *nonpareil* of the age.

That thoughtless ease (so peculiar to yourself) with which you have run through many strange and unaccountable vicissitudes of fortune, is an undeniable proof of the native indolent sweetness of your temper. With what fortitude of mind have you vanquished sorrow, with the fond imagination and promissary hopes (only from yourself) of a succession of happiness, neither within your power or view?

Your exquisite taste in building must not be omitted: the magnificent airy castles, for which you daily drew out plans without foundation, must, could they have been distinguishable to sight, long ere this have darkened all the lower world; nor can you be matched in oddity of fame, by any but that celebrated knight-errant of the moon, G—e A—r St—s*, whose memoirs and yours

---

*A few months before the publication of Mrs Charke's *Narrative*, on 28 January 1755, George Alexander Stevens appeared at the Haymarket Theatre delivering a 'Praemium and Peroration' entitled 'The Female Inquisition', 'with a debate on superiority of the Fair Sex'. This performance was followed by a display by Miss Isabella Wilkinson on the slack wire.

Stevens, a part-time strolling player who, like Mrs Charke, had been imprisoned for debt, was born in London in 1710. He was well-known for reckless practical jokes, including one in which he threw a waiter out of the window and demanded that he should be put down on his bill. After a severe illness in 1750 he wrote a poem of repentance – 'Religion or The Libertine Repentant'. On his recovery, however, he went straight back to his old ways, and in Dublin in 1752, with his friend 'Lord Chief Joker Sparks', he set up the 'Nasau Court', where mock trials were performed. Shortly after this he published *Distress Upon Distress, a Heroi-Comi-Parodi-Tragedi-Farcical Burlesque* in two acts. This work is not only amusing as a short play, but also for the

conjoined would make great figures in history and might justly claim a right to be transmitted to posterity, as you are, without exception, two of the greatest curiosities that ever were the incentives to the most profound astonishment.

My choice of you, madam, to patronize my works, is an evidential proof that I am not disinterested in that point, as the world will easily be convinced (from your natural partiality to all I have hitherto produced) that you will tenderly overlook their errors, and, to the utmost of your power, endeavour to magnify their merits. If by your approbation the world may be persuaded into a tolerable opinion of my labours, I shall, for the novelty-sake, venture for once to call you friend – a name, I own, I never as yet have known you by.

I hope, dear madam, as Manly says in *The Provok'd Husband*,* that 'last reproach has struck you', and that you and I may ripen our acquaintances into a perfect knowledge of each other that may establish a lasting and social friendship between us.

Your two friends, Prudence and Reflection, I am informed, have lately ventured to pay you a visit, for which I heartily congratulate you, as nothing can possibly be more joyous to the heart than the return of absent friends after a long and painful peregrination.

Permit me, madam, to subscribe myself for the future what I ought to have been some years ago.

Your real friend,

And humble servant,

Charlotte Charke.

---

pseudo-academic footnotes provided by Stevens under the pseudonym Paulus Purgantius Pedasculus.

After working a short time in London, writing songs, acting, etc., he published (after the death of Mrs Charke) his disguised autobiography, *The History of Tom Fool*. His 'Lecture Upon Heads', a pioneer of monologue entertainment, was a great success in the mid-1760s, toured Britain and America and earned him, it is said, over £10,000. He retired to Hampstead by 1780 and died insane in Hertfordshire in September 1784.

*Comedy by John Vanbrugh and Colley Cibber

Chapter One

THE NARRATIVE

As the following history is the product of a female pen, I tremble for the terrible hazard it must run in venturing into the world, as it may very possibly suffer, in many opinions, without perusing it. I, therefore, humbly move for its having the common chance of a criminal, at least to be properly examined before it is condemned, and should it be found guilty of nonsense and inconsistencies, I must consequently resign it to its deserved punishment – instead of being honoured with the last row of a library, undergo the indignancy of preserving the syrup of many a choice tart, which, when purchased, even the hasty child will soon give an instance of its contempt of my muse by committing to the flames, or perhaps cast it to the ground to be trampled to death by some threadbare poet, whose works might possibly have undergone the same malevolence of fate.

However, I must beg leave to inform those ladies and gentlemen whose tenderness and compassion may excite them to make this little brat of my brain the companion of an idle hour, that I have paid all due regard to decency wherever I have introduced the passion of love, and have only suffered it to take its course in its proper and necessary time, without fulsomely inflaming the minds of my young readers or shamefully offending those of riper years, a fault I have often condemned, when I was myself but a girl, in some female poets. I shall not descant on their imprudence, only wish that their works had been less confined to that theme which too often led them into errors, reason and modesty equally forbid.

In regard to the various subjects of my story, I have, I think, taken care to make them so interesting that every person who reads my volume may bear a part in some circumstance or other in the perusal, as there is nothing inserted but what may daily happen to every mortal breathing.

Not that I would have the public conceive, though I am endeavouring to recommend it to their protection, that my vanity can so far overcome my small share of reason as to impute the success it should meet with to any other motive than a kind condescension in my readers to pity and encourage one who has used her utmost endeavours to entertain them.

As I have promised to give some account of my unaccountable life, I shall no longer detain my readers in respect to my book, but satisfy a curiosity which has long subsisted in the minds of many. And I believe they will own, when they know my history, if oddity can plead my right to surprise and astonishment, I may positively claim a title to be shown among the wonders of ages past and those to come. Nor will I, to escape a laugh, even at my own expense, deprive my readers of that pleasing satisfaction or conceal any error which I now rather sigh to reflect on, but formerly, through too much vacancy of thought, might be idle enough rather to justify than condemn.

I shall now begin my detail of the several stages I have passed through since my birth, which made me the last born of Mr Colley Cibber, at a time my mother began to think, without this additional blessing (meaning my sweet self), she had fully answered the end of her creation, being just forty-five years of age when she produced her last, 'though not least in love'. Nor was I exempted from an equal share in my father's heart; yet partly through my own indiscretion (and I am too well convinced from the cruel censure of false and evil tongues) since my maturity I lost that blessing, which, if strongest compunction and uninterrupted hours of anguish, blended with self-conviction and filial love, can move his heart to pity and forgiveness, I shall with pride and unutterable transport throw myself at his feet to implore the only benefit I desire or expect – his blessing and pardon.

But of that more hereafter, and I hope, ere this small treatise is finished, to have it in my power to inform my readers, my painful separation from my once tender father will be more than amply repaid by a happy interview, as I am certain neither my present or future conduct shall ever give him cause to blush at what I should esteem a justifiable and necessary reconciliation, as it is the absolute ordination of the Supreme that we should forgive when the offender becomes a sincere and hearty penitent. And I positively declare, were I to expire this instant, I have no self-interested views in regard to worldly matters, but confess myself a miser in my wishes so far, as having the transcendent joy of knowing that I am restored to a happiness which not only will clear my reputation to the world in regard to a former want of duty, but, at the same time, give a convincing proof that there are yet some sparks of tenderness remaining in my father's bosom for his repentant child.

I confess, I believe I came not only an unexpected, but an unwelcome guest into the family (exclusive of my parents) as my mother had borne no children for some few years before, so that I was rather regarded as an impertinent intruder, than one who had a natural right to make up the circular number of my father's fireside; yet, be it as it may, the jealousy of me from her other children laid no restraint on her fondness for me, which my father and she both testified in their tender care of my education. His paternal love omitted nothing that could improve any natural talents heaven had been pleased to endow me with – the mention of which, I hope, won't be imputed to me as a vain self-conceit, of knowing more, or thinking better than any other of my sister females. No! Far be it from me, for as all advantages from nature are the favourable gifts of the power divine, consequently no praise can be arrogated to ourselves for that which is not in ourselves possible to bestow.

I should not have made this remark, but, as it is likely my works may fall into the hands of people of disproportioned understand-ings, I was willing to prevent an error a weak judgement might have run into by inconsiderately throwing an odium upon me I could not possibly deserve, for, alas, all cannot judge alike.

As I have instanced that my education was not only a genteel, but in fact a liberal one, and such indeed as might have been sufficient for a son instead of a daughter, I must beg leave to add that I was never made much acquainted with that necessary utensil which forms the housewifery part of a young lady's education called a needle, which I handle with the same clumsy awkwardness a monkey does a kitten, and am equally capable of using the one as Pug is of nursing the other.

This is not much to be wondered at, as my education consisted chiefly in studies of various kinds, and gave me a different turn of mind than what I might have had if my time had been employed in ornamenting a piece of canvas with beasts, birds, and the alphabet; the latter of which I understood in French rather before I was able to speak English.

As I have promised to conceal nothing that might raise a laugh, I shall begin with a small specimen of my former madness, when I was but four years of age. Having, even then, a passionate fondness for a periwig, I crawled out of bed one summer's morning at Twickenham, where my father had part of a house and gardens for the season, and taking it into my small pate that by dint of a wig and a waistcoat I should be the perfect representative of my sire, I crept softly into the servants' hall, where I had the night before espied all things in order, to perpetrate the happy design I had framed for the next morning's expedition. Accordingly I paddled down stairs, taking with me my shoes, stockings, and little dimity* coat, which I artfully contrived to pin up as well as I could to supply the want of a pair of breeches. By the help of a long broom I took down a waistcoat of my brother's and an enormous bushy tie-wig of my father's, which entirely enclosed my head and body, with the knots of the ties thumping my little heels as I marched along with slow and solemn pace. The covert of hair in which I was concealed, with the weight of a monstrous belt and large silver-hilted sword that I could scarce drag along, was a vast impediment in my procession, and what still added to the other inconveniences I laboured under was whelming myself under one of my father's large beaver hats,† laden with lace as thick and as broad as a brickbat.‡

Being thus accoutred, I began to consider that it would be impossible for me to pass for Mr Cibber in girl's shoes, therefore took an opportunity to slip out of doors after the gardener, who went to his work, and rolled myself into a dry ditch, which was as deep as I was high, and in this grotesque pigmy state walked up and down the ditch bowing to all who came by me. But, behold, the oddity of my appearance soon assembled a crowd about me, which yielded me no small joy, as I conceived their risibility on this occasion to be marks of approbation and walked myself into a fever in the happy thought of being taken for the squire.

When the family arose, till which time I had employed myself in this regular march in my ditch, I was the first thing enquired after and missed, till Mrs Heron, the mother of the late celebrated actress of that name, happily espied me, and directly called forth the whole family to be witnessed of my state and dignity.

The drollery of my figure rendered it impossible, assisted by the fondness of both father and mother, to be angry with me, but, alas, I was borne off on the footman's shoulders, to my shame and disgrace, and forced into my proper habiliments.

*stout cotton fabric woven with raised stripes or fancy figures†.
†a hat made of beaver fur.
‡size of half a brick – 4½ in.

The summer following our family resided at Hampton Town, near the Court. My mother being indisposed, at her first coming there, drank every morning and night asses' milk. I observed one of those little health-restoring animals was attended by its foal, which was about the height of a sizeable greyhound.

I immediately formed a resolution of following the fashion of taking the air early next morning, and fixed upon this young ass for a pad-nag,* and, in order to bring this matter to bear, I communicated my design to a small troop of young gentlemen and ladies whose low births and adverse states rendered it entirely convenient for them to come into any scheme Miss Charlotte Cibber could possibly propose. Accordingly, my mother's bridle and saddle were secretly procured, but the riper judgements of some of my followers soon convinced me of the unnecessary trouble of carrying the saddle, as the little destined beast was too small and indeed too weak to bear the burden; upon which it was concluded to take the bridle only, and away went Miss and her attendants, who soon arrived at the happy field where the poor harmless creature was sucking. We soon seized and endeavoured to bridle it, but I remembered it was impossible to bring that point to bear, the head of the foal being so very small the trappings fell off as fast as they strove to put them on. One of the small crew, who was wiser than the rest, proposed their garters being converted to that use, which was soon effected, and I rode triumphantly into town astride, with a numerous retinue, whose huzzas were drowned by the dreadful braying of the tender dam, who pursued us with agonizing sounds of sorrow for her oppressed young one.

Upon making this grand entry into the town, I remember my father, from the violent acclamations of joy on so glorious an occasion, was excited to enquire into the meaning of what he perhaps imagined to be an insurrection; when, to his amazement, he beheld his daughter, mounted as before described, preceded by a lad who scraped upon a twelve-penny fiddle of my own to add to the dignity and grandeur of this extraordinary enterprise.

I perfectly remember, young as I was then, the strong mixture of surprise, pleasure, pain, and shame in his countenance on his viewing me seated on my infantical Rosinante,† which, though I had not then sense enough to distinguish, my memory has since

*an easy-going horse
†Don Quixote's wretched jade of a horse

afforded me the power to describe, and also to repeat his very words, at his looking out of the window, 'Gad demme! An ass upon an ass!'

But, alas, how momentary are sometimes the transports of the most happy? My mother was not quite so passive in this adventure as in that before related, but rather was, as I thought, too active, for I was no sooner dismounted than I underwent the discipline of birch, was most shamefully taken prisoner in the sight of my attendants, and with a small packthread* my leg was made the sad companion with that of a large table.

'O! fall of honour!'

It is not to be conceived the violent indignation and contempt my disgrace raised in my infant breast, nor did I forgive my mother, in my heart, for six months after, though I was obliged to ask pardon in a few moments of her, who, at that time, I conceived to be most in fault.

Were I to insert one quarter part of the strange mad pranks I played even in infancy, I might venture to affirm I could swell my account of them to a folio, and perhaps my whimsical head may compile such a work, but I own I should be loath, upon reflection, to publish it, lest the contagion should spread itself and make other young folks as ridiculous and mischievous as myself. Though I cannot charge my memory with suffering other people to feel the ill effects of my unaccountable vagaries, except once, I remember, a cross old woman at Richmond having beat me, I revenged myself by getting some of my playfellows to take as many as they could of her caps and other small linen that hung in the garden to dry, and who sent them sailing down a brook that forced its current to the Thames, whilst I walked into the parlour, secretly pleased with the thoughts of my revenge.

This is the only piece of malice that occurs to my remembrance, but I have too much reason to know that the madness of my follies have generally very severely recoiled upon myself, but in nothing so much as in the shocking and heart-wounding grief for my father's displeasure, which I shall not impudently dare deny having justly incurred. But I dare confidently affirm, much pains have been taken to aggravate my faults and strengthen his anger, and in that case I am certain my enemies have not always too

*parcel string

strictly adhered to truth, but meanly had recourse to falsehood to perpetrate the ruin of a hapless wretch, whose real errors were sufficient, without the addition of malicious slanders. The persons I mean, who did me these unfriendly offices, are still in being, but, *qui capit ille facit.**

I formerly wrote to my father, as I thought it an incumbent duty to enquire after his health, and at the same time implore his pardon, but could never have the happiness of even a distant hope of obtaining it. For the forementioned reasons I flatter myself, as reflection and contrition have brought me to a just sense of all past failings, humanity will plead her right in his relenting heart and once again restore me to a joy which none can conceive, who never felt the pain arising from the family in which they originally drew breath.

My obligations to him in my bringing up are of so extensive a nature I can never sufficiently acknowledge them, for, notwithstanding it is every parent's duty to breed their children with every advantage their fortunes will admit of, yet, in this case, I must confess myself most transcendently indebted, having received even a superfluity of tender regard of that kind, and, at the same time, beg pardon for not having put it to a more grateful and generous use, both for his honour and my own credit.

However, I shall lay it down as a maxim for the remaining part of life, to make the utmost amends by prudent conduct, for the miscarriages of the former, so that, should I fail in my hopes, I may not draw any further imputation on myself by not endeavouring to deserve what I think so particularly my duty, if possible, to achieve.

I shall now proceed in my account. At eight years of age I was placed at a famous school in Park Street, Westminster, governed by one Mrs Draper, a woman of great sense and abilities, who employed a gentleman called Monsieur Flahaut, an excellent master of languages, to instruct her boarders. Among the number of his pupils I had the happiness of being one, and as he discovered in me a tolerable genius and earnest desire of improvement, he advised my mother, in a visit to me at school, to let him teach me Latin and Italian, which she, proud of hearing me capable of receiving, readily consented to.

*'If the cap fits, wear it.' Charlotte uses this motto for *The Art of Management*; Colley Cibber for *The Careless Husband*.

Nor was my tutor satisfied with those branches of learning alone, for he got leave of my parents to instruct me in geography (which, by the by, though I know it to be a most useful science, I cannot think it was altogether necessary for a female) but I was delighted at being thought a learned person, therefore readily acquiesced with my preceptor's proposal.

Accordingly I was furnished with proper books and two globes, celestial and terrestial, borrowed of my mother's own brother, the late John Shore Esq., Sergeant-Trumpet of England, and pored over them until I had like to have been as mad as my uncle, who has given a most demonstrative proof of his being so for many years, which I shall hereafter mention.

The vast application to my study almost distracted me, from a violent desire I had to make myself perfect mistress of it. Mr Flahaut, perceiving that I was too close in the pursuit of knowledge not absolutely needful, shortened the various tasks I had daily set me, thinking that one mad mortal in a family was rather too much without further addition.

After I had received, in two years' schooling, a considerable share of my education (in which music and singing bore their parts), I was, through my indulgent parents' fondness, allowed masters at home to finish my studies.

Mr Flahaut, my master of languages, was continued. Mr Young, late organist of St Clement Danes, instructed me in music, though I was originally taught by the famous Dr King, who was so old when I learnt of him, he was scarce able to give the most trifling instructions. The celebrated Mr Grosconet was my dancing master and, to do justice to his memory, I have never met with any that exceeded him in the easy sublime taste in dancing, which is the most reasonable entertainment can be afforded to the spectators who wish only to be delighted with the genteel movement of a singular or plurality of figures with becoming gracefulness (in which no performer ever so eminently distinguished themselves as Mrs Booth,* widow of the late incomparable and deservedly esteemed Barton Booth, Esq., one of the patentees of Drury Lane Theatre, conjunctive with my father and Mr Wilks).†

*the actress Hester Santlow (c. 1690–1773), second wife of Barton Booth
†Barton Booth (1681–1733) and Robert Wilks (1665–1732), actors and co-managers, with Colley Cibber, of Drury Lane Theatre

The present taste in dancing is so apposite to the former, that I conceive the high-flown caprioles* which distinguish the first performers to be the result of violent strength and unaccountable flights of spirits, that rather convey an idea of so many horses *à la manège*,† than any design formed to please an audience with the more modest and graceful deportment with which Mrs Booth attracted and charmed the hearts of every gazer.

When it was judged that I had made a necessary progression in my learning and other accomplishments, I went to Hillingdon, within one mile of Uxbridge, where my mother, who was afflicted with the asthma, chose to retire for the preservation of her health.

This was an agreeable retreat my father had taken a leasé of for some years, but a winter residence in the country was not altogether so pleasing to me as that of the summer, I therefore began to frame different schemes for rendering my solitude as agreeable to myself as possible. The first project I had was in frosty mornings to set out upon the common and divert myself with shooting, and grew so great a proficient in that notable exercise that I was like the person described in Farquhar's *The Recruiting Officer*:‡ capable of destroying all the venison and wild fowl about the country.

In this manner I employed several days from morning till evening, and seldom failed of coming home laden with feathered spoil, which raised my conceit to such a pitch I really imagined myself equal to the best fowler or marksman in the universe.

At length, unfortunately for me, one of my mother's strait-laced old-fashioned neighbours, paying her a visit, persuaded her to put a stop to this proceeding, as she really thought it inconsistent with the character of a young gentlewoman to follow such diversions, which my youth, had I been a male, she thought would scarce render me excusable for, being but fourteen. Upon this sober lady's hint I was deprived of my gun, and with a half-broken heart on the occasion I resolved to revenge myself by getting a muscatoon§ that hung over the kitchen mantelpiece, and use my utmost endeavours towards shooting down her chimneys. After having wasted a considerable quantity of powder and shot to no purpose, I was

*balletic leaps
†fancily trained
‡the husband (Act v, scene v)
§short handgun with a large bore

obliged to desist and give up what I had, though wishfully, vainly attempted.

I remember upon having a fit of illness, my mother, who was apprehensive of my death, and consequently, through excessive fondness, used all means to prevent it that lay within her power, sent me to Thorly, in Hertfordshire, the seat of Dr Hales, an eminent physician and relation, with a design not only to restore and establish my health, but with the hopes of my being made a good housewife – in which needful accomplishment, I have before hinted, my mind was entirely uncultivated. But, alas, she ended where, poor dear soul, she ought to have begun, for by that time, from her desire of making me too wise, I had imbibed such mistaken, pedantic notions of superiority of scholarship and sense, that my utmost wisdom centred in proclaiming myself a fool, by a stupid contempt of such qualifications as would have rendered me less troublesome in a family, and more useful to myself and those about me.

Learning is undoubtedly a glorious and happy acquisition when it is encountered by a genius capable of receiving and retaining the powerful efficacy of its worth, yet, notwithstanding this assertion, I am certain that its greatest advantages are to be infinitely improved by launching into the world, and becoming acquainted with the different places and objects we go through and meet in travelling.

The observations to be made by that means refine the under-standing and improve the judgement, as something is to be gathered from the various dispositions of people in the highest and lowest stations of life, which persons of reflection may render greatly conducive in clearing and purging themselves of those dregs of learning, which too often, for want of this method of purifying the mind, reduce many a fine genius to sour pedantry and ill humour, that make them uneasy to themselves and obnox-ious to all who converse with them.

Even in my slender capacity, I have found this remark to be just, for notwithstanding my vanity might have excited me to a fond belief of my being wonderfully wise, in nine years' peregrination I began to find out, till I had seen something of the world, I was but rough in the mine. Observation had a little polished me, and I was soon convinced the additional helps I received from travel almost rendered my former knowledge nothing, so that I cannot but join in Polydore's opinion:

I would be busy in the world, and learn;
Not like a coarse and useless dunghill weed,
Fix'd to one spot, and rot just as I grew.*

Though I must acknowledge it is an equal error for youth to set out too soon to see the world before they are capable of digesting what they hear or see, and too frequently come back with the same light load of understanding with which they set out. I therefore think it proper, instead of saying such-a-one is lately returned from his travels (who is so unadvisedly sent forth) rather to have it said, 'He is lately returned from his delightful jaunts and parties of pleasure.'

In the second chapter of *Mr Dumont's History*† I have expatiated on this error, and refer my readers thereto; who, I believe, will not think my argument offensive or unreasonable.

While I stayed at Thorly, though I had the nicest examples of housewifery perfections daily before me, I had no notion of entertaining the least thought of those necessary offices by which the young ladies of the family so eminently distinguished themselves, in ornamenting a well-disposed and elegant table, decently graced with the toil of their morning's industry, nor could I bear to pass a train of melancholy hours in poring over a piece of embroidery, or a well-wrought chair, in which the young females of the family (exclusive of my mad-cap self) were equally and industriously employed, and have often, with inward contempt of them, pitied their misfortunes, who were, I was well assured, incapable of currying‡ a horse, or riding a race with me.

Many and vain attempts were used to bring me into their working community, but I had so great a veneration for cattle and husbandry it was impossible for them, either by threats or tender advice, to bring me into their sober scheme.

If anything was amiss in the stable, I was sure to be the first and head of the mob, but if all the fine works in the family had been in the fire I should not have forsook the curry comb to have endeavoured to save them from the utmost destruction.

During my residence in the family I grew passionately fond of the study of physic, and was never so happy as when the doctor employed me in some little offices in which he durst entrust me without prejudice to his patients.

*Thomas Otway's *The Orphan* (Act I, scene i)
†novel by Charlotte Charke published in 1755
‡rubbing down and dressing

As I was indulged in having a little horse of my own, I was frequently desired to call upon one or other of the neighbouring invalids to enquire how they did, which gave me a most pleasing opportunity of fancying myself a physician, and affected the solemnity and gravity which I had often observed in the good doctor. Nor am I absolutely assured, from the significant air which I assumed, whether some of the weaker sort of people might not have been persuaded into as high an opinion of my skill as my cousin's, whose talents chiefly were adapted to the study of physic. To do him justice, he was a very able proficient, and, I dare say, the loss of him in Hertfordshire and some parts of Essex is not a little regretted, as he was necessary to the rich, and tenderly beneficent to the poor.

At the expiration of two years his lady died, and I was remanded home, and once again sent to our country house at Hillingdon, where I was no sooner arrived than I persuaded my fond mother to let me have a little closet, built in an apartment seldom used, by way of dispensary. This I easily obtained and summoned all the old women in the parish to repair to me whenever they found themselves indisposed. I was indeed of the opinion of Leander in *The Mock Doctor*,* that a few physical hard words would be necessary to establish my reputation, and accordingly had recourse to a Latin dictionary and soon gathered up as many fragments as served to confound their senses and bring them into a high opinion of my skill in the medicinal science.

As my advice and remedies for all disorders were designed as acts of charity, it is not to be imagined what a concourse of both sexes were my constant attendants, though I own I have been often obliged to refer to myself to Salmon, Culpeper† and other books I had for that purpose before I was able to make a proper application, or indeed arrive at any knowledge of their maladies. But this defect was not discovered by my patients, as I put on significancy of countenance that rather served to convince them of my incomparable skill and abilities.

Fond as I was of this learned office, I did not choose to give up that of being lady of the horse, which delicate employment took up some part of my time every day, and I generally served myself in

*by Henry Fielding, after Molière (scene xiv)
†William Salmon (*Practical Physick*, 1692) and Nicholas Culpeper (*The English Physician Enlarged*, 1653)

that capacity, when I thought proper to pay my attendance on the believing mortals who entrusted their lives in my hands. But providence was extremely kind in that point, for though, perhaps, I did no actual good, I never had the least misfortune happen to any of the unthinking credulous souls who relied on me for the restoration of their healths, which was ten to one I had endangered as long as they lived.

When I had signified my intention of becoming a young Lady Bountiful,* I thought it highly necessary to furnish myself with drugs etc. to carry on this notable design. Accordingly I went to Uxbridge, where was then living an apothecary's widow whose shop was an emblem of that described in *Romeo and Juliet*. She, good woman, knowing my family, entrusted me with a cargo of combustibles which were sufficient to have set up a mountebank for a twelvemonth, but my stock was soon exhausted, for the silly devils began to fancy themselves ill because they knew they could have physic for nothing, such as it was. But, oh woeful day, the widow sent in her bill to my father, who was entirely ignorant of the curious expense I had put him to, which he directly paid, with a strict order never to let Doctor Charlotte have any further credit on pain of losing the money so by me contracted.

Was not this sufficient to murder the fame of the ablest physician in the universe? However, I was resolved not to give up my profession, and, as I was deprived of the use of drugs, I took it into my head, to conceal my disgrace, to have recourse to herbs. But one day a poor old woman coming to me, with a violent complaint of rheumatic pains and a terrible disorder in her stomach. I was at a dreadful loss what remedies to apply, and dismissed her with an assurance of sending her something to ease her, by an inward and outward application, before she went to bed.

It happened that day proved very rainy, which put it into my strange pate to gather up all the snails in the garden, of which, from the heavy shower that had fallen, there was a superabundant quantity. I immediately fell to work, and of some part of them, with coarse brown sugar, made a syrup, a spoonful of which was to be taken once in two hours. Boiling the rest to a consistence, with some green herbs and mutton fat, I made an ointment, and, clapping conceited labels upon the phial and gallipot,† sent my

*character in George Farquhar's *The Beaux' Stratagem*
†apothecary's small glazed pot for ointment

preparation, with a joyous bottle of hartshorn and sal volatile* I purloined from my mother, to add a grace to my prescriptions.

In about three days' time the good woman came hopping along to return me thanks for the extreme benefit she had received, entreating my goodness to repeat the medicines, as she had found such wonderful effects from their virtues.

But fortune was not quite kind enough to afford me the means of granting her request at that time, for the friendly rain, which had enabled me to work this wonderful cure, was succeeded by an extreme drought, and I thought it highly necessary to suspend any further attempts to establish my great reputation until another watery opportunity offered to furnish me with those ingredients whose sanative qualities had been so useful to her limbs and my fame. I therefore dismissed her with a word of advice not to tamper too much; that as she was so well recovered, to wait until a return of her pains, otherwise a too frequent use of the remedy might possibly lose its effect by being applied without any absolute necessity. With as significant an air as I could assume, I bid her be sure to keep herself warm, and drink no malt liquor, and, that if she found any alteration, to send to me.

Glad was I when the poor creature was gone, as her harmless credulity had raised such an invincible fit of laughter in me, I must have died on the spot by the suppression, had she stayed a few minutes longer.

This relation is an instance of what I have often conceived to be the happy motive for that success which travelling physicians frequently meet with, as it is rather founded on faith of the patient than any real merit in the doctor or his prescriptions. But the happiness I enjoyed, and still continue to do, in the pleasing reflection of not having, through inexperience, done any harm by my applications, I thank the great Creator for, who (notwithstanding my extreme desire of being distinguished as an able proficient) knew my design was equally founded on a charitable inclination which, I conceive, was a strong guard against any evils that might have accrued from merely a wild notion of pleasing myself.

My being unfortunately deprived of the assistance of the widow's shop to carry on this grand affair made me soon tire in the pursuit, and put me upon some other expedient for my amusement, I therefore framed the tenderest excuses I could possibly

*smelling salts

invent to drop my practice, that those who had before thought themselves indispensably obliged to me might not conceive I had lost that charitable disposition which they had so often blessed me for, and which, indeed, I heartily regretted the not having power still to preserve and maintain.

My next flight was gardening; a very pleasing and healthful exercise, in which I passed the most part of my time every day. I thought it always proper to imitate the actions of those persons whose characters I chose to represent, and, indeed, was as changeable as Proteus.

When I had blended the groom and gardener, I conceived, after having worked two or three hours in the morning, a broiled rasher of bacon upon a luncheon of bread in one hand, and a pruning knife in the other (walking, instead of sitting to this elegant meal), making seeds and plants the general subject of my discourse, was the true characteristic of the gardener, as, at other times, a halter and horse-cloth brought into the house and awkwardly thrown down on a chair were emblems of my stable profession; with now and then a shrug of the shoulders and a scratch of the head, with a hasty demand for small beer, and a 'God bless you make haste. I have not a single horse dressed or watered, and here 'tis almost eight o'clock, the poor cattle will think I have forgot 'em – and tomorrow they go a journey, I am sure I'd need take care of 'em.' Perhaps this great journey was an afternoon's jaunt to Windsor, within seven miles of our house; however, it served me to give myself as many airs as if it had been a progress of five hundred miles.

It luckily happened for me that my father was gone to France, and the servant who was in the capacity of groom and gardener, having the misfortune one afternoon to be violently inebriated, took it in his head to abuse the rest of his fellow-servants, which, my mother hearing, interfered, and shared equally the insolence of his approbrious tongue. Upon which, at a minute's warning, he was dismissed, to the inexpressible transport, my gentle reader, of your humble servant, having then the full possession of the garden and stables.

But what imagination can paint the extravagance of joy I felt on this happy acquisition! I was so bewildered with the pleasing ideas I had framed, in being actually a proper successor to the deposed fellow, I was entirely lost in a forgetfulness of my real self, and went each day with that orderly care to my separate exployments that is generally the recommendatory virtue for the first month only of a new-hired servant.

The rumour of the man's dismission was soon spread, and reached, to my great uneasiness, to Uxbridge, and every little adjacent village. Upon which I soon found it necessary to change my post of gardener, and became, for very near a week, porter at the gate, lest some lucky mortal might have been introduced, and deprived me of the happy situation I enjoyed.

I began to be tired with giving denials and, in order to put an end to their fruitless expectations, gave out that we had received letters from France to assure us that my papa had positively hired a man at Paris to serve in that office, and therefore all future attempts would be needless on that account.

I kept so strict a watch at the gate, during the apprehensions I had of being turned out of my places, the maids wondered what made me so constantly traversing the court yard for near eight days successively. But,

'Alas! They know but little of Calista'!*

It was really to secure my seat of empire, which at that time I would not have exchanged for a monarchy, and I conceived so high an opinion of myself, I thought the family greatly indebted to me for my skill and industry.

One day, upon my mother's paying me a visit in the garden and approving something I had done there, I rested on my spade, and, with a significant wink and a nod, asked whether she imagined any of the rest of her children would have done as much at my age, adding, very shrewdly, 'Come, come, madam, let me tell you, a pound saved is a pound got', then proceeded in my office of digging, in which I was at that time most happily employed, and with double labour pursued, to make the strongest impression I could on my admiring mother's mind, and convince her of the utility of so industrious a child.

I must not forget to inform the reader, that my mother had no extraordinary opinion of the fellow's honesty whom she had turned away, and what confirmed it was tracing his footsteps under the chamber windows the night after his dismission, and the neighbours had observed him to have been hovering round the house several hours that very evening.

*character in Nicholas Rowe's *The Fair Penitent*

As we had a considerable quantity of plate, my mother was a good deal alarmed with an apprehension of the man's attempting to break in at midnight, which might render us not only liable to be robbed, but murdered. She communicated her fears to me, who most heroically promised to protect her life, at the utmost hazard of my own. Accordingly, I desired all the plate might be gathered up and had it placed in a large flasket by my bedside. This was no small addition to my happiness, as it gave me an opportunity of raising my reputation as a courageous person, which I was extremely fond of being deemed, and, in order to establish that character, I stripped the hall and kitchen of their firearms, which consisted of my own little carbine* (I had, through the old maid's persuasion, been barbarously divested of not long before), a heavy blunderbuss, a muscatoon, and two brace of pistols, all which I had loaded with a couple of bullets each before I went to bed, not with any design, on my word, to yield to my repose, but absolutely kept awake three long and tedious hours, which was from twelve to three, the time I thought most likely for an invasion.

But no such thing happened, for not a mortal approached, on which I thought myself undone, till a friendly dog, who barked at the moon, gave a happy signal, and I bounced from my repository with infinite obligations to the cur, and fired out of the window piece after piece, recharging as fast as possible, till I had consumed about a pound of powder and a proportionable quantity of shot and balls.

It is not to be supposed but the family was, on my first onset in this singular battle (having nothing to combat but the air), soon alarmed. The frequent reports and violent explosions encouraged my kind prompter to this farce to change his lucky bark into an absolute howl, which strongly corroborated with all that had been thought or said in regard to an attempt upon the house. My trembling mother, who lay half expiring with dreadful imaginations, rang her bell, which summons I instantly obeyed, firmly assuring her that all danger was over, for that I heard the villain decamp on the first firing, which decampment was neither more nor less than the rustling of the trees, occasioned by a windy night, for the fellow was absolutely gone to London the very morning I declared war against him, as was afterwards proved.

*gun smaller than a musket, bigger than a pistol

Notwithstanding, I was fully convinced I had nothing to conquer but my unconquerable fondness and resolution to acquire the character of a courageous person, I settled that point with the whole family, in begging them not to be under the least apprehension of danger, urging that my constant firing would be the means of preventing any, and bid them consider that the loss of sleep was not to be put in competition with the hazard of their lives.

This reflection made them perfectly easy, and me entirely happy, as I had an unlimited power, without interruption, once in ten minutes to waste my ammunition to no purpose, and, retiring to my rest as soon as my stock was exhausted, enjoyed in dreams a second idea of my glorious exploits.

It is certain, nothing but my mother's excessive fondness could have blinded her reason, to give in to my unprecedented, ridiculous follies, as she was, in all other points, a woman of real good sense. But where the heart is partially engaged, we have frequent instances of its clouding the understanding and making dupes of the wisest.

I shall add one unfortunate circumstance more, and then proceed to give an account of my marriage with Mr Richard Charke, whose memory will, by all lovers of music who have heard his incomparable performance on the violin, be held in great estimation. But to my story – I had received information that there was a very fine young horse to be disposed of at Uxbridge, qualified to draw a chaise, and, having heard my father say, before he went to France, he would purchase another when he came home, I flew with distracted joy to the man's house, where this horse was to be seen, and accordingly had him harnessed and put to. This excursion was entirely unknown to my mother, who, at that time, lay extremely ill of the asthma.

The owner of the horse, knowing my family, and seeing me often drive my father's horses, made no doubt but that I was sent in fact to make trial of his, and, being willing to make his market as quick as possible, got the horse and chaise ready in a few minutes, and out I set, at the extreme hazard of my neck, when I got upon Uxbridge Common, for the creature was very young and ungovernable, and dragged me and the chaise over hills and dales with such vehemence that I despaired of ever seeing Hillingdon again. However, the subtle devil, knowing his way home, set up a barbarous full gallop, and made to his master's house with dreadful expedition beyond my power to restrain, and, in the cart-rut, ran over a child three years of age that lay sprawling there for its unfortunate amusement.

The violent rapidity of his course luckily prevented the death of the child, but was very near effecting mine, for grief and surprise took such hold of my spirits I became speechless. The child was soon brought after me by the parents, attended by a numerous mob, and, as soon as I regained my speech, I ordered the infant to be examined by a surgeon. But, no harm being done more than a small graze on the neck, the affair was made up with a shilling and a shoulder of mutton.

Notwithstanding this happy acquittance from so terrible a disaster (as ignorant people are naturally fond of striking terror), some doubly-industrious courier, who had more expedition than brains, ran with the news to my mother of my having killed a child, which threw her into such agonizing frights as greatly hazarded her life, and for some time was an aggravation to the illness she laboured under, for though I came home as soon as possible and convinced her of the error of the stupefied wretch that had so cruelly alarmed her, the surprise and shock so strongly possessed her, it was with difficulty she retained her senses.

This misfortune threw me into a kind of melancholy that lasted as long as could be expected from one of my youth and volatile spirits, and, to the extreme surprise of the neighbourhood, Miss Charlotte became for a little while, I believe, rather stupidly dull than justly reflecting, for I don't remember any impression left on my mind by this acccident after my mother's recovery, and the assurance I had of the boy's being living and well. However, it put a period to the fertility of my mischievous genius, and, upon being soon after acquainted with Mr Charke, who was pleased to say soft things and flatter me into a belief of his being an humble admirer, I (as foolish young girls are apt to be too credulous) believed his passion the result of real love, which indeed was only interest. His affairs being in a very desperate condition, he thought it no bad scheme to endeavour at being Mr Cibber's son-in-law, who was at that time a patentee in Drury Lane Theatre, and I in the happy possession of my father's heart, which, had I known the real value of, I should never have bestowed a moment's thought in the obtaining of Mr Charke's, but preserved my father's.

THE FACTS

1713–29

Charlotte Cibber was born on 13 January 1713, probably at her parents' home in Southampton Street West, London. She was christened three weeks later, on 8 February at the parish church, St Martin-in-the-Fields.

She was the last of eleven children born to the actor-playwright Colley Cibber and his wife Katherine. By the time of her birth, Charlotte's father was joint-manager of Drury Lane Theatre and (thanks to various jobs on the side, among them literary manager) the highest paid actor in the company. Her mother, once an actress and singer, had given up all thoughts of a career years before.

Colley Cibber was born on 6 November 1671, the eldest son of the Danish sculptor Caius Gabriel Cibber and his second wife Jane Colley, a Rutlandshire heiress.

He wed Katherine Shore, daughter of Matthias Shore (Sergeant of the Trumpeters, Drummers and Fifes in Ordinary to Kings James II and William III), at St James, Dukes Place, on 6 May 1693. His twenty-first birthday had been six months earlier. Katherine Shore's father did not attend the wedding ceremony.

In his autobiography, *An Apology for the Life of Colley Cibber*, Colley describes his marriage in terms of its productivity:

'My Muse and my spouse were equally prolific . . . the one was seldom the mother of a child, but in the same year the other made me the father of a play. I think we had about a dozen of each sort between us, of which kinds, some died in their infancy, and near an equal number of each were alive when I quitted the theatre.'[1]

(It is worth noting that this reference to his wife is about the only one in his *Apology*.)

Their first child, Veronica, was born on 18 January 1694 and christened the same day. Almost a year later on 14 January 1695, the second daughter, Mary, was born and baptized. In December of the same year Katherine gave birth to another girl, Catherine. A break of seventeen months preceded the birth of the first son, Colley junior, and Lewis (named after Colley senior's brother) was born within a year on 28 March. Anne was born 1 October 1699, and Elizabeth in early March 1701. Theophilus, who was to have an existence even more notorious than his baby sister, was born amid a great storm on 25 November 1703. James (who, according to a chancery suit on his uncle William's will, was blind) was born 25 July 1706 and christened two weeks later on 7 August. Another son was christened Colley on 23 November 1707.[2]

After the birth of these ten children, Katherine had a six-year break from pregnancy. So it is not surprising that Charlotte arrived 'not only an unexpected, but an unwelcome guest' and was regarded as 'an impertinent intruder'. Her eldest surviving sister, Catherine, was seventeen; her nearest surviving sibling, Theophilus, was ten.

Presumably exhausted after thirteen years of almost continuous childbearing, the middle-aged Katherine could not have had an easy time during her pregnancy with Charlotte, for, on 22 June 1712, her husband was arrested and charged with 'getting Mary Osbourne, spinster, with a bastard child'.[3] A shareholder in the theatre's royal patent, Henry Brett, paid the £40 bail and Cibber was released. The case was settled out of court before the appointed trial at Westminster Sessions. The day after her husband's arrest, Katherine sent for police to apprehend David Seale, a yeoman, for making a 'rout and tumult about her door'.[4] It seems more than likely that the two events were linked, and neither episode can have been very pleasant for an asthmatic, pregnant woman in her mid-forties.

This was not the first upset Katherine had suffered over her husband's activities. Shortly after the birth of the first infant Colley, in July 1697, Colley senior was arrested, charged with assault and imprisoned at the request of Jane Lucas, an actress and dancer in the Drury Lane company. Cibber was by this time one of the ten major stars at Drury Lane, one of the 'Gentlemen of the Great Chamber' and as such under the protection of the Lord Chamberlain. Accordingly, he wrote to the new Lord Chamberlain, the Earl of Sunderland, was released from prison and the case was dropped before it was due to come to court.[5]

Although Jane Lucas stayed on with the Drury Lane company (there was very little alternative work with a similar status), she was never promoted from small roles: maids and singing and dancing bit-parts. She disappeared from cast lists altogether in 1703.[6]

There were other times when Colley Cibber failed to treat his wife with the respect she deserved. During the summer of 1706, when Katherine was heavily pregnant with their blind son James, rather than stay with her in London, or indeed find a country retreat they both could share, he went alone to spend a luxurious summer with his rich friends Colonel Henry Brett (who had bailed him out after the bastardy charge) and his wife, the Countess of Macclesfield, at their Gloustershire estate, Sandywell Park. Through the Bretts, who had rich and influential friends and relations, Cibber built up an impressive array of patrons and supporters.

A few months after Charlotte's birth, in August 1713, her aunt, Rose Shore, widow of her mother's recently deceased brother, William, died, leaving a will which was ambiguous. Katherine Cibber, presumably under pressure from her husband, took the matter to the Court of Chancery.

Katherine's brother, William Shore, had left his money to his wife and, after her death, promised some to Katherine ('for her own separate use') and some for Katherine's children. Rose complicated matters by drawing up a will of her own. She left the money to Charlotte's sister Elizabeth.

It is hard to imagine a man resenting his own daughter receiving a bequest from a close relative. Elizabeth was presumably very close to Rose Shore as she had been sent to stay with her when her mother was pregnant and ill in 1707, and had stayed with her for a long time. It is possible that Rose Shore willed the money to Elizabeth knowing that (even if she inserted clauses like 'for her own separate use' as her husband had done) any money left to Katherine would, under English law, be the property of Colley anyway. ('By marriage, the husband and wife are one person in law: that is, the very being and legal existence of the woman is suspended during the marriage', William Blackstone, *Commentaries on the Laws of England*, 1765.) By leaving the money in trust to Elizabeth there was some hope that Shore money was not to be lavished on the self-centred Colley Cibber. But Rose had not realized that he was not only self-centred, but greedy and shameless with it.

In court Colley Cibber claimed all the Shore money, asserting that his income was small and uncertain. Actually it was over £1000 per annum. The English legal procedures have a tendency to be more advantageous to the wily than the truthful, and his perjury won him the case. His daughter Elizabeth's money became his.[7]

This episode seems even more disgraceful in the light of Colley's lack of generosity when years later Elizabeth fell on hard times.

Cibber's parsimonious attitude towards his wife and children was a recurrent theme in the press.

In a letter to *The Original Weekly Journal* for 1 March 1719 Charles Johnson claimed that Cibber had gambled away the £1000 profit from his play *The Non-Juror* at the Groom Porters Club and asserted that 'the other masters of the playhouse, seeing his daughter very bare in clothes, kindly offered him a private benefit for her; and I am credibly informed that it amounted to fourscore pounds, which this unhuman father, rather than let his child have necessaries, made away with also'. (This must have been Charlotte; by 1719 the other Cibber girls were too old to be described as 'child'.)

The playwright John Dennis, whose play *The Invader of His Country* had been in his opinion ruined in the presentation by Cibber and his company, attacked Cibber in a pamphlet directed mainly against Sir Richard Steele – *The Character and Conduct of Sir John Edgar*:

'Tis credibly reported that he [Cibber] spit on the face of our Saviour's picture at the Bath, with words too execrable and too horrible to be repeated . . . He has neither tenderness for his wife, or natural affection for his children, nor any sympathizing regard for the rest of men . . . He has, in the compass of two years, squandered away six thousand pounds at the Groom Porters without making the least provision for either his wife or his children.'[8]

Cibber offered a £10 reward for the author's name.[9]

An anonymous pamphleteer (possibly Cibber himself) answered the allegations: 'you fall foul of Mr Cibber, the deputy governor as you call him, and tell a notorious lie in saying he lost £6000 one season without providing for his family, when everyone that knows him can tell you that he settled £3000 that very year upon his children.'

This defence of Cibber fails on one psychological point: the type of father who boasts to 'everyone that knows him' that he has settled a large amount of money on his children is more likely to be justifying his ability to gamble wads of money on a regular basis, and to spend a small fortune on himself, than telling the truth. Fathers who make generous settlements on their children rarely boast of it to all and sundry.

It cannot be denied that Colley Cibber was a great actor in his own field. In foppish and affected roles he reigned supreme, although even his good reviews were not entirely complimentary:

'As to his person, his shape was finely proportioned yet not graceful, easy but not striking. Though it was reported by his enemies that he wanted a soul, yet it was visible enough that he had one, because he carried it in his countenance; for his features were narrowly earnest and attentively insignificant. There was a peeping pertness in his eye, which would have been spirit had his heart been warmed with humanity or his brain been stored with ideas. In his face was a contracted kind of passive yet protruded sharpness, like a pig half roasted; and a voice not unlike his own might have been borrowed from the same suffering animal while in a condition a little less desperate. With all these comic acomplishments of person, he had an air and a mind which completed the risible talent, insomuch that, when he represented a ridiculous humour, he had a mouth in every nerve and became eloquent without speaking. His attitudes were pointed and exquisite, and his expression was stronger than painting; he was beautifully absorbed by the character, and demanded and monopolized attention; his very extravagances were coloured with propriety; and affectation sat so easy about him that it was in danger of appearing amiable.'[10]

Charlotte has described many escapades which can be vaguely dated by their location.

By royal command of King George I, the Drury Lane company performed seven times at Hampton Court at the end of September 1718. It is probable that Colley Cibber, as actor-manager-playwright, would have spent much of the summer near the Palace overseeing the construction of the theatre and sets in the Palace's great old hall and the arrival of the touring wardrobe by chaise-marine. Charlotte was then five years old.[11]

The Cibber family lived for a while in a cottage at Strawberry Hill, Twickenham (on the site of what was to become Horace Walpole's famous coterie). Locally nicknamed 'Chopped Straw Hall', the cottage was built in 1698 by one of the Earl of Bradford's coachmen. It was thought by villagers that this coachman got the money to build the cottage by feeding his Grace's horses chopped straw instead of hay. Colley Cibber was one of the first tenants. Some sources suggest that Cibber stayed there over a number of summers and while in residence at Twickenham wrote *The Refusal:*

or, The Ladies' Philosophy. This would place the family there in 1721, when Charlotte was eight. (There are no relevant documents for this period in the Uxbridge archives.)

According to Charlotte a handful of influential people were engaged in her education.

Mrs Draper certainly occupied a very large property in Park Street (titled in the rate-books *Madam* Draper), but I cannot find a direct reference to her school. It was possibly associated with either James Palmer's or Emery Hill's boys schools in nearby Tuthill Fields. Girls' schools of the time were usually linked with a local boys' school.

Charlotte's first music teacher was Robert King, a violinist and composer. King was private musician to five monarchs, from Charles II onwards. Composer in ordinary to William and Mary, he remained a member of the royal band until 1728, at about which time he is thought to have died. He wrote many songs and airs, and incidental music to plays by Nahum Tate, John Crowne and Thomas Shadwell. His first printed music appeared in 1676. Assuming he was about twenty then, he would have been well over sixty (in those days a good old age) when he taught Charlotte.

Her next teacher was Anthony Young (born *c.* 1685), organist of St Clement Danes from 1707, and a composer of songs.

Like her sister, Elizabeth, Charlotte was farmed out for a few years when her mother was not well. She went to Thorly, Hertfordshire, to stay with Dr William Hales and his wife Elizabeth Beaumont at their home, Twyford House, Thorly. Dr Hales, though not listed in Munks Roll (an eighteenth-century medical register), is listed in Cussan's *The History of Hertfordshire* as William Hale MD, son of William Hale DD, rector of Great Hallingbury, Essex (a village only a few miles from Thorly). Histories of Essex refer to the rector as William Hales.

The medical Dr Hales's wife Elizabeth died in 1726, so Charlotte must have picked up her interest in medicine between 1724 and 1726. She was therefore eleven when she arrived at Twyford House, thirteen when she returned home.

Charlotte writes of 'the young ladies of the family'. Cussans mentions Elizabeth Hales, describing her as the second daughter (born 1707). I have found another daughter, Mary, christened at Thorly in 1709. Presumably this means there were three daughters 'poring over their embroidery' while Charlotte was out currying horses in the stables.

Dr Hales died in 1752, and so the reference in the 1755 *Narrative* to 'the loss of him in Hertfordshire' is a fairly topical remark.

Before Charlotte's fifteenth birthday her surviving brothers and sisters were all busily establishing themselves: Catherine was five years married; Anne had her own shop in Charles Street; Theophilus was married and had been acting for eight years; Elizabeth, now Mrs Brett, had been acting for some years; and in the summer of 1718 Elizabeth's daughter, Anna, made her début, dancing with the Drury Lane company.

With the rest of the Cibber family fully occupied elsewhere, it is hardly surprising that Charlotte and her mother Katherine, alone together in their rented Hillingdon house, formed a very strong bond.

1 Apology p. 138.
2 Cibber children: Veronica, St Martin-in-the-Fields; Mary, St Martin-in-the-Fields; Catherine, Christened 10 December 1695, St Clement Danes; Colley, born 8 May, christened 23 May 1697, St Martin-in-the-Fields; Lewis christened 17 April 1698, St Martin-in-the-Fields; Anne, christened 15 October 1699, St Martin-in-the-Fields; Elizabeth, christened 16 March 1701, St Paul's, Covent Garden; Theophilus christened 19 December 1703, St Martin-in-the-Fields; James, St Martin-in-the-Fields; Colley, born 29 November 1707, St Martin-in-the-Fields.
3 Middlesex Record Office WJ/SR/2192, 11 June O.S. 1712.
4 MRO WJ/SR/2192. ind. 24 and recog. 75.
5 Public Record Office LC7/3, 6 October 1697; MJ/SR (W), no. 113; and WSP/1697/Oct/1.
6 Philip Highfill etc., *Dictionary of Actors*.
7 PRO Chancery decrees 1713 A.p.643; 1733 A.p.183; Master's Records vol. 335 (1716).
8 John Dennis, *The Critical Works of John Dennis*, ed. E.N.Hooker, 1939–43, II, p.188–9.
9 Richard Steele, *The Theatre*, ed. Nichols, 1791, II, p.401.
10 Aaron Hill, *The Prompter*, 19 November 1734.
11 *The London Stage 1700–29*, ed. Emmett L. Avery, p.xxxiv; Colley Cibber, *Apology for the Life of Colley Cibber*, Everyman edn., 1976. p. 277–83.

Chapter Two

THE NARRATIVE

Alas! I thought it a fine thing to be married, and indulged myself in a passionate fondness for my lover, which my father perceiving, out of pure pity, tenderly consented to a conjugal union. The reader may suppose that I thought, at that time, it was the greatest favour he ever conferred on me, as indeed I really did, but I have some modest reasons to believe, had he indulged me under the guardianship of some sensible trusty person, or have taken a small tour into the country, without letting me know it was done with a design to break off my attachment to my then intended husband, it would have prevented the match, and both parties, in the main, might have been better pleased; for I am certain that absence, and an easy life, would soon have got the better of the violence of my fondness, being then of too indolent a disposition to let anything long disturb my mind.

I do not advance this as a reproach for my father's indulgence, but to give the reader a perfect idea of the oddity of my youthful disposition, for, as Sir Charles Easy says to his lady, 'He is often rude and civil without design',* the same inadvertency had an equal dominion over me, and I have avoided or committed errors without any premeditation either to offend or oblige.

But to my tale: After six months' acquaintance, I was, by consent, espoused at St Martin's Church to Mr Charke, and thought at that time the measure of my happiness was full, and of an ever-during nature. But, alas, I soon found myself deceived in that fond conceit, for we were both so young and indiscreet we ought rather to have been sent to school than to church, in regard to any qualifications on either side towards rendering the marriage state comfortable to one another. To be sure, I thought it gave me an air of more consequence to be called Mrs Charke, than Miss Charlotte, and my spouse, on his part, I believe, thought it was a fine feather in his cap to be Mr Cibber's son-in-law, which indeed it would have

*in *The Careless Husband* (Act v, scene vi) by Colley Cibber

proved, had he been skilful enough to have managed his cards rightly, as my father was greatly inclined to be his friend, and endeavoured to promote his interest extremely among people of quality and fashion. His merit as a proficient in music, I believe, is incontestable, and being tolerably agreeable in his person, both concurred to render him the general admiration of those sort of ladies who, regardless of their reputation, make them the unhappy sacrifices to every pleasing object (which, *entre nous*, was a most horrible bar to my escutcheon* of content, insomuch that married miss was, the first twelvemonth of her connubial state, industriously employed in the pursuit of fresh sorrow by tracing her spouse from morn to eve through the hundreds of Drury).†

I had, indeed, too often very shocking confirmations of my suspicions, which made me at last grow quite indifferent; nor can I avoid confessing that indifference was strongly attended with contempt. I was in hopes that my being blessed with a child would, in some degree, have surmounted that unconquerable fondness for variety, but 'twas all one, and I firmly believe nothing but the age of Methuselah could have made the least alteration in his disposition.

This loose and unkind behaviour consequently made me extravagant and wild in my imagination, and, finding that we were in the same circumstances in regard to each other that Mr Sullen and his wife‡ were, we agreed to part. Accordingly, I made our infant my care, nor did the father's neglect render me careless of my child, for I really was so fond of it I thought myself more than ample made amends for his follies in the possession of her.

When Mr Charke thought proper he paid us a visit, and I received him with the same good nature and civility I might an old decayed acquaintance that I was certain came to ask me a favour, which was often the case, for I seldom had the honour of his company but when cash ran low, and I as constantly supplied his wants, and have got from my father many an auxiliary guinea, I am certain, to purchase myself a new pair of horns.§

When I married it was in the month of February, the beginning

---

*heraldic terms. Escutcheon is a shield; bar a horizontal stripe.
†area of London famous for its bordellos and bagnios
‡characters in George Farquhar's *The Beaux' Stratagem*
§cuckold's horns

of benefit time* at both theatres. Mrs Thurmond's† coming on soon, who understood that I was designed for the stage the season following, requested that I might make my first appearance on her night, in the character of Mademoiselle in *The Provok'd Wife*.‡ And I particularly remember, the first time of my playing was the last in which that matchless performer Mrs Oldfield§ ever charmed the town with her inimitable exhibition. She sickened soon after and lingered till October following, when she expired, to the inexpressible loss of her acquaintance in general and all connoisseurs in acting; though I am apt to think, had she survived that illness, the stage would not have been less liable to have sustained her loss, as she had acquired a considerable fortune and was in the decline of life, but, in her business, still in the utmost height of perfection.

This excellent actress, from her encouragement, gave me lively hopes of success, and being possessed with a youthful transport, was rendered quite insensible of those fears which naturally attend people on their first essay on the theatre.

My father and Mrs Oldfield's approbation was no trifling addition to my self-conceit. It is true, I was happy in a genius for the stage, but I have, since my riper years, found that the success I met with was rather owing to indulgent audiences that good-naturedly encouraged a young creature, who they thought might one day come to something, than any real judgement I had in my profession, and that I was more indebted to chance than I was aware of for the applause I received when I accidentally stumbled on the right.

I must beg leave to give the reader an idea of that ecstasy of heart I felt on seeing the character I was to appear in the bills; though my joy was somewhat dashed when I came to see it inserted, 'By a young gentlewoman, who had never appeared on any stage before'. This melancholy disappointment drew me into an unavoidable expense in coach-hire to inform all my acquaintance that I was the person to set down in Mrs Thurmond's benefit bills –

---

*There were days in spring when actors could supplement their wages with performances held on behalf of individually named actors who took that night's profits.
†the actress Sarah Thurmond (*fl.* 1715–37)
‡comedy by John Vanbrugh
§the celebrated actress Anne Oldfield (1683–1730). Personally encouraged by Colley Cibber, she went on to become the leading comic actress of her generation

though my father's prudent concern intended it to be a secret till he had proof of my abilities.

To my inexpressible joy, I succeeded in the part, and the play was in about six weeks after re-chosen for the benefit of Mr Charke and Miss Raftor, now Mrs Clive,* who was then a young but promising actress, of which she has given demonstrative proofs in various lights, therefore I shall not expatiate on that subject, lest the weakness of my pen should fall short of her merit.

My name was in capitals on this second attempt, and I dare aver that the perusal of it from one end of the town to the other, for the first week, was my most immediate and constant business. Nor do I believe it cost me less, in shoes and coaches, than two or three guineas, to gratify the extravagant delight I had, not only in reading the bills, but sometimes hearing myself spoken of, which luckily was to my advantage. Nor can I answer for the strange effect a contrary report might have wrought on a mind so giddily loaded with conceited transport. I am not quite certain whether my folly and indignation might not have caused a drawn battle on such an occasion.

It happened that Mrs Horton† (who played Lady Fanciful‡ the time before), was indisposed, and my sister-in-law, the late Mrs Jane Cibber,§ was appointed to do the part, who, notwithstanding her having been a few years on the stage, and indeed a meritorious actress, had not overcome the shock of appearing the first night in any character. I, who was astonished at her timidity, like a strange gawky as I was, told her I was surprised at her being frightened, who had so often appeared, when I, who had never played but once, had no concern at all. 'That's the very reason,' said she. 'When you have stood as many shocks as others have done, and are more acquainted with your business, you'll possibly be more susceptible of fear.' The apprehensions she laboured under gave her a grave aspect, which my insensible head at that time took as an affront, and, I remember, I turned short on my heel as we were waiting for our cue of entrance and broke off our conversation, nor could I bring myself, but on the stage, to speak to her the whole evening.

*the low comedienne Kitty Clive (1711–85)
†Christiana Horton (1699–1756), a versatile actress who specialized in female fops, was described in 1735 by Aaron Hill as 'the finest figure on any stage at present'
‡in John Vanbrugh's *The Relapse*
§the actress Jane Johnson, first wife of Charlotte's brother Theophilus

This ridiculous circumstance we have both laughed at since, and I found her words very true, for I'll maintain it: the best players are the most capable of fear, as they are naturally most exact in the nicety of their performance. Not that I would insinuate, by this observation, that I think myself better than in the common run of those theatrical gentry who are lucky enough to be endured through the course of a play, without being wished to be no more seen after the first act.

Such melancholy instances I have been witness of, both in town and country: whilst the poor player has bawled and bellowed out his minute on the stage, and the groaning audience hissingly entreated he might be heard no more.

The second character I appeared in was Alicia,* and found the audience not less indulgent than before. Mrs Porter's† misfortune of being overturned in her chaise at Highwood Hill was the means by which I was possessed of that part. The third was *The Distressed Mother*,‡ in the summer, when the young company were under my brother Theophilus Cibber's direction.

Now I leave to any reasonable person what I went through in undertaking two such characters after two of the greatest actresses in the theatre, viz: Mrs Oldfield and Mrs Porter. By this time I began to feel I feared, and the want of it was sufficiently paid home to me in the tremor of spirits I suffered in such daring attempts. However, fortune was my friend, and I escaped with life, for I solemnly declare that I expected to make an odd figure in the bills of morality – 'Died one, of capital characters'.

Soon after this *George Barnwell*§ made his appearance on the stage, in which I was the original Lucy, and, beginning to make acting my business as well as my pleasure, the success I had in that part raised me from twenty to thirty shillings per week, after which, having the good fortune to be selected from the rest of the company as stock-reader¶ to the theatre in case of disasters, I acquitted myself tolerably to the satisfaction of the masters and audience.

My first attempt of that kind was Cleopatra,‖ for the benefit of Mr

*in Nicholas Rowe's *Jane Shore*
†the tragic actress Mary Ann Porter (?–1765)
‡Ambrose Phillips's adaptation of Racine's *Andromache*
§frequently used alternative title to George Lillo's *The London Merchant*
¶a sort of universal understudy
‖in John Dryden's *All For Love*

Worsdale,* who was honoured with the presence of His Royal
Highness, the late Prince of Wales. Mrs Heron† having that
afternoon the misfortune to bruise her knee-pan,‡ she was immov-
able, and I was, at the second music,§ sent for to read the part.

Had I been under sentence of death, and St Sepulchre's dreadful
bell tolling for my last hour, I don't conceive I could have suffered
much greater agony, and thought of my sister's words to some
tune, for I absolutely had not a joint or nerve I could command for
the whole night, and, as an addition to the terror I laboured under,
Mr Quin,¶ that worthy veteran of the stage, played Ventidius. The
apprehension I laboured under in respect to the audience, which
was a numerous one, to the amount of three hundred and odd
pounds, was nothing in comparison to the fright his aspect threw
me into.

But even this shock I got through, and was soon after induced to
a second of the same nature. Mrs Butler‖ was taken ill and the
Queen in *Essex* was to be filled up. Accordingly, I was sent for to
supply the deficiency, which, in justice to the memory of the
deceased gentlewoman, I must inform the reader she rewarded me
for, by sending me, in a very polite manner, a couple of guineas
next morning. I must needs say I did not think it worth so
handsome an acknowledgement, but she sent it in such a manner
that, had I refused it, I must have been guilty of a very great
absurdity, as her station and mine at that time were upon very
different footings, I being but a baby in the business, and she an
established person of a very good salary.

---

*the actor James Worsdale who acted occasionally in 1735 and again in 1750. He
wrote the play *Cure for a Scold*, an adaptation of *The Taming of the Shrew*.
†Mary Heron (?–1736), a young actress of great promise. She was one of the
leaders of the 1733 stage mutiny, who before her accident planned to join the
management at Drury Lane.
‡kneecap
§It was the custom in eighteenth-century London theatre to play three overtures, or concertos, before each performance. On a typical day in 1735 (8 May)
the first, second and third music were: a concerto for hautboys etc., a concerto of
Geminiani and the overture to *Ariadne*. Between the end of the play and the
afterpiece Handel's 'Water Music' was played. The whole musical pre-show
programme would last about 30–40 minutes.
¶the huge, arrogant leading actor, James Quin (1693–1766). He was, by 1734,
earning over twice as much per year as any other actor in London.
‖the actress Elizabeth Butler (?–1748)

I continued for that season at the before-mentioned revenue, but, upon Mr Highmore's* making a purchase in the theatre, there immediately happened a revolt of the greatest number of the company to the new theatre in the Haymarket. My brother being principally concerned, I also made a decampment, and was by agreement raised from thirty shilling to three pounds, had a very good share of parts, and continued with them till the whole body returned to Mr Fleetwood,† who for some time carried on the business with great industry, attended with proportionable success; though, poor gentleman, I fear that super-extraordinary success was the foundation of his ruin.

It happened he and I had a dispute about parts, and our controversy arose to such a height, I, without the least patience or consideration, took a French leave of him, and was idle enough to conceive I had done a very meritorious thing. I cannot say, in the affair, he used me entirely well, because he broke his word with me, but I used myself much worse in the main by leaving him, as I have since experienced. As there are too many busy meddlers in the world, who are ever ready to clinch the nail of sedition when once it is struck, so some particular people thought it worth while, by villainous falsehoods, to blow the spark of fire between Mr Fleetwood and myself into a barbarous blaze, insomuch that I was provoked to write a farce on the occasion, entitled *The Art of Management*, wherein the reader may be assured I took no small pains to set him in a most ridiculous light, and spared not to utter some truths which I am sensible ought rather to have been concealed, and I cannot but own I have since felt some secret compunction on that score, as he, notwithstanding my impertinent and stupid revenge, at my father's request restored me to my former station.

What further aggravates my folly and ingratitude, I made, even then, but a short stay with him, and joined the late Henry Fielding, Esq., who at that time was manager at the Haymarket Theatre, and running his play, called *Pasquin*, the eleventh night of which I played the part of Lord Place, which till then had been performed by Mr Richard Yates,‡ but as he had other parts in that piece, Mr Fielding begged the favour of him to spare that to make room for

*the gentleman-manager John Highmore (1694–1759)
†the manager Charles Fleetwood (?–1747)
‡actor (c. 1706–96)

me, and I was accordingly engaged at four guineas per week, with an indulgence in point of charges at my benefit by which I cleared sixty guineas, and walked with my purse in my hand till my stock was exhausted lest I should forget the necessity I then laboured under of squandering what might have made many decayed family truly happy.

As I stand self-convicted for all the follies I have been guilty of, I hope my behaviour to Mr Fleetwood will fix no imputation that may not be removed; and the less so, as I might say to him from the origin of our quarrel, with Peachum: 'Brother, brother, we were both in the wrong.'*

My motive for leaving him the second time proceeded from a cause he had no share in, which I confess is a further aggravation to my ingratitude. I can only acknowledge my error, and beg pardon for the folly, and, at the same time, apologize for my concealment of the reason of my second elopement, as it was partly a family concern, though perhaps I might be condemned were I to reveal it. But notwithstanding I've done a thousand unaccountable things, I cannot absolutely think myself blameable for that last project further than in using a gentleman ill, who had behaved to me agreeably to that character, when he might have taken any advantages against me, without being thought quilty of inhumanity or injustice.

Soon after *Pasquin* began to droop, Mr Lillo, the author of *George Barnwell*, brought Mr Fielding a tragedy of three acts, called *The Fatal Curiosity*, taken from a true tragic tale of a family at Penryn, in Cornwall, who lived in the reign of King James the First. In this play are two well-drawn characters, under the denominations of Old Wilmot and his wife Agnes, an aged pair, who had, from too much hospitality on the husband's part, and unbounded pride on the wife's, outrun a vast estate, and were reduced to extremest poverty.

The late Mr John Roberts,† a very judicious speaker, discovered a mastership in the character of the husband, and I appeared in that of the wife. We were kindly received by the audience, the play had a fresh run the season following, and, if I can obtain a grant for one night only, I intend to make my appearance once more as Mrs Agnes, for my own benefit, at the Haymarket Theatre, on which

*in John Gay's *The Beggar's Opera* (Act II, scene x)
†John Roberts was the original George Barnwell in Lillo's *The London Merchant*

occasion I humbly hope the favour and interest of my worthy friends.

At the time I was engaged with Fielding, I lodged in Oxendon Street, and boarded with my sister Brett,* who was but an inmate as well as myself. But I and my little daughter swelled up the number of her family. I, being a sort of creature that was regarded as a favourite cat or mischievous monkey about the house, was easily put off with what reasonable people might have deemed not only an inconvenience, but an affront; I accordingly was put into the worst apartment, and was entirely insensible of its oddity, until a blustery night roused me into an observation of its extraordinary delicacy. When I had thoroughly surveyed it, I sat down and wrote the following description of the room, and exact inventory of my chattels.

> Good people for a while give ear,
>   Till I've describ'd my furniture:
> With my stately room I shall begin,
> Which a part of Noah's ark has been:
> My windows reach from Pole to Pole;
> Strangely airy – that in winter, O' my soul,
> With the dear delight of – here and there a hole.
>
> There is a chest of drawers too, I think,
> Which seems a trough, where pigeons drink;
> A handkerchief and cap's as much as they'll contain:
> O! but I keep no gowns – so need not to complain.
>
> Then, for my fire; I've an inch of stove,
> Which I often grieve I cannot move
> When I travel from the chimney to the door,
> Which are miles full three, if not fourscore.
>
> By that time I, shiv'ring, arrive,
> I doubtful grow if I'm alive.
> Two foreign screens I have, in lieu
> Of tongs and poker – nay, faith, shovel too.
>
> Sometimes they serve to fan the fire,
> For 'tis seldom that to bellows I aspire
> I'll challenge England's king, and the Pretender,
> To say, that e'er I rust my fender.

*Elizabeth Cibber married Dawson Brett in about 1718.

That fashion's old, I've got a newer,
And prudently make use of iron skewer.
Now for my lovely bed, of verdant hue,
Which, ere Adam liv'd, might possibly be new.

So charming thin, the darns so neat
With great conveniency expel the heat:
But these things will not ever last;
Each day a curtain I, in breathing, waste.

Then, for chairs; I indeed have one;
But, since ruin draws so swiftly on,
Will let my room, ere chair, screens,
And curtains all are gone.

These curious lines were for nineteen years preserved by my foolish, fond sister, who, in her turn, has been a universal friend to her brethren, or rather her sisterhood. I wish fortune had been less rigorous, and gratitude more predominant, that the former might have prevented, or the latter have been the tender motive to assuage those sorrows and inconveniences of life, she at present labours under: from which, as far as she has a claim in me and my poor capacity extends, I will make it the business of my life to extricate her, as I have, when fortune was in her power, been a participator of her bounty.

I don't make this design public with any regard to myself, but with the pleasing hope of being the happy example of others from whom she may have an equal claim, both from nature and gratitude. Poor thing! she is now in the five and fiftieth year of her age, and, as she has had no faults the family can allege against her, it is a pity but she should be tenderly considered by them all, that the remaining part of life may pass away without those corroding cares that are too often the impediment to our casting our thoughts beyond the present state, which, alas, is the sad and dreadful consequence of a forgetfulness and disregard of the future.

I don't apprehend that to be my unhappy sister's case, for I am certain her reason and good sense can never be reduced to such a stupefaction; yet the strongest intellects and most resolute minds may possibly be vanquished in some degree by an oppressive load of anguish and uninterrupted hours of care.

Now I am speaking of her, I must not omit the mention of Mr

Joseph Marples,* her second husband, the faithful partner of her sorrows, who is worthy the consideration of every human heart as he tenderly endeavours to soften all her distresses, which doubly prey on his mind from want of power totally to dissipate, and wears to her a pleasing aspect with a bleeding heart. But I hope providence has still an unforeseen happiness in store for them, and that I shall see their clouds of grief brightened with smiles of joy, from the possession of a happier fortune.

I must now leave them in the industrious and pleasing search of what I hope they'll shortly obtain, and pursue my story by informing my reader, when I removed from my airy mansion before described, I took it into my head to dive into trade. To that end, I took a shop in Long Acre, and turned oil-woman and grocer.

This new whim proved very successful, for every soul of my acquaintance, of which I have a numerous share, came in turn to see my mercantile face, which carried in it as conceited an air of trade as it had before in physic, and I talked of 'myself and other dealers', as I was pleased to term it. The rise and fall of sugars was my constant topic, and trading abroad and at home was at frequent in my mouth as my meals. To complete the ridiculous scene, I constantly took in the papers to see how matters went at Bear Quay,† what ships were come in, or lost, who in our trade was broke, or who advertised teas at the lowest prices, ending with a comment upon those dealers who were endeavouring to undersell us, shrewdly prognosticating their never being quiet till they had rendered the article of tea a mere drug and that I and many more of the business should be obliged entirely to give it up; an injury to traffic in general that must be allowed.

I must beg leave, gentle reader, to tell you that my stock perhaps did not exceed ten or a dozen pounds at a time of each sort, but that furnished me with as much discourse as if I had the whole lading of a ship in my shop. Then as to oils, to be sure, the famous Nobbes‡ and fifty more were not to be put in competition with mine for their excellence and, though I seldom kept above a gallon

---

*After the death in 1738 of Brett, Elizabeth Cibber married Mr Marples. In 1753 *The Gentleman's Magazine* listed Joseph Marples in their bankruptcies column.
†specialized in the landing and shipment of corn and other foodstuffs. A market held there on Mondays, Wednesdays and Fridays.
‡Thomas Nobbes's oil shop in the Strand

of a sort in the house, I carried on the farce so far as to write to country chapmen* to deal with me.

Then I considered, until I had established a universal trade, I'd save, for the first year, the expense of an out-rider, as I was a very good horsewoman, and go the journeys myself, concluding with a significant nod, that money was as well in my own pocket as another's. But, providentially for me, I could gain no country customers, for, as the case stood, I must positively have let them had the goods considerably to my own loss, and, as a proof, will relate a circumstance that occurred to me in the selling a quarter of a hundred of lump sugar to a good-natured friend, who came to buy it for no other reason but that I sold it.

It is customary in buying of sugars by the hundred to be allowed a treat of six pound extra. I was so insufferably proud of hearing so large a quantity demanded by my friend, that I really forgot the character of grocer, and, fancying myself the sugar baker, allowed in the twenty-five pounds the half of what I got in the hundred, alleging that it was our way when people dealt for large quantities to make an allowance over and above the common weight.

My friend, who knew no better than myself, promised me all the custom she could bring, which, if she had been as good as her word, might in due course of time have paved the way for me either to Newgate, the Fleet, or Marshalsea.†

After my friend was gone with her bargain, I began, as I thought trade increasing, to think it proper to purchase a large pair of scales to weigh by hundreds and a large beam to hang them on, and set out next morning to that purpose, traversing through Drury Lane, Holborn, Fleet Ditch, etc., but, meeting with nothing to my mind, returned home with a resolution to have a pair made.

The good woman who kept the house, upon hearing I had been endeavouring to make this needless purchase, made bold to enquire into the necessity of it, upon which it told her what had happened the day before and mentioned, as a proof of my knowledge of trade, the advantage I allowed to my friend. She for sometime left me amazed at her meaning, while she was almost strangled with laughing at my folly.

When she came to herself, I gravely asked where the joke lay and what mighty wonder there was in my having an increasing trade, who had such an universal acquaintance? As soon as she was able

*pedlars
†London prisons used for debtors

40

to convince me of the error I had committed, in giving one half of the over-weight in a quarter of a hundred which was allowed in a whole hundred only, I began to drop my jaw and looked as foolish as any reasonable person may suppose on so ridiculous an occasion.

Links and flambeaux* are a commodity belonging to the oil trade (at least generally sold in shops of that kind) and constant and large demands I had for both. But I remember, in particular, one of those nocturnal illuminators, who are the necessary conductors for those who did not choose chairs or coaches, came every night just before candle time, which is the dusky part of the evening, the most convenient light for perpetrating a wicked intent, as will be proved in the sequel of my story.

To be sure, I thought myself infinitely obliged to the sooty-coloured youth for using my shop, and was mighty proud of his handsel† every evening, and sometimes, as I dealt in spiritous liquors, treated him with a dram and many thanks for his own and other gentleman's custom of his profession. The arch villain smiled, and expressed great satisfaction that even, in his poor way, he had the power of serving his good mistress. He bowed and I curtseyed till, walking backwards out of my shop, he had complimented me out of every brass weight I had in it.

He had not been gone five minutes ere I had occasion to make use of some of them, when, to my great amazement and confusion, not one was to be found. Unluckily for me, they were piled up one within the other and injudiciously placed in the corner of the window next the door, quite pat to his purpose, and he was really so perfect a master of his art in filching, that, notwithstanding the great ceremony that passed between us from the upper end of the shop to the lower, he went off entirely undiscovered in his villainy.

I need not tell the reader it was the last interview we ever had till I (to his great misfortune) saw him making a small tour in a two-wheeled coach from Newgate to Tyburn,‡ a college where many industrious squires like himself have frequently and deservedly taken their degrees.

This second fracas so closely pursuing the former, I had some secret thoughts of shutting up my shop for ever to conceal my misfortunes and disgrace, though I altered my mind for that time,

*torches used for lighting people along the unlit streets
†handshake on a deal
‡place of execution; now Marble Arch

but I think, in about three months after, I positively threw it up possessed of a hundred pounds' stock, all paid for, to keep a grand puppet-show over the Tennis Court in James Street, which is licensed, and is the only one in this kingdom that has had the good fortune to obtain so advantageous a grant.

When I first went into my shop, I was horribly puzzled for the means of securing my effects from the power of my husband, who, though he did not live with me, I knew had a right to make bold with any thing that was mine, as there was no formal article of separation between us. And I could not easily brook his taking anything from me to be profusely expended on his mistress, who lived no further from me than the house next to the coachmaker's in Great Queen Street, and was sister to the famous Mrs Sally K—g,* one of the ladies of the highest irreputable reputation at that time in or about Covent Garden. However, to prevent any danger, I gave and took all receipts (till Mr Charke went to Jamaica, where he died in about twenty months after his leaving England) in the name of a widow gentlewoman who boarded with me, and I sat quiet and snug with the pleasing reflection of my security, though he suspected I had a hand in the plot.

But he did not stay long enough to trouble me on that score, for his lady was one day unfortunately arrested for a hundred pounds, as they sat *tête-à-tête* at dinner, and he, to show his gallantry, went directly into the City and immediately purchased her redemption by taking up that sum of the merchants who were agents for the gentleman he went over with, and whom, till then, he left in uncertainty whether he would go or not.

It was concerted between this happy pair that madam should follow and, I suppose, pass in the Indies for his wife, which she had my leave to do, though she were a lady.

As I have, among many other censures, laboured under that of being a giddy, indiscreet wife, I must take this opportunity of referring myself to the superior judgement of those who read my story, whether a young creature, who actually married for love (at least I thought so – nay, was foolish enough to think myself equally beloved) must not naturally be incensed, when, in less than a month after marriage, I received the most demonstrative proofs of disregard where I ought to have found the greatest tenderness; to

*Sarah King paid rates on a fashionable property in Bridges Street East, Covent Garden, next door to Charles Fleetwood.

be, even to my face, apparently convinced of his insatiate fondness for a plurality of common wretches that were to be had for half-a-crown. This consequently raised in me both aversion and contempt, and, not having years enough to afford me much reflection, nor patience sufficient to sit down, like Lady Easy,* contented with my wrongs till experience might by chance have made him wiser.

Had he entertained a reciprocal affection for me, he had, when I married him, so absolute a possession of my heart it was in his power to have moulded my temper as he thought fit. But the ungrateful returns my fondness met with could not fail of the unhappy effects of a growing disregard on my side.

I was in hope the birth of my little girl might have made some impression on his mind, but it was the same thing after as before it. Nor did he make the least provision for either of us when he went abroad. It is true I was then in Lincoln's Inn Fields Playhouse, and from thence engaged at a good salary with the late Mr Fielding,† but then I was as liable to death or infirmities as any other part of the creation, which might have disimpowered me from getting my own or my child's bread.

Pray what was to become of us then? I laboured under the melancholy circumstance of being newly under my father's displeasure, and consequently no redress to be hoped or expected from that quarter, which he very well knew, and, as I have been since informed, was one of the principal sowers of sedition betwixt us. (Though, at the same time, he would explode my father behind his back, and condemn him to me for the very things he had partly urged him to.)

However, though he did not chose to be a husband or a father, he proved himself a son, by making an assignment of twenty pounds a year during his life to his mother, who constantly made it her practice to be one of the party with him and his lady, and very confidently come from them to my apartment and give me a history of the chat of the day that had passed between them.

But peace to his manes,‡ and I hope heaven has forgiven him, as I do from my soul and wish, for both our sakes, he had been master of more discretion, I had then possibly been possessed of more prudence.

*character in Colley Cibber's *The Careless Husband*
†the playwright, manager, novelist and judge Henry Fielding (1707–54)
‡ghost or spirit

About a year before he went to the Indies, I had the misfortune to lose my dear mother, otherwise I should not have undergone that perturbation of mind I suffered from his not leaving anything, in case of accidents, for mine and the child's support, as my mother's tenderness would have made us equally her care, in any exigence that might have occurred to me. But, alas, she was gone, to my sorrow, even to the present minute in which I mention her, and shall ever revere her memory, as is quite incumbent on me for her inexpressible fondness and tender regard for me, to the latest moment of her life.

This dear woman was possessed of every personal charm that could render her attractive and amiable. Her conquest over my father was by a visit he made to her late brother, whom I have before mentioned, and, as he passed by the chamber where she was accompanying her own voice on the harpsichord, his ear was immediately charmed, on which he begged to be introduced, and at first sight was captivated. Nor, as I hear, was she less delighted with the sprightliness of his wit, than he was with the fund of perfection with which art and nature had equally endowed her. In short, a private courtship began, and ended in a marriage against her father's consent, as Mr Colley Cibber was then rather too young for a husband, in the old gentleman's opinion, he not coming to age till after, as I have been told, the birth of his second child. But, notwithstanding, my grandfather in the end gave her a fortune, and intended a larger, but this marriage made him convert the intended additional sum to another use and, in revenge, built a folly on the Thames, called Shore's Folly, which was demolished some years before I was born.

Her father's family, exclusive of her children, is now entirely extinct, by the death of my uncle, who, poor man, had the misfortune to be ever touched in his brain, and, as a convincing proof, married his maid, at an age when he and she both had more occasion for a nurse than a parson.

We have proof positive of his being incapable of making a will that can stand good; for which reason I am determined, as being one of the heirs at law, to have a trial of skill with the ancient lady, and see whether a proper appeal to the court of chancery won't be the happy means of setting aside a madman's will, and make way for those who have a more legal and justifiable claim to his effects than an old woman, whose utmost merit consisted in being his servant. I am only astonished they have let her alone so long, but I promise her she shall not find me quite so passive – and that right soon.

> 'And heaven give our arms success,
> As our cause has justice in it.'

For some time I resided at the Tennis Court with my puppet-show, which was allowed to be the most elegant that was ever exhibited. I was so very curious that I bought mezzotintos of several eminent persons and had the faces carved from them. Then, in regard to my clothes, I spared for no cost to make them splendidly magnificent, and the scenes were agreeable to the rest.

This affair stood me in some hundreds, and would have paid all costs and charges, if I had not, through excessive fatigue in accomplishing it, acquired a violent fever, which had like to have carried me off and consequently gave a damp to the run I should otherwise have had, as I was one of the principal exhibitors for those gentry; whose mouths were, like many others we have seen move, without any reality of utterance, or at least so unintelligible in the attempt they might as well have closed their lips without raising an expectation they were unlucky enough to disappoint, whether orators or players, is not material. But as I have myself been lately admitted into the number of the former, and from my youth helped to fill up the catalogue of the latter, I hope no exception will be taken, as the cap may as reasonably fit myself as any other of either profession, though I must beg leave to hint, however deficient I, or some of my contemporaries may be, every tragic player, at least, should be an orator.

It is no compliment to Mr Garrick* to say he is both; consequently encomiums are needless to prove what the nicest judges have for some few years past been so pleasingly convinced of.

It is, I own, natural and necessary to apologize for disgressing from a subject, but I hope when the reader considers the merit of the person who occasioned it, I may, in the eye of reason and judgement, stand excused. Perhaps, as Mr Garrick is a person who many may undoubtedly wish to pay their court to, this remark may be deemed adulation, bu I must beg their pardons and assure them they would in that point be guilty of a very great error, for I am the last creature in the world to be picked out for that piece of folly, nay, I think so meanly of it as to set it down as servility which I

*The great actor-manager, David Garrick (1717–79)

heartily condemn and have been often blamed for a too openness of temper, that has sometimes hazarded the loss of a friend.

In regard to the above-mentioned gentlemen, there is not any mortal breathing that enjoys the benefit of hearing and of sight but must receive infinite delight from his performance, though they should be ever so indifferent to him when off the stage. But that is not my case, I have received some acts of friendship from him, therefore of course must revere him as a benefactor, and am proud of this opportunity to make him a public acknowledgement.

It is certain, there never was known a more unfortunate devil than I have been, but I have, in the height of all my sorrows, happily found a numerous quantity of friends, whose commiseration shall be taken notice of with the utmost gratitude before I close this narrative. Now, on to the affairs of state.

When I quitted the Tennis Court, I took a house in Marsham Street, Westminster, and lived very privately for a little while, till I began to consider that my wooden troop might as well be put in action and determined to march to Tunbridge Wells at the head of them. When I arrived, there was a general who had taken the field before me: one Lacon,* a famous person, who had for many successive years, and indeed very successfully, entertained the company with those inanimate heroes and heroines. I therefore was obliged to sound a retreat and content myself with confining my forces and fighting against Lacon *in propria persona* at Ashley's great room.

I had living numbers sufficient to play two or three of our thinnest comedies, and our only tragedy we had to our backs was *George Barnwell*, which I played for my own benefit the last night, and set out next morning for London.

When I arrived there, I began to consider which way I should turn myself. Being then out of the houses, and in no likelihood of future restoration, I resolved to make the best use I could of my figures without fatiguing myself any further, and let my comedians out for hire to a man who was principally concerned in the formation of them. But business not answering his ends and my expectations, I sold, for twenty guineas, what cost me near five hundred pounds. Another proof of my discretion, and, indeed, of the honesty of the purchaser, that knew the original expense of them, and the reality of their worth. But as I have condemned him

*famous puppeteer, waxwork exhibitor and watercolourist (?–*c*.1757)

for taking the advantage of my necessity, shall conceal his name, and hope he'll have modesty enough, if this paragraph should be read to him (by some who knew the affair), to add one sin more, in denying that he was the person.

I even gave him the privilege, as I had a licence, to make use of that and my name, which now, whenever I think proper (as I shall never exhibit anything than can possibly give offence), shall always employ Mr Yeates,* who is a skilful person, and one who has made it his business from his youth upwards.

As it is very possible I may entertain the town with some unacountable oddity of that kind very shortly; those that like to laugh I know will encourage me, and I am certain there is no one in the world more fit than myself to be laughed at. I confess myself an odd mortal, and believe I need no force of argument beyond what has been already said to bring the whole globe terrestial into that opinion.

It has been hinted (and indeed luckily came to my ear), that I should never have patience to go through the process of my life. I don't suppose those who could advance such a piece of folly in me could possibly be my friends and am sorry for their want of humanity, as this work is at present the staff of my life, and such an insinuation must naturally deter many from taking it on, if they suppose me capable of such an inconsistency. So far from it, that were I, by miracle, capable of riding in my own coach, I would still pursue my scheme, till I had brought it to a conclusion, for a happy change of circumstances makes

'Misfortunes past prove stories of delight'

and what now is my support would then be my amusement.

It is strange, but true, let people use the most honest endeavours to support themselves, there is generally some ridiculous mortal that, without rhyme or reason, and for the sake of saying something, without any real views (good or ill), are often detrimental to the industrious or oppressed. Be it as it may, it is an error, I fear, invincible and hurtful to both and, sure, unprovoked to offer an injury, is unpardonable! If the contrary were the case, it is nobler far to overlook than resent, but, as I have no reason to believe that I have offended, I hope for the future no person will be indiscreet

*Richard Yeates, actor, puppeteer and manager

enough to assert that for a truth, which time will prove to be a real falsehood.

Not long after I had parted from what might really by good management have brought me in a very comfortable subsistence (and in a genteel light), I was addressed by a worthy gentleman (being then a widow) and closely pursued till I consented to an honourable though very secret alliance, and, in compliance to the person, bound myself by all the vows sincerest friendship could inspire never to confess who he was. Gratitude was my motive to consent to this conjunction, and extreme fondness was his inducement to request it. To be short – he soon died, and, unhappily for me, not only from sustaining the loss of a valuable and sincere friend, but by the unexpected stroke of death I was deprived of every hope and means of a support.

As I have overcome all the inconveniences of life this terrible shock of fate rendered me liable to, I am contented and think myself happy, but not even the most inexplicable sorrows I was immersed in ever did, nor shall any motive whatever, make me break that vow I made to the person by a discovery of his name.

This was a means indeed by which I hoped to have secured myself far above those distresses I have known, but, alas, proved the fatal cause of all. I was left involved with debts I had no means of paying, and, through the villanous instigation of a wicked drunken woman, was arrested for seven pounds, when, as heaven shall judge me, I did not know where to raise as many pence.

THE FACTS
1730–9

Charlotte Cibber married her first husband Richard Charke at St Martin-in-the-Fields, the church where she had been baptized, on 3 February 1730. Her father gave his consent. (A Richard Charke was born in Bodmin in March 1703. Charlotte's husband must have been born at about this time, and it is possible that this parish register entry refers to him.)

An actor, violinist and composer, Richard Charke had been working for Charlotte's father's Drury Lane Theatre company for just under a year. He began his career as a dancing master, but by 1729 he was leader of the orchestra at Drury Lane. He played small to medium-sized roles, also usually singing solo songs or playing his violin at some point during the performance, or during one or more of the intervals.

The same year as this marriage, he published a collection of theatre songs. His later *Medley or Comic Overtures* are said to be the original models for the overtures now played at the start of musical comedies. The first known performance of one of these medley overtures was Charke's overture to *Harlequin Restored* in 1732, in which he arranged fragments from the march from Handel's *Scipione*, a short burst from Purcell's *King Arthur* and *Lillibulero*. Music historians praise Charke's clever setting of a 3/4 melody to a 6/8 accompaniment in the adagio of this overture.[1]

He was still acting and playing in 1733, when he joined the rebels and moved with his wife and her brother Theophilus to the Haymarket Theatre, where he played Osric in *Hamlet*.

In the summer of 1736 he was still in London, and shortly afterwards borrowed £100 from Henry Moore's London agent, presumably to bail out his mistress. Mrs Charke identifies this woman as the sister to Sally King of Covent Garden. Mrs Sarah King lived next to the theatre manager, Charles Fleetwood, in Bridges Street, Covent Garden.[2]

It has been suggested that Moore invited Charke to join him in Jamaica, after helping him bail out Charke's mistress. Wright's *Revels in Jamaica* states that Charke died about eighteen months after his arrival in Jamaica, and that his mistress never left London; certainly Richard Charke was dead by 20 October 1744, when his medley overture was announced as by 'the late Mr Charke'.[3]

In choosing a musician for a husband, Charlotte was forging yet another link with her mother, for Katherine Cibber (née Shore) and her brothers were all musicians. Katherine herself, before she met Colley, had been taken seriously as a performer in her own right. She was the soprano Miss Shaw often connected with performances by Henry and Daniel Purcell. She also played the harpsichord. But she gave up all thoughts of a musical career when she married Colley Cibber and devoted her time to bearing their entourage of children.

Katherine Cibber's father, Matthias Shore, spent a great deal of money on a house-boat on the Thames shortly before Katherine's marriage. Four days before the wedding Narcissus Luttrell made a note of a visit by Queen Mary to Shore's boat: 'The queen went lately on board of Mr Shore's pleasure boat against Whitehall, and heard a consort of music, vocal and instrumental; it was built for entertainment, having 24 sash windows, and 4 banqueting houses on top.' 'A timber building erected on a strong barge', it lay at anchor near Cupid's Stairs, and was 'commonly called the Folly'.[4]

Although Matthias Shore may have spent his cash in this way to indicate his displeasure at his daughter's choice of husband, he did relent before his death on 27 May 1700, and left money to his daughter in his will. None the less, throughout that document, he referred to her in each case as Katherine *Shore*, and never by her married name, Cibber.[5]

William, Katherine's elder brother, succeeded his father as royal Sergeant-Trumpeter. He died in 1707 and his will sparked off the chancery proceedings mentioned in Chapter 1.

Charlotte's other uncle, John, was the most versatile and the most famous member of the Shore family. He played trumpet, lute and violin, and was a musician in the royal orchestra along with John Blow, and Henry, John and Solomon Eccles. He succeeded his brother as Sergeant-Trumpeter, but split his lip and had to give up performing. He not only played but also made instruments, and was also an inventor: in 1711 he invented the tuning fork, still regarded as the most convenient and reliable tool for determining pitch.[6]

John Shore died in November 1752 and in his will left to 'Mr Colley Cibber, the Poet Laureate and to each of his children as shall be living at the time of my death, the sum of one shilling to every of them that shall demand the same of my said executrix, and I give them no more by reason of their evil behaviour towards me.' The bulk of his estate he left to his 'dear and well-beloved wife, Hannah Shore, in reward for her tender care, regard and affection towards me'.[7] Despite her threats to sue Hannah Shore, Charlotte does not seem to have instigated any chancery proceedings on this will.

Charlotte's career in the theatre can be followed very accurately.

Mrs Sarah Thurmond had a benefit performance of Vanbrugh's *The Provok'd Wife* on 8 April 1730. It is now agreed that the actress, billed as 'a young gentlewoman', who took the role of Mademoiselle at that performance was Charlotte Charke. The casting of Mademoiselle had been unstable for some time. In the previous three performances of the play that season the cast was the same as at this performance, *except* that Mademoiselle was played on each occasion by a different actress: Mrs Wetherilt on

16 October, Mrs Shireburn on 17 December 1729, and Mrs Laguerre on 16 March 1730.

At the next performance of that play, on Tuesday 28 April, Charlotte played Mademoiselle again, but this time she was billed – the advertisments read: 'Mrs Charke, being the Second Time of her Appearance upon the Stage.' As she tells us in the *Narrative*, it was a benefit for her husband and Miss Raftor, soon to become better known as Kitty Clive.

Charlotte was pregnant at the time of her first appearances, and her daughter, Catherine Maria Charke, was probably born in late November, as she was christened at St Clement Danes on 6 December 1730.

Mrs Charke was back on stage as Mademoiselle a month later, and played the part for the rest of the season. She also appeared as Aurora in the afterpiece *Cephalus and Procris*, and Flora in *Don John*. On Tuesday 22 June 1731 she created the part of Lucy in George Lillo's tragedy *The London Merchant: or George Barnwell*, one of the most successful and enduring of eighteenth-century plays.

As stock reader (general understudy) Mrs Charke also found herself occasionally going on at the last minute for sick actresses. Mary Porter, one of the company's leading tragic actresses, lived near Hendon and drove herself home each night in a one-horse chaise. As a precaution, she always carried a brace of pistols. One night in the summer of 1731 she was stopped by a highwayman. She took out her gun, and the startled highwayman explained that he was not a professional thief but had been driven to it: he was poor and had to support a large family. Mrs Porter gave him about ten guineas, all she had on her, and took his address before leaving him. Unfortunately her horse stumbled on the way home, the chaise overturned and Mrs Porter broke her thigh bone. Although she was so badly injured she was unable to work for two years, she made enquiries into the highwayman's circumstances, discovered his story was true, and raised about £60 for the relief of his family. In August 1732, a year after Mrs Porter's accident, Mrs Charke was *billed* to play Mrs Porter's role of Alicia in Rowe's tragedy *Jane Shore*, opposite Mrs Butler. She played it again in April 1733.

On 9 June 1732, Mrs Charke played Andromache in Philips's *The Distressed Mother*. This was not an understudy performance but part of a short season for the junior actors organized by Charlotte's brother, Theophilus. Mrs Butler was in the other female leading role, Hermione, and Theophilus played Orestes. Theophilus's experiment was over by 7 November that year when the leading actress Mrs Horton was back in her role of Andromache and Mills again played Orestes.

In August 1732 Charlotte appeared at her first Bartholomew Fair, and, a few days later, at Drury Lane, she played her first male role, Roderigo in *Othello*.

In the 1732–3 Drury Lane season, apart from her old roles, (Mademoiselle, Lucy, etc.) she played Mrs Slammekin, the first of many different roles she attempted in Gay's *The Beggar's Opera*, Hoyden in *The Relapse* (her brother was Foppington), Molly in *The Boarding School Romp*, and Fainlove in *The Tender Husband*. In December, while Charlotte was playing Mrs Lupine in Charles Johnson's *Caelia or The Perjured Lover*, the author 'had the mortification to see this play acted . . . and to hear the characters of Mother Lupine and her women disapproved by several of the audience, who, as if they thought they were in bad company, were very severe'.[8]

Then in May, shortly after she played Damon in the afterpiece *Damon and Daphne* (ascribed to Theophilus, and in which Mrs Grace played Daphne, Kitty Clive played Venus, and Richard Charke played one of his concertos during the interval), Charlotte, along with other members of the company, joined her brother in a rebellion over salaries and management in general.

The story of London's theatrical patent is a long and complicated one, but the actors' mutiny of 1733 came about largely because of the way Colley Cibber handled the disposal of his share of the patent. Having retired as an actor, Cibber senior at first rented his share of the theatre's patent to his son Theophilus. Naturally enough Theophilus, as a practical acting-writing-managing member of the company (not to mention son of the share-owner), expected his father to sell or at least continue renting him the share. However, when Colley decided he needed the money, he chose to realize the whole value of his share at its top market price. Going over Theophilus's head, for 3000 guineas he sold out to John Highmore, a gentleman who knew little of theatrical business, but as an amateur actor fancied himself a great judge of acting. On 16 May Highmore and his fellow patentees, sensing rebellion in the air, removed the costumes and properties from the theatre and locked Theophilus and the other actors out.

Theophilus and his crew, including the Charkes, soon broke into the building and locked the managers out. While a pamphlet and newspaper war raged, Theophilus and many of the company decamped to the Haymarket and set up a rival company. Highmore made several attempts to close them down, and even had the mutinous actor John Harper arrested as vagrant under the statute of 12 Anne. This was a bad mistake, as Harper was a much-loved corpulent personality, and as a householder could not legally *be* a vagrant.

Charlotte played the weeks of August and September 1733 at Theophilus's booth at Bartholomew and Southwark Fairs,[9] where she played a male role – Haly in Nicholas Rowe's *Tamerlane*. Her brother played Bajazeth, and Adam Hallam, who was to come to her aid later in her life, played Tamerlane.

The new Haymarket company played from early October 1733 to the end of the following February (when Highmore eventually admitted defeat and sold the share of Charles Fleetwood), and Mrs Charke added to her repertoire the roles of Sylvia in *The Recruiting Officer*, Charlotte Welldone in Southerne's *Oroonoko* and Doll Common in Ben Jonson's *The Alchemist*.

Charlotte's mother Katherine died after an asthma attack on 17 January 1734. It seems that when she died, although Colley Cibber had a house in Berkeley Square, the most fashionable address in London, his wife was living in the more countrified area of Kensington.[10] Charlotte gives the impression that her mother spent much time living in the country while her father worked in town, but by this time he was only making the odd guest appearance on stage, and writing. Neither of these occupations would have necessitated his living separately from his wife, who preferred the clearer air of the suburbs. (Remember, the pistol-toting Mary Porter lived out at Hendon.) His well-known hobbies of club-going, gambling and hobnobbing with the gentry, however, would have made a bachelor townhouse a must.

On the day that her mother died, Charlotte was playing one of her big roles with Theophilus's Haymarket company, Alicia in *Jane Shore*. It was just before all her major troubles started. She returned to Drury Lane for a few performances in March and April 1734, before embarking on management for the first time. The large London theatres usually closed for the summer, and most actors found some alternative employment, some in the provinces, some at the Fairs. Charlotte took over a main London house as a showcase for her bizarre talent.

For her Drury Lane benefit performance (maybe she used the

profits from this to finance her summer season), she chose to play Roderigo.

On 20 May an advertisement in the *Daily Advertiser* proclaimed: 'A mad company of comedians having lately taken the Haymarket Theatre, propose to convert it into a mad-house, and humbly hope the Town will be as mad as themselves and come frequently to see their mad performances which will be madly exhibited, two or three times a week, during the summer season.' Another announcement in the next day's *Daily Journal* may sound satirical, but give a very accurate description of Mrs Charke's forthcoming season: 'We hear that the mad company of the Haymarket design to keep up that character, by performing *The Beggar's Opera* in Roman dresses, and exhibiting *Hurlothrumbo*, in which Mrs Charke attempts the character of Lord Flame.'[11]

Three days after the second announcement she made one appearance at Lincoln's Inn Fields, playing Lucy, the second the five roles she eventually played in *The Beggar's Opera*.

Then her season started. In less than three months she played a mind-boggling list of parts including Macheath (her third role in *The Beggar's Opera*) in Roman dress, Falstaff and Pistol (on separate occasions – in *The Humours of Sir John Falstaff, Justice Shallow and Ancient Pistol*), Mr Townly (*The Provok'd Husband*), Rovewell (her husband's most famous role) in *The Contrivances*, Sir Charles (*The Beaux' Stratagem*), Lothario (*The Fair Penitent*) and the name parts in *The Mock Doctor* and *George Barnwell*. She also took supporting roles, and played Lucy for Mrs Roberts's benefit while that Lady took the role of Macheath.

On 20 August, two days before the end of her season at the Haymarket, she played Townly in *The Provok'd Husband* in a performance 'at the desire of Tomo Chaci, Micho or King of the Indians of Yamacrow, Banauki his wife, Tooanahowi, his nephew, and the rest of the Indians'. It is possible that this was a genuine visit by foreign dignitaries, but it sounds as though it was one of her joke announcements (the style of which were to be taken up with glee by Henry Fielding).

She was back at Drury Lane for the autumn season, but, compared with the frantic activity of her own summer season, had little to do. She played much the same repertoire of support roles as she had always done at Drury Lane. She also took on two very important parts at a quarter of an hour's notice.

Dryden's tragedy *All For Love* was performed, for the first time in seven years, in April 1734, with Mrs Heron as Cleopatra. In December Mrs Heron repeated her performance, and the following January played it again. *The Plot*, 'a new tragi-comi-farcical oper-atical grotesque pantomime', an afterpiece by John Kelly was played the same night. In that piece Charlotte took the role of 'a French-woman'.

The tragedy's next appearance was on Monday 5 May 1735, by command of His Royal Highness, and for the benefit of Mr Worsdale, who had also written the afterpiece, *A Cure for a Scold*. Charlotte Charke was not advertised among the all-star cast, but this performance includes all the peripheral evidence discussed by Mrs Charke, and must have been the day that Mary Heron broke her kneecap and the young Charlotte was sent for at the second music.

Elizabeth Butler was scheduled for performances of Queen Elizabeth in John Banks's *The Unhappy Favourite: or the Earl of Essex* in February, October and December 1735. Charlotte's take-over performance in this role could not have been, as she claims, shortly after her trial as Cleopatra. She had walked out of the Drury Lane company by June 1735 (only weeks after her understudy performance of Cleopatra) so she either played the February performance of *Essex*, or perhaps she confused the Queen Elizabeths. Banks's *The Unhappy Favourite* is about Queen Elizabeth and Essex, his *Albion Queens* explores an earlier episode in Queen Elizabeth's reign, her relationship with Mary Queen of Scots. Charlotte Charke was billed to appear as Douglas, a supporting (female) role in this play on 21 April 1735, a few weeks *before* her attempt at Cleopatra. Mrs Butler was announced in the role of Queen Elizabeth, and it is possible that Charlotte was called at the last minute to take over as the Queen on this occasion. In fact her appearance as Cleopatra for Mrs Heron must be one of her last appearances before she took her 'French leave' of Fleet-wood's company and spent five months working here and there, sometimes managing her own troupe, sometimes working for others.

Her first performance away from Drury Lane was a one night stand on 19 June at Lincoln's Inn Fields. She played Lord Fopping-ton, the role which 'belonged' to her father. She also spoke the epilogue in the character of Foppington, and after the afterpiece (*The Devil to Pay*, in which she played Sir John) she and Miss Brett, her sister Elizabeth's daughter Anne, performed a dance called

'The Black Joke' (with a song sung by somebody and nobody; the characters dressed in black and white, and presumably, with trick lighting, disappearing at relevant moments during the song). The whole performance was for the benefit of 'a family in distress', presumably Mrs Charke and Miss Brett's own, and was designed 'for the entertainment of Che-Sazan Outsim, Hindy-Gylesangbier, Charadab-Sinadab, Coacormin, the Chinese Mandarins, lately arrived in England on a tour through Europe, being the only people of that nation who have been in England since the reign of King James I'. Was this another of Mrs Charke's joke announcements?

On 1 July she was back at Drury Lane (the main company were on summer leave), playing the leading female role, Milwood, in *The London Merchant*. Ten days later she was playing the male lead, George Barnwell, in the same show at Lincoln's Inn Fields. Over the next four months she played Grizzle in *The Tragedy of Tragedies*; Marius Jr in *Caius Marius*: Pickle Herring in *Bartholomew Fair*; Polly, her fourth role in *The Beggar's Opera*; and the French Harlequin in her own (unpublished) play, *The Carnival*, at Lincoln's Inn Fields; Alicia in *Jane Shore* at the Haymarket and then Alicia, Polly and Milwood at the theatre in York Buildings, Villiers Street.

At York Buildings she committed one of the worst of theatrical crimes: she made some very serious allegations about actors and managers at Drury Lane in her own play *The Art of Management*. In this piece she took the role of Mrs Tragic, an unfairly treated actress. An article concerning the first night appeared in the *Daily Advertiser* for 26 September: 'We hear that Mrs Charke . . . drew tears from the whole audience and in her prologue, which she spoke very pathetically, and the new farce . . . was very much applauded notwithstanding the impotent attempts of several young clerks to raise a riot, who were for that purpose properly marshalled by the running lawyer their master. Their rude behaviour was so extraordinary that several gentlemen were provoked to threaten them with the discipline of their canes, upon which they thought proper to desist.'

Not content with trying to disrupt the first night, Charles Fleetwood bought as many copies of the printed play as he could lay his hands on, hoping to burn them all. Luckily a few survive. The play was dedicated to him:

Sir,

It may appear something strange that I chose you for a patron, but as I hate ingratitude, whom could, or ought I so soon address as yourself? The many obligations I have received from you would make it an unpardonable error in me, were I to lose this opportunity of returning you my sincerest thanks. And at once convince you how just a sense I have of your worth and honour. That you are a gentleman of a most profound judgement, every action of your life is a sufficient testimony. But since you have kindly condescended to distract the poor players with your understanding you are become an inimitable original. In short sir, there's no doing you justice; thou excellent young man.

Since therefore 'tis not in my power to pay your merits due, I must content myself with only saying that take you for all in all, I hope I ne'er shall look upon your like again. I have such an implicit regard for you that I would not have you encumber your head with theatric affairs any longer, but leave it to the fools who are used to it, and make no more vacancies but with yourself, as being, in my opinion, the least use and consequently the easier spared,
I am, sir,
with all due respect,
your most obliged, and super abundant, humble servant,
Charlotte Charke.[12]

In the preface she describes (with much passion and little grammar) the events which led her to write the play:

'I shall give a just account of the manner of my being discharged, as to the reasons, that will be as difficult a task for me as for the gentleman who did it, for he has often spoke of me as one whom he thought worth acceptance (as a player) in any theatre; therefore any contrary reason after such a declaration would be ridiculous; but I had a letter sent me to inform me the charge being too high made it necessary to lessen it by dismissing me. I confess it was what I did not in the least expect as being ignorant of having deserved it. When a mention was made for my being recalled (tho' not by me) I was refused, and it was not long before we left off playing. That I at a quarter of an hour's warning twice read two capital parts, viz: the Queen in Essex and another night Cleopatra—which I believe I did not appear scandalous in, if I may be allowed to judge by the good nature of the audience, tho' on such occasions they are generally tender to young players.

I can't but say 'tis hard to be deprived of a means of an honest livelihood without giving some immediate provocation, and for my private misconduct, which it seems has been (for want of a better alleged reason) tho' a bad one; for while my follies are only hurtful to myself, I know no right that any persons, unless relations or very good friends, have to call me to account, I'll allow private virtues heighten public merits, but then the want of those private virtues won't affect an actor's performance.

And for me, tho' I confess it with a blush, I have paid so little regard to myself that I rather have made my faults too conspicuous, than that I have concealed them, so the Town will hardly be surprised at what they have so long been acquainted with.'

In the play itself she addresses some of the age-old problems which actors find themselves labouring under due to the whim of the moneymen.

BLOODBOLT (Macklin): I'll engage to furnish the house with a much better company, and at a cheaper rate, ay, and have business carried on as it should be. I'll make a bear play, Pierrot, or a monkey, Harlequin, that shall outdo anything we have now upon the stage!

MRS GLIDEWELL: For that matter, sir, I don't doubt seeing your own cook-maid exhibiting a tragedy-queen before it's long, and your ostler play Sir Harry Wildair!

BLOODBOLT: And no ill thing neither. Egad! I'll soon teach 'em to come up to anything we have here.[13]

And as to pay:

BRAINLESS (Fleetwood): We are resolved to bring all our five pounders down to twenty shillings, for I don't think any actress worth more.[14]

For some of the advertised performances of *The Art of Management*, Mrs Charke was indisposed, and the performances were cancelled. This was possibly due to harassment from Fleetwood, or maybe because Mrs Charke, exhausted by the anxieties of the previous months, was genuinely ill.

Thanks to a diplomatic word from her father she was reinstated at Drury Lane in November 1735, playing Doll Common (*The Alchemist*), Mrs Otter (*The Silent Woman*) and Lucy in *The London Merchant*. Obviously, this selection of parts was very dull for a woman who had not only been her own mistress but her own master for the best part of two years, and by the new year she walked out again, regardless of the long-term results for her reputation or indeed of the embarrassment it might cause her father.

To add insult to injury, after a two-month break she joined Henry Fielding's 'Great Moghul's company of English comedians, newly imported . . . N.B. The clothes are old but the jokes are new'. Fielding was, and would remain, one of the most vociferous Colley Cibber haters.

Cibber had already inspired the wrath and disdain of many Grub Street hacks, but by this time, thanks mainly to his aspirations towards the post of Poet Laureate, his list of enemies-in-print included great wits like Jonathan Swift and Alexander Pope.

Although Fielding had actually worked for Cibber at Drury Lane, and had some of his plays accepted and performed by Cibber's company, he thought nothing of abusing him publically, criticizing his grammar and his style in poetry (or, rather, his lack of it). When Cibber had been announced Poet Laureate in November 1730, Henry Fielding inserted a new scene, *The Battle of the Poets* (featuring Sir Fopling Fribble, alias Cibber), into his satire *Tom Thumb*. In another of his plays, the revised version of *The Author's Farce*, the character representing Cibber, Marplay senior, advises his son how to choose plays for theatrical production, and gives him a few notes on playwriting:

MARPLAY SR: If thou writest thyself . . . it is thy interest to keep
   back all other authors of any merit, and be as forward to advance
   those of none . . . The arts of writing, boy, is the art of stealing
   old plays by changing the name of the play, and new ones by
   changing the name of the author.

In Fielding's newspaper, the *Champion*, he made fun of Cibber's learning: 'I know it may be objected that the English Apollo, the prince of poets, the great laureate abounds with such a redundancy of Greek and Latin that, not contented with the vulgar affectation of a motto to a play, he hath prefixed a Latin motto to every act of his *Caesar in Egypt* . . . Nay, his learning is thought to extend to the Oriental tongues, and I myself heard a gentleman reading one of his odes cry out, "Why, this is all Hebrew!"'[15]

Later Fielding was to write *An Apology for the Life of Mrs Shamela Andrews* (the title, a satire on Colley Cibber's autobiography *An Apology for the Life of Colley Cibber*; the work, a satire on *Pamela* by

Samuel Richardson, one of Cibber's close friends) and ascribe it to
Mr Conny Keyber. He also made a more personal attack on Cibber
in the opening pages of his novel *Joseph Andrews*.

Cibber, in his own *Apology* (1740), made an attempt to redress
the balance, describing Fielding's theatrical seasons, in which, it
should be remembered, *Charlotte* had been a leading player: 'These
so tolerated companies gave encouragement to a broken wit
[Fielding] to collect a fourth company, who for some time acted
plays in the Haymarket, which house the Drury Lane comedians
had lately quitted.

'This enterprising person, I say (whom I do not chose to name,
unless it could be to his advantage, or that it were of importance)
had sense enough to know that the best plays, *with bad actors*,
would turn but to a very poor account; and therefore found it
necessary to give the public some pieces of extraordinary kind, the
poetry of which he conceived ought to be so strong that *the greatest
dunce of an actor could not spoil it.*'[16]

The first part Charlotte took with Fielding's company was Lord
Place in his own satire *Pasquin*. As Lord Place, a role modelled on
and critical of Cibber, she performed part of the following dialogue:

SECOND VOTER: I am a devilish lover of sack.
LORD PLACE: Sack, say you? Odso, you shall be poet laureate.
SECOND VOTER: Poet! No, my lord, I am no poet, I can't make verses.
LORD PLACE: No matter for that – you'll be able to make odes.
SECOND VOTER: Odes, my lord! What are those?
LORD PLACE: Faith, sir, I can't tell well what they are; but I know
you may be qualified for the place without being a poet.

According to the advertisements, she took over on the 19 March
1737 (the twelfth night). *Pasquin* was a huge hit, and ran, tagged
with a selection of afterpieces, until May.

On the 25th of that month she opened in Lillo's follow-up to *The
London Merchant – Guilt its own Punishment: or Fatal Curiosity*. She
played the leading female role, Agnes. The next morning the *Daily
Advertiser* described the first night. 'Last night . . . *Guilt its own
Punishment* . . . was acted . . . with the greatest applause that has
been shown to any tragedy for many years. The scenes of distress
were so artfully worked up and so well performed that there scarce
remained a dry eye among the spectators at the representation, and

during the scene preceding the catastrophe an attentive silence possessed the whole house, more expressive of an universal approbation than the loudest applauses.'[17]

A month later she was back as Macheath.

The season made a great impact on the theatre of the eighteenth century. Fielding's choice of plays, in particular Mrs Haywood's adaptation of the Elizabethan domestic tragedy *Arden of Faversham*, and *Fatal Curiosity*, was a significant move from rant towards the less sensational middle-class domestic drama. He did not include the usual pot-boilers: pantomimes or harlequinades. In fact he more than fulfilled Mrs Charke's hopes, as expressed by Mrs Tragic, the role she herself played in *The Art of Management*:

> 'Men (not apes, nor rough-hewn bears,
> Nor mimic Andrews, from the Smithfield fairs)
> Shall our stage again, in pomp, explore,
> And to her proper rights the tragic muse restore.'

After the season ended she made appearances at the summer fairs.

In the autumn she was working for Henry Giffard at Lincoln's Inn Fields. She spent from October 1736 to February 1737 playing a wide variety of roles including Flora, the maid, in Centlivre's *The Wonder*, Tattle in Congreve's *Love For Love*, Lady Grace in Vanbrugh and Cibber's *The Provok'd Husband*, Mrs Peachum, her fifth role in Gay's *Beggar's Opera*, Alibech in Dryden's *The Indian Emperor* and Mrs Hamilton's husband (Pistol) in the anonymous *The Beggar's Pantomime* – a satire on the row, started by Theophilus Cibber, between his second wife, Susannah, and Kitty Clive over the role of Polly in *The Beggar's Opera*.

In March 1737 she was back with Fielding. His company was now billed as 'A company of comedians dropped from the clouds, late servants to their thrice-renowned majesties, Kouly Kan and Theodore. . . . 2nd N.B. Considering the extraordinary expense that must necessarily attend equipping so many monarchs of different nations the proprietor hopes the Town will not take umbrage at the prices being raised. 3rd N.B. The proprietor begs leave to enter his caveat against all (what names soever distinguished) who may hire, or be hired, to do the drudgery of hissing, catcalling &c. and entreats the town would discourage, as much as in them lies, a practice at once so scandalous and prejudicial to author, player, and every fair theatre adventure.' The play was *The Rehearsal of*

Kings; or, The Projecting Gingerbread Baker: With the unheard of catastrophe of Macplunderkan, King of Roguomania and the ignoble fall of Baron Tromperland, King of Clouts. The cast of characters included King Bombardino, King Pamper Gusto, King Taxyburndus, Campanardicoff and Mynheer Maggot, and, in the role of First Queen Incog. was Mrs Eliza Haywood, the celebrated novelist and playwright. Mrs Charke played Don Resinando.

The double bill of *Fatal Curiosity* and *The Historical Register for 1736* (Fielding's satirical look at the year's events), featured Mrs Charke in her old role of Agnes and, in the second piece, playing the auctioneer, Christopher Hen (based on the famous London auctioneer, Christopher Cock). It was 'received with the greatest applause ever shown at the theatre'.[18] The bills announced: 'All persons are desired to cry at the tragedy and laugh at the comedy, being quite contrary to the present general practice. Mr Hen gives notice that if any joke is both hissed and clapped such division will be considered an encore and the said joke be put up again.'

Colley Cibber was responsible for one of the most enduring adaptations of Shakespeare, *Richard III*, and it was he who inserted the famous line: 'Off with his head. So much for Buckingham.' In *The Historical Register* Fielding ridiculed Cibber's attempts to improve Shakespeare – the character of Ground-Ivy (a satire on Bayes, the anglification of the title Laureate) represented Cibber:

APOLLO'S BASTARD SON: Was not Shakespeare one of the greatest geniuses that ever lived?

GROUND-IVY: No, sir, Shakespeare was a pretty fellow, and said some things which only want a little of my licking to do well enough.

On the first night Cibber is reputed to have sat in one of the side boxes, and, when the audience looked at him during the Ground-Ivy scenes, to have laughed and applauded.[19]

During Passion week the Prime Minister, Sir Robert Walpole, attended a performance, and, understanding one of the lines to refer to himself and the Excise Bill, climbed on to the stage and 'immediately corrected the comedian with his own hands very severely'.

Thus began Walpole's theatrical clean-up campaign. By 20 May Walpole and his ministers had brought in a new bill seriously curbing the freedom of the theatre. It was passed within a week and became law the following month (10 George II c.19) At the end of the parliamentary session, Walpole had craftily put the Bill before a deserted House, for most MPs had already left town. The Earl of Chesterfield noted that the Act was passed 'at a very extraordinary season, and pushed with most extraordinary dispatch'.[20]

This Act was a disaster for most actors and playwrights, but particularly so for Charlotte Charke, whose behaviour at Drury Lane had spoiled her chances with one of the two patent theatres.

From the moment the Licensing Act became law the whole structure of English theatre changed. Theatrical performances were limited to the two patent houses in London. Theatre Royal Drury Lane, and Theatre Royal Covent Garden. A theatrical performance was deemed to be any presentation in which actors played for 'hire, gain, or reward'. On top of this all new plays had to have a special licence from the Lord Chamberlain, and legitimate drama (including Shakespeare) could not be performed except by the patent houses unless a specific temporary licence was granted. Henry Fielding, master of London's alternative theatre movement, retired altogether from the theatre and his company disbanded.

With the Act Mrs Charke lost not only an employer who gave her the sort of mad opportunities she relished (and who, in the course of these opportunities, had alienated her from the figurehead of the establishment, her father), but found she had *nowhere* to turn. She had publically disclaimed all interest in the patent companies, vehemently casting her lot with London theatre's 'new wave'. Had theatrical matters moved in the usual fashion, where new wave inevitably becomes establishment; if Fielding's company (and others like it) had been able to develop and expand, it is possible that Mrs Charke would have been a major figure in the London theatre of the eighteenth century. But this was not to be.

In the winter of 1737 one of the actors from Fielding's company, James Lacy, attempted to find a loop-hole in the new law, performing his one-man show. He was arrested and imprisoned in Bridewell. It is probable that Mrs Charke spent this difficult time during the months following the passing of the Act, setting up her oil shop in Long Acre.

Having had a few months to think through the theatrical problem, by the spring of 1738 the indefatigable Mrs Charke had found a loop-hole. On 13 March the *London Daily Post* and the *General Advertiser* announced 'By permission, according to Act of Parliament. At Punch's Theatre, at the Old Tennis Court in James

Street, near the Haymarket. *Henry VIII* written by Shakespeare; *Damon and Phillida*, written by Colley Cibber, Esq., Poet Laureate' together with 'a new ode, written by Mrs Charke, the music composed by an eminent hand'.

She was on the road again. By using puppets for her productions she had technically evaded the Licensing Act, while managing to organize and perform in theatrical productions – of a sort. Just to be safe, though, she really had obtained a licence for her shows.[21]

During the rest of the season Mrs Charke presented performances of *The Beggar's Wedding*, *The Covent Garden Tragedy*, *Damon and Phyllida*, *Henry IV part 1*, *The Mock Doctor*, *The Old Debauchees*, *The Unhappy Favourite* and *Richard III* – a sturdy classical season, not a pantomime or harlequinade in sight.

In her advertisements she kept reminding her audience that the plays were to be performed by puppets while announcing them exactly as if they were to be acted by actors: 'The part of the Mock Doctor by Punch, Dorcas by his wife Joan, Leander by the gentleman who performed the part of Damon in the pastoral; Charlotte by Miss Blunt who never appeared on any stage'; 'N.B. Very speedily will be performed a comedy called *Amphitryon; or the Two Sosias*. The part of the two Sosias to be performed by two Punches'; 'The part of Father Martin performed by Signior Punch from Italy'; 'The part of Mother Punchbowl by Punch, being the first time of his appearing in pettticoats'; and in the tragedy of *Richard III* 'the parts of the Prince Edward and the Duke of York by the two master Tottys . . . [in *The Beggar's Wedding*]. The part of Hunter by Farinelli; taken from the picture of that celebrated singer'.[22]

Like most Punches, hers spoke through a squeaker. Farinelli was a famous Italian castrato of the time. A book of that year refers to Charlotte's joke at his expense: ''Tis said she intends, by their artificial voices to cut out the Italians; for it has been found that Punch can hold his breath and quiver much better and longer than Farinelli; I wish this may be true, for then we may expect to have Italian songs at a moderate rate, without the use of a knife.'[23]

Her use of likenesses of well-known figures of the day for her puppets makes her possibly the earliest precursor of TV's *Spitting Image* team.

Some days her friend Job Baker performed 'jigs and country dances on the single kettle drum, accompanied by the whole band' during or after the entertainment. Job Baker's performances on the drums caused a big stir in the eighteenth century. He had beat his drums before the Duke of Marlborough after the victory at Mal- plaquet in 1709, and after this on almost all the stages of London. He was an immensely popular entertainer.

The season at the James Street Tennis Court came to an abrupt halt in mid-May 1738. This presumably was due to the 'violent fever' she describes in the *Narrative*. By summer 1739 she had recovered well enough to make her abortive trip to Tunbridge Wells.

Soon after this, in the autumn of 1739, she hired her puppets to Yeates, at the Tennis Court, but they were sold by August 1740 when they made an appearance at the Bartholomew Fair, billed as 'Punch's celebrated company of comedians, formerly Mrs Charke's'. Fawkes, a famous fairground conjuror, announced them at the booth he shared with Pinchbeck and Terwin, and we may presume that he was the villain she could never forgive, who bought her puppets for a song, knowing how much they had cost.

While she was working in Fielding's Haymarket company Char- lotte Charke lodged with her elder sister Elizabeth Brett in Oxen- den Street. This would have been a convenient location, as Oxenden Street was just round the corner from the Haymarket. Unfortunately for her sister, by harbouring Charlotte, the black sheep of the family, while she was committing her anti-father felonies on stage each day, Elizabeth Brett probably put herself in the firing-line from both her father and eldest sister Catherine. I presume that in the family conferences designed to call Charlotte to order Elizabeth spoke in her defence. There seems to be no other explanation for Colley Cibber's later lumping both daughters together and all but disowning them.

Dawson Brett junior, Elizabeth's husband, died in November 1738, the same year as their daughter Anne married the Drury Lane prompter William Rufus Chetwood.

Although Mrs Charke places her own second marriage during this period of her life, in fact it was much later. And I will discuss it in its chronological place.

1 R. Fiske, *English Theatre Music in the Eighteenth Century*, 1973; entry in Groves' *Dictionary of Music and Musicians*.
2 P. Highfill, *Dictionary*; Westminster Poor Rates.
3 P. Highfill, *Dictionary*; The London Stage.

4 *A Brief Relation of State Affairs* III, p.88; Edward Hatton, *A New View of London*, 1708, II, p.785.

5 PRO PROB 11/456, Q98.

6 *Roger North on Music*, ed. John Wilson, 1959; Groves' *Dictionary*.

7 PRO PROB 11/798 Q287.

8 Preface to *Caelia*.

9 See note to illustration *Southwark Fair* by Hogarth.

10 St Martin-in-the-Fields parish register, 20 January.

11 *Daily Journal* 21 May 1734.

12 Dedication to *The Art of Management*.

13 p.16.

14 p.25.

15 25 December 1739.

16 Cibber, *Apology*, pp. 146–7; my italics throughout.

17 28 May 1736.

18 *Daily Advertiser*, 22 March.

19 This is his own story from his publication *The Egoist*, pp. 27–8.

20 Quoted in Richard Findlater, *Banned*, p. 41.

21 Lord Chamberlain warrant book; LC 5/161, fol. 8.

22 *London Daily Post*, 25 March 1738; 22 April; 6 May; 25 April; 2 May.

23 *The Usefulness of the Stage*, second edition, April 1738.

Chapter Three

THE NARRATIVE

The officer who had me in custody, on hearing my story, really compassionated me and was exceeding angry at the woman, who without cause worked up the creditor to believe I had a fortune of five hundred per annum left me, which was not in the power of the deceased to leave; nor, as the affair was a secret and death sudden, any probability of such a happiness.

This misfortune was occasioned first by the stupidity and cruelty of the woman, and effected by dint of a very handsome laced hat I had on (being then, for some substantial reasons, *en cavalier**) which was so well described, the bailiff had no great trouble in finding me.

Undoubtedly I was extremely happy when he told me his business, having nothing in view but the Marshalsea, the gates of which I thought, though at that time in the middle of Covent Garden, stood wide open for my reception! But as the man had humanity, he eased me of those fears, and, by dint of a trifling favour, conferred by poor Mrs Elizabeth Careless (whose name will, I believe, be for some years in remembrance) I was set at large till matters could be accommodated.

It is not to be expressed, the transport I felt on his leaving me behind him with Mrs Careless and her good-natured friend, who, being an attorney, was incapable of becoming my bail, but compassionated my distress and sent me directly to Mr Mytton, who kept the Cross Keys, requesting him to do that friendly office for me, and sent by me a note of indemnification, which Mr Mytton could by no means make any exceptions to, as the gentleman was a person of worth and honour and, besides, a particular good customer to the other.

The next thing was to procure another bail to join with the former. I soon obtained one, whose good nature was easily excited to do a kind action, but, when I went to the officer and told who it

*dressed as a man

67

was, objections were made against him, as he was obliged himself to keep close for fear of equal disaster and, to convince me of his danger, produced a writ which had been two or three times renewed, to no purpose.

What to do in this terrible exigence I could not tell, as I had but a day and a half longer to be at large, if I could not produce a second bail. I tried all means, but in vain, and on the Friday following was obliged to surrender and lay that night in Jackson's Alley, at the officer's house.

I had not been there half an hour, before I was surrounded with all the ladies who kept coffee houses in and about the garden, each offering money for my ransom. But nothing could be done without the debt and costs, which, though there was, I believe, about a dozen or fourteen ladies present, they were not able to raise. As far as their finances extended, they made an offer of them, and would have given notes jointly or separately, for the relief of poor Sir Charles, as they were pleased to style me. It is true, the officer would willingly have come into their kind propositions, as he was truly sensible of my indigence, but, being closely watched by the creditor, who would on no terms be brought to any composition, all their efforts were ineffectual.

After two or three hours wasted in fruitless entreaties, it growing late, they left me to bewail the terrible scene of horror that presented to my tortured view, and, with a heart overcharged with anguish and hopeless of redress, I retired to my dormitory, and passed the night in bitterest reflections on my melancholy situation.

My poor child, who was then but eight years of age, and whose sole support was on her hapless, friendless mother, knew not what was become of me, or where to seek me and, with watchful care, wore away the tedious night in painful apprehensions of what really had befallen me.

About seven next morning I dispatched a messenger to my poor little suffering infant, who soon came to me with her eyes overflowed with tears and a heart full of undissembled anguish. She immediately threw her head upon my bosom and remained in speechless grief, with which I equally encountered her. For some time, the child was so entirely sensible of our misfortunes, and of the want of means of being extricated from them, it was with difficulty I soothed her into a calm. Alas, what has the poor and friendless to hope for, surrounded with sorrows of such a nature, that even people in tolerable circumstances find some perplexity when so assailed to overcome?

I sat down and wrote eight and thirty letters before I stirred out of my chair, some of which went where I thought Nature might have put in her claim, but I could obtain no answer, and, where I least expected, I found redress!

My poor little wench was the melancholy messenger, and neither ate or drank till she had faithfully discharged the trust I reposed in her. To be short, the very ladies who had visited me the night before brought with them the late Mrs Elizabeth Hughes, who, by dint of her laying down a couple of guineas and a collection from the rest, with a guinea from Mrs Douglas in the Piazza, I was set at liberty, and the officer advised me to change hats with him, that being the very mark by which I was unfortunately distinguished and made known to him.

My hat was ornamented with a beautiful silver lace, little the worse for wear, and of the size which is now the present taste; the officer's a large one, cocked up in the coachman's style and weightened with a horrible quantity of crepe to secure him from the winter's cold.

As to my figure, it is so well known it needs no description, but my friend the bailiff was a very short, thick, red-faced man, of such a corpulency he might have appeared in the character of Falstaff without the artful assistance of stuffing, and his head proportionable to his body, consequently we each of us made very droll figures: he with his little laced hat, which appeared on his head of the size of those made for the Spanish ladies, and my unfortunate face smothered under his, that I was almost as much incommoded as when I marched in the ditch under the insupportable weight of my father's.

However, this smoky conveniency (for it stunk insufferably of tobacco) was a security and absolute prevention from other threatening dangers, and I prudently retired into a most dismal and solitary mansion in Great Queen Street, where I was hourly apprehensive of having the house fall upon my head (though if it had, according to the old proverb, it would not have been the first misfortune of the kind that had befallen me). It was the old building which has since been formed into several new and handsome houses.

When my kind redeemers took me away, they treated me with an elegant supper and sent me home to my child with a guinea in my pocket, which they very politely desired me to accept as a present to her.

I passed the night in grateful thoughts, both to heaven and those appointed by that great power to save me from the gulf of absolute destruction. I, never having been in a distress of that kind before, laid my sorrow deeper to heart, and the inexpressible delight of being restored to my child and liberty was almost too much for my fluttered spirits at that time to bear. So unexpected a relief may be deemed a prodigy! But what is there so difficult or unlikely in the imagination of thoughtless mortals, that the all-gracious ruler of the world cannot bring to bear?

This very circumstance convinces me that no misfortune, of ever so dreadful a nature, should excite us to despair. What had I to conceive, but the miserable enforcement to linger out a wretched life in prison; a child who might possibly have been despised only for being mine, and perhaps reduced to beggary?

These were the entertaining ideas I had the night of my confinement, but when I found providence had been so tenderly and industriously employed in my behalf, I began to arraign myself for supposing that my relations, in such extremity, though they were regardless of me, would have abandoned an innocent and hapless child to that rigorous fate my fears suggested.

During my solitary residence in Queen Street, I never made my appearance for a considerable time but on a Sunday, and was obliged to have recourse to as many friends as I could muster up to help me to a support for myself and my little fellow sufferer. She, poor child, was so deeply affected with the malevolence of my fortune, it threw her into a very dangerous illness, but, even in that distress, heaven raised a friend. My brother, Theophilus Cibber, kindly sent an apothecary at his own expense, for which I shall always acknowledge myself extremely his debtor, and am sorry I have not the power of making a more suitable return.

I left the poor girl one Sunday, to prog* for her and myself by pledging with an acquaintance a beautiful pair of sleeve buttons, which I effected in about two hours, and on my return, asking the landlady how the child did (having left her very much indisposed), she told me, Miss went up about an hour and a half ago to put on some clean linen but, by her staying, she concluded she was lain down, having complained of being very sleepy before she went up.

*poke about for food

But, oh heaven! how vast was my grief and surprise, when I entered the room and found the poor little soul stretched on the floor in strong convulsion fits, in which she had lain a considerable time and no mortal near to give her the least assistance.

I took her up and, overcome with strong grief, immediately dropped her on the floor, which I wonder did not absolutely end her by the force of the fall, as she was in fact a dead weight. My screaming and her falling raised the house and, in the hurry of my distraction, I ran into the street with my shirt-sleeves dangling loose about my hands, my wig standing on end,

'Like quills upon the fretful porcupine',

and proclaiming the sudden death of my much-beloved child. A crowd soon gathered round me and, in the violence of my distraction, instead of administering any necessary help, wildly stood among the mob to recount the dreadful disaster.

The people's compassion was moved, it is true, but as I happened not to be known to them, it drew them into astonishment to see the figure of a young gentleman so extravagantly grieved for the loss of a child. As I appeared very young, they looked on it as an unprecedented affection in a youth, and began to deem me a lunatic, rather than that there was any reality in what I said.

One of the people who had been employed in the care, as I then thought, of my expiring infant, missing me, sought me out and brought me home, where I found the child still in violent convulsions, which held her from Sunday, eleven o'clock in the forenoon, without intermission, till between the hours of eight and nine next morning.

In the midst of this scene of sorrow Mr Adam Hallam, who lived next door to my lodging, hearing of my misfortune, in a very genteel and tender manner proved himself a real friend unasked. The first instance I had of his humanity was a letter of condolence, in which was enclosed that necessary and never-failing remedy for every evil incidental to mankind in general, and, what was more extraordinary was his constantly sending to enquire after the child's health with the same respectful regard as might have been expected had I been possessed of that affluence I but some few months before enjoyed.

At his own request, his table was my own, and I am certain his good nature layed an embargo on his person, as he often dined at home in compliment to me, rather than leave me to undergo the shock of mingling with his servants, or be distinguished by them as his pensioner, by leaving me to eat by myself.

It happened very *à propos* for me, that Mr Hallam had a back door into his house, which prevented the hazards I might otherwise have been liable to by going into the street, and, indeed, as Sharp says to Gayless,* the back door I always thought the safest, by which means I had a frequent opportunity of conversing with a sincere friend, whose humanity assuaged the anguish of my mind, and whose bounty was compassionately employed for a considerable time, to protect me and mine from the insupportable and distracting fears of want.

After what I have said in regard to the favours I received, I am certain no person who ever knew what it was to be obliged, and had honesty enough to dare to be grateful, will condemn me for making this public acknowledgement, who have no other means of doing justice to one that had no motive or right to give such an instance of benevolence, but excited alone from a natural propensity to do a good action.

Favours, when received, are too often forgot, and I have observed gratitude to be a principle that bears the smallest share in the hearts of those where it ought to be most strongly president, so that I begin to imagine one half of the world don't understand the real etymology of the word.

But that I may give further assurances of my detestation of that sin of unkindness and insolence, I shall proceed to give a further account of my obligations I received from strangers, and shall begin with those conferred on me by the late Mr Delane,† comedian, who, though almost a stranger to my person, grew intimate with my affliction, and testified his concern by raising a timely contribution to alleviate my distress, and redoubled the favourable remedy in the politeness of the application.

Mrs Woffington‡ stands equally in the rank of those whose merits must be sounded in the song of grateful praise, and many

---

*in David Garrick's *The Lying Valet*

†(?–1750) Dennis Delane was a minor tragic actor with a voice 'Like a passing bell'. He was famous enough for Garrick to impersonate him in the 1740s, but became an overweight alcoholic and died relatively young.

‡ the celebrated Peg Woffington (*c.* 1717–60). She appeared when a child as Macheath, and although she was renowned for coquets (Millament, Lady Townly, Lady Betty Modish) her mature attempts at male roles (Sir Harry Wildair, Lothario, etc.) made her the toast of the town.

more of the generous natives of Ireland, who are in nature a set of worthy people when they meet with objects of pity, and I have made bold to expatiate, in a particular manner, on that subject in my history of Mr Dumont, which will be immediately published after the conclusion of this narrative.

I must now mention the friendly assistance of Mr Rich, Mr Garrick, Mr Lacey (the several governors of the two theatres), Mr Beard,* and many more of the gentlemen of the stage, to whose bounty I shall ever think myself indebted.

I am now going to take notice of a person who, at friendly distance, has many times afforded a happy relief to my bitterest wants, namely, the present Mrs Cibber,† whose pity was once the means of saving my life by preventing my going to a gaol, and more than once or twice fed both myself and child by timely presents, only from hearing of the sad circumstances we laboured under. Whatever the world may think in regard to my taking this public notice of her humanity, I must beg to be excused, if I insist on my being justifiable by the laws of gratitude, and, as I was glad to be obliged, should think it the height of insolence to be ashamed to make the acknowledgement.

As soon as my poor girl began a little to recover, I sometimes used by owl-light to creep out in search of adventures, and, as there was frequently plays acted at the Tennis Court, with trembling limbs and aching heart, adventured to see (as I was universally studied) whether there was any character wanting – a custom very frequent among the gentry who exhibited at that celebrated slaughterhouse of dramatic poetry.

One night, I remember *The Recruiting Officer* was to be performed, as they were pleased to call it, for the benefit of a young

*John Rich (c. 1692–1761) managed Covent Garden Theatre, established pantomime as a major force in British theatre and produced John Gay's *The Beggar's Opera*; **David Garrick** co-managed Drury Lane with actor **James Lacy**. Lacy had appeared alongside Charlotte in Fielding's company. He was imprisoned for his attempts to evade the Licensing Act. Gentleman actor John Beard (c. 1716–91) married Lady Herbert, whose father disowned her for it. Handel praised his singing, and Smollett described him as 'respected and beloved by all the world'. He did charity work for the Sublime Society of Beefsteaks and the Royal Society of Musicians. During a performance a spaniel walked on to the stage and stood at his feet. Beard adopted it, named it Phillis, and brought it on for every subsequent performance of that play. After his wife died in 1753 he married John Rich's daughter, Charlotte.
†Susannah Maria Cibber, née Arne, Theophilus's second wife. She was Thomas Arne's sister, and an immensely successful actress and singer.

creature who had never played before. To my unbounded joy, Captain Plume was so very unfortunate, that he came at five o'clock to inform the young gentlewoman he did not know a line of his part. I (who though shut up in the mock green-room) did not dare to tell them I could do it, for fear of being heard to speak and that the sound of my voice, which is particular and as well known as my face, should betray me to those assailants of liberty who constantly attend every play night there, to the inexpressible terror of many a potentate, who has quiveringly tremored out the hero, lest the sad catastrophe should rather end in a sponging-house,* than a bowl of poison or a timely dagger – the want of which latter instrument of death I once saw supplied with a lady's busk,† who had just presence of mind sufficient to draw it from her stays, and end at once her wretched life, and more wretched acting.

Some of these kind of meritorious exhibitors were to massacre poor Farquhar that night, but not one among them capable of playing, or rather going on for Plume, which they would have done, perhaps, like a chair set up to fill up the number in a country dance. At last the question was put to me. I immediately replied (seeing the coast clear) I could do such a thing, but, like Mosca,‡ was resolved to stand on terms and make a merit of necessity. 'To be sure, ma'am,' says I, 'I'd do anything to oblige you, but I'm quite unprepared. I have nothing here proper. I want a pair of white stockings, and clean shirt.' Though, between friends, in case of lucky hit, I had all those things ready in my coat pocket, as I was certain, let what part would befall me, cleanliness was a necessary ingredient.

Then I urged that it would be scarce worth her while to pay me my price, upon which she was immediately jogged by the elbow and took aside to advise her to offer me a crown. I, being pretty well used to the little arts of those worthy wights, received the proposal soon after and, without making any answer to it, jogged the lady's other elbow and withdrew, assuring her that under a guinea I positively would not undertake it, that to prevent any demur with the rest of the people she should give me the sixteen shillings privately and publicly pay me five.

Her house was as full as it could hold and the audience clattering

*bailiff's house, used as preliminary confinement for debtors
†strip of wood or whalebone used to stiffen corset
‡character in Ben Jonson's *Volpone*

for a beginning. At length she was obliged to comply with my demands and I got ready with the utmost expedition. When the play (which was, in fact, a farce to me) was ended, I thought it mighty proper to stay till the coast was clear, that I might carry off myself and guinea securely. But in order to effect it, I changed clothes with a person of low degree, whose happy rags, and the kind covert of night, secured me from the dangers I might have otherwise encountered. My friend took one road, I another, but met at my lodgings, where I rewarded him, poor as I was, with a shilling, which, at that time, I thought a competent fortune for a younger child.

It happened, not long after, that I was applied to by a strange, unaccountable mortal called Jockey Adams, famous for dancing the Jockey Dance to the tune of 'Horse to Newmarket'. As I was gaping for a crust, I readily snapped at the first that offered and went with this person to a town within four miles of London, where a very extraordinary occurrence happened, and which, had I been really what I represented, might have ridden in my own coach in the rear of six horses.

Notwithstanding my distresses, the want of clothes was not amongst the number. I appeared as Mr Brown (a name most hateful to me now, for reasons the town shall have shortly leave to guess at) in a very genteel manner and not making the least discovery of my sex by my behaviour, ever endeavouring to keep up to the well-bred gentleman, I became, as I may most properly term it, the unhappy object of love in a young lady, whose fortune was beyond all earthly power to deprive her of, had it been possible for me to have been what she designed me, nothing less than her husband.

She was an orphan heiress and under age, but so near it that at the expiration of eight months her guardian resigned his trust and I might have been at once possessed of the lady and forty thousand pounds in the Bank of England, besides effects in the Indies that were worth about twenty thousand more.

This was a most horrible disappointment on both sides; the lady of the husband, and I of the money, which would have been thought an excellent remedy for ills by those less surrounded with misery than I was. I, who was the principal in this tragedy, was the last acquainted with it, but it got wind from the servants to some of the players (who, as Hamlet says, 'can't keep a secret'), and they immediately communicated it to me.

Contrary to their expectation, I received the information with infinite concern, not more in regard to myself than from the poor lady's misfortune, in placing her affection on an improper object, and whom, by letters I afterwards received, confirmed me 'she was too fond of her mistaken bargain'.

The means by which I came by her letters was through the persuasion of her maid, who, like most persons of her function, are too often ready to carry on intrigues. It was no difficult matter to persuade an amorous heart to follow its own inclination and accordingly a letter came to invite me to drink tea, at a place a little distant from the house where she lived.

The reason given for this interview was the desire some young ladies of her acquaintance had to hear me sing, and, as they never went to plays in the country, it would be a great obligation to her if I would oblige her friends, by complying with her request.

The maid who brought this epistle informed of the real occasion of its being wrote and told me, if I pleased, I might be the happiest man in the kingdom before I was eight and forty hours older. This frank declaration from the servant gave me but an odd opinion of the mistress, and I sometimes conceived, being conscious how unfit I was to embrace so favourable an opportunity, that it was all a joke.

However, be it as it might, I resolved to go and know the reality. The maid too insisted that I should, and protested her lady had suffered much on my account from the first house she saw me, and, but for her, the secret had never been disclosed. She futher added I was the first person who had ever made that impression on her mind. I own I felt a tender concern and resolved within myself to wait on her and, by honestly confessing who I was, kill or cure her hopes of me for ever.

In obedience to the lady's command, I waited on her, and found her with two more, much of her own age, who were her confidantes, and entrusted to contrive a method to bring this business to an end by a private marriage. When I went into the room I made a general bow to all, and was for seating myself nearest the door, but was soon lugged out of my chair by a young madcap of fashion, and, to both the lady's confusion and mine, awkwardly seated by her.

We were exactly in the condition of Lord Hardy and Lady Charlotte, in *The Funeral*,* and I sat with as much fear in my

*by Richard Steele

countenance as if I had stolen her watch from her side. She, on her part, often attempted to speak, but had such a tremor on her voice she ended only in broken sentences. It is true, I have undergone that dreadful apprehensions of a bum-bailiff,* but I should have thought one at that time a seasonable relief and, without repining, have gone with him.

The before-mentioned madcap, after putting us more out of countenance by bursting into a violent fit of laughing, took the other by the sleeves and withdrew, as she thought, to give me a favourable opportunity of paying my addresses. But she was deceived for when we were alone I was in ten thousand times worse plight than before, and what added to my confusion was seeing the pour soul dissolve into tears, which she endeavoured to conceal.

This gave me freedom of speech, by a gentle enquiry into the cause and, by tenderly trying to soothe her into a calm, I unhappily increased, rather than assuaged, the dreadful conflict of love and shame which laboured in her bosom.

With much difficulty I mustered up sufficient courage to open a discourse, by which I began to make a discovery of my name and family, which struck the poor creature into astonishment. But how much greater was her surprise when I positively assured her that I was actually the youngest daughter of Mr Cibber, and not the person she conceived me! She was absolutely struck speechless for some little time, but when she regained the power of utterance, entreated me not to urge a falsehood of that nature, which she looked upon only as an evasion, occasioned, she supposed, through a dislike of her person, adding that her maid had plainly told her I was no stranger to her miserable fate, as she was pleased to term it (and, indeed, as I really thought it).

I still insisted on the truth of my assertion, and desired her to consider whether it was likely an indigent young fellow must not have thought it an unbounded happiness to possess at once so agreeable a lady and immense fortune, both which many a noble-man in this kingdom would have thought it worth while to take pains to achieve.

Notwithstanding all my arguments, she was hard to be brought into a belief of what I told her and conceived that I had taken a dislike to her from her too readily consenting to her servant's

*a bailiff of the meanest kind

making that declaration of her passion for me, and for that reason she supposed I had but a light opinion of her. I assured her of the contrary, and that I was sorry for us both, that providence had not ordained me to be the happy person she designed me, that I was much obliged for the honour she conferred on me and sincerely grieved it was not in my power to make a suitable return.

With many sighs and tears on her side, we took a melancholy leave and in a few days the lady retired into the country, where I have never heard from or of her since, but hope she is made happy in some worthy husband that might deserve her.

She was not the most beautiful I have beheld, but quite the most agreeable: sang finely, and played the harpsichord as well, understood languages, and was a woman of real good sense. But she was (poor thing!) an instance, in regard to me, that the wisest may sometimes err.

On my return home, the itinerant troop all assembled round me to hear what had passed between the lady and me – when we were to celebrate the nuptials? – besides many other impertinent, stupid questions; some offering, agreeable to their villainous dispositions, as the marriage they supposed would be a secret, to supply my place in the dark to conceal the fraud; upon which I looked at them sternly and, with the contempt they deserved, demanded to know what action of my life had been so very monstrous, to excite them to think me capable of one so cruel and infamous?

For the lady's sake, whose name I would not for the universe have had banded about by the mouths of low scurrility, I not only told them I had revealed to her who I was, but made it no longer a secret in the town, that, in case it was spoke of, it might be regarded as an impossibility, or at worst, a trumped-up tale by some ridiculous blockhead who was fond of hearing himself prate, as there are indeed too many such (of which, in regard to my own character, I have been often a melancholy proof, and, as it just now occurs to my memory, will inform the reader).

As misfortunes are ever the mortifying parents of each other, so mine were teeming and each new day produced fresh sorrow. But, as if the very fiends of destruction were employed to perpetrate mine, and that my real miseries were not sufficient to crush me with their weight, a poor beggarly fellow (who had been sometimes a supernumerary in Drury Lane Theatre, and part-writer) forged a most villainous lie, by saying I hired a very fine bay gelding and borrowed a pair of pistols, to encounter my father upon Epping Forest (where I solemnly protest I don't know I ever saw my father in my life), that I stopped the chariot, presented a pistol to his breast and used such terms as I am ashamed to insert; threatened to blow his brains out that moment if he did not deliver, upbraiding him for his cruelty in abandoning me to those distressses he knew I underwent when he had it so amply in his power. I would force him to a compliance and was directly going to discharge upon him, but his tears prevented me, and asking my pardon for his ill-usage of me, gave me this purse with threescore guineas and a promise to restore me to his family and love, on which I thanked him and rode off.

A likely story – that my father and his servants were all so intimidated (had it been true) as not to have been able to withstand a single stout highwayman, much more a female, and his own daughter too! However, the story soon reached my ear, which did not more enrage me on my own account than the impudent, ridiculous picture the scoundrel had drawn of my father in this supposed horrid scene. The recital threw me into such an agonizing rage, I did not recover it for a month. But the next evening I had the satisfaction of being designedly placed where this villain was to be, and, concealed behind a screen, heard the lie re-told from his own mouth.

He had not sooner ended than I rushed from my covert, and, being armed with a thick oaken plant, knocked him down without speaking a word to him and, had I not been happily prevented, should, without the least remorse, have killed him on the spot. I had not breath enough to enquire into the cause of his barbarous falsehood but others, who were less concerned than myself, did it for me, and the only reason he assigned for his saying it was he meant it as a joke, which considerably added to the vehemence of my rage. But I had the joy of seeing him well caned and obliged to ask my pardon on his knees – poor satisfaction for so manifest an injury!

This is, indeed, the greatest and most notorious piece of cruelty that was ever forged against me; but it is a privilege numbers have taken with me, and I have generally found in some degree or other my cause revenged, though by myself unsought, and it is more than morally possible I may live to see the tears of penitence flow from the eyes of a yet remaining enemy, to whose barbarity I am not the only victim in the family. But,

'– Come what come may,
Patience and time run through the roughest day.'

If the person I mean was herself guiltless of errors, she might 'stand in some rank of praise' for her assiduity in searching out the faults of others, as it might be reasonably supposed the innocent could never wish to be the author of ill to their fellow-creatures, and those especially nearly allied in blood. We have all realities of folly too sufficient to raise a blush in thinking minds, without the barbarous imposition of imaginary ones, which I, and others in the family, have been cruelly branded with. I shall only give a hint to the lady, which I hope she'll prudently observe:

'The faults of others we with ease discern,
But our own frailties are the last we learn.'

I shall now give a full acount of, I think, one of the most tragical occurrences of my life, which but last week happened to me. The reader may remember, in the first number of my narrative I made a public confession of my faults and, pleased with the fond imagination of being restored to my father's favour, flattered myself, ere this treatise could be ended, to ease the hearts of every human breast, with an account of reconciliation.

But how fruitless was my attempt! I wrote, and have thought it necessary, in justification of my own character, to print the letter I sent my father, who, forgetful of that tender name and the gentle ties of nature, returned it me in a blank.* Sure that might have been filled up with blessing and pardon, the only boon I hoped for, wished, or expected. Can I then be blamed for saying with the expiring Romeo,

'– Fathers have flinty hearts! No tears
Will move 'em! – Children must be wretched.'

This shocking circumstance has since confined me to my bed, and has been cruelly aggravated by the terrible reflection of being empowered to say, with Charles in *The Fop's Fortune*,† 'I'm sorry that I've lost a father!'

I beg pardon for this intrusion on the reader's patience, in offering to their consideration the following letter.

*paper or form with spaces left to be filled by the recipient
†A most apposite quote, as it is from the comedy *Love Makes a Man: or, The Fop's Fortune* by her own father Colley Cibber.

To Colley Cibber, Esq. at his house in Berkeley Square.

Saturday 8 March 1755

Honoured Sir,

I doubt not but you are sensible I last Saturday published the first number of a Narrative of my Life, in which I made a proper concession in regard to those unhappy miscarriages which have for many years justly deprived me of a father's fondness. As I am conscious of my errors, I thought I could not be too public in suing for your blessing and pardon, and only blush to think my youthful follies should draw so strong a compunction on my mind in the meridian of my days, which I might have so easily avoided.

Be assured, sir, I am perfectly convinced I was more than much to blame, and that the hours of anguish I have felt have bitterly repaid me for the commission of every indiscretion, which was the unhappy motive of being so many years estranged from that happiness I now, as in duty bound, most earnestly implore.

I shall, with your permission, sir, send again to know if I may be admitted to throw myself at your feet and, with sincere and filial transport, endeavour to convince you that I am,

Honoured sir,

Your truly penitent and dutiful daughter,

CHARLOTTE CHARKE.

When I sent, as is specified in the letter, for an answer, I engaged a young lady, whose tender compassion was easily moved to be the obliging messenger. She returned with friendly expedition and delivered me my own epistle, enclosed in a blank, from my father. By the alteration of my countenance she too soon perceived the ill success of her negotiation, and bore a part in my distress.

I found myself so dreadfully disconcerted, I grew impatient to leave my friend, that I might not intrude too far on her humanity, which I saw was sensibly affected with my disappointment. A disappointment indeed! To be denied that from mortal man which heaven is well pleased to bestow, when adressed with sincerity and penitence, even for capital offences.

The prodigal, according to Holy Writ, was joyfully received by the offended father. Nay, mercy has even extended itself at the place of execution to notorious malefactors. But as I have not been

guilty of those enormities incidental to the forementioned characters, permit me, gentle reader, to demand what I have done so
hateful, so very grievous to the soul, so much beyond the reach of
pardon, that nothing but my life could make atonement? – which, I
can bring witness, was a hazard I was immediately thrown into.

The shock of receiving my own letter did not excite a sudden
gust of unwarrantable passion, but preyed upon my heart with the
slow and eating fire of distraction and despair till it ended in a
fever, which now remains upon my spirits, and which I fear I shall
find a difficult task to overcome.

The late Mr Lillo's character of Thoroughgood, in his tragedy of
George Barnwell, sets a beautiful example of forgiveness, where he
reasonably reflects upon the frailties of mankind, in a speech apart
from the afflicted and repenting youth: 'When we have offended
heaven, it requires no more; and shall man, who needs himself to
be forgiven, be harder to appease?' Then turning to the boy,
confirms his humanity, by saying: 'If my pardon or my love be of
moment to your peace, look up, secure of both.'*

How happy would that last sentence have made me; as the want
of it has absolutely given me more inexpressible anguish than all
the accumulated sorrows I had known before, being now arrived to
an age of thinking, and well weighing the consequences arising
from the various occurrences of life. But this I fear will prove the
heaviest and bitterest corrosive to my mind and the more I reflect
on it, find myself less able to support such unkindness from that
hand which I thought would have administered the gentle balm of
pity.

I am very certain my father is to be, in part, excused, as he is too
powerfully persuaded by his cruel monitor, who neither does, or
ever will, pay the least regard to any part of the family, but herself,
and though within a year of threescore, pursues her own interest to
the detriment of others, with the same artful vigilance that might
be expected from a young sharper of twenty-four. I am certain I
have found it so, and am too sure of its effects from the hour of my
birth; and my first fault was being my father's last born. Even the
little follies of prattling infancy were by this person construed into
crimes before I had a more distinguishing sense than a kitten. As I
grew up, I too soon perceived a rancorous disposition towards me,
attending with malice prepense to destroy that power I had in the

The London Merchant; or George Barnwell, II, iv

hearts of both my parents, where I was perhaps judged to sit too triumphant, and maintained my seat of empire in my mother's to her latest moments, and, it is possible, had she lived, my enemy might not have carried this cruel point, to prevent what I think I had a natural right to receive, when I so earnestly implored it.

One thing I must insert for her mortification: that my conscience is quite serene, and though she won't suffer my father to be in friendship with me, I am perfectly assured that I have, in regard to any offences towards him, made my peace with the Power Supreme, which neither her falsehood nor artful malice could deprive me of. It is now my turn to forgive, as being the injured person, and, to show her how much I choose to become her superior in mind, I not only pardon, but pity her – though I fear she rather pursues the rules observed in the following lines:

'Forgiveness to the injured does belong;
But they ne'er pardon who have done the wrong.'

That I have suffered much is too evidential, and though I neither proposed nor expected more than what my letter expresses, I hope my father's eyes, for the sake of his family who are oppressed, may be one day opened. For my part, I cease to think myself belonging to it, and shall conclude this painful subject with an assurance to my brother's two daughers:* that I am sincerely pleased they are so happily provided for, and hope they will have gratitude and prudence enough to preserve their grandsire's blessing, and never put it in the power of artful treachery to elbow them out of his favour, as I have been, and that most cruelly.

I remember, the last time I ever spoke with my father, a triumvirate was framed to that end, and I was sent for from the playhouse to put this base design in execution. After being baited like a bull at a stake, and perceiving they were resolved to carry their horrid point against me, I grew enraged and obstinate and, finding a growing indignation swelling in my bosom, answered nothing to their purpose, which incensed my father. Nor can I absolutely blame him, for it was undoubtedly my duty to satisfy any demand he should think proper to make. But then again, I considered that his judgement was sufficient to correct the errors of my mind, without the insolent assistance of those whose wicked hearts were too fraught with my ruin.

*Betty and Jenny, Theophilus's daughters by his first wife, Jane Johnson

My father, having been worked up to a strong fit of impatience, hastily quitted his house, with a declaration not to return to till I was gone. This, I am too well assured,

> 'Was a joyful sound to Cleopatra's ear.'

I stayed a few moments after him, when she who was once my eldest sister was pleased to ask the rest of her colleagues if they had done with me, who answering in the affirmative, in a peremptory manner turned me out of doors.

I was then married, and had been so near four years, therefore did not conceive that anyone had a right to treat me like a child, and could not easily brook being forced into a submission of that nature. But the main design was to deprive me of a birthright – and they have done it. For which, in obedience to the laws divine, I beseech heaven to forgive them and bring them to repentance ere it be too late. And let Goneril take care: she has found a brace of Cordelias in the family: which that they may ever continue is my heartiest wish and earnest prayer. Nor would I have the poor children think, because they are made happy, that I envy them the advantages they possess. No! So far from it, I am rather delighted than displeased, as it convinces me my father has yet some power over himself, and, though deaf to me, has listened to the tender call of mercy by a seasonable protection of their youth and innocence.

I apprehend I shall be called in question for my inability in conveying ideas of the passions which most tenderly effect the heart, by so often having recourse to abler pens than my own – by my frequent quotations – but, in answer to that, I must beg to be excused, and also justified, as mine and others' griefs were more strongly painted by those authors I have made bold with, than was in the power of my weak capacity. I thought there was greater judgement in such references, than in vainly attempting to blunder out my distress, and possibly by that means tire the reader in the perusal.

THE FACTS
1740–2

The apparently fictional newspaper account of Charlotte's attempt at highway robbery reads as follows:

'The amazing Mrs Charke equipped herself with a horse, mask and pistols, made herself up as a highwayman and waylaid her father in Epping Forest. Poor Cibber handed over his money, making only the rueful reproof: "Young man, young man! This is a sorry trade. Take heed in time." "And so I would," replied his disguised daughter, "but I've a wicked hunks of a father, who rolls in money, yet denies me a guinea. And so a worthy gentleman like you, sir, has to pay for it!"'[1]

Charlotte presumably believed that her father would have the same morals as the characters in his sentimental plays. When writing to him, begging for a reconciliation, at the age of forty-two, she must have imagined that she would be welcomed back into his affections: the prodigal daughter returned, the Christian father forgiving and giving her his blessing. When she received her letter back, unopened, she obviously believed that her father had not known of its arrival, and that, by publishing it in her book, that he would get to hear about it, read it and forgive her misdemeanours. But this was not to be.

Charlotte's quarrel with her father, obviously well established before the publication of the *Narrative* in 1755, has been given various causes, usually with Charlotte as the aggressor. It seems to me that there was blame on both sides. But, as a man who was proud of his moral stance within the theatre, Colley Cibber's behaviour as a real-life father left a lot to be desired.

His appearance at the licensing office to give Charlotte away to Richàrd Charke when she was only seventeen probably seemed an act of kindness to a young, impetuous girl. But a father who really cared, knew her wild ways, and presumably knew of Charke's too, would have done better to take a firm stance and send her away for a while, as she suggested he might have done. Perhaps (as is usual with Colley Cibber) financial benefit was more important to him than Charlotte's future happiness: by marrying her off he would have had no more daughters to support.

It is interesting to note that Charlotte's grandfather, Matthias, faced with a similar problem when his daughter – Charlotte's mother – wanted to marry Charlotte's father, did not put his name to the licence, and Katherine was instead given away by a friend, George Bingham.[2]

Despite Cibber's standing at the Drury Lane Theatre Charlotte was given a very ordinary list of parts for her first few years. After three seasons, Charlotte joined the rebellion sparked off by her father selling his share of the patent to Highmore. Once out of the strict hierarchy of the patent house, she found herself not only better paid, but with a much wider range of parts to play. She also experienced her first, heady moments in management.

After a few months back in her dull repertoire at Drury Lane she set up her whirlwind summer season. She returned to the fold for the main season, acquitted herself reasonably in her two major take-overs, and was sacked. She admits (in her preface to the subsequent *The Art of Management*) to 'private misconduct', and, in the *Narrative*, she describes her own pomposity and tactlessness with more experienced actresses, for instance her ungracious reception of Mrs Butler's present for having gone on for her.

Modern scolars have tried to read into the phrase 'private misconduct' all sorts of sexual innuendo. One repeatedly refers to her having been discharged by Fleetwood for 'immorality'.[3]

Anyone who has ever worked in a theatre knows that, backstage, almost anything can be forgiven except for the grumbling of the disgruntled actor – especially a young actor who constantly criticizes, and behaves in a condescending manner to the more experienced leading players.

It is quite clear from the substance of *The Art of Management* that her grievances against the Drury Lane company went further than her own dismissal. She did not approve of Fleetwood's policy of filling his bills with variety turns and pantomimes.

Despite her bad behaviour within the company and her public criticism of it elsewhere, her father arranged for her reinstatement. But within two months of her return, Charlotte, with her customary lack of grace, walked out again.

I believe that, for her father, the final straw came when Charlotte joined Henry Fielding's company. Earlier she had had a stab at playing Cibber's most famous role, Lord Foppington. It is well known that Cibber was a vain man, and his own daughter's mimicry must have been galling to him, but Fielding grabbed this opportunity of a truly vicious swipe at Cibber and exploited Charlotte's talents to humiliate him. In *Pasquin*, her own, maybe affectionately intended, imitation Cibberisms were played through barbs designed to wound. It is a wonder indeed that, as a daughter, Charlotte accepted the role; as an actress it is not.

Henry Fielding was witty, spirited, and, especially, in his theatrical offerings, possessed of the same anarchic spirit as

Charlotte; his style of theatre a real alternative to the staid patent companies. Her father's work represented everything of the older generation; Fielding's could have been seen as the vanguard of the new. On top of this she was offered the type of parts that she enjoyed most – cracking leads, both male and female.

Presumably the family conference, where she was 'baited like a bull at the stake', took place while she was working with Fielding, although, if, as she says, she never saw her father or sister again, it must have occurred after 21 March 1737, when Cibber is known to have laughed at and applauded the first night of *The Historical Register*.

It would have been important to Cibber to save face, and be seen to accept jokes about himself with good grace. But it seems highly possible that he was actually appalled by the play and all its implications. Most likely, after the show, having put on a good face in public, he sent for Charlotte to lambast her in private.

Colley Cibber's comments on the standards of acting in Fielding's company (already quoted in Chapter 2: The Facts) give a clue as to the true meaning of an undated letter he wrote to Charlotte.

Tavistock Square, Cvt Gdn   27 March

Dear Charlotte,
I am sorry I am not in a position to assist you further. You have made your own bed, and therein you must lie. Why do you not dissociate yourself from that worthless scoundrel, and then your relatives might try and aid you. You will never be any good while you adhere to him, and you most certainly will not receive what otherwise you might from your father,
Colley Cibber[4]

No doubt Charlotte's belief that her eldest sister, Catherine, fanned the flames of her quarrel with her father was true.

Catherine Cibber was eighteen years older than her baby sister. A few days after Charlotte's seventh birthday, Catherine married Colonel James Brown at St Benet Pauls Wharf.[5] Perhaps as an in-joke (maybe she did as ripping a take-off of Colonel Brown as she did of her father), when she later took to disguising herself as a man, Charlotte assumed the name Brown, a name that by 1755 was 'hateful' to her.

Catherine Brown did the right thing by her father by naming her son Colley (he died, like Colley's own two Colleys, in infancy), but, not long afterwards, she was widowed and, around the same time as her mother's death, Catherine Brown (and her daughter) moved in with Colley. She devoted her time to looking after her father, getting him doctors when he was ill and travelling with him to fashionable spa towns like Bath and Tunbridge Wells.

Catherine and Charlotte were possessed of quite opposite characters. In choosing a husband, Catherine went for a respectable army man; Charlotte a wild, young musician. Catherine stayed at home to be a wife and mother; Charlotte worked, shortly after both her wedding and the birth of her child. Catherine kept herself out of the limelight; Charlotte flung herself into it.

It must have been especially difficult for Charlotte to understand why she, by trying to make a name for herself in the same profession as her father, should be less highly favoured than her sister, who was entirely dependent all her life, first on her father, then her husband, then on her father again.

Catherine's influence over her father lasted until his death. Like the wicked step-mother of fairy tales, her squashing of the claims of others' demands on her father's affection had a practical basis. Not only was she dependent on her father for her own and her daughter's upkeep, but she had only him to provide her daughter with a dowry, so that she too might attract the right type of husband. Catherine's years of service paid off. Her father left her most of his estate, and her daughter married John Thomas Esq. on 4 June 1761.

In 1758, a few months after Colley Cibber's death, Charlotte wrote *The Lover's Treat*, a 'true narrative' about hate within families.

'In this last century there has been no vice more generally rooted in the minds of men than a discordancy in families and which flows from the very springs from which we should naturally expect to find the most agreeable harmony; but interest, whose power is invincible, too frequently creates us enemies where we are most nearly, and consanguinity, which ought most especially to endear to each other, is now become a standing maxim to forget those tender principles which nature claims and the world must necessarily approve.

This unfortunate depravity of sense, laid want of fraternal affection, was the unhappy cause of many sufferings and severest hardships, which a very worthy youth for many years endured; and from whom I had a particular account of a long series of misery, occasioned by his elder brother. (*The Lovers Treat: or, Unnatural Hatred. Being a true narrative as delivered to the author by one of the family who was principally concerned in the following account.* 1758)'

The laws of debt in eighteenth-century England were very severe. Landlords, merchants and professional men could have a debtor imprisoned for *life* if they could not pay up. Criminals were at least sentenced on the weight of their own case, and could hope for a short spell in prison. Daniel Defoe described the problem:

'For debt only, men are condemned to languish in perpetual imprisonment, and to starve without mercy, redeemed only by the grave. Kings show mercy to traitors, to murderers, and thieves; and general pardons are often passed to deliver criminals of the worst kinds, and give them an opportunity to retrieve their characters and show themselves honest for the future; but in debt, and we are lost for this world. We cannot obtain the favour of being hanged or transported, but our lives must linger within the walls till released by the grave; our youth wastes away inactive, grey hairs cover us, and we languish in all the agonies of misery and want, while our wives and children perish for mere hunger, and our creditors themselves see themselves paid by death and time; . . . Tell me, what nation condemns poor, incapable debtors to perpetual imprisonment, for no offence but not being able to pay what they owe?'[6]

The punishment was all the more cruel in that it only applied to those with petty debts, and that the misfortune of imprisonment itself ran the debt up, for debtors were charged legal and prison fees, and these were added to the original debt until the debt became impossible to pay. Nield's *Observations on the Law of Civil Imprisonment* expands:

'Suppose that an unfortunate man, unable even to pay a debt of 10 shillings, is arrested on the eve of a law term, and thrown into prison for his inability; and that in the same number of days as he owes pounds he will be involved in a fresh debt, of equal or greater amount, for the costs of his detainer in prison . . . Let us suppose that his attachment by one creditor alarms the rest (nor is it unnatural that it should be so), and that he has ten detainers laid against him for debts of the same amount; what will then be his situation? Why, he will in a few days be encumbered with additional debts put together, at the very time that he is immured in prison, without subsistence, or the means of earning any for himself, or the wretched dependents on his affections . . . . The Bankrupt laws, which, to the fair trader who has had the good fortune to deal with humane creditors, afford relief, are not open to his assistance; he has been too modest in all his transactions in trade to have ventured sufficiently to come within their purview; his debts are not of the required amount to entitle him to their relief.' (p. 24)

Charlotte was neither the first, not the last member of the Cibber family to have been troubled with debt. *She* narrowly avoided actual imprisonment, but her paternal grandfather Caius Gabriel Cibber, a monumental sculptor, was released by day to cut the bas reliefs on the Monument between 1673–5, while confined in the King's Bench prison. Ironically, he cut, at about the same time, the City Arms and the King's Arms for Newgate prison. (Earlier in his career he carved the beautiful Melancholy and Raving Madness for the gates of Bedlam, and the statue of King Charles II which still stands – though severely damaged by acid rain – in Soho Square.)

Her brother Theophilus was imprisoned for debt on more than one occasion, and spent a long time in France hiding from creditors.

Charlotte's night at the bailiff's house in Jackson's Alley must have taken place during 1741–2 (if all the given facts of her story tally), for Richard Mytton was proprietor of the Cross Keys, on the corner of Bedford Street and Henrietta Street, for these years only. By 1743 Mytton had taken over the Shakespeare's Head in Covent Garden Piazza, north side.[7]

The 'celebrated' Mrs Elizabeth Careless, who helped Charlotte find bail, started her career as an actress. She played Polly in *The Beggar's Opera* at the Haymarket in December 1728, and Cherry in *The Stratagem* in September 1730.

During the summer of 1733 she appeared alongside Charlotte at the Bartholomew Fair booth run by Theophilus Cibber, and his partners Griffin, Bullock and Hallam. She played Mariana in Fielding's *The Miser* in a double bill with *Tamerlane* (which featured Mrs Charke as Haly). At that year's fair Mrs Careless also played a lady of pleasure in *Ridotto al' Fresco* and Miss Witless in *The Comical History of Sir John Falstaff*.

After a break of a few years, Betty Careless returned briefly to the stage in 1741 to dance a minuet and play Polly at her own benefit at the St James Street Theatre. Although she was, according to her playbills, 'in distress', and having 'terrible fits of the vapours proceeding from bad dreams', that same year she had opened her own coffee house in Playhouse Passage, Covent Garden.

Elizabeth Careless's most famous moment came when Hogarth used her and her link boy, Little Cazey, for the central figures in the engraving 'Morning'. Her last few years were supported by the poor house; she died in April 1752, and was buried in the actor's church, St Paul's, Covent Garden.

As Mrs Careless was, in 1741–2, in close contact with the ladies who ran coffee houses in and around Covent Garden, and indeed a coffee-house proprietress herself, this also helps to date the episode, but shows that Mrs Charke's 'poor little suffering infant' would have been nearer twelve than eight. (I think it highly probable that Mrs Charke had many scrapes with the bailiffs other than this one.)

Her other benefactors are also identifiable: Mrs Jane Douglas ran a large tavern on the Covent Garden Piazza, which apparently doubled as a brothel. Mrs Betty Hughes, not to be confused with the coffee-house ladies, made and hired 'all sorts of masquerade dresses . . . together with a great variety of very fine Venetian and silk masks'.[8] She lived, between 1739 and 1744, four doors down from Charlotte's father, in Charles Street, Covent Garden. Possibly, as his neighbour, she heard about Charlotte's predicament and, seeing that he intended to do nothing about it, offered her assistance. Perhaps Mrs Hughes, along with most of London's polite society, had heard that Colley Cibber was currently far too preoccupied to have the time to think of bailing out his own daughter. For in 1740 Charlotte's father had struck up a close friendship with the would-be poetess Letitia Pilkington.

Miss Pilkington was the same age as Charlotte, and had similar financial tendencies, but, unlike Charlotte, was very good at getting money out of ladies and gentlemen of quality.

In about 1740, she sent verses to Charlotte's father, by then Poet Laureate, and shortly afterwards took a flat opposite his gambling club, White's. He would visit her there, between card games, and burst into tears as she read him her poems (and not because they were awful, which they were).

He won her commissions and redeemed her furniture when she

told him she had been forced to pawn it. But, ironically, in 1742, when Charlotte had one of her brushes with debtors' prison, Letitia Pilkington was seized by bailiffs and taken to Marshalsea. As soon as he heard, Colley Cibber sent her money and raised a subscription from sixteen dukes to set her free. She was accordingly released on 24 December 1742.

It is possible that Charlotte deliberately used her tale of redemption by the ladies of Covent Garden to show up the hypocrisy of her father, who, for all his sentimental morality and dramatic feminization of women, felt more compassion for a young gold-digger, who blatantly used all her female wiles, than for his own energetic daughter.

Charlotte's failure with her father was, to an extent, the result of her independence. Letitia Pilkington played on Colley Cibber's desire to be the respected father-figure. She oozed with syco-phantic flattery and gushed with gratitude; he responded with hard cash – four guineas here, five guineas there.

Charlotte's neighbour, Adam Hallam, who did support her at this time, had acted with her when she made her début in 1730. He was with Theophilus's group of rebels who took off to the Haymarket in 1733 and he played the lead, Tamerlane, at the 1733 Bartholomew Fair with Mrs Careless and Mrs Charke.

He was apparently also a pyrotechnic artist and one of his benefit performances boasted the first firework display ever completed by a European.

In 1734 he joined the Covent Garden company. In May 1735 his father, Thomas, was involved in a row in the theatre's green room with the Irish actor Charles Macklin (who Charlotte satirized as Bloodbolt in her play *The Art of Management*). Macklin poked Thomas Hallam in the eye with his stick, it penetrated his skull and he died. The cause of their quarrel was a wig.

After this Adam Hallam spent some time in Dublin, Covent Garden and Drury Lane before retiring in about 1743.

Hallam's house in Great Queen Street was one of three, Nos. 66, 67 and 68) singled out by *The Survey of London*. Very much later, when Charlotte was touring the provinces, Theophilus's wife's brother, Thomas Arne, composer of 'Rule, Britannia', owned one of them. These houses seem to have been rather grand, with large gardens (for central London). Hallam was there from 1735 to 1751. His house had a chapel on one side and a Madam Paign on the other. Presumably Mrs Charke rented an apartment from Madam

Paign, or, indeed, from Adam Hallam, for she described being grateful for the use of his back door.

As Hallam and others of his family were members of the Ancient and Honourable Society of Free and Accepted Masons, it is possible that his generosity towards Charlotte extended to commissioning some of her puppet performances which were billed as 'at the desire of several gentlemen of the Ancient and Honourable Order of Freemasons'.[9]

Charlotte's one-night stand at the Tennis Court, for which she took over the role of Captain Plume, took place on Tuesday 29 September 1741. She is not billed, of course, but it is one of the few performances of *The Recruiting Officer* at that theatre. The other billing for this performance provides the vital clue: 'Sylvia – Miss Rogers, first time on any stage . . . benefit Miss Rogers.' I suggest that the 'young creature' described by Mrs Charke, whose benefit this was, and who had never appeared before (and who apparently never appeared again), was Miss Rogers.

Charlotte had employed Jockey Adams in her Haymarket company in 1736; he played the part of James in *The Female Rake*. So it was fair enough that, when times were hard for her, he reversed the offer. After his early touring operation folded, he became famous for dancing at fairs, and in particular for dancing the Jockey Dance.

The venue she played with Adams's company, four miles south of London, would, in those days, have been somewhere like Clapham or Peckham. (On Clapham Common there is still an old stone which reads Whitehall 4 miles; Royal Exchange 4½ miles.)

Charlotte had two other benefactors: her brother Theophilus and his second wife Susannah Cibber (née Arne).

Theophilus Cibber was a drunk, a womanizer, and a bully. However, he was a popular and hard-working actor who threw himself into his work with enthusiasm and gusto. Charlotte's story indicates that he was also capable of generosity.

Born at the tail end of a great storm which wreaked havoc over Europe in November 1703, Theophilus was educated at Winchester College and joined his father's company in 1719, when Charlotte was six. He tackled a wide variety of leading and character roles, but his portrayal of the character Pistol was a huge popular success, and in prints of the day he was usually depicted in his Pistol costume: huge wading boots, a large hat, a diagonal sash over a full-sleeved jacket and a sword hanging from a thick leather belt.

By 1723 he was managing the junior summer companies, and two years after this married his first wife, actress Jane Johnson. The couple had two children, Jenny in 1730 and Betty in 1733, but his wife died giving birth to his second child.

As we have heard, when Colley Cibber sold the share of the patent to John Highmore, Theophilus led the mutiny of actors who set up a rival company at the Haymarket. His father made the underhand deal with Highmore during the couple of months after the death of his wife, when Theophilus himself was laid flat with a violent cold, fever and inflamed stomach.

Soon after the rebel company returned to Drury Lane, in April 1734, Theophilus married again. His second wife, Susannah Arne, was also an actress. In his attempts to promote his wife, he alienated Kitty Clive, by trying to steal parts which were Mrs Clive's and give them to Mrs Cibber. This led to 'the Polly war'. In *The Beggar's Opera*, Kitty Clive had for some time been playing the role of Polly. Theophilus expected Mrs Clive to stand down and take the smaller role of Lucy, while his wife played Polly, and soon both parties engaged in a slanging match in the press. Undaunted, Mrs Clive stood firm, and did not relinquish her role to Mrs Cibber.

These negotiations on behalf of his wife were not strictly without self-interest, for Susannah brought in a thumping profit which, as her husband, Theophilus regularly pocketed, and hoped to increase.

His attempts to make money out of his wife reached an all-time low when in 1737 he took money from William Sloper, a country squire. In exchange Sloper, who Theophilus nicknamed 'Mr Benefit', was permitted to spend time with Susannah. At first reluctant, Susannah soon formed a sexual relationship with Sloper. She would undress in Theophilus's room, and, taking her pillow with her, Theophilus would then lead her to Sloper's room for the night. She would return in the morning.

When the affair became a bit too exclusive for Theophilus, and seemed likely to threaten his financial claims on Susannah (and after he had kidnapped Susannah from the hideaway she shared with Sloper, imprisoned her in a room, and she had been rescued by her brother), he sued his wife for adultery, and claimed £5000 damages from Sloper. Sloper was found guilty, but Theophilus was only awarded £10.

Throughout his first appearance after the sensational trial, Theophilus was hissed and booed. Undeterred he acted till the end of the show and indeed the end of the season. The following year, deeply in debt, he filed another case against Sloper, this time for depriving him of the financial benefits of his wife, and claiming £10,000 damages. He won, for Susannah was now openly living with Sloper and had borne him a daughter. Theophilus was only awarded £500, but Susannah's career was ruined, for the time being.

Colley Cibber had not been pleased with Theophilus's choice of a second wife. Questioned at the first Sloper trial as to why he had been against the match, Cibber senior barefacedly replied: 'Because she had no fortune.' He also admitted having admonished Theophilus for giving her 'valuable presents of rings and jewels'.[10]

With a little training, however, Susannah Cibber soon proved to be a very popular tragic actress, and as such managed to raise all the money she had not brought in dowry.

A women who committed adultery (even if she had been talked into it at gunpoint by her husband) was regarded as a social outcast during the eighteenth century, and Susannah Cibber was wise enough to keep off the stage for the few years following the trials. But in autumn 1742, having secured guarantees that she would not have to work in the same building as her husband, she returned to the London stage. She went on to become one of the most popular and successful actresses of the century, and by the time Charlotte was writing her *Narrative* she was David Garrick's leading tragic actress. When she died in 1766, Garrick declared 'then tragedy expired with her'.

As Charlotte claims that the coffee-house ladies saved her from the clutches of the bailiffs and the gates of the Marshalsea, and later asserts that 'the present Mrs Cibber' prevented her going to gaol, I think it fair to assume that Charlotte Charke was caught by bailiffs on more than one occasion.

1 Clipping in Robinson Locke's scrapbooks, New York Public Library theatre collection – unfortunately not dated.
2 Bishop of London's Marriage Licences; Guildhall Library.
3 L.R.N. Ashley, *Colley Cibber*, and his introduction to facsimile edition of the *Narrative*.
4 Letter in the Guildhall Library; MS 542.
5 Parish register, 5 February 1719.
6 Defoe, quoted in William Lee, *Life of Defoe*, p.11.
7 Westminster rates books.
8 Her own advertisements in the *General Advertiser*.
9 12 April 1738, *London Daily Post* and *General Advertiser*.
10 *The Tryal of a Cause for Criminal Conversation.*

Chapter Four

THE NARRATIVE

As I have finished my tragical narration, I shall return to the town where I was honoured with the young lady's regard. Our departure from thence happened soon after, and kings, queens, lords and commons were all tossed up in an undistinguished bundle from that place and, like Scarron's itinerants,* escorted to another in a cart.

As my unlucky stars were ever employed in working on the anvil of misfortune, I, unknowingly, took a lodging in a bailiff's house, though not as Clodio† did, who had three writs against him, but I was not absolutely certain how long it might be, ere so terrible a catastrophe might be the case, being then but ten miles from London, and every hour of my life liable to be seen by some air-taking tradesman, to whom it was twenty to one I might be indebted.

Under such a circumstance as this, to be sure, I passed my time mighty pleasingly! But that I might be delivered of the anxiety and constant fears that attended me, I persuaded our manager (who was under the same unfortunate circumstance) that there was, to my certain knowledge, a writ issued against him, with which he was soon alarmed, and in order to elude the hunters suddenly took away his company by night.

I own this was a base trick, to deprive the town of the infinite pleasure they must have received form the incomparable representations of our sonorous collection, who, if noise could plead any claim to merit, they were undoubtedly the greatest proficients of the age. I have often wondered that these bawling heroes do not as tenderly compassionate their brains, as the retailers of flounders in London streets, by an application of their hand to one ear, to preserve the drum by that necessary caution.

*The French novelist Paul Scarron's *Roman Comique* (1651 – 7) follows a troupe of strolling players.
†alias Don Dismallo-Thick-scullo-de-Half-witto in Colley Cibber's *Love Makes a Man*

However, away we went, and to the great surprise of the inhabitants of the next place we adventured to, about six o'clock on the Sunday morning we made our entry, and beseiged the town. But as our commander was one of a most intrepid assurance, he soon framed some political excuses for the unseasonableness both of the hour and day. The landlord, who happened luckily for us to be an indolent, good-natured man, seeing so large a company, and such boxes full of nothing come into his house, easily dispensed with the oddity of our arrival, and called out lustily for his maid and daughter to set on the great pot for the buttock of beef, and to make a fine fire to roast the loin of veal. He also ordered the ostler to help up with the boxes, which, I own, where weighty, but I believe the chief of the burden consisted of scabbardless, rusty swords and departed mopsticks transmigrated into tragedy truncheons.

For the first week we lived like those imaginary sons of kings we frequently represented, but, at length, we played a night or two, and no money coming, upon enquiry what was for dinner, the good host, with an altered countenance, signified he thought it would be better for us to find our own provision, and apprehending it would not do, he advised us to make a good house, to pay him and march off. Upon which one, whose appetite was extremely keen, discovered such a sudden paleness; another, enraged at the disappointment, and feeling the same demands from nature, thought not equally passive in his disposition, thundered out a volley of oaths, with the addition of terrible threats to leave the house, which the landlord would have been well pleased had he put in force, and with a calm contempt signified as much.

As I had a child to support as well as my unfortunate self, I thought it highly proper to become a friendly mediator between these two persons, and very judiciously introduced myself into further credit by endeavouring to palliate the matter. But the insensible puppy, paying more regard to his offended honour than his craving appetite, scolded himself out of the house, and my daughter and I were continued, by my prudently preserving the gentleman, instead of launching into the barbarous enormities of the Billingsgate* hero.

Business continuing very shocking, I really was ashamed to presume any longer on the partial regard paid to me by the injured

*foul-mouthed (after the reputation of fish-sellers at Billingsgate market)

man, and at last proposed his using his interest to put off as many tickets as he possibly could, in order to make up the several deficiencies of the company. This proposition was kindly accepted, and he soon dispersed a sufficient number of tickets to defray all charges, with many acknowledgements to me for the hint, and, that I might not run the hazard of losing the reputation I had gained, I set off the day after, well knowing that a second misfortune of this nature would not have so happy an end.

With a solitary shilling I went to London and took a lodging in about two hours afterwards at a private house in Little Turnstile, Holborn, but being soon enquired after by another manager, set out from London for Dartford about three o'clock in the afternoon on foot, in a dreadful shower of rain, and reached the town by eight in the evening.

I played that night, for it is losing their charter to begin before nine or ten, but my pumps being thin and the rain heavy, I contracted such a hoarseness, I was the day following turned off with half-a-crown and rendered incapable. An excellent demonstration of the humanity of those low-lived wretches, who have no further regard to the persons they employ but while they are immediately serving them, and look upon players like pack-horses, though they live by them!

When I got to London I had, on account of my hoarseness, no view of getting my bread, as it was impossible to hear me speak without a close application of an ear to my mouth. I was then reduced to the necessity of pledging, from day to day, either my own or my child's clothes for our support, and we were stripped to even but a bare change to keep us decently clean by the time I began to recover my voice.

As soon as I was capable of speaking to be heard, I took a second owl-light opportunity to seek for business and happily succeeded in my endeavour, and, as from evil often unexpected good arises, so did it then to me. I went to play a part in Gravel Lane, where I met with a woman who told me she had scenes and clothes in limbo for two guineas, and, if I could propose any means for their redemption, she would make me manager of her company, if I thought fit to set out with her. I assured her, so far from raising two guineas, I really did not know where to levy as many pence, but, in the night, contemplating on my hapless fate, I recollected a friend that I believed would, on trial, oblige me with that sum.

To strengthen my cause, I wrote a letter as from a sponging-house, and sent one of the performers, who had extremely the air of a bum-bailiff, to represent that character. My friend, moved at my supposed distress, directly granted my suit, the goods were redeemed, and the next morning we set sail, with a few hands, for Gravesend.

For about a month we got, one week with another, a guinea each person. From thence we proceeded to Harwich, where we met with equal success for three weeks more, but unfortunately the manageress's husband, who was no member of the company, was under sentence of transportation in Newgate, and she being frequently obliged to pay her devoirs to her departing spouse in the dismal castle of distress, we broke up, and I returned to London.

My projecting brain was forced again to set itself to work to find fresh means of subsistence, but for some time its labours were ineffectual, till even the last thread of invention was worn out. At last, I resolved to pay circular visits to my good-natured friends who redeemed me from the jaws of destruction when under confinement in Jackson's Alley. I thought the best excuse I could make for becoming so importunate was to fix it on a point of gratitude, in taking the earliest opportunity my circumstances would admit of, to return my sincerest thanks for so infinite an obligation, and, after having starved all day, by the friendly assistance of the night, I adventured, and was, by each person in my several visits, kindly received and constantly sent home with a means to subsist for sometimes a day or two; which, as my circumstances stood, was no small comfort to one who proceeded in paralytic order upon every excursion.

Among the distressful evening patrols I made, I one evening paid my brother a visit, who kindly compassionated my sorrow and, clapping half-a-crown in my hand, earnestly enjoined me to dine next day with him at a friend's house, who he knew had a natural tendency to acts of humanity, and conceived would, in a genteel manner, be serviceable to me. His good-natured design had the desired effect, and in less than three days I was, by my brother's friend, introduced to L—d A—a, who wanted a gentleman, being newly come from I—d, and nice in regard to the person he intended for that office. One well-bred, and who could speak French, were two necessary articles; upon which, mention was made of me, and an open declaration who I really was, with a piteous account of my misfortunes, which his lordship very tenderly considered, and received me upon the recommendation of my brother's friend.

The day following I entered into my new office, which made me the superior domestic in the family. I had my own table, with a bottle of wine and any single dish I chose for myself, extra of what came from my lord's, and a guinea paid me every Wednesday morning, that being the day of the week on which I entered into his lordship's service.

At this time my lord kept in the house with him a *fille de joie*.* Though no great beauty, yet infinitely agreeable, a native of Ireland, remarkably genteel, and finely shaped, and a sensible woman, whose understanding was embellished by a fund of good nature.

When there was any extraordinary company, I had the favour of the lady's at my table, but when there was no company at all, his lordship permitted me to make a third person at his, and very good-naturedly obliged me to throw off the restraint of behaviour incidental to the servant, and assume that of the humble friend and cheerful companion. Many agreeable evenings I passed in this manner, and when bedtime approached I took leave and went home to my own lodgings, attending the next morning at nine, my appointed hour.

I marched every day through the streets with ease and security, having his lordship's protection, and proud to cock my hat in the face of the best of the bailiffs and shake hands with them into the bargain. In this state of tranquillity I remained for about five weeks, when, as the devil would have it, there came two supercilious coxcombs, who, wanting discourse and humanity, hearing that I was his lordship's gentleman, made me their unhappy theme, and took the liberty to arraign his understanding for entertaining one of an improper sex in a post of that sort. His lordship's argument was, for a considerable time, supported by the strength of his pity for an unfortunate wretch, who had never given him the least offence, but the pragmatical blockheads teased him at last into a resolution of discharging me the next day, and I was once again reduced to my scenes of sorrow and desolation.

I must do justice to the peer, to confess he did not send me away empty-handed, but so small a pittance as he was pleased to bestow was little more than a momentary support for myself and child.

*illicit girlfriend; good-time girl

When my small stock was exhausted, I was most terribly puzzled for a recruit.

Friendship began to cool! Shame encompassed me, that where I had the smallest hope of redress remaining I had not courage sufficient to make an attack. In short, life became a burden to me, and I began to think it no sin not only to wish, but even desire to die. When poverty throws us beyond the reach of pity, I can compare our beings to nothing so adaptly as the comfortless array of tattered garments in a frosty morning.

But providence, who has ever been my friend and kind director, as I was in one of my fits of despondency, suddenly gave a check to that error of my mind, and wrought in me a resolution of making a bold push, which had but two chances, either for my happiness or destruction – which is as follows:

I took a neat lodging in a street facing Red Lion Square, and wrote a letter to Mr Beard,* intimating to him the sorrowful plight I was in and, in a quarter of an hour after, my request was most obligingly complied with by that worthy gentleman, whose bounty enabled me to set forward to Newgate market, and buy a considerable quantity of pork at the best hand, which I converted into sausages, and with my daughter set out, laden with each a burden as weighty as we could well bear, which, not having been used to luggages of that nature, we found extremely troublesome; but *necessitas non habeat leges*† – we were bound to that, or starve.

Thank heaven, our loads were like Aesop's, when he chose to carry the bread, which was the weightiest burden, to the astonishment of his fellow-travellers; not considering that his wisdom preferred it, because he was sure it would lighten as it went. So did ours, for, as I went only where I was known, I soon disposed, among my friends, of my whole cargo, and was happy in the thought that the utmost excesses of my misfortunes had no worse effect on me than an industrious and honest inclination to get a small livelihood, without shame or reproach. Though the archduchess of our family, who would not have relieved me with a halfpenny roll or a draught of small beer, imputed this to me as a crime.

I suppose she was possessed with same dignified sentiments

---

*John Beard lived near Charlotte's lodgings in the Red Lion Square area from 1740 to 1751.
†necessity know no bounds

Mrs Peachum is endowed with, and thought the honour of their family was concerned. If so, she knew the way to have prevented the disgrace, and, in a humane, justifiable manner, have preserved her own from that taint of cruelty I doubt she will never overcome.

My being in breeches was alleged to me as a very great error, but the original motive proceeded from a particular cause; and I rather choose to undergo the worst imputation that can be laid on me on that account, than unravel the secret, which is an appendix to one I am bound, as I before hinted, by all the vows of truth and honour everlastingly to conceal.

For some time I subsisted as a higgler,* with tolerable success, and, instead of being despised by those who had served me in my utmost exigencies, I was rather applauded. Some were tender enough to mingle their pitying tears with their approbation of my endeavouring at an honest livelihood, as I did not prostitute my person or use any other indirect means for support that might have brought me to contempt and disgrace.

Misfortunes, to which all are liable, are too often the parents of forgetfulness and disregard in those we have, in happier times, obliged. Too sure I found it so, for I could name many persons, who are still in being, that I have both clothed and fed, who have since met with success, but, when strong necessity reduced me to an attempt of using their friendship, scarce afforded me a civil answer, which closed in an absolute denial, and consequently the sting of disappointment on such occasions struck the deeper to my heart; though none so poignant as the rebuffs I met with from those who ought, in regard to themselves, to have prevented my being under such universal obligations, but, instead of acting agreeably to the needful sentiments of compassion and sorrowful regret for the sufferings of a near relation, where a villainous odium could not be thrown, a ridiculous one was sure to be cast, even on the innocent actions of my life.

Upon being met with a hare in my hand, carried by order to the peer I had then lately lived with, this single creature was enumerated into a long pole of rabbits; and it was affirmed as a truth that I made it my daily practice to cry them about the streets.

This falsehood was succeeded by another, that of my selling fish, an article I never thought of dealing in; but notwithstanding, the wicked forger of this story positively declared that I was selling

*an itinerant dealer in foods such as poultry and dairy produce

some flounders one day, and, seeing my father, stepped most audaciously up to him, and slapped one of the largest I had full in his face. Who that has common sense could be so credulous to receive the least impression from a tale so inconsistent; or that, if it had been true, if I had escaped my father's rage, the mob would not, with strictest justice, have prevented my surviving such an unparalleled villainy one moment?

I always thought myself unaccountable enough in reality, to excite the various passions of grief and anger, pity or contempt, without unnecessary additional falsehood to aggravate my misdeeds. I own I was obliged, till seized with a fever, to trudge from one acquaintance to another with pork and poultry, but never had the honour of being a travelling fishmonger, nor the villainy of being guilty of that infamous crime I was inhumanly charged with.

When I was brought so low by my illness as to be disempowered to carry on my business myself, I was forced to depend upon the infant industry of my poor child, whose strength was not able to bear an equal share of fatigue, so that I consequently was obliged to suffer a considerable deficiency by the neglect of my customers. And though I could scarce afford myself the least indulgence in regard to my illness, I found, though in a trifling degree, it largely encroached upon my slender finances, so that I was reduced to my last three pounds of pork, nicely prepared for sausages, and left it on the table covered up. As I was upon recovery, I took it in my head a little fresh air would not be amiss, and set forth into Red Lion Fields. But, on my return (oh disastrous chance!) a hungry cur had most savagely entered my apartment, confounded my cookery, and most inconsiderately devoured my remaining stock, and from that hour a bankruptcy ensued, the certificate of which was signed by the woefulness of my countenance at the horrid view.

The child and I gaped and stared at each other and, with a despondency in our faces very natural on so deplorable an occasion, we sat down and silently conceived that starving must be the sad event of this shocking accident, having at that time neither meat, money, nor friends. My week's lodging was up the next day, and I was very sure of a constant visit from my careful landlord, but how to answer him was a puzzling debate between me and myself, and I was very well assured could only be answered but by an affirmative in that point.

After having sighed away my senses for my departed pork, I began to consider that sorrow would not retrieve my loss or pay my landlord and, without really knowing where to go or to whom I should apply, I walked out till I should either meet an acquaintance, or be inspired with some thought that might happily draw off the scene of distress I was then immersed in.

Luckily, I met with an old gentlewoman whom I had not seen many years, and who knew me when I was a child. She, perceiving sadness in my aspect, enquired into the cause of that, and my being in men's clothes; which, as far as I thought proper, I informed her. When we parted, she slipped five shillings into my hand, on which I thankfully took leave, went home with a cheerful heart, paid my lodgings off next morning, and quitted it.

The next vexation that arose was how to get another, for the child was too young to be sent on such an errand, and I did not dare to make my appearance too openly. However, that grief was soon solved by the good nature of a young woman, who gave a friendly invitation to us both, and, though not in the highest affluence, supported myself and child for some time, without any view of hopes of a return, which has since established a lasting friendship between us, as I received more humanity from her indigence than I could obtain even a glimpse of from those whose fortunes I had a more ample right to expect a relief from.

I had not been many days with my friend before I relapsed, my fever increasing to that degree my death was hourly expected, and, being deprived of my senses, was left without means of life in this unhappy situation, and, had it not been for the extensive goodness of the person before-mentioned, my child must have either begged her bread, or perished for the want of it.

When I was capable of giving a rational answer, she was my first care, and I had, in the midst of this extremity, the pleasing relief of being informed my friend's humanity had protected her from that distress I apprehended she must have otherwise suffered from the severity of my illness. I was incapable of writing, and therefore sent a verbal message, by my good friend, to my Lord A—a, who sent me a piece of gold, and expressed a tender concern for my misfortunes and violent indisposition.

As soon as I was able to crawl, I went to pay my duty there, and was again relieved through his bounty, and might have returned to my place till something else had fallen out, but that his lordship was obliged to go suddenly out of England, which, as I had a child, was not suitable to either him or me.

Mr Yeates's New Wells* being open, and he having occasion for a singer in the serious part of an entertainment, called *Jupiter and Alcmena*, I was sent for to be his Mercury, and by the time that was ready for exhibition I began to be tolerably recovered. And a miracle indeed it was that I overcame a dreadful, spotted fever without the help of advice. Nor had I any remedy applied, except an emetic, prescribed and sent me by my sister Marples, who was the only relation I had that took any notice of me.

As I have no power of making her amends equal to my inclinations, I can only entreat the favour of my acquaintance in general, and those whom I have not the pleasure of knowing, whenever it is convenient and agreeable for them to use a neat, well-accommodated house of entertainment, they will fix a lasting obligation on me by going to hers, which she opened last Thursday, the 20th instant, in Fullwood's Rents, near Gray's Inn, where they will be certain of flesh, fish and poultry dressed in an elegant manner (at reasonable rates), good wines, etc., and a politeness of behaviour agreeable to the gentlewoman, whose hard struggles through seas of undeserved misfortunes will, I hope, be a claim to that regard I am certain she deserves, and will, wherever she finds it, most gratefully acknowledge.

For some months I was employed, as before-mentioned, till Bartholomew Fair, and, as I thought it would be more advantageous to me to be there, obtained leave of Mr Yeates to quit the Wells for the four days, and returned to him at the expiration thereof.

The rumour of my being in business having spread itself among my creditors, I was obliged to decamp, being too well assured, my small revenue, which was but just sufficient to buy bread and cheese, would not protect me from a jail, or satisfy their demands. Had not my necessities been pressing, my service would not have been purchased at so cheap a rate, but though I must have been everlastingly condemned, had I, through pride, been so repugnant to the laws of nature, reason and maternal love, as to have rejected with insolent scorn this scanty maintenance, when I was conscious I had not sixpence in the world to purchase a loaf. I therefore found it highly necessary to set apart the remembrance of what I had been:

'I then was what I had made myself';

*the New Wells Theatre, Clerkenwell, open from 1734 to about 1748, mainly a pantomime house

and, consequently, obliged to submit to every inconvenience of life my misfortunes could possibly involve me in.

The amount of all I owed in the world did not arise to five and twenty pounds, but I was as much perplexed for that sum as if it had been as many thousands. In order to secure my person and defend myself from want, I joined with a man who was a master of legerdemain, but, on my entering on an agreement with him, he commenced manager and we tragedized in a place called Petticoat Lane, near Whitechapel; I then taking on me that darling name of Brown, which was a very great help to my concealment, and indeed the only advantage I ever received from it, or those who have a better claim to it.

But to my purpose. I soon grew tired of leading such a life of fear, and resolved to make trial of the friendship of my late uncle, and wrote a melancholy epistle to him, earnestly imploring his assistance, for the sake of his deceased sister, my dear mother, to give me as much money as would be necessary to set me up in a public house. I told him I would not put it upon the foot of borrowing, as it was ten millions to one whether he might ever be repaid, and, in case of failure of a promise of that nature, I knew I must of course be subject to his displeasure, therefore fairly desired him to make it a gift, if he thought my circumstances worthy his consideration; which, to do him justice, indeed he did, and ordered me to take a house directly, that he might be assured of the sincerity of my intention.

I obeyed his commands the next day, and, as I have been in a hurry from the hour of my birth, precipitately took the first house where I saw a bill, and which, unfortunately for me, was in Drury Lane, that had been most irregularly and indecently kept by the last incumbent, who was a celebrated dealer in murdered reputations, wholesale and retail.

This I, through a natural inadvertency, never considered, nor what ill consequences must reasonably attend so imprudent a choice of my situation. Choice I can't properly call it, for I really did not give myself time to make one, it was sufficient that I had a house; and rattled away, as fast as a pair of horses could gallop, to inform my uncle how charmingly I was fixed.

He, according to his word, gave me a bank note directly, and a sum of money in gold besides. Providence was merciful enough to afford me a decent quantity of patience to stay long enough to thank him in that respectful manner which duty obliged me to, and his bounty truly deserved; but, I remember, as soon as I got into the coach, I began to think the happiness I then enjoyed to be too great and too substantial to be true.

Having been so long the slave of misery and child of sorrow, it appeared to me like a dream; and I was in Nell Jobson's * condition on that score, who never wished, from a surmise of exactly the same kind, ever to wake again. I had not patience to go home, but stopped at a tavern to count my money, and read my note as often, I believe, as there were shillings in each separate pound, till o' my conscience, I had enumerated every shilling in imagination to a pound.

The first thing I did was to hasten to my principal creditor, who, by the by, had issued out a writ against me a month before, but was, through a fruitless search, obliged to drop his action; though really the man was so good-natured as to hope I would consider the expenses he had been at on that account, and that not finding me had put him to a supernumerary charge, which I was undoubtedly strangely obliged to him for! As a proof how much I thought myself so, I begged the favour of him to give me a receipt for the money, and when he could prevail upon a reprieved criminal to pay for the erecting of Tyburn Tree, because he was not hanged there, he should be perfectly assured of all costs he had been at in tenderly endeavouring to confine me in a prison.

The chap, I believe, was glad of his money, but cursedly vexed he had not stayed till the report of an amendment of my circumstances, which woul have run me to an equal expense of the debt, through the unnecessary charges the dear man would have put me to.

When I had given this Cerberus a sop, I flew with impatient joy to all the brokers in town to buy household furniture, gave the asking price for everything I bought, and in less than three hours my house was thoughtlessly furnished with many things I had no real occasion for.

I dare answer for it that some delicate old maid or prudent wife will bless themselves at this strange recital, and, with vacant uplifted eyes, thank heaven I was no relation of theirs: that they did not wonder such an inconsiderate wretch should be so unhappy, when, poor devils, the same fate would have drawn

*heroine of Charles Coffey's *The Devil to Pay*

equal incumbrances upon their gravities, and perhaps without the advantage of spirits to surmount them, as I have done, for which,

'Thank heaven alone.'

I hope, as I have been often deservedly, and sometimes undeservedly, the motive of laughter in others, I may be allowed to come in for my share, and beg to inform the town that I can as heartily join with them in that respect as they could wish, and more than they may probably expect.

But this affair was attended with such numerous unaccountable proceedings, I can't blame anybody for being thrown into a speechless astonishment. As for example – as soon as I had cluttered an undistinguishable parcel of goods into my house (which was after the hour of five in the evening), I resolved to lie there that night. Beds were to be put up, and everything ranged in proper order. By the time these matters were accomplished, I was forced to forgo my resolution of sleeping there that night, it being near six in the morning before I could advance to my repository, where, when I was imagined to take my rest, my impatient and elevated spirits would not let me continue till the reasonable hour of rising throughout the neighbourhood. But, through excess of joy, I arose and contrived fresh means to unlade me of part of the treasure my uncle had possessed me of.

I dare venture to affirm, I had not been two days and a half in the house before it was opened, and, as is customary on such occasions, gave away an infinity of ham, beef, and veal, to every soul who came and called for a quart of beer, or a single glass of brandy. The faces of many of them I never saw before or since, but was, from the number of people that came the first day, fully convinced that I should carry on a roaring trade; though I afterwards found I had successfully run myself out very near seven pounds, in less than twenty-four hours, to acquire nothing at all.

The next great help I had towards getting an estate was the happiness of the unprofitable custom of several strolling actors, who were unfortunately out of business, and though they had no money, I thought it incumbent on me, as they styled themselves comedians, to credit them till they got something to do; not considering, when that happened, they might in all probability be many score miles out of my reach, which indeed proved to be the very case.

Another expedient towards the making my fortune was letting

three several rooms to as many different persons, but in principle were all alike and conjunctive in the perpetration of my destruction, which I shall define in few words. One of the party has very narrowly escaped hanging, more from dint of mercy than desert; another reduced to common beggary, and lying on bulks,* being so notorious a pilferer as to be refused admittance into the most abject, tottering tenement in or about St Giles's; and the third is transported for life.

Very unfortunately for me, the water was layed into my cellar, and I having no design of doing injuries, suspected none; but found, too late, that my tap had run faster than the water-cock, and my beer carried in pails to the two pair of stairs and garrets, which too frequently set the house in an uproar, as the gentry, at poor Pilgarlick's† expense, got themselves excessively drunk, and constantly quarrelled; insomuch that they began at length to impeach one another, by distant hints and winks, assuring me that they believed it would be very proper to observe Mrs Such-a-one when she went about the house, what she carried up stairs. Presently the person of whom I was warned would come to me and give the same caution of the other, and, in about half an hour's time, the husbands of these people would come and do the same by each other.

These hints made me begin to be a little peery, and resolved to look round the house to see if anything was missing. In short, they had taken violent fancies to my very candlesticks and saucepans, my pewter terribly shrunk, and my coals daily diminished, from the same opportunity they had in conveying off my beer; and, as I kept an eating-house also, there was very often a hue and cry after an imaginary dog, that had run away with three parts of a joint of meat.

As my stock was thus daily and cruelly impaired, consequently my profits were not able to make up for the horrid deficiency, and, as I did not dare to make a second attempt on my uncle, I prudently resolved to throw up my house before I ran myself into such inconveniencies, by endeavouring to keep it, I might not easily have overcome; so suddenly disrobed my own apartments of their furniture, and quitted them, on which the thieving crew were then obliged to disperse, being deprived of all future hopes of making me thus inhumanly their prey.

*small wooden frames.
†mock-pitiful euphemism – 'poor old me'

I must beg pardon of the reader for omitting a circumstance that happened about a year before I was thus intendedly settled by my uncle. Being, as I frequently was, in great distress, I went to see a person who knew me from my childhood, and though not in a capacity of serving me beyond their good wishes and advice, did their utmost to convince me, as far as that extended, how much they had it at heart to serve me; and upon enquiry into what means I proposed for a subsistence, I gave the good woman to understand there was nothing which did not exceed the bounds of honesty that I should think unworthy of my undertaking; that I had been so inured to hardships of the mind, I should think those of the body rather a kind relief, if they would afford but daily bread for my poor child and self.

The woman herself knew who I was, but her husband was an entire stranger, to whom she introduced me as a young gentleman of a decayed fortune, and, after apologizing for half an hour, proposed to her spouse to get me the waiter's place, which was just vacant, at one Mrs Dorr's, who formerly kept the King's Head, at Marylebone.

I thankfully accepted the offer, and went the next morning to wait on the gentlewoman, introduced by my friend's husband, and neither he nor Mrs Dorr in the least suspected who I was. She was pleased to tell me, she liked me on my first appearance, but was fearful, as she understood I was well born and bred, that her service would be too hard for me. Perceiving me to wear a melancholy aspect, she tenderly admonished me to seek out for some less robust employment, as she conjectured that I should naturally lay to heart the impertinence I must frequently be liable to from the lower class of people, who, when in their cups, pay no regard either to humanity or good manners.

I began to be half afraid her concern would make her talk me from my purpose, and, not knowing which way to dispose of myself, begged her not to be under the least apprehensions of my receiving any shock on that account; that notwithstanding I was not born to servitude, since misfortunes had reduced me to it, I thought it a degree of happiness that a mistaken pride had not foolishly possessed me with a contempt of getting an honest livelihood, and choosing rather to perish by haughty penury, than prudently endeavour to forget what I had been, and patiently submit to the severities of fortune, which at that time was not in my power to amend.

To be short, the gentlewoman bore so large a share in my affliction, she manifested her concern by a hearty shower of tears, and, as she found I was anxious for a provision with her, we agreed, and the next day I went to my place; but when I informed her I had a daughter about ten years of age, she was doubly amazed, and the more so to hear a young fellow speak so feelingly of a child.

She asked me if my wife was living. I told her no, that she died in child-bed of that girl (whom she insisted should be brought to see her next day, and entertained the poor thing in a very genteel manner, and greatly compassionated her and her supposed father's unhappiness).

I was the first waiter that was ever permitted to sit at table with her, but she was pleased to compliment me that she thought my behaviour gave me a claim to that respect, and that it was with the utmost pain she obliged herself to call me anything but 'sir'.

To her great surprise, she found me quite a handy creature, and, being light and nimble, tripped up and down stairs with that alacrity of spirit and agility of body that is natural to those gentlemen of the order of the tap-tub;* though, as Hob† says, we sold all sorts of wine and punch, etc.

At length Sunday came and I began to shake in my shoes for fear of a discovery, well knowing our house to be one of very great resort, as I found it, for I waited that day upon twenty different companies, there being no other appearance of a male, except myself, throughout the house, exclusive of the customers, and, to my violent astonishment, not one soul among them all that knew me.

Another recommendation of me to my good mistress was my being able to converse with the foreigners who frequented her ordinary‡ every Sabbath-day and to whom she was unable to talk but by signs, which, I observing, prevented her future trouble by signifying in the French tongue I perfectly well understood it. This was a universal joy round the table, which was encompassed by German peruke-makers and French tailors, not one of whom could utter one single syllable of English.

*bowl to catch drips from beer tap
†in John Hippisley's *Flora* – an immensely popular play inspired by Colley Cibber's *Hob; or, the Country Wake*
‡ eating house with set-price meals

As soon as Mrs Dorr heard me speak French, away she ran with her plate in her hand and, laughing, left the room to go down and eat an English dinner, having, as she afterwards told me, been obliged once a week to dine pantomimically, for neither she or her company were able to converse by any other means.

When I came down with the dishes I thought the poor soul would have eat me up, and sent as many thankful prayers to heaven as would have furnished a saint for a twelvemonth, in behalf of the man who brought me to her. Her overjoy of her deliverance from her foreign companions wrought a generous effect on her mind, which I had a convincing proof of by her presenting me with half-a-crown, and made many encomiums I thought impossible for me ever, in such a sphere of life, to be capable of deserving.

In regard to my child, I begged not to be obliged to lie in the house, but constantly came to my time in a morning, and stayed till about ten or eleven at night; and often wondered I have escaped without wounds or blows from the gentlemen of the pad, * who are numerous and frequent in their evening patrols through these fields, and my march extended as far as Long Acre, by which means I was obliged to pass through the thickest of them. But heaven everlastingly be praised, I never had any encounter with them, and used to jog along with the air of a raw, unthinking, penniless apprentice, which I suppose rendered me not worthy their observation.

In the week-days, business (though good) was not so very brisk as on Sundays, so that when I had any leisure hours I employed them in working in the garden, which I was then capable of doing with some small judgement; but that, and everything else created fresh surprise in my mistress, who behaved to me as if I had been rather her son than her servant.

One day, as I was seting some Windsor beans,† the maid came to me, and told me she had a very great secret to unfold, but that I must promise never to tell that she had discovered it. As I had no extraordinary opinion of her understanding or her honesty I was not over-anxious to hear this mighty secret, lest it should draw me into some praemunire;‡ but she insisted upon disclosing it,

*highwaymen
†broad beans
‡predicament

assuring me it was something that might turn to my advantage if I would make a proper use of it. This last assertion raised in me a little curiosity, and I began to grow more attentive to her discourse; which ended in assuring me, to her certain knowledge, I might marry her mistress's kinswoman, if I would pay my addresses, and that she should like for a master extremely, advising me to it by all means.

I asked her what grounds she had for such a supposition? To which she answered she had reasons sufficient for what she had said, and I was the greatest fool in the world if I did not follow her advice. I positively assured her I would not, for I would not put it in the power of a mother-in-law to use my child ill, and that I had so much regard, as I pretended, to the memory of her mother, I resolved never to enter into matrimony a second time.

Whatever was the motive I am entirely ignorant of, but this insensible mortal had told the young woman that I intended to make love to her (which had I really been a man would have never entered in my imagination, for she had no one qualification to recommend her to the regard of anything beyond a porter or a hackney-coachman). Whether she was angry at what I said to the wench in regard to my resolution against marrying, or whether it was forgery of the maid's, of and to us both, I cannot positively say, but a strangeness ensued, and I began to grow sick of my place, and stayed but a few days after.

In the interim somebody happened to come who hinted that I was a woman. Upon which, Madam, to my great surprise, attacked me with insolently presuming to say she was in love with me, which I assured her I never had the least conception of. 'No, truly, I believe,' said she, 'I should hardly be enamoured with one of my own sect!' Upon which I burst into a laugh, and took the liberty to ask her if she understood what she said. This threw the offended fair into such an absolute rage, and our controversy lasted for some time, but in the end I brought, in vindication of my own character, the maid to disgrace, who had, uncalled-for, trumped up so ridiculous a story.

Mrs Dorr still remained incredulous in regard to my being a female, and, though she afterwards paid me a visit, with my worthy friend (at my house in Drury Lane) who brought my unsuccessful letter back from my father, she was not to be convinced – I happening on that day to be in the male habit, on account of playing a part for a poor man, and obliged to find my own clothes.

She told me she wished she had known me better when I lived with her, she would on no terms have parted with her man Charles, as she had been informed I was capable of being master of the ceremonies in managing and conducting the musical gardens; for she had a very fine spot of ground, calculated entirely for that purpose, and would have trusted the care of it to my government. But it was then too late, which I am sorry for, on the gentlewoman's account, who might have been by such a scheme preserved in her house, from which, through ill-usage, in a short time after she was drove out, and reduced to very great extremities, even by those most nearly related to her; but I find it is become a fashionable vice, to proclaim war against those we ought to be most tender of, and the surest and only way to find a friend is to make a contract with the greatest stranger.

After I left my unfortunate mistress, I was obliged to look out for acting jobs, and luckily one soon presented itself. One Mr Scudamore, a serjeant of dragoons, who had been some years before a player, on his return from battle (where our royal youthful hero* had immortalized his fame in his father's and country's defence) took *The Recruiting Officer* for his benefit, played Captain Plume, and engaged me for Sylvia; and also to write him a prologue on the occasion, which he spoke himself.

I don't pretend to have any extraordinary talents in regard to poetry in verse, or indeed in prose; but as it speaks the warmth of my heart towards the royal family, whose illustrious line may heaven to latest posterity extend, I will venture to insert what I wrote, and hope, though I am but an insignificant and humble subject, every true Briton will let my zeal plead an excuse for my deficiency in attempting so noble and glorious a theme.

> From toils and dangers of a furious war,
> Where groans and death successive wound the air;
> Where the fair ocean, or the crystal flood,
> Are died with purple streams of flowing blood,
> I am once more, thank providence, restored,
> Though narrowly escaped the bullet and the sword.
> Amidst the sharpest terrors I have stood,
> And smiled at tumults for my country's good.
> But where's the Briton dare at fate repine,
> When our great William's foremost of the line?

*the Duke of Cumberland

With steady courage, dauntless he appears,
And owns a spirit far beyond his years;
With wisdom, as with justice, be spurred on,
To save this nation from a papal throne.
May gracious heaven the youthful hero give
Long smiling years of happiness to live:
And Britons, with united voices, sing
The noblest praises of their glorious king;
Who, to defend his country and its rights,
Parted from him in whom his soul delights.
Then with a grateful joy Britannia own,
None but great George should fill the British throne.

Though my poetry may be lame, my design was good and, as I am sensible it has no other merit than that, shall say no more about it, but that it was well received at the Haymarket Theatre, and I was handsomely rewarded by the person whose benefit it was wrote for.

I must acknowledge the story of my situation at Marylebone is not properly ranged in my history according to the time it happened; but as it made up the number of my oddities, I have made bold to haul it in, as I think it is as remarkable as any other part of my life before-mentioned.

After I left my house (which to my uncle's kind pail of milk enabled me to go into, though soon after kicked down by his ridiculous marriage) I went to the Haymarket, where my brother revived the tragedy of *Romeo and Juliet* (and would have succeeded by other pieces he got up, in particular by the run of *Cymbeline*, but was obliged to desist by virtue of an order from the L—d C—n – I imagine, partly occasioned by a jealousy of his having a likelihood of a great run of the last-mentioned play, and which would of course have been detrimental, in some measure, to the other houses.

While we were permitted to go on, my brother and I lived together, where I passed my time both cheerfully and agreeably, and it is no compliment to own the pleasure and advantage I reaped from his daily conversation was the foundation of that pleasing content I enjoyed whilst he was a resident of that theatre.

But as my happiness was never of very long duration, my brother was invited, on the suppression, to Covent Garden Theatre, and I was left to make the best I could with the remaining few who had a mind to try their fortunes with me: and, indeed, to do my brother justice, he promised me I should have the advantage of his daughter Jenny's performance, as I was left suddenly, and in distress.

As she was a promising actress in a tender, soft light, I designed to set her forth to the best advantage, and there was nothing wanting but her father's presence to carry everything on as orderly as before; though his going was the only means that rendered it practicable for me to keep the house open; for, when he was removed,

> We did our safety to our weakness owe,
> As grass escapes the scythe by being low.

Yet I was determined, had my neice remained with me, to have been as industrious as possible, both for her sake and my own, and, as I had appeared in some first characters, was resolved to endeavour at filling up all those with which she was most concerned, as our figures were agreeably matched, I being but of the bulk and stature of most of our modern fine gentlemen, and Miss Jenny, who was a growing girl of sixteen, exactly tallied with me in that respect.

When my brother governed the theatre, he got up *The Conscious Lovers*,* which we played four nights successively to full houses, in which I appeared in the character of Young Bevil, the child in Indiana, and her father in Tom.

As I had been not only endured, but really well received in such a part, during my brother's reign, I could not conceive that his throwing up the reins of empire could lessen me in the esteem of the good-natured part of the town, who had been kind enough to afford me, perhaps, more than my share of applause. But it was otherwise thought by some of my dear friends, who prevailed on my father to send his positive commands to his son to withdraw his daughter, on pain of his displeasure.

I was then reviving an old play, call *Pope Joan*,† in which I afterwards exhibited that character to a dreadful house, which I partly attribute to being deprived of my niece, who was to have performed the part of Angeline. When the bills were up, and her name not there, all those who were fond of seeing and encouraging

---

*by Sir Richard Steele
†probably Elkanah Settle's *The Female Prelate*

her growing genius, sent back their tickets, with various excuses for their non-attendance, and it was debated in the family: it would be a scandal for her to play with such a wretch as I was, it was letting her down to be seen with me, as her father was not there to keep her in countenance.

I should be glad to know what mighty degree of theatrical dignity the harmless child was possessed of preferable to myself as a player? I was, when even under age, received in capital characters at Drury Lane, where I made my first appearance, and in such parts my riper judgement makes me tremble to think I had, only with an uncultivated genius, courage enough to undertake.

In regard to her birth, I presume I was upon a par with her, as her grandfather's daughter and her father's sister. The only disgrace was, my being under misfortunes; the very worst reason for my family's contributing to a perpetration of that which nature and humanity should rather have excited them to have helped me to overcome.

In respect to an improvement in her business, I was thought worthy to instruct her in the part of Indiana, which another of her aunts can testify the truth of, who came with her into my own apartment several days for that purpose.

I suppose the reason of an application to me on that account proceeded from my brother's hurry of business, which prevented his doing it. There could be no other motive, for I am certain there was no mortal in the universe more capable of leaving the impressions of any character whatever on the minds of those who were endowed with the necessary talents to receive them.

I don't mention this with the least tincture of disregard to the dear child, for I am well assured she would have been glad to have rendered her abilities useful to her unfortunate aunt, and I dare say, unless her principles are perverted (which, for her own sake, I hope are not), she still retains in her heart a secret pity for my sufferings: though to avow it might perhaps hazard the forfeiture of that blessing heaven has been pleased to make her grandfather the happy instrument of bestowing, which I would not for the universe be the miserable motive of, therefore shall not only excuse, but even advise her to think, as some other relations do, that I am a stranger to her blood.

It is plain the rancorous hate to me had spread itself to so monstrous a degree that they rather chose to make themselves, I may say in this case, ridiculously cruel, than not load me with an additional weight of misery. The low malice of taking away the child, as I had her father's consent, I put upon the level of schoolboys' understandings, who quarrel with their play-fellow from a jealousy of one's having more plums in his cake than the other.

Had she stayed it might have been useful to both; as time, experience and observation had furnished me with some little knowledge of the stage, I would, to the extent of my power, have rendered it serviceable to my niece, and I am confident she would, on her part, by her performance, have been greatly beneficial to me.

As I am foolishly flattered, from the opinion of others, into a belief of the power of cultivating raw and unexperienced geniuses, I design very shortly to endeavour to instruct those persons who conceive themselves capable of dramatic performances, and propose to make the stage their livelihood.

Some very good friends of mine have lately advised me to this scheme, which I shall put in force as soon as I can with conveniency, and will, on reasonable terms, three times a week, pay constant attendance from ten in the morning till eight in the evening at my intended academy, where ladies and gentlemen shall be, to the utmost of my power, instructed both in the art of speaking and acting; that though they should never come upon the stage, they shall be enabled even to read a play more pleasingly to the auditor, by a few necessary hints, than it is likely they ever would without them.

If I should qualify those who may design to offer themselves to the theatres in such a manner as may render them worthy the manager's acceptance, I shall receive a double satisfaction, both in regard to my pupils' advancement, and rendering my academical nursery useful to the masters of both houses, by a cultivation of a good genius; which has been often thrown away, like a piece of fertile ground overrun with weeds, through neglect or want of good husbandry.

When this narrative is ended I shall advertise to that purpose in the daily papers, and must now beg leave to apologize for swelling out my numbers with my own history, which was originally designed to have consisted only of a short sketch of my strange life, but, on the appearance of the first number, I was enjoined (nay, it was insisted on) by many, that if it was possible for me to enlarge the account of myself to a pocket volume, I should do it.

In compliance with so obliging a request, which I receive as a compliment from my good friends, I have deferred the publication of *Mr Dumont's History* till this is finished, and I hope that, though the town is not so well acquainted with the above-mentioned gentleman, they will be equally curious to become so with his story as they have been with mine, and I dare promise that it will afford them such a satisfaction in the reading they won't repent their encouragement of the author.

As morality is the principal foundation of the work, I venture to recommend it to the perusal of the youthful of both sexes, as each will find a character worthy their observation, and I hope won't blush to make their example.

I intended to have made writing my support, if possible, when I was dispossessed of the happiness of getting my bread with my brother, but, my cares increasing, I had not time to settle myself properly, or collect my mind for such an undertaking, therefore was obliged to decline it, and trust to providence from time to time for what I could get by occasionally acting.

Though I was unfortunate in the main, yet once in five or six weeks something or other generally happened to relieve my afflicted spirits, and I met with two cards running that turned up trumps, which led me into an imaginary hope that the measures of my griefs were so completely filled, that it was probable they would contain no more.

The first of these unexpected joys arose from the tender compassion of his late grace the Duke of M—gu,* who, having been told of my hapless fortune, gave so tender an attention to it, it encouraged the person who related it to advise me to write to his Grace.

I instantly did, and, without the least trouble of obtaining admission for the messenger or letter, was relieved with several guineas, enclosed in a line of soft commiseration, under the bounteous hand of my noble benefactor; the honour of which, notwithstanding my poverty, afforded me a more elevated transport than the liberal donation, and naturally claims a real sorrow for his loss, attended with a grateful and sincere respect for his memory to the last hour of my existence, to which he has a right from hundreds more besides myself, having been a universal

---

*John (1690–1749), 2nd (and last) Duke of Montagu from 1709, son of Ralph Montagu his mother insisted on being addressed as Empress of China. He himself was married to John Churchill's daughter, Mary.

physician and restorer of peace and comfort to afflicted minds, variously oppressed.

This comfort was, in about two days, succeeded by an engagement with the late unfortunate Mr Russell, who was then a man of vogue, and in universal favour with every person of quality and distinction. This gentleman had an Italian opera at Mr Hickford's Great Room, in Brewer Street, exhibited by puppets, which I, understanding the management of, and the language they sung, was hired, after the first night's performance, at a guinea per diem, to move his Punch in particular.

This affair was carried on by subscription, in as grand a manner as possible. Ten of the best hands in town completed his band of music, and several of the female figures were ornamented with real diamonds, lent for that purpose by several persons of the first quality.

During the short run, I was in respect of my salary (which was paid me every day of performance) extremely happy, but so unfortunately circumstanced, I was forced to set out between five and six o'clock in the morning, traversing St James's Park till Mr Hickford's maid arose, and, for security, stayed there all day, mingling with the thickest of the crowd at night to get home.

The benefaction of my noble friend, and Mr Russell's salary, enabled me to new-rig myself and child; that is, upon the score of redemption. But this flowing tide of joy soon came to an ebb, both with my friend and self, for, in a few months after, I heard the unpleasing tidings of his being under confinement in Newgate for debt.

Compassion led me to visit him there, though I had not power to deliver him from that dismal abode but in my wishes, though afterwards, had he taken my advice, he might possibly have proved me a friend by endeavouring to extricate him, in bringing on the Haymarket stage a humorous piece of his own composing; which I believe is still in the hands of some of his creditors, where it is of no use to the person who possesses it, but, as it has merit, might be rendered so, if properly disposed of.

I offered this unhappy gentleman to provide performers, with my own service inclusive, and to take the entire management of it upon myself, without fee or reward, unless his nightly receipts empowered him to gratify me for my trouble, which, had he but been barely set free, I should have thought myself amply rewarded in being partly the happy instrument.

As to the money, I told him I would have nothing to do with it; that door and office keepers should be of his own providing – but that if I engaged the people they should be nightly paid, according to the agreement I should make with them; and for myself, would, if the thing succeeded, leave it to his generosity to reward me as he thought proper, which I make no doubt would have been done in the genteelest manner, had the affair been brought to any issue.

But this distressed gentleman was madly exasperated with the terrible and sudden revolution of his fortune, and, instead of receiving my offered friendship with that regard a reasonable person might have thought it deserved, he rather seemed offended at the proposal; which startled me at first, but on our further conversation I was convinced of his growing misfortune, and too plainly perceived that he was not entirely in his senses, on which I dropped the discourse, and, with a real concern, left him that evening, but returned to see him in about two days, when, instead of finding him in a more settled order, he was absolutely changed from the man of sense to the drivelling idiot, nor was there the least consistency in one single syllable he uttered.

I found myself too much shocked to lengthen my visit and more so, when I gathered from him an account, delivered with heart-breaking sighs and bitter sobs, that a person he had entrusted to raise a contribution for him among the nobility had run away with the bounty intended for his relief, and which would have more than affected it, as there was upwards of a hundred pounds amassed for that purpose.

This piteous narration was recounted to me afterwards by a gentleman who was his intimate friend, and had served him to the extent of his power through the whole scene of misery that ended him.

In about a fortnight after my interview with him in Newgate, passing through, I called to know how he did, and was informed he was removed by a habeas* to the Fleet. As it lay in my way, I stopped there and enquired after him, upon which I was desired to walk up two pair of stairs and in such a room I should find him.

I expressed to the persons who directed me a great concern for him, and they, as naturally, answered it was very kind and good in me, and desired me very civilly to walk up, which accordingly I did; and, after having rambled into several people's rooms through

*court order

mistake, I arrived at that where Mr Russell's remains only were deposited, for he was absolutely in a coffin, which some friend had sent in respect to him.

I conceive a description of my surprise on this account quite necessary, but I really for some time was very near as motionless as the deceased person, and in my heart very angry with the woman who sent me up to him without informing me he was dead.

When I came down, she very reasonably excused herself, by reminding me that the tenor of our discourse consisted of nothing more than a tender concern on my side for the unhappy gentleman, and she concluded that friendship and curiosity had brought me there to see his sad remains, he having been dead two days, and therefore she thought I knew it.

I assured her I did not, and further told her I was pleased to see he had so handsome a shroud and coffin. But she shocked me excessively by telling me he was to be removed out of that one and disrobed of the other, to be put into one provided by the parish – for it was a law, when a debtor died without any effects or means to satisfy their creditors, they must be so interred, otherwise an indulgence of being buried by friends rendered the warden of the Fleet liable to pay all the debts of the deceased, if it could be proved that he had suffered it. It is a hard case, nothwithstanding, that humanity should not extend itself even to the dead, without hurting those whose principles of Christianity excite them to it.

Thus ended the life of one who was universally admired, and had been for some time as much the fashion in families as their clothes. But, alas, misfortunes are too apt to wear out friendship, and he was cast off in two or three months with as much contempt as an old coat made in Oliver's * time.

Though it was represented by his acquaintance how cruelly he had been used by the person he intrusted to solicit them in his behalf, it was scarce believed, even by those who not long before had laid him nearest to their hearts. This is one very remarkable instance of the uncertainty of friendship, and the instability of people's minds who are only fashionably kind.

I was in hopes, after Mr Russell's death, to have got his figures upon reasonable terms, and have taken them into the country, as they were very small, and rather an incumbrance to one who did not understand how to make use of them, but, when I made an

*Oliver Cromwell

enquiry into the price of them, his landlord valued them at threescore guineas, and the money down.

That last assertion soon ended my project, as the reader may conceive, so I engaged myself at May Fair, and lived on my profits there till the ensuing Bartholomew. From thence I went into the country, where I remained till last Christmas, for very near nine years.

THE FACTS
1742–6

The episode at Mrs Dorr's King's Head, Marylebone, most probably took place much earlier, in 1737–8, for it was when she had lodged at Long Acre. Unfortunately the victuallers' licences for the King's Head at that time have not survived, so I have been unable to positively date her stay with Mrs Dorr.

The King's Head public house is the one featured on the right side of Hogarth's *March of the Guards to Finchley*. It was at the top of Tottenham Court Road, on the site of the ancient Manor of Tottenhall (where Tottenham Court Road now crosses Euston Road), and was surrounded by miles of countryside. From it, the walk back to town would certainly have entailed a long walk over fields, for then the first streets of London were on the site of today's Oxford Street.

Mrs Charke claims to have performed at the theatre in Gravel Lane. This could possibly be one of the Southwark theatres which occasionally managed the odd performance, or possibly Goodman's Fields, which was near another Gravel Lane, in Houndsditch.

Her spell as *valet de chambre* to the Earle of Anglesey (she obviously thought it was spelled Anglesea) most probably took place in 1742. Richard Annesley, Earl of Anglesey, Viscount Valentia, Baron Mountnorris, Baron Altham, took his seat in England on 10 May 1737. He was quite a ladies' man.

On 25 January 1715, at the age of twenty-one, he married Ann Prust, a nineteen-year-old Captain's daughter from Devon, and they lived together in Westminster and on his estates in Ireland at Waterford and Ross. She brought him a considerable fortune, but left him and returned to Devon in 1719. Also in 1715 he is said to have married a fifteen-year-old Dublin girl, Anne Simpson, the daughter of a wealthy clothier, who in 1726 signed a document for him promising never to sue him for bigamy. She had three daughters by the earl.

On 15 September 1741 (first wife four weeks dead; second one still alive and well), he married, privately at his Irish home, Camolin Park, Juliana Donovan, the daughter of a Wexford merchant. The witnesses both conveniently died before anyone wanted to check the documents, and the couple re-married in 1752, just to tie up any loose ends. In 1744 Juliana Donovan bore him a son, Arthur Annesley (whose claims to his father's titles were quashed by the House of Lords in 1771). In London, he also had an illegitimate son by Anne Salkeld, daughter of a London merchant. It is possible that this relationship was solemnized in 1742.

I surmise that his lordship's *fille de joie*, described by Mrs Charke as 'a native of Ireland, remarkably genteel', must have been Juliana Donovan (although a man of Anglesey's proclivities could well have had other undiscovered live-in mistresses).

Anglesey was certainly in London in 1741–2 and Juliana Donovan would, so early in the marriage, most likely have accompanied him. I suggest that Mrs Charke's stint as gentleman's gentleman was during those year's.[1]

Quite possibly, among the begging letters she wrote was the letter to her father which prompted this reply:

To Mrs C. Charke   21 September

Madam,
The strange career which you have run for some years (a career not always unmarked by evil) debars my affording you that succour which otherwise would naturally have been extended to you as my daughter. I must refuse therefore – with this advice – try Theophilus.
Yours in sorrow, Colley Cibber.[2]

By the early 1740s the effects of the 1737 Licensing Act were really starting to bite. Except at the patent houses, acting jobs were now hard to come by, unless the actor was willing to give up all the trappings of a respectable life.

Unlicensed managers attempting to present plays had to couch their advertisements in terms which could be interpreted ambiguously, boldly offering a play which appeared to be the least important thing on the bill. Giffard was the first to use the 'concert formula', in which a concert of music was announced, with a play performed 'gratis' during the interval. Soon afterwards, Macklin attempted to perform by announcing that a play would be performed by gentlemen for their own diversion, but this formula was not successful.

The pantomime, *Jupiter and Alcmena* (with rope-dancing, juggling and performances on the slack wire) was being performed at New Wells, Clerkenwell, in the summer of 1742 (as it was many times after this), and it would fit into the rest of Mrs Charke's story if she played Mercury then, for she appeared, with her troupe, Punch's Company of Comical Tragedians, at the 1742 Bartholomew Fair, performing *The Humours of Covent Garden; or the Covent Garden Tragedy*, in which she played Lovegirlo, and *The Universal Monarch Defeated; or the Queen of Hungary Defeated*, the subtitle of which was one of Mrs Charke's recurring jokes.

It is practically certain that she also played that year's Southwark Fair, for the first known appearance of her twelve-year-old daughter, Catherine, was as Princess Elizabeth at Southwark in 1742.

In November 1742 (using the concert formula), she announced her next venture:

'For the benefit of a person who has a mind to get money; At the new Theatre in James Street, near the Haymarket, on Monday next, will be performed a concert of vocal and instrumental music, divided into two parts . . . Between the two parts of the concert will be performed a tragedy called *Fatal Curiosity*, written by the late Mr Lillo, auther of *George Barnwell*. The part of Mrs Wilmot by Mrs Charke, who originally performed it at the Haymarket. The rest of the parts by a set of people who will perform as well as they can, if not as well as they would, and the best can do no more.

With variety of entertainments, viz: Act 1. A preamble on the kettle drums by Mr Job Baker, particularly Larry Grovy, accompanied with French horns. Act 2nd. A new peasant dance by Mons. Chemont and Madam Peran, just arrived piping hot from the opera at Paris. To which will be added a ballad opera called *The Devil to Pay*: the part of Nell by Miss Charke, who performed Princess Elizabeth at Southwark. Servants will be allowed to keep places on the stage – particular care will be taken to perform with the utmost decency, and to prevent mistakes.'

The following Charke season skirted very near to infringement of the Licensing Act, for it appears that although many of the shows were billed as puppet shows, they included live actors. Although, given the nervousness about performing straight plays at all, it was a very strong one, and included Dryden's *Aureng-Zebe* and *Don Sebastian*, Fielding's *The Miser*, Lillo's *London Merchant*, Farquhar's *The Recruiting Officer* and *The Constant Couple*, Carey's *The Honest Yorkshireman* and *Chrononhotonthologos*, Cibber's *Love Makes a Man*, Garrick's *The Lying Valet*, *The Stratagem*, Howard's *The Committee* and Baker's *Tunbridge Walks*. Her own 'whimsical, comical, farcical, operatical, allegorical, emblematical, Pistolatical impromptu medley' called *Tit for Tat; or, Comedy and Tragedy at War* came into the repertoire in February 1743. It was not published.

As the season came to an end in March 1744, she must have pestered her uncle John for the money for her tavern, for during 1744 she was paying the rates (wrongly transcribed as Charlot Clarke) on a small property in Prince's Court on its corner with Drury Lane and Colson's Court. Colson's Court was being rebuilt, and that same year was renamed Stuart's Rents (it contained some of the first numbered properties in Camden's rates books).

She advertised a benefit performance on 28 March 1744, Rowe's *The Fair Penitent*, in which she played Lothario. The tickets, at 4 shillings, 2 shillings and 1 shilling, were to be bought at 'Mrs Charke's Steak and Soup house in Drury Lane, near Stuart's Rents'.[3]

In May 1744 another of her companies played a heavy schedule at Hallam's New Theatre in Mayfair. In *The Royal Hero; or the Lover of his Country (intermixed with several comical and diverting scenes called the blundering brother, with the merry adventures of Timothy Addlepot and Davy Dunce)* featured Mrs Charke as Eumenes and her daughter as Lucia. On the same bill was *Harlequin Sclavonian; or The Monsieurs in the Suds*, with the lady who had saved her from debtors' prison, 'the celebrated Mrs Careless' as Colombine. Her quondam manager, Jockey Adams, was also in the company and some of the performances were followed by his Jockey Dance. For two months she presented more plays, playing her old roles of Barnwell, Archer, Plume, Lothario and Foppington, while her daughter started to build up her repertoire, playing Gipsey in *the Beaux' Stratagem* and Edging in her grandfather's comedy *The Careless Husband*.

The most important thing about this season was Mrs Charke's

new tactic for evading the infamous Licensing Act. On 8 June she announced 'each person to be admitted for 6 pence at the door, which entitles them to a pint of fine ale, upon delivering the ticket to the waiter'. Thus she was not selling the tickets for a dramatic performance, but for a (very expensive) pint of ale. The entertainment was technically being offered for free. This method of by-passing licensing laws is still regularly used all over the world, usually with tea, coffee, or a programme, replacing ale. Note also that, as mistress of a tavern, she probably supplied her own ale, or, possibly, her career as inn-keeper coming to an end, she found a way to use up the stock.

Jenny Cibber, Theophilus and Jane Cibber's first child, was born in 1730, the year Mrs Charke made her début. Jenny made her own first appearancce in December 1741, playing the Duke of York, one of the princes in the Tower, in *Richard III*. Over the next two years she occasionally played similar roles – pages, young princes, etc.

In September 1744 (at the age of fourteen) Theophilus gave her her first big chance. He impudently announced a season of plays, at the Haymarket which he declared was 'By Permission, by Act of Parliament' although it was not. In *Romeo and Juliet*, Charlotte played the Nurse, Jenny played Juliet, and her father, Theophilus, played Romeo. He also spoke the prologue. Garrick witnessed it.

'I never heard so vile and scandalous a performance in my life; and, excepting the speaking of it, and the speaker of it, nothing could be more contemptible. The play was tolerable enough, considering Theophilus was the hero . . . Mrs Charke played the Nurse to his daughter, Juliet; but she was so miserable throughout, and so abounded in airs, affectation and Cibberisms, that I was quite shocked at her. The girl I believe may have genius, but unless she changes her preceptor, she must be entirely ruined.'

Aaron Hill thought Jenny Cibber showed 'considerable merit' but criticized Theophilus ('Too old for her choice, too little handsome, to be in love with, and, into the bargain, her father').[4]

Father and daughter continued their double act in *Othello*, *The Recruiting Officer*, *The Conscious Lovers*, *The Distressed Mother*, and *Cymbeline* before the Lord Chamberlain closed them down on 22 October.

Theophilus then devised yet another method of evading the Act – the rehearsal formula. He announced an 'Academy' at which a concert would be performed, followed by a rehearsal of *Romeo and*

Juliet, 'the characters personated by the master of the academy, his assistants, pupils and servants'. The Lord Chamberlain stopped the show before it opened.

Jenny Cibber, however, was granted permission for a benefit performance in mid-December. Charlotte tried to cash in on Jenny's temporary licence with a proposed performance of *The Beggar's Opera* on 26 December 1744. Mrs Charke, as Macheath, was to lead 'The Queen of Hungary's company of comedians' – with so many cancelled shows she probably was getting hungry by this time.

Mrs Charke's portrayal of Pope Joan in Settle's *The Female Prelate*, with a cast including her niece, Jenny, was announced for 4 March 1745. A few days earlier a mysterious letter had appeared in the *Daily Advertiser*:

Sir,
I find by the daily papers that there is an old play reviving (and which is to be performed on Monday next at the Haymarket Theatre) called Pope Joan, wherein Mrs Charke represents the character of the Pope. I must confess it gave me pleasure when I read her name for a female character and take this public manner of congratulating her on her appearing in her proper sphere, and hope there will be a crowded audience to encourage her to persevere in the resolution of laying aside the hero and giving them the pleasure of her performance for the future as the heroine. I hope this friendly hint will be received as it is meant purely to serve her, having been informed that her throwing herself into male characters have proved detrimental to her; if so, allowing that she is sensible of her error I think it is pity she should be lost to the Town, having sufficient merit, in my opinion, to entitle her to its favours.
Sir,
Your constant reader,
Q.Z.

This letter has been served up against Mrs Charke many times, as proof that the town was revolted by her frequent playing of male characters. But certain things should be noted which indicates that it was her own work: the unlikely initials of the writer, the slightly pompous tone, the joke against herself (the same type of humour as her announcement of a benefit 'for a person who has a mind to get money'), and the reference in the letter to hopes for 'a crowded audience'. Add to this the fact that the letter was printed, not in the main heart of the paper where other letters can be found, but in a square box amid the adverts for theatrical presentations. It is quite clearly an advert which *she* placed to arouse interest in her one-off performance.[5]

In November 1745 she appeared for Adam Hallam's brother, William, with his company at Goodman's Fields. She played Lady Townly (*The Provok'd Husband*), Sylvia (*The Recruiting Officer*), Lucy (*The Beggar's Opera*), Belvidera (*Venice Preserv'd*) and Abigail (*The Drummers; or the Haunted House*). Adam Hallam's other brother Lewis played male leads in the same season.

During the year she also moved Punch for John Russell (previously only identified as Mr Russel) at Hickford's Great Room in Brewer Street. Horace Walpole saw Russell's programme and was not impressed: 'One Russell, a mimic, has a puppet-show to ridicule operas; I hear very dull, not to mention its being twenty years too late; it consists of three acts, with foolish Italian songs burlesqued in Italian.'[6]

On 28 January 1746 John Russell, gentleman, was taken into custody for debt. His other creditors soon leapt on to the bandwagon, and his original conviction for £42 was soon increased by a further £227 owed to seven others. He was committed by Habeas Corpus to the Fleet prison, as case 1522, on 31 May 1746. A note in the margin of Russell's entry in the Fleet committals register dates Mrs Charke's trip to the Fleet in which she found him in his coffin: 'July 1746. Departed this life within the prison'.[7]

On Wednesday 30 April 1746, Mrs Charke returned to the legitimate stage for the first time in over a year, playing Sylvia in *The Recruiting Officer* at the Haymarket Theatre. She is not on the bills, but there is supporting evidence that she did appear. 'An occasional prologue in honour of his Royal Highness, the Duke of Cumberland . . . by Scudamore' was announced. No professional actor called Scudamore is appearing anywhere at this time. However the performance is to 'benefit a gentleman under misfortunes, lately arrived from the army in Flanders'. Surely this is Scudamore, sergeant of dragoons, himself. The prologue, quoted in full in the *Narrative*, was presumably written by Mrs Charke, and *performed* by Scudamore.

Two days later, on 2 May 1746, she appeared in person at St George's Chapel, Mayfair, where she married the mysterious John Sacheverell of St Andrew's, Holborn.

After two weeks she was back on stage, this time at the New Wells, Clerkenwell, where, from 19 May to 14 June, she spoke her own 'occasional epilogue' (presumably the prologue in disguise), and proudly billed herself 'Mrs Sacheverell, late Mrs Charke'. She spoke this epilogue after an evening consisting of rope-dancing, tumbling, a musical entertainment called *Britannia Rediviva* and a new grotesque piece called *The Fortunate Volunteer; or, the Amours of Harlequin*, 'the whole to conclude with the exact view of the battle fought under the command of our glorious hero the Duke of Cumberland, and the cannonading the walls of Culloden House, with the horse in full pursuit of the rebels, and the complete victory over them'. Admission was by pint of wine or punch and printed books of the entertainment were given free to the audience. The whole evening was a perfect example of the type of entertainment she had been so against in *The Art of Management*. But times were changing.

After this, for some reason, Mrs Charlotte Sacheverell, née Cibber, late Charke, disappeared from the London playbills for many years.

1 All information on Anglesey from GEC, *The Complete Peerage*, 1901.
2 Enthoven Collection, British Theatre Museum.
3 Camden Rate Books; *The London Stage*.
4 *Garrick: Letters*, ed. David Little and George Kahrl, 1963; Aaron Hill, *The Actor*, 1750.
5 The *Daily Advertiser*, 27 February 1745.
6 Letter to Horace Mann; 29 March 1745.
7 PRO MS PRIS 1;10 f.162.

Chapter Five

THE NARRATIVE

My first expedition was to Sunning Hill, where I had the joy of playing Captain Plume and blending it with the part of Sylvia.* The lady who should have represented it, as I suppose, was so strongly affected with the death of her brother Owen, she was not able to speak a plain word, or indeed to keep her ground.

This gave me an early touch of the quality of strollers, and, but that it was rather convenient than otherwise to keep out of town, would soon have brought me back again. But, alas, this was trifling to what I afterwards beheld. I have seen an emperor 'as drunk as a lord', according to the old phrase, and a lord as elegant as a ticket-porter; a queen with one ruffle on, and Lord Townly without shoes, or at least but an apology for them.

This last circumstance reminds me of the queen in Dryden's *The Spanish Friar* once playing without stockings; though I must do the person justice to say it proceeded from an unprecedented instance of even a superfluity of good nature, which was excited by Her Majesty's observing Torrismond to have a dirty pair of yarn stockings with above twenty holes in sight, and, as she thought her legs not so much exposed to view, kindly strips them of a pair of fine cotton, and lends them to the hero.

I played Lorenzo, and, having no business with the Queen, had a mind to observe how she acquitted herself in her part, being a person I had known many years, and was really anxious for her success. I found she spoke sensibly, but to my great surprise observed her to stoop forward, on which I concluded she was seized with a sudden fit of the colic, but she satisfied me of the contrary, and on her next appearance I remarked that she sunk down very much on that side I stood, between the scenes, on which I then conjectured her to be troubled with a sciatic pain in her side, and made a second enquiry, but was answered in the negative on that score; upon which I desired to know the reason of

* the leading roles in George Farquhar's comedy *The Recruiting Officer*

her bending forward, and sidling so. She told me it was a trick she had got. 'It is a very new one then,' says I, 'for I never saw you do so before!' But I began to suspect something was the matter and resolved to find it out. Presently the royal dame was obliged to descend from the stage into the drawing room, and made a discovery, by the tossing up of her hoop of a pair of naked legs.

I own I was both angry and pleased. I was concerned to find my friend's humanity had extended so far as to render herself ridiculous, besides the hazard she ran of catching cold, but must confess I never saw so strong a proof of good nature, especially among travelling tragedizers, for, to speak the truth of them, they have but a small share of that principle subsisting amongst them.

If a person is but a lame hand, he or she is despised for that, and it is a common rule when benefits come on, to say among their different parties (which they all herd in): 'Mr and Mrs Such-a-one, to be sure, will have a great house', meaning perhaps the manager and his wife, who very often are the worst in the whole set; and it is very seldom that one couple shall both prove good, but the merit of the one is forced to make up for the deficiency of the other.

The least glimmering or shade of acting, in man or woman, is a sure motive of envy in the rest, and if their malice can't persuade the townspeople into a dislike of their performer, they'll cruelly endeavour to taint their characters, so that I think going a-strolling is engaging in a little, dirty kind of war in which I have been obliged to fight so many battles I have resolutely determined to throw down my commission. And to say truth, I am not only sick, but heartily ashamed of it, as I have had nine years' experience of its being a very contemptible life; rendered so through the impudent and ignorant behaviour of the generality of those who pursue it, and I think it would be more reputable to earn a groat a day in cinder-sifting at Tottenham Court than to be concerned with them.

It is a pity that so many who have good trades should idly quit them to become despicable actors, which renders them useless to themselves, and very often nuisances to others. Those who were bred up in the profession have the best right to make it their calling, but their rights are horribly invaded by barbers' apprentices, tailors, and journeyman weavers, all of which bear such strong marks of their professions that I have seen Richard the Third murder Henry the Sixth with a shuttle,* and Orestes jump off the shopboard† to address Hermione.‡

Another set of gentry who have crept into their community are servants out of place, and I very lately saw the gallant Marcian§ as well rubbed and curried as ever the actor did a horse in his master's stable. This worthy wight, having the happiness to write an exceeding fine hand and living formerly with a gentleman in one of the inns of court, wisely palms himself upon strangers for a lawyer, when his real and original profession was that of a groom.

How such sort of people, without the help of at least a little education, can presume to pick the pockets of an audience is to me astonishing; though they have the vanity and assurance to say they please, but it is only themselves, and were the spirits of departed poets to see their works mangled and butchered as I have too often been a melancholy witness of, they would certainly kick the depredating heroes out of this world into the next.

I have had the mortification of hearing the characters of Hamlet, Varanes,¶ Othello, and many more capitals, rent in pieces by a figure no higher than two sixpenny loaves, and a dissonancy of voice which conveyed to me a strong idea of a cat in labour, all of which, conjoined with an injudicious utterance, made up a complete tragical emetic for a person of the smallest degree of judgement. And yet these wretches very impudently style themselves players – a name, let me tell them, when properly applied, is an honour to an understanding, for none can deserve that title who labour under the want of a very considerable share of sense.

In the course of my travels I went to a town called Cirencester, in Gloucestershire, where an odd affair happened, which I beg leave to relate as follows:

I happened to be taken violently ill with a nervous fever and lowness of spirits that continued upon me for upwards of three years before I was able to get the better of it. When I came to the before-mentioned town I was so near death that my dissolution was every moment expected, but, after my illness came to a crisis, I very slowly amended, and as soon as I could creep about the house,

*instrument used in weaving
†bench sat on by tailors while at their trade
‡in Ambrose Phillips's *The Distressed Mother*
§in Nathaniel Lee's *Theodocius*
¶another character in *Theodocius*

was advised by my apothecary to ride out, if I was able to sit a horse.

As soon as I found myself capable of it, I followed his advice, and had one lent me for myself, and another for my friend, the good-natured gentlewoman who commiserated poor Torrimond's * misfortunes, and to whom I am most infinitely and sincerely obliged for her tender care in nursing me in three years' illness without repining at her fatigue, which was uninterrupted, and naturally fixes on me a lasting grateful sense of the favour.

The person who furnished me with the horses was a reverend-looking elder, about sixty years of age, with a beautiful curling head of hair and florid complexion, that bespoke at once both admiration and respect. His temper was agreeable to his aspect, extremely pleasing, and his company entertaining; with which he often obliged me, while my friend attended her business of a play night.

After riding out two or three days, the old gentleman, perceiving me to grow better, asked me if I liked the horse, which I told him I greatly approved, as it was an easy and willing creature. He said he was at my service. I very thankfully accepted the favour, and, before many witnesses, the present was made, as also the other for my friend's use, which belonged to a young fellow he called his nephew.

He told me that if I thought proper to quit the stage, which he imagined in my weak condition was better avoided than pursued, he would take me to his estate, situate at a place called Brill in Oxfordshire; and, if I and my friend would stay with him as long as either he or we should live, I should be superintendent over his affairs abroad, and my friend should have the entire management of the family at home; which he said consisted only of himself and nephew, and about seven or eight servants that were employed in husbandry, he being, as he informed us, a wealthy grazier.

It was soon resolved that we should give warning to Mr Linnett, who was manager of the company, to leave him at the expiration of a month. This was accordingly done and, as a confirmation of his intentions in taking us with him, gave Mrs Brown an old-fashioned gold necklace, with a large locket of the same metal, which all together, I dare believe by the weight, could not be worth

---

* in John Dryden's *The Spanish Friar*

less than twenty pounds, there being several rows, and the beads not small.

I desired the old gentleman not to insist on her wearing it till she went home. It being an old-fashioned thing, I knew, as an actress, people would stare to see her so equipped; though it was a valuable gift, but more proper to ornament the neck of a country housewife, than a tragedy queen. I therefore desired him to keep it till we were settled, and pretended, for fear of afronting him, that she might run a hazard in losing it of a play night. He thought my care was just, but insisted on her laying it up herself, and I luckily insisted he should have it in his possession till we went away.

The thoughts of being so well settled and provided for both our lives, was, in fact, greatly conducive towards the restoration of my health, and our friendship with the old gentleman daily increased, as also with his nephew, whom he frequently sent into different parts of the country after cattle, and, with the utmost ceremony, begged the favour of borrowing my horse till he could send an order to Brill for another.

The least I could do was to comply with the request of so valuable a friend, and away went the nephew, who, at length, happened to stay three or four days longer than was intended, which gave his uncle a great deal of seeming uneasiness that, to all appearance, was worked into a downright passion, with threats of cutting him off with a shilling for rambling about when he had sent him upon business of weighty concern.

As I observed him to be very much out of humour, I thought it would be but a friendly part to endeavour to appease the uncle, for the nephew's sake, which the old man took very kindly of me, and bid me want for nothing that might be necessary toward the recovery of my health, assuring me, when Jemmy came home, fifty pounds should be at my service to put to what use I pleased.

So generous an offer, unasked, made me conceive that this man was dropped from heaven to be my kind deliverer from all the sorrows of life, but before Mr James came back, there came a sudden order from the magistrate of the town to insist on the old man's leaving it at a moment's warning, on pain of being sent to Gloucester jail if he refused to obey.

In the interim, home comes the nephew, who received the same charge, but they huddled up their affairs in a strange manner and ventured to stay three days longer, though very little seen.

This put my friend and self into a terrible consternation, for still we could neither of us arrive at the real truth of the affair, until Mr Linnett, who had heard it from the townspeople, and with a frighted aspect and real concern came, almost breathless, to let me know that my pretended friends were positively gamblers and house-breakers; that if we listened any longer to them we should be sure not only to be deceived, but in all human probability be made innocent sufferers for their guilt.

Mr Linnett's concern was expressed with all the symptoms of strong truth, which startled us both with fear and wonder, and made us heedfully attentive to all he related. We immediately gave up all right and claim to our horses, and my friend did the same to her gold necklace, all of which were stolen goods; and, had she been seen with it about her neck by the right owner, it is possible the poor soul might have been provided with one of a rougher kind, and each of us disgracefully exalted for being harmlessly credulous.

I afterwards found out their scheme was to have got our boxes into their possession, which, as both the old and young man were frequent in their visits to play at cards with me, by way of amusement in my illness, they had observed were well furnished with very good linen, and my friend had just received a present of clothes from her relations. Had they got those into their possession they would have proved a tolerable booty.

But our better stars shone forth that time and, though we lost only an imaginary fortune, we secured our lives, and the little all we were both worth upon the face of the earth.

In about a year after, the old man dangled into the next world upon a gibbet, either at Salisbury or Oxford, which I cannot positively affirm, but that was his deserved fate; and the young one died raving mad in a prison, in or near London.

I thought proper to insert this story, not only as it is a particular occurrence of my life, but to warn the undesigning part of the world of heedlessly falling into company of strangers, and being taken in by them.

This man, by his discourse and appearance, would have deceived a much wiser person than myself, as he really wore the venerable marks of bearded sanctity and wisdom, but his principles were as opposite to that description as an angel to a demon, having been upwards of forty years a noted gambler, pickpocket, and sometimes highwayman.

I often lift up my heart to heaven with grateful sense of its providential care of us in preventing the dismal scenes of misery to which we should have been exposed had this wicked man perpetrated his design; and we might have been made innocent sacrifices to save his horrid life, through villainy imposed, and branded with the guilt of crimes we never should have thought of committing. I therefore hope our fortunate escape will set others on their guard, who may be liable to an accident of the same kind.

When we left Cirencester we made a short progress to Chippenham, an agreeably situated market town in the road to Bath, where I met with many friends, as indeed I generally had the good fortune to do, go where I would: in particular, Mr Thomas Stroud, who keeps the Angel Inn, and Mr Lodge, master of the White Hart, were conjunctive in forwarding my interest, and I think, without the compliment to either, they are remarkable for keeping two of the most elegant and best accommodated houses throughout Great Britain. A thing seldom known that one little market town should produce two such agreeable repositories for travellers, and I am very glad they meet with the success they deservedly enjoy.

From thence we took a short trip to a little village called Corsham, four miles distant from Chippenham, where we had little else to do than to walk out and furnish our keen stomachs with fresh air and come home and gape at each other for want of a dinner.

Bad business is a sure means to produce ill blood in a company, for, as they grow hungry, they naturally grow peevish and fall out with one another, without considering that each bears a proportionable part of the distress, the manager excepted, who never fails, in all companies, to eat, as Bombardinian* says,

'Though all mankind should starve.'

This happening to be my case, I was refused a small, but needful supply, which occasioned a disagreeable argument, and I wrote to Mr Richard Elrington to inform him, agreeable to an invitation I received some months before, upon his sending me three guineas, my friend, daughter, and self, would immediately join him.

Accordingly, as soon as the letter could reach him, which was as far as Tiverton in Devonshire, he dispatched a messenger on horseback, with two guineas and a half, and a letter full of joy with the hopes of my speedy arrival, which was no small advantage as

* General in Henry Covey's *Chrononhotonthologos* (scene v)

the company then stood, as it consisted but of few hands, and one of the women so unfortunate that she was dead drunk in bed the first night of their opening, when she should have been soberly employed in the performance of Lucy in *The Beggar's Opera*. Mrs Elrington, who was perfect in all the characters in that piece, artfully contrived to double the parts of Polly and Lucy, which I suppose she must do, as Sosia represents himself and Alcmena,* by the assistance of a lanthorn.

So dismal a disappointment naturally offended the audience, and their nightly receipts fell very short of their expectations from this disastrous chance, which reduced them to the necessity of playing three times a week at a little market town called Cullompton within five miles of Tiverton, or at least attempting so to do, that they might have a probability of eating once in six days; and a terrible hazard that was, for the Cullompton audience never amounted to more than twenty shillings at the fullest house, which, when the charges were paid, and the players, like so many hungry magpies, had gaped for their profits, might very possibly afford what they call a stock-supper, which was generally ended in a quarrel by way of dessert.

That barbarous word 'merit' has been the occasion of more feuds in those communities than the whole court of chancery can ever be able to decide, or His Majesty's army overcome. I own it surprises me that a single syllable, which in itself is truly valuable, should be so constant an invader of the peace of those who, if I may judge by their abuse of it on the stage, are perfect strangers to its derivation, and not in the least relative to them who nightly claim an unlawful title to it.

However, I shall, though I find fault with the multitude, do justice to those who deserve it. Mrs Elrington has the first demand on my judgement in that case among the travelling comedians. She has a great deal of spirit, and speaks sensibly. Her genius is calculated for low comedy entirely, and the smallness of her person, which rendered her unsuccessful in her attempt on Covent Garden Theatre, is no detriment on a country stage, as the difference of them is upon an equality with a mouse-trap and a mountain.

When we arrived at Tiverton they were gone for a night or two to their more rural retreat, and I, having a man and two horses to

---

* in John Dryden's *Amphitryon and The Two Sosias*

discharge, was really, with our keeping upon the road for near seventy miles, under some sort of confusion and concern for want of the half-guinea which was short of our demands.

After some private consultation with my friend and daughter, who were both trembling with terrible apprehensions of some immunities arising from this misfortune, I took heart and resolved to set the best face upon a bad matter. As Mr Elrington was not present to receive us, I enquired what houses he used in town, and was, to my great joy, soon informed that there was one in particular, the mistress of which was a great friend to him, on which I undauntedly set forward, and very luckily found the person to be the young man's mother who brought us the money into Wiltshire.

In Mr Elrington's name I borrowed the half-guinea, which to our general joy was immediately granted, and the man and horses discharged; though a second thought came into my head, that as the company was absent, and hearing but a terrible account of their progress there, I began to be doubtful whether their faith was strong enough to keep so many poor, penniless devils from starving till their return, which I was told would not be so soon as they proposed, there being a play bespoke, to which they were promised a great house.

This gave me fresh spirits, and I thought it quite proper to engage our guide to walk the other five miles and escort us to the players. The splendour of a shilling soon prevailed, and we mounted directly; my friend single, and my daughter and self double, upon a strapping beast, which was of a proper size to have been ranked in the number of dragoons.

I was not a little pleased, notwithstanding their ill success, to find Mr Elrington's credit so good and his character so justifiable that even in his absence a stranger could be entrusted on his account.

When we came to our journey's end, Mrs Elrington, who was the first person we saw, received us with inexpressible joy, and gave us a second relation of the miserable state of their affairs. But, as Lady Grace says of Lady Townly,* she rallied her misfortunes with such vivacity that, had not her wit been too strong for my

---

* Colley Cibber's and John Vanbrugh's *The Provok'd Husband* (V; i): 'she rallied her own follies with such vivacity, and painted the penance she knows she must undergo for them in such ridiculous lights, that had not my concern for a brother been too strong for her wit, she had almost disarmed my anger.'

resolution, I should have certainly gone back again by the return of the next post.

As we were just entering the town, a good-looking farmer met us, by our appearance guessed what we were, and asked if we were not comedians? We answered in the affirmative, on which he desired, if we had any pity for ourselves, to turn back, and rapping out a thundering oath, affirmed to us that we were going to starve, which threw my friend (who is not the best horsewoman in the world) into such a fright she dropped her bridle, from which advantage her hungry steed fairly ran her into a hedge and dropped her into the ditch.

When she recovered her surprise she was for going directly back without seeing the company, but when I assured her the money would not hold out she was prevailed on to go forward.

At length the bespoke play was to be enacted (which was *The Beaux' Stratagem*), but such an audience I dare believe was never heard of before or since. In the first row of the pit sat a range of drunken butchers, some of whom soon entertained us with the inharmonious music of their nostrils; behind them were seated, as I suppose, their unsizeable consorts, who seemed to enjoy the same state of happiness their dear spouses were possessed of, but having more vivacity than the males, laughed and talked louder than the players.

Mrs Elrington (who played Mrs Sullen) having such a lovely prospect before her, and being willing to divert me from any design she might suspect of my not staying, in the drunken scene between Archer and Scrub* (the former of which I played), unexpectedly paid us a visit and, taking the tankard out of Scrub's hand, drank Mr Archer's health, and to our better acquaintance. The least I could do was to return the lady's compliment by drinking to hers, after which she ordered my brother Scrub to call the butler in with his fiddle, and insisted on my dancing a minuet with her, while poor Scrub comforted himself with the remains of the tankard.

This absurdity led us into several more, for we both took a wild-goose chase through all the dramatic authors we could recollect, taking particular care not to let any single speech bear in the answer the least affinity, and while I was making love from Jaffier, she tenderly approved my passion with the soliloquy of Cato.†

*in Act iii, scene iii
†both characters from tragedies: Thomas Otway's *Venice Preserv'd* and Joseph Addison's *Cato*

In this incoherent manner we finished the night's entertainment, Mrs Sullen, instead of Archer, concluding the play with Jane Shore's tag at the end of the first act of that tragedy,* to the universal satisfaction of that part of the audience who were awake and were the reeling conductors of those who only dreamt of what they should have seen.

For some time we dragged on our unsuccessful lives, without the least prospect of an alteration, that I at last gave up all hopes and expectations of ever enjoying a happy moment. This, according to the usual custom, made each wear an eye of coldness and dislike, till, after a long series of plagues, Madam Fortune, in one of her frolics, was pleased to pay us a small visit, and during her short stay we began to be better reconciled, till the trumpery slut tucked up her tail of good nature, and reduced us to our primitive nothing; and sour looks with disaffected minds resumed their empire in the breast of every malcontent.

In process of time we went to Cirencester where, I informed the reader, I had been once before with Mr Linnett's company, but Mr Elrington, without any previous notice, took a place in the stage-coach for London, and, the very night we came to the town, left his

---

*The play they were performing should end:

> Both happy in their sev'ral states we find:
> Those parted by consent, and those conjoin'd.
> Consent, if mutual, saves the lawyer's fee;
> Consent is law enough to set you free.

Mrs Elrington and Mrs Charke instead provided the tag:

> Why should I think that man will do for me
> What yet he never did for wretches like me?
> Mark by what partial judges we are judged:
> Such is the fate unhappy women find,
> And such the curse entailed upon our kind,
> That man, the lawless libertine, may rove
> Free and unquestioned through the wilds of love,
> White woman, sense and nature's easy fool,
> If poor weak women swerve from virtue's rule,
> If, strongly charmed, she leave the thorny way,
> And in the softer paths of pleasure stray;
> Ruin ensues, reproach and endless shame,
> And one false step entirely damns her fame.
> In vain with tears the loss she may deplore,
> In vain look back to what she was before,
> She sets, like stars that fall, to rise no more.

wife to manage the company, in which I gave my assistance to take off from her as much of the trouble as I possibly could.

Mr Linnett, wanting at that time some auxiliaries, sent one of his company to engage me and my friend to join him at Bath, where he then was, in a new erected theatre in Kingsmead Street. But my honour was so deeply engaged in Mrs Elrington's behalf, I would on no terms leave her, as she was pleased to compliment me with being her right hand; and at that time not knowing the real design of her husband's going to London, looked on her as an injured person, which doubly engaged my attachment to her interest – though I afterwards found it was a concerted scheme to fix himself, if possible, with Mr Rich; which proved almost abortive, he staying but one season, from what cause I shan't pretend to judge, and then went to Bath.

His wife soon followed, and I was left with six more besides myself. One scene and a curtain, with some of the worst of their wardrobe, made up the paraphanalia* of the stage, of which I was prime minister, and, though under as many disadvantages as a set of miserable mortals could patiently endure, from the before-mentioned reasons and an inexhaustible fund of poverty through the general bank of the whole company (even to a necessity to borrowing money to pay the carriage of the next town), we all went into a joint resolution to be industrious, and got a sufficiency to support ourselves and pay the way, not only to that town, but were decently set down in the next with just enough to dismiss our waggoner with reputation, and were then left to proceed upon

---

*Very interesting that she uses this word, and spells it incorrectly. Her father's misspelling of it – 'paraphonalia' – led to much ridicule from other writers, including Henry Fielding. In *The Pleasures of the Town*, the play-within-the-play, *The Author's Farce*, a ballad, is sung to the air 'Hunt the Squirrel', and is introduced thus: 'Gentlemen, pray observe and take notice how Sir Farcical's song sets Nonsense asleep.'

> Can my Goddess then forget
> Paraphonalia,
> Paraphonalia?
> Can she the crown to another head set,
> Than of her Paraphonalia?
> If that had not done too,
> Remember my bone too,
> My bone, my bone, my bone:
> Sure my goddess never can
> Forget my marrow bone.

fresh credit and contract the strongest friendship we could with each believing landlord.

As it is very common for even the lowest in understanding to fancy themselves judges of acting, I must give a curious specimen of it in a person who saw me, for want of a better, attempt the part of Hamlet, I was lucky enough to gain a place in his opinion, and he was pleased to express his approbation of me by saying no man could possibly do it better because I 'so frequently broke out in fresh places'.

But I had a much larger share of his esteem after playing Scrub, which was indeed infinitely more suitable to his taste, and left so strong an impression on his mind that a night or two after, when I was tragedizing in the part of Pyrrhus in *The Distressed Mother*, he stepped from the pit, and desired me to oblige some of his friends, as well as himself, by mixing a few of Scrub's speeches in the play, assuring me it would give much more satisfaction to the spectators, though they liked me very well, he said, in the part I was acting.

This revived in my memory the curious performance at Cullompton and rendered me for the rest of the night infinitely a properer person for Scrub than Pyrrhus, as the strangeness of his fancy had such an effect on my risible faculties I thought I should never close my mouth again in the least degree of seriosity.

I imagine it is such judges as these that occasion that indolent stupefaction in most travelling players, and, as the lower sort are foolish enough to be pleased with buffoonery in comedy and bellowing in tragedy without a regard to sense or nature in either, it makes them forgetful that there are, among the country

---

The jokes about bone refer to another Cibber clanger, this time in his adaptation from an unfinished play by John Vanbrugh – *The Provok'd Husband*. After the assignation scene Mrs Motherly asks Sir Francis Wronghead, 'Will you give me leave to get you a broiled bone, or so, till the ladies come home, sir?' It brought the performance to a standstill, the audience, picking up the *double entendre* (actually provided by Vanbrugh, but obviously not understood by the sentimental Cibber), were amused and scandalized.

In 1730, the same year as *The Author's Farce*, Fielding wrote another 'paraphonalia' ballad for *Tom Thumb*:

> Sure no wretch will ever dare
> With me to compare,
> Nor meagre grim satirist flout me;
> For the highest degree
> Of quality see
> The paraphonalia about me.

gentlemen and ladies, very great judges, whose good nature overlooks those monstrous absurdities, but, at the same time, if they took more pains to please them, they would certainly find them more frequent in their visitation.

It is for want of this consideration in the players, which makes the favours they receive from families of distinction rather a charity than a genteel reward, for, at best, their weak endeavours to entertain a set of sensible people who would be glad to encourage the least spark of decency and industry.

I know this will be a kind of choke-pear to many of the travelling gentry, but I am under no sort of uneasiness on that account, and think, if they make a proper use of the hint, they will have more reason to thank me than be offended at it.

After traversing through some few towns more, Mr and Mrs Elrington rejoined their company, and we went to Minchinhampton, in Gloucestershire, where we were kindly invited by the lord of the manor, a worthy gentleman, who was not only a great benefactor in respect of the business, but our guardian and protector from the terrible consequences that might have ensued from a most shocking cruelty designed for the company in general. But, luckily for the rest, only put in force against me and two more – which was, by dint of an information, encouraged by a C—r at S—d, who meanly supported a decayed relation by procuring him a special warrant to apprehend all persons within the limits of the Act of Parliament.

This ignorant blockhead carried his authority beyond a legal power, for almost every traveller that went through the town was examined by him before they could pass freely, and often made sacrifices to his interest.

My landlord, who was a worthy wight likewise, was privy to the plot laid against us (though affected infinite concern when we were taken and violently exclaimed against his partner in this contrivance, though they were equally concerned). The scheme was not intended to do justice in regard to the laws, but extort money from the players and the worthy gentleman, who, they were well assured, would stand by us in a case of extremity, as indeed he did. They carried on their process so far as to take me and two of our men to jail, where we were not under the least apprehension of going, from what my landlord had told us.

We waited in court, expecting every moment to be called upon and dismissed with a slight reprimand. But, alas, it was not so easy as we thought, for we were beckoned to the other end of the court and told that the keeper of the prison insisted on our going into the jail, only for a show and to say we had been under lock and key. An honour, I confess, I was not in the least ambitious of; and for the show, I thought it would never be over, for it lasted from nine in the morning till the same hour of the next, and, had it not been for the generous and friendly assistance of the before-mentioned gentleman, I believe it would have held out till doomsday with me, for another day must have absolutely put an end to my life.

Rage and indignation having wrought such an effect on my mind, it threw me almost into a frenzy and arose to such a height that I very cordially desired my fellow-prisoners would give me leave to cut their throats, with a faithful promise to do the same by my own, in case we were doomed to remain there after the trial.

They were sorry to see me, they said, so very much disconcerted, but could by no means comply with my request, endeavouring, as much as possible, to keep up my spirits and bring me into temper.

Several times my landlord came backwards and forwards, giving us false hopes of our being every minute called upon. The last visit he made, I began to be quite outrageous, and told him all I conceived of him, uttering several bold truths, not in the least to the advantage of his character.

Away he went grumbling, and I never saw him till the next morning when he came to summon us to the hall. The evening wore apace, and the clock struck eight, the dreadful signal for the gates to be locked up for the night.

I offered half a guinea apiece for beds, but was denied them, and, if I had not fortunately been acquainted with the turnkey, who was a very good-natured fellow, we must have been turned into a place to lie upon the bare ground and have mixed among the felons, whose chains were rattling all night long and made the most hideous noise I ever heard, there being upwards of two hundred men and boys under the different sentences of death and transportation.

Their rags and misery gave me so shocking an idea, I begged the man, in pity, to hang us all three rather than put us among such a dreadful crew. The very stench of them would have been a sufficient remedy against any future ills that could have happened to me, but those dreadful apprehensions were soon ended by the young fellow who was our warder for the night making interest with a couple of shoemakers who were imprisoned in the women's condemned hole, which, till they came, had not been occupied for a considerable time.

These two persons were confined, one for debt, the other for having left his family with a design to impose his wife and children on the parish.

Extremely glad were we to be admitted into the dismal cell, which, though the walls and flooring were formed of flint, at that time I was proud of entering, as the men were neat, and their bed (which my companions only took part of) entirely clean.

The two gentlemen of the craft had, the day we were brought in, furnished themselves, with each a skin for under-leathers, which, being hollow, one within the other, I chose for my dormitory, and, having a pair of boots on and a great coat, rolled into my leather couch, secure from every evil that might occur from such a place – except a cold, which I got, occasioned by the dampness of my bedchamber.

As we were not there for any crime but that committed by those who informed against us, I had the good fortune to prevail on my friend the turnkey to permit me to send for candles and some good liquor, to reward our kind hosts, and preserve us from the dreadful apprehensions of getting each an ague in our petrified apartment.

I continued for the most part of the night very low-spirited and in very ill-humour, till I was roused by the drollery of one Mr Maxfield, my fellow-sufferer, a good-natured man, and of an odd turn of humour, who would not let me indulge my melancholy, which he saw had strongly possessed me, and insisted, as he had often seen me exhibit Captain Macheath in a sham prison, I should, as I was then actually in the condemned hold, sing all the bead-roll of songs in the last act, that he might have the pleasure of saying I had once performed in character.

I own I was not in a condition to be cheerful, but the tender concern of those about me laid a kind of constraint on me to throw off my chagrin and comply with their request, which, when ended, I fairly fell asleep for about an hour and dreamt of all the plagues that had tormented my spirits in the day.

As soon as the dawn of day appeared I sat with impatient expectation of the turnkey's coming to let me into the fresh air, and, to do him justice, he came an hour earlier on my account to let us all look into the yard, which is formed into gravel-walks, not unlike Gray's Inn gardens, though not kept up in that regular and nice order.

But, rough as it was, I thought it comparable to the Garden of Eden, and question much, when the first pair beheld their paradise, whether they were more transported at the view, than I was when let out of my cell.

After I had sauntered about for a quarter of an hour, deeply immersed in thought, down came the rattling crew, whose hideous forms and dreadful aspects gave me an idea of such horrors which can only be supposed to centre in hell itself. Each had his crime strongly imprinted on his visage, without the least tincture of remorse or shame, and, instead of imploring for mercy, impudently and blasphemously arraigned the judgement of the power divine in bringing them to the seat of justice.

While I was surveying these miserable and dreadful objects I could not possibly refrain from tears to see so many of my fellow-creatures entered volunteers in the service of that being which is hourly preying upon the weak and negligent part of mankind, and, as I too plainly saw, both age and infancy plunged in total undistinguished ruin.

About the hour of eight, we received the pleasing news of our being ordered to appear in court at nine, and the joy of being removed, though but for a few moments, from the sight of these unhappy wretches, was superior to that I felt when delivered from the torturing apprehension I had some years before of ending my life, by famine, in the Marshalsea.

But then the dread of being remanded back to prison suddenly gave a damp to my transport, but, heaven be praised, our kind benefactor sent in the night a special messenger to be ready in the sessions house, with a large quantity of gold, to protect us from any threatening danger.

I had not been in the pen five minutes before I was called upon to receive a letter of comfort to myself and friends, who, though they assumed a gaiety the night before, were heartily shocked at appearing at the bar among a set of criminals, the least of whose crimes not one of them would have dared to have been guilty of, though but in thought.

However, we had the pleasure to see the wise J— (who, for dint of interest to his kinsman, committed us) march out of court just before our cause came on, which ended in a very few words, our kind protector having laid our plan of safety so securely with his interest and power, we were soon dismissed, and can never, I think, be sufficiently grateful in our acknowledgements for so tender and generous a commiseration of our misfortunes.

It was a secret pleasure to us to know that the C— was obliged to walk off, having rendered himself so contemptible to the gentlemen on the bench, by dabbling in such dirty work, that he was not only heartily despised by them, but stood a ridiculous chance, if he had stayed till our dismission, of being hooted out of court, and I believe if he were to live to the age of Methuselah, this great action of his life would not be forgot.

It is no small comfort to me that two of the best gentlemen in and about that place have dropped his acquaintance on the account, as they conceived a man of sense might have employed his time and thoughts more laudably than in giving countenance and encouragement to an action which was founded upon avarice, not justice; for I can be upon oath, and bring many more to justify the truth of my assertion, that they brought in a bill of different charges to the amount of near twelve pounds, besides a quantity of guineas it cost the gentleman who stood our friend in the affair.

I have often heard of persons paying money to avoid a jail, but we were so cruelly imposed on they made us pay half-a-guinea apiece for going into one, and, though we had but twelve post miles to ride, charged a guinea a head for conducting us to G—, besides the expenses of our horses, which they ought to have found us, as we were afterwards informed.

Power, when invested in the hands of knaves or fools, generally is the source of tyranny, which has been too often experienced: and had not our worthy friend stood firmly by us we must have innocently suffered, for labouring to keep ourselves just above the fears of starving.

As we were not guilty of any misdemeanour, everybody pitied our distress and heartily despised the author of it. Our friend, who gave us partly an invitation, as he was a person of great worth and power, was highly exasperated, and took it as a high indignity offered to himself, after he had given us encouragement, to presume to object against his entertaining his family (which was a numerous one) in an inoffensive manner, and which, as he reasonably urged kept many an idle person from lavishing their substance at alehouses, equally destructive to their health and the interests of their wives and children.

On our return from G—, the gentleman bespoke a play, and removed us out of the little town hall into the great one, which was his property, and, in despite of our adversaries, supported us with a firm promise to protect us, in case of a second invasion, if it cost him half his estate. But, as they knew his power and resolution both invincible, they never attempted to molest us afterwards.

Our stay was but short after this unlucky stroke of fortune, though it was a bad matter well ended, thanks to the humanity of our generous friend. We were heartily glad when we left the place, and whenever I go to that, or any other, upon the same expedition, I'll give them leave to imprison me for every hour of life to come.

The autumn following, Mr Elrington and his spouse went again to Bath, and I was left as conductor to the company a second time. Just before they went, a plot was laid to draw us into another dilemma at Dursley, but we were upon our guard, and luckily escaped their persecution. In order to get quite out of their reach, we went into another county, to a town called Ross in Herefordshire, where we met with tolerable success, and from thence proceeded to Monmouth in Wales, which, though a very large place, we found it very difficult to get a bare livelihood.

Chepstow was our next station, where I met with many friends, particularly a widow lady, to whom, and her family in general, I am under great obligations, and shall ever with pride acknowledge.

I had the honour and happiness of obtaining the friendship of another lady, who lived within a quarter of a mile of Chepstow, and often favoured me with friendly letters when I went to Abergavenny, at the end of which town I left Mr Elrington, with a firm design, at that time, to quit all thoughts of playing.

I immediately took a very handsome house with a large garden, consisting of near three quarters of an acre of ground, belonging to my friend's papa, a very worthy gentleman who had eminently distinguished himself in battle in the reign of King William and Queen Anne, but in the decline of life quitted the service and retired, having a very considerable state, to which his daughter is sole heiress.

Perhaps the reader may think that the repeated rebuffs of fortune might have brought me to some degree of reflection, which might have regulated the actions of my life, but, that I may not impose upon the opinions of the good-natured part of the world, who might charitably bestow a favourable thought on me in that point, I must inform them that the aversion I had conceived for vaga-bondizing (for such I shall ever esteem it), and the good nature of my friends in Chepstow, put it strongly into my head to settle there, to which end I determined to turn pastry-cook and farmer;

and, without a shilling in the universe, or really a positive knowledge where to get one, took horse from Abergavenny to visit the young lady and hire the house.

I must do her the justice to say she advised me to forgo my resolution, and set before me all the inconveniencies I afterwards laboured under, but she found me so determined, she dropped her argument and, being of an obliging temper, forwarded the repairing of the house, that it might be ready at the appointed time for my reception.

To be short, I went to it, but, that the whole scene of my unaccountable farce might be complete, I not only involved myself, but the gentlewoman (whom I have before mentioned that travelled with me), in the same needless and unreasonable difficulties; for which I think myself bound in honour to ask her pardon, as I really was the author of many troubles from my inconsiderate folly, which nothing but a sincere friendship and an uncommon easiness of temper could have inspired her either to have brooked or to have forgiven.

THE FACTS
1747–53

The life of a strolling player in the mid eighteenth century was hard in every way. Managers were notorious for underpaying, tricking the actors into accepting an engagement at a certain rate of pay and then, once they were on the road, reducing it, and then leaving the company high and dry when a better personal offer or chance presented itself. Costumes and props were pitiful in comparison with those on the London stage. (The point made in Hogarth's engraving 'Strolling Actresses in a Barn' is that the costumes were years out of date.) Travel arrangements were very rough and ready, accommodation similar, and the theatres themselves could be anything from a private theatre in a manor house to a pigsty.

'To earn a living an actor "must go cap in hand [to the local gentry] and with the humblest demeanour, paint his distress, and solicit their support: or he must attend their nocturnal revels, wait upon their smiles, and feed them with his jests. He must spout, sing, and be every way subservient to their wishes, and, after thus debasing human dignity, it is well if he finds himself enriched with a few guineas."'[1]

Charlotte's first provincial managers, Mr and Mrs Linnet, had worked briefly in London in 1740. Their acting credentials were dreadfully inferior to hers. Long after Mrs Charke's stint with his company, Mr Linnet was the subject of an amusing anecdote: applying for a licence to perform, Linnet accidentally sent the Justice of the Peace a property letter used in a production of Mrs Centlivre's *A Bold Stroke for a Wife* (Act V). The note read:

> There is a design formed to rob your house this night and cut your throat, and for that purpose there is a man disguised like a Quaker who is to pass for one Simon Pure; the gang whereof I am one, though now resolved to rob no more, has been at Bristol; one of them came up in the coach with the Quaker, whose name he hath taken, and from what he gathered from him, formed that design and did not doubt but he should impose so far upon you as to make you turn out the real Simon Pure and keep him with you. Make the right use of this Adieu.

Luckily, before the Justice had time to issue documents for Linnet's arrest, the mistake came to light. (Incidentally, Linnet got his licence.)

Cirencester, described by Defoe in *A Tour through the Whole Island of Great Britain* as 'a very good town, populous and rich, full of clothiers, and driving a great trade in wool', was one of Mrs Charke's venues. Another clothing town, Chippenham, followed. There the company played Addison's *Cato*.

The *Bath Journal* for 27 February 1749 reported the performance of *Cato*, which had taken place the previous Thursday 'to the general satisfaction of the audience, who allowed the performance surpassed their expectation; and that the Roman habits were not inferior to those at the theatres in London'.

Shortly after this Mrs Charke travelled to Tiverton to join Richard Elrington's company. Tiverton was, 'next to Exeter . . . the greatest manufacturing town in the county', and its people were 'all fully employed, and very few, if any, out of work, except such as need not be unemployed, but were so from mere sloth and idleness, of which, some will be found everywhere'.[2]

Her new manager, Richard Elrington, started his career as a child-actor in Dublin, playing typical children's roles such as the Duke of York in *Richard III*. In 1746 he married Elizabeth Martin, and the couple toured the south of England in 1749.

Mr Elrington went to Dublin in the spring of 1750 (maybe before Charlotte joined the company). Both Mr and Mrs Elrington played at Covent Garden during the 1750–1 season: Mrs Elrington played Lady Froth in *The Double Dealer* (billed as 'a young gentlewoman who never appeared on this stage before'), on 25 April 1750; her husband joined the main Covent Garden company in October 1750, and played through to the following May. He played some pretty dull secondary roles including Bernardo (*Hamlet*), Blunt (*Henry IV part 1*), Oxford (*Richard III*) and Westmoreland (*Henry V*).

Richard Elrington rejoined his troupe in June 1751, but, by 11 November, had again left Charlotte at the reins, this time while he tried his chances at the newly built Orchard Street Theatre in Bath.

Two years later, while Mrs Charke prompted for Simpson, the Elringtons led their troupe to Manchester, where Elizabeth Elrington had a brush with the law. She resisted arrest in the most spectacular manner: '"Yes, let me be instantly manacled, shackled, or closed up in a brazen bull, as the infernal Phalarius used, as recorded in the Grecian story." She had no sooner said this than she rose and tore a valuable wig from her bald pate, which had long before been despoiled by a cruel disorder of its flaxen locks. Thus, in a state of affected distraction she ran like fury about the room.'[3]

Mrs Charke's old friend Jockey Adams seems to have crossed her path again during 1750–1. Till now his name is thought to have vanished from the bills after February 1749. I have tracked him down to Bristol in 1750–1. Using the concert formula, he played at the Merchant Taylor's Hall, Broad Street, in December 1750. A month later he advertised another of his shows which included 'manual exercise with Hannah Snell, a female soldier who went by the name of James Grey'. In June 1751 his company performed at the New Inn, without Lawford's Gate, for the benefit of his wife Mrs Adams. The plays performed were *The Orphan* and *Tit for Tat: or, Comedy and Tragedy at War*.[4]

In February 1743 Charlotte Charke had put on one of her own, unpublished, plays: *Tit for Tat: or Comedy and Tragedy at War*. Could this be the same play? Could Mrs Charke have worked briefly with Adams in Bristol? Perhaps Mrs Adams was one of the performers from Mrs Charke's 1743 season and had kept the play in her repertoire since then. We shall probably never know the truth, but I think the questions posed by this new information on Adams are worth throwing open.

When, in 1750, Richard Elrington left his company to try and secure positions in a London company for himself and his wife, Mrs Charke mistakenly looked on Mrs Elrington as 'an injured person'. Mrs Charke may have got it wrong this time, but Mrs Elrington's record with husbands was even worse than her own.

She was born Elizabeth Grace, but, after spending some time in Dublin known as Mrs Barnes, she had a son, Thomas, by Mr Martin, who lived off her salary, and was eventually imprisoned for robbery. She married Elrington in 1746, but in 1760, at the age of forty-four, he left her, urged on by his mother, to marry a woman of property. After joining another touring company at Caernarvon, Mrs Elrington found a new consort, Mr Workman, a painter, who soon afterwards died of lead poisoning. She managed a company at Mansfield for a short time in 1766, before marrying a young actor, Richard Wilson, who left her within months of the marriage. Nothing more was heard of Mrs Elrington.

Mrs Charke had encountered, and pays compliment to, two innkeepers in Chippenham. These two gentlemen, Thomas Stroud (died 1762) and George Lodge the elder (died 1752), ran inns which still exist today. Both, now listed buildings, were famous eighteenth-century coaching inns. The Angel was used by Tobias Smollett in his novel *Peregrine Pickle*. Its former courtyard is now a motel extension. The White Hart, however, survives only as a frontage: the rest of the building was demolished in 1973. Behind the remaining wall is a supermarket.[5]

Apart from the old problems of licensing, strolling players were wide open to the law passed in 1714 which classified actors as 'rogues, vagabonds, sturdy beggars and vagrants'. Householders were exempt, but no strolling actor was likely to have that fortunate defence. In the unhappy event of an actor being imprisoned under this statute or under the 1737 Act, they would, in addition to the discomfort and anxiety of being imprisoned, incur certain charges – for instance the cost of travel to court if that should be necessary, and legal costs: the warrant for their own arrest, fees, including a garnish, or charge made on admission to prison, affidavits, registration costs, etc. Charges were made for beds and for cells apart from the rabble.

They were prosecuted by a coroner, councillor, or maybe clothier, from Stroud, Their protector, the Lord of the Manor at Minchinhampton, must have been Samuel Sheppard, who inherited the title in 1724 and died in 1754.[6] I have not found a record of her imprisonment.

CHAPTER FIVE

1 William Temp, *The Strolling Player*, 1802; quoted in Sybil Rosenfeld, *Strolling Players and Drama in the Provinces 1660–1765*, 1939.
2 Defoe. pp. 249–50.
3 Charles Lee Lewes; quoted in P. Highfill, *Dictionary*.
4 *Bristol Weekly Intelligencer*.
5 Various records in Wiltshire Records Office.
6 *Victoria County History of Gloucestershire*, vol. 11, p. 192.

Chapter Six

THE NARRATIVE

As soon as I arrived at Chepstow I began to consider, that though I had got a house without either bed or chair to lie or sit on, it would be highly proper to seek out a place of rest, and, that I might live as cheap as possible, took a ready-furnished lodging for nights, and wandered for a fortnight up and down my empty house till fortune came that road to drop some furniture into it.

I own it, I was secretly chagrined at my exploit, but did not dare to make the least discovery of it to Mrs Brown, who had very justifiable reasons to reproach me for an indiscretion she had prudently taken much pains to prevent.

My first design was to set forth in pastry: it is true I had an oven, but not a single penny to purchase a faggot to light it, and for the materials to make the pies they were equally un-come-atable. But I took courage and went to inform the widow lady of my intention and entreat the favour of her custom.

As she is, without compliment, a person of sense and discernment, she very humorously asked me all the natural and necessary questions concerning the motive and means by which I was to settle myself, as she well knew I had not a grain of the principal ingredient towards exciting me to such a resolution, or the effecting it.

I confess I was strangely puzzled to answer her, and, after several hums and haws, told her I hoped fortune would favour my design, as I only wanted to get an honest and decent living, which was no small recommendation to her favour. After having smiled at my rash undertaking, she administered that kind of comfort I stood most in need of that time.

To baking we went, and, partly through pity and curiosity, we took twenty shillings the first day. I then began to triumph greatly at my success and thought it my turn to upbraid my friend for having reproached me for leaving the stage.

I must not forget to insert a strong desire I had to go to the Major on the strength of my success and hire a large field of grass, and, instead of a bed, thought of purchasing a horse to carry goods to the neighbouring markets, but, that I might not appear more conspicuously ridiculous than I had done, Mrs Brown wisely dissuaded me from such a mad scheme and in a few weeks convinced me I had not occasion for such a chargeable conveyance of my pastry – for when everybody's curiosity was satisfied, I found a terrible declension of business.

However, I met with unprecedented friendships especially from Val—ne M—s, Esq., who lives at P—d, a young gentleman of a fair character and a fine estate. His generosity enabled me to put the main part of my furniture into my house, and, as to linen and many necessary materials besides, my good friend, the young lady before-mentioned, supplied me with them.

As I found one business fall off, I resolved to set up another, and went in one my extraordinary hurries to buy a sow with pig; but, to my great disappointment, after having kept it for near three months, expecting it hourly to bring forth, it proved to be an old barrow, and I, to make up the measure of my prudent management, after having put myself to double the expense it cost me in the purchase, was glad to sell it to a butcher for a shilling or two less than I gave for it.

Thus ended my notion of being a hog merchant, and I, having a garden well stored with fruits of all sorts, made the best I could of that, till some villainous wretches, in one night's time, robbed me of as much as would have yielded near three guineas, besides barbarously tearing up the trees by the roots, and breaking the branches through fearful haste, being well assured that the gentleman who owned them would have punished them to the utmost rigour of the law had they been discovered.

One plague succeeding another, I resolved to leave the place and try my fate in some other spot, but, behold, we were run a little aground, so that we were positively obliged to sell the best part of our furniture to make up some deficiencies, and we were once more in a bedless condition.

With the necessary utensils for the pastry-cook's shop, and the friendly assistance of some of our good friends, we took leave, and set out for a little place called Pill, a sort of harbour for ships, five miles on this side of Bristol. The place itself is not unpleasant, if it were inhabited with any other kind of people than the savages who infest it, and are only in outward form distinguishable from beasts of prey. To be short, the villainies of these wretches are of so heinous and unlimited a nature, they render the place so unlike any other part of the habitable world, that I can compare it only to the ante-chamber of that abode we are admonished to avoid in the next life by leading a good one here.

A boy there of eight or ten years of age is as well versed in the most beastly discourse, and the more dreadful sin of blasphemy and swearing, as any drunken reprobate of thirty, and he who drinks hardest and excels most in these terrible qualifications stands foremost in his father's favour.

There are some few that don't belong to the boats that are reasonable creatures, and I am amazed they can patiently bear to reside where there is such a numerous set of cannibals. A name they very justly deserve, for I believe there are some among them who would not scruple to make a meal of their fellow-creatures.

I have seen many a suffering wretch who has been wind-bound sent away half naked after they had spent their ready money, who have been obliged to strip themselves of their clothes and glad to part from a thing worth twenty shillings to obtain with difficulty one to keep them from starving, and that without any view of ever seeing it again, nay, their want of principle and Christianity is such that if they out-stay the means of raising a sixpence for a bed, they will charitably turn them into the street to

> 'Rest their heads on what cold stone they please.'

For near six months my friend and I resided in this terrible abode of infamy and guilt, but, being ignorant at our first coming of what kind of mortals they were, we settled amongst them and did not find it an easy matter to remove, though we went trembling to bed every night with dreadful apprehensions of some ill-treatment before the break of day.

I took a little shop, and because I was resolved to set off my matters as grand as possible, I had a board put over my door with this inscription:

BROWN, PASTRY-COOK, FROM LONDON

– at which place I can't charge myself with ever having, in the course of my life, attempted to spoil the ingredients necessary in the composition of a tart. But that did not signify, as long as I was a Londoner, to be sure, my pastry must be good!

While the ships continued coming in from Ireland, in the months of June, July, and August, I had a good running trade, but, alas, the winter was most terrible, and if an uncle of my friend's (who died while we were there) had not left her a legacy, we must inevitably have perished.

About the time the news came of her money, we were involved to the amount of about four or five and thirty shillings, and if a shilling would have saved us from total destruction we did not know where to raise it.

On the receipt of the letter, I showed it to the landlord, hoping he would lend me a guinea to bear my charges to Mrs Brown's aunt, who lives in Oxfordshire, where I was to go to receive her legacy, which was a genteel one, and I should have left her as a hostage till my return.

But the incredulous blockhead conceived the letter to be forged, and, as he himself was capable of such a fraud, imagined we had artfully contrived to get a guinea out of him, and would reward him by running away in his debt. But he was quite mistaken, as he was afterwards convinced, and made a thousand awkward excuses for his unkindness when we received the money and had discharged his trifling demands.

I consulted on my pillow what was best to be done, and communicated my thoughts to my friend. Upon which we concluded, without speaking a word to anybody, both to set out and fetch the money, according to order from her relation, though there were two very great bars to such progress in the eye of reason, but I stepped over both.

One was having no more than a single groat in the world between us, and the other my having been obliged to pledge my hat at Bristol a fortnight before for half-a-crown, to carry on the anatomical businesss we haplessly pursued.

Yet, notwithstanding these terrible disasters, I was resolved at all events to go the journey. I took my fellow-sufferer with me, who was lost in wonder at so daring an enterprise, to set out without either hat or money fourscore miles on foot. But I soon eased the anxiety of mind she laboured under by assuring her that when we got to Bristol I would apply to a friend who would furnish me with a small matter to carry us on to Bath.

This pacified the poor soul, who could scarce see her way for tears before I told her my design, which never entered my imagination till we had got two miles beyond the detested place we lived in. Our circumstances were then so desperate, I thought

'Whatever world we next were thrown upon,
Could not be worse than *Pill*.'

As we were on our march we were met by some of our unneigh-
bourly neighbours, who took notice of my being in full career
without a hat, and of Mrs Brown with a bundle in her hand which
contained only a change of linen for us on our travel.

They soon alarmed our landlord with the interview, with many
conjectures of our being gone off, and concluded my being
bareheaded was intended as a blind for our excursion. But, let their
thoughts be what they would, we were safe in Bristol by the time
they got home to make their political report, and I obtained at the
first word the timely assistance our necessities required to procure
a supper and bed that night, besides what served to bear our
charges to Bath next morning.

The only distress I had to overcome was to procure a covering for
my unthinking head. But providence kindly directed us to a house
where there was a young journeyman, a sort of Jemmy Smart* who
dressed entirely in taste, that lodged where we lay that night. As I
appeared, barring the want of a hat, as smart as himself in dress, he
entered into conversation with me, and, finding him a good-
natured man, ventured (as I was urged by downright necessity) to
beg the favour of him to lend me a hat, which by being very dusty I
was well assured had not been worn some time, from which I
conceived he would not be in a violent hurry to have it restored,
and, framing an excuse of having sent my own to be dressed, easily
obtained the boon.

Next morning at the hour of five we set out, and stayed at Bath
till the morning following; though I remember I was obliged to
give the landlady my waistcoat for the payment of my lodging
before we went to bed, which I had the comfort of redeeming by
the help of Mr Kennedy and company, and set forwards on my
journey with the favour they were pleased to bestow on me.

I never received an obligation in my life that I was ashamed to
acknowledge, though I have very lately incurred the displeasure of
a fine lady, for mentioning a person in my third number to whom I
shall ever think myself most transcendentally obliged, and shall
never be persuaded to forget their humanity, or to reconcile
contradictions, and believe in impossibilities.

* a dandy

As soon as I was empowered by the help of a little cash, we set out from Bath to Oxfordshire, and in three days arrived at the happy spot, where we were furnished with that opiate for grief, the want of which had many tedious nights kept us waking.

Our journey home was expedited by taking a double horse from Witney to Cirencester, and now and then, for the rest of the way, mounting up into a hay cart or a timely waggon.

When we returned to Bristol we met with several of the Pill gentry, who were surprised to see us, and informed us how terribly we had been exploded as being cheats and runaways, and, though they themselves in our absence were as inveterate as the rest of the vulgar crew, were the first to condemn others for a fault they were equally guilty of.

I returned the borrowed hat, and went home triumphant in my own, paid my landlord, and, as long as the money lasted, was the worthiest gentleman in the county. But when our stock was exhausted and we were reduced to a second necessity of contracting a fresh score, I was as much disregarded as a dead cat, without the remembrance of a single virtue I was master of while I had a remaining guinea in my pocket.

Business daily decreasing from the want of shipping coming in, and the winter growing fast upon us, we had no prospect before us but of dying by inches with cold and hunger, and what aggravated my own distress was having unfortunately drawn in my friend to be a melancholy partaker of my sufferings.

This reflection naturally roused me into an honourable spirit of resolution not to let her perish through my unhappy and mistaken conduct, which I meant all for the best, though it unfortunately proved otherwise, and, that I might not stay at Pill till we were past the power of getting away, I sat down and wrote a little tale, which filled up the first and second columns of a newspaper, and got a friend to introduce me to Mr W—d, a printer on the T—y, who engaged me at a small pittance per week, to write, and correct the press when business was in a hurry, which indeed it generally was as he is a man of reputation and greatly respected. I believe, if he had been perfectly assured who I was, and had known how much I had it in my power to have been useful to him, as well as myself, it had been much better for us both. However, it was kind in him to employ a distressed person, and a stranger, to whom he could not possibly be under the least obligation.

Having secured something to piddle on, for I can call it not better, I ran back to Pill to bless my friend with the glad tidings, and, as it was a long and dirty walk from thence to Bristol and infinitely dangerous over Leigh Down, which is three miles in length besides two miserable miles before that to trudge, we thought it better to give up what we had to the landlord, to whom we were but eighteen shillings indebted, though we left him as much as fairly stood us in five pounds ready money. But if we had offered to have made a sale of it, I knew their consciences would have given us sixpence for that which might be worth a crown or ten shillings, so we even locked up the shop and went with the key in my pocket to Bristol, and in two days' time I sent it back with a note to let him know what we had left was entirely his own, for that we should never more return.

In truth I have been as good as my word, and shall continue so, for, if business or inclination should ever excite me to take a trip to Ireland, I would go Chester way, and if travellers knew as much as I do of that horrid seat of cruelty and extortion, they would all come into the same determination.

Having thus comfortably withdrawn ourselves from this hated place, we took a lodging at two shillings per week, and if I had not had the good fortune to be kindly accepted on by a few friends who were constantly inviting me, the remaining part of my wages would not have been sufficient to have afforded us, with other expenses, above two good meals in a week.

But thanks to my friends, who empowered me to consign it all to the use of one, to whom I should have thought on this occasion, if every shilling had been a guinea, I had made but a reasonable acknowledgement, after having immersed her in difficulties which nothing but real friendship and a tender regard to my health (which through repeated grievances was much impaired) could have made her blindly inconsistent with her own interest to give into, and so patiently endure.

This business lasted for one month exactly, and I found it impossible to subsist without being troublesome to friends, and, Mr W—d not caring to enlarge my income, I took it into my head to try for a benefit, and to that end printed some bills in the style of an advertisement, which were kindly presented to me by my master.

All was to be done under the rose,* on account of the magistrates, who have not suffered any plays to be acted in the city for many

*sub rosa, i.e. secretly, furtively

years. But notwithstanding I slyly adventured to have *Barnwell* exhibited in the very heart of it, at the Black Raven in High Street, where I had as many promises as would have filled the room (which was a large one) had it been twice as big. But alas, they were but promises, for, instead of five and twenty pounds, I had barely four, and abominably involved by the bargain, insomuch, I was obliged to march quietly off and say nothing.

After I was gone, several pitied my misfortune, and declared if I would make a second attempt I should be made amends for the disappointment of the former. But I thought it mighty well as it was, and, as I was safe in a whole skin, would not run the chance of being a second time deceived, nor the hazard of being more deeply engaged than I was.

I was so miserably put to my shifts, that the morning after my 'malefit'* I was obliged to strip my friend of the only decent gown she had, and pledged it to pay the horse-hire for the players who came from Wells to assist me, which, to do them justice, was a difficulty they were entirely ignorant of.

It was no small mortification to me not to have it in my power to reward them genteelly for their trouble, and more especially so as my own daughter was one of the number with her husband, whom she prudently married, contrary to my inclination, about three years before.

Though I had no fortune to give her, without any partiality, I look on her as a more advantageous match for a discreet man than a woman who might bring one and confound it in unnecessary expenses (which I am certain Kitty will never do), and, had she met with as sober and reasonable a creature as herself, in the few years they have had a company, might have been worth a comfortable sum of money to have set them up in some creditable business that might have redounded more to their quiet and reputation.

But I fear that is as impossible to hope or expect as it would be likely to unmarry them, which, had it been in my power, should have been done the first moment I heard of the unpleasing knot's being tied. But as it is

> 'I here do give him that with all my heart
> Which, but that he has already,
> With all my heart I would keep from him.'

*opposite of a benefit

As my child was at Wells with her company, nature was more prevalent in that point than necessity to fix me there, for there was another set of people I could have gone to thirty miles off, a different road. But, notwithstanding my dislike to her marriage, I wanted to be as near her as I could, and joined them at Wells, where I was very well acquainted, and, as much as players can expect, well regarded by the best in town.

About three years before, I had been there with Mr Elrington's company, and we met with uncommon success, but the last time the smallpox raged violently there, and if the ladies and gentlemen had not been extremely kind, the poor exhibiters might have been glad to have shared the fate of the invalids, to have been insured of a repository for their bones.

It is a common observation that evils often produce good effects, and such my daughter found from the generosity of the ladies, who made her several valuable presents, which enlarged their wardrobe considerably, and, being a well-behaved girl, that recommended her to their consideration in respect of her private character, and her public performance on the stage rendered her very pleasing to the audience in general.

I humbly entreat to be believed, when, without partiality, I aver her genius would recommend her to a station in either theatre, if properly made use of, as she has an infinite share of humour that calculates her for an excellent low comedian; though she is obliged, having none equal to herself, to appear in characters in which her chief merit consists in being positively a sensible speaker.

I once saw her play Horatia, in *The Roman Father*,* and was astonished to find her so truly affected with the scene where she comes to upbraid Publius for the murder of her lover and provoke her own death from her brother's hand. I confess I was pleasingly surprised, and beg pardon for degenerating so far as to speak in praise of so near a relation, who really deserved it, an error my family is not very apt to run into.

A second time she gave me equal delight in the part of Boadicea,† which I should never have suspected from her uncultivated genius; but she proved she had one in very justly acquitting herself in that character, but yet I had rather see her in low comedy, as it is more agreeable to her figure, and entirely so to the oddity of her

*by William Whitehead
†in *Boadicea: or, the Queen of Britain* by Richard Glover

humorous disposition; and I wish she was so settled as to constantly play in that walk, which is a very pleasing one, and most useful when players come towards the decline of life: for when they have outlived the bloom and beauty of a Lady Townly or a Monimia, they may make very pleasing figures in a Mrs Day* or a Widow Lackitt.†

I wish the girl may take this friendly hint now she is young, as I am certain, in respect to her years, she may in all probability live long enough to make a considerable figure in characters of that cast.

I stayed with her the run of six towns, the last but one of which was Honiton in Devonshire, where I had the happiness of gaining many friends of distinction, and perhaps should have continued longer, but that I received a letter from my brother to inform me Mr Simpson of Bath had a mind to engage me to prompt and undertake the care of the stage incidental to that office.

As I was heartily tired of strolling (and being too frequently impertinently treated by my daughter's husband), I readily embraced the offer and set out for Bath with my friend (who had been as often, and equally, insulted by the little insignificant), and on my arrival Mr Simpson, in a gentlemanlike manner, received me and lent me a sum of money to equip me in my proper character, which I repaid him weekly out of my salary and thank him most sincerely for the favour.

From the month of September to March I continued there, but the fatigue of the place was more than my health or spirits could easily support, for I am certain the prompters of either theatres in London have not half the plague in six months that I have had in as many days.

It is true Mr Simpson was owner, and ought to have been master of the house, but his good nature and unwillingness to offend the most trifling performer made him give up his right of authority, and rather stand neuter when he ought to have exerted it.

The hurry of business in his rooms, which were more methodically conducted than his theatre, took up so much of his time it was impossible for him to pay a proper attention to both. By this means, what ought to have been a regular government was reduced to anarchy and uproar. Each had their several wills, and but one, which was myself, bound to obey them all.

*a translated kitchenmaid in Sir Robert Howard's *The Committee*
†in Thomas Southerne's *Oroonoko*

This any reasonable person will allow to be a hard and difficult task, as I was not inclined to offend any of them, and, though they herded in parties, I was resolved to be a stranger to their disputes, till open quarrels obliged me to become acquainted with them, and in such cases I was often made use on as a porter to set these matters to rights.

This I confess my spirit could not easily brook, both in respect to my father, as well as having been on a much better footing in a superior theatre than any I was obliged to pay a daily attendance on.

I can be upon my oath, during the whole time of my residence in Bath I had not, even on Sundays, a day I could call my own; Mr Bodley the printer can testify I have often left fresh orders while he has been at church either for alteration of parts or of capital distinctions in the bills, without which very indifferent actors would not otherwise go on.

I think it would have been a greater proof of judgement to have distinguished themselves on the stage than upon a post or brick wall, and I have often thought, when I wrote the word 'performed', it would have been no error to have changed it to 'deformed', of which I have often had melancholy proofs from a brace of heroes, who, I believe (one in particular) thought none equal to them. And truly I can't but be of their minds, for two such great men were never seen before, and it is hoped never will again.

As to the women, the principal, which is Miss Ibbott, is really deserving of praise and admiration, as all she does is from the result of a very great and uncommon genius. I own myself not very apt to be partial, but this gentlewoman struck me into a most pleasing astonishment by her performance of many characters; but most particularly in the part of Isabella, in *The Fatal Marriage*.* She not only drew the audience into a most profound attention, but absolutely into a general flood of commiserating tears, and blended nature and art so exquisitely well that it was impossible not to feel her sorrows and bear the tenderest part in her affliction.

I must confess I never was more truly affected with a tragical performance and was rendered incapable of reading a single syllable, but, luckily for Miss Ibbott, she is always so perfect, a prompter is a useless person while she is speaking, and it is no compliment to insert what I told her when she came off: that

* by Thomas Southerne

'. . . Her whole function suited
With forms to her conceit.'

I am very certain there were several people of quality down at
Bath who can testify the truth of what I have said of her, and I
should think it very well worth the while of the masters of either of
the theatres to take her merit into consideration, and if she had the
advantage of seeing Mrs Cibber, Mrs Woffington or Mrs Pritchard*
in their different lights, it would make her as complete an actress as
ever trod the English stage.

The merit of this person was not a little conducive to the interest
of the players in general, which was demonstrated in the deficiency
of the night's receipts whenever it happened that she was out of a
play, which indeed was very seldom. But, as merit generally creates
envy, her contemporaries would scarce allow her, either publicly or
privately, notwithstanding the politest audiences testified it by a
universal applause, and they themselves proved it by the odds of
their revenues when first characters have been stuffed up by those
who would have made better figures as her attendants while she
had performed them.

The business in general was, according to all accounts, that
season better than they had known it for many past, and was
greatly heightened by the universal admiration of the performance
of the justly celebrated Mr Maddox, who engaged with Mr Simpson at a considerable salary, though not more than he truly
deserved.

I believe the comedians found him worthy of his income, as he
not only brought in what paid his agreement but more than
doubled that sum, which they shared among them. Yet to my
certain knowledge there was private murmuring even in respect to
him, though they profited by his success, and in spite of their
grudging hearts could not help being delighted at his surprising
feats of activity on the wire, which he is at Whitsuntide engaged to
perform at Mr Hallam's Wells in Goodman's Fields, and intends to
entertain the town with several new things, which he has never as
yet publicly exhibited. I hope, not only in respect to Mr Maddox,
but in regard to Mr Hallam, who is an honest worthy man, he will
be constantly visited by all the people of true taste.

Soon after Mr Maddox left Bath (as Mr Fribble says†) a most

*Hannah Pritchard (1711–68), Garrick's principal tragic actress
†in David Garrick's A Miss in Her Teens

terrible fracas happened to the states-general of both theatres, occasioned by a mercenary view of gain in an old scoundrel, who was chiefly supported by charitable donations, in which Mr Simpson (whose humanity frequently prompts him to such acts) had been often very liberal to this viper, who rewarded him by lodging an information against him and the company in Orchard Street.

This put a stop to the business for about three weeks, and was brought to a public process, but I believe an attempt of the kind will never be made again.

As Bath is the seat of pleasure for the healthful and a grand restorative for the sick, it is looked on as a privileged place, and those who come only to please themselves expect a free indulgence in that point, as much as the infirm do the use of the baths for their infirmities, therefore a suppresson of any part of their innocent diversions was deemed by the people of quality as the highest affront that could be offered them, especially as they, and others of distinction, are the absolute supports of the place, which, without them, would be but a melancholy residence for the inhabitants, if custom had not made it fashionably popular, being a town of no particular trade.

This reflection ought to put the strongest guard upon them, not to be guilty of offences themselves, or countenance it in others, which was positively the case in relation to this affair, as it was proved a certain A— raised a contribution of twenty guineas to bribe the old knave to put this cruel design in force against the players.

This greatly exasperated every person of condition, who, as it was an infringement upon their liberty of entertainment, interested themselves greatly in behalf of each theatre, and carried their point against the insolent invader of their privileges.

During the suspension, I could scarce walk through the grove but the very chairmen had something to say, by way of exultation, on the misfortunes of the poor show-folk, as they impudently and ignorantly termed them, not considering that play nights very greatly enlarged their incomes.

Among this set of two-legged horses were scattered some of the new-fangled methodical tribe,* who blessed their stars that there was an end put to profanation and riot.

* Methodists

It is surprising that the minds of those who wear the human form can be so monstrously infatuated, to be the constant attendants on the canting drones whose talents consist only in making a shoe or a pair of breeches. Have we not thousands of fine gentlemen, regularly bred at universities, who understand the true system of religion? And are not the churches hourly open to all who please to go to them, instead of creeping into holes and corners to hear much less than the generality of the auditors are able to inform their hypocritical pastors?

I very lately visited Mr Yeates's New Wells and was persecuted for an hour with words without meaning and sound without sense. I own I should as soon think of dancing a hornpipe in a cathedral, as having the least tincture of devotion where I had myself been honoured as a heathen deity and dreaded as a roaring devil.

No mortal but Mr Yeates could have thought of letting the place for that use, and, I believe, the first symptoms of his religion will be discovered (if there ever should be a suppression of this mockery of godliness), in the loss of his sanctified tenants and the sad chance of the tenement standing empty.

He must pardon me for this liberty, but as we are both equally odd, in separate lights, neither of us can ever be surprised or offended at what the other says or does.

My warmth, I fear, has led me into an unnecessary digression from my story; but, I confess, I think the following these people so inconsistent with the rules of reason and sense, I have not patience to think that any creature, who is capable of distinguishing between right and wrong, should listen to such rhapsodies of nonsense, which rather confound than serve to improve their understandings, and consequently can be no way instrumental to the salvation of their souls.

If public devotion four times a day is not sufficient for that torrent of goodness they would be thought to have, their private prayers at home, offered with sincerity and penitence, they may be assured will be graciously received, and prevent that loss of time bestowed in hearing the gospel turned topsy-turvy by those who really are as ignorant of it as the rostrum they stand in, and whose heads seem to be branches of the same root.

Notwithstanding the gaiety of Bath, they swarm like wasps in June, and have left their stings in the minds of many. I am certain rancour and malice are particularly predominant in them, which they discovered in an eminent degree when the houses were shut up, by saying and doing all they could to have them remain so, to the destruction of many families who were happy in a comfortable subsistence arising from them.

I know it was some guineas out of my pocket, and though I grew heartily tired of my office, I intended to have finished the season if this disaster had not happened. But the uncertainty of their opening again fixed in me a resolution to leave them, which was strengthened by some ill-natured rebuffs I had met with from the lower part of the company, which I scarce thought worth my notice, having secretly determined to withdraw myself from that, and the fatigue being, I think, more proper to be undertaken by a man than a woman.

One thing I took monstrously ill, which I cannot help mentioning: some persons of fashion who had seen me in London had a mind that I should appear in the part of Lord Foppington, in *The Careless Husband*, and, at their request, I rehearsed it in a visit, which they were so obliging to tell me made them more anxious for my playing it. As a proof that they desired it, they communicated their design to him who ought to have been their commander-in-chief, and he agreed to their proposal, till two of his subalterns, neither of which were qualified to appear in the character, opposed it – each hoping to supply it themselves, without the advantage either of that ease in their action necessary to the part, or being able to utter a syllable of French. But what provoked me further was trumping up a story of my brother's having laid an injunction on Mr Simpson, never to permit me to go on the stage, but particularly in that character.

I believe the town has had too many proofs of my brother's merit to suppose it possible for me to be vain enough to conceive I should eclipse it by my performance, or that he was weak enough to fear it, and, though I may be judged to have raised my thoughts to the highest pitch of vanity in believing that to be the real case of my two opponents in this cause, I am positively assured it was the main motive of their being so industriously employed in preventing my coming on the stage.

To say truth, I began to be very angry with myself for ever condescending to sit behind the scenes to attend a set of people, that, I was certain, whatever faults I might have in acting, not one of them, Miss Ibbott excepted, was capable of discerning.

The intention of my playing was framed by my friends to give me an opportunity of recommending myself to a benefit, who faithfully promised to exert their interest for me, but their scheme was soon frustrated, through the mean and dirty artifices of these two people, who, I am certain, ought to endeavour at making every one their friends, of which I have some modest reasons to believe they frequently stand in need of.

Mr Falkener* very kindly offered to enter into the immediate study of Lord Morelove,† that the play might not wait for him, and was pleased at a seeming opportunity of my being more agreeably engaged than I was. But his good nature is no wonder, for I must do him the justice to say I never heard him utter or do a thing that was inconsistent with the true character of a gentleman.

This ill-natured disappointment raised such indignation and contempt in me, that I as much abhorred to go to the house as some people do to undergo a course of nauseous physic, but I soon removed myself, and, if they will forgive my ever having been there at all, I will promise them never to do so again.

Before I conclude the account of my Bath expedition, I cannot avoid taking notice of a malicious aspersion, thrown and fixed on me as a reason for leaving it, which was that I designed to forsake my sex again, and that I positively was seen on the streets in breeches.

This I solemnly avow to be an impertinent falsehood, which was brought to London and spread itself, much to my disadvantage, in my own family, where I was informed it was delivered to them as a reality by an actress that came to town soon after I quitted Bath. I guess at the person, but, as I know her to be half mad, must neither wonder or be angry at her folly, yet, as she has sometimes reason sufficient to distinguish between truth and falsehood, am surprised she should meanly have recourse to the latter to make me appear ridiculous, who never gave her the least provocation to do me so apparent an injury. My only reason for not staying was an absolute abhorrence to the office I was in, and which I would not again undertake for ten guineas per week.

It happened at the time I left Bath there was, without exception, the most deplorable set of non-performers at Bradford that ever wrecked the heart of tragedy or committed violence on the ears of the groundlings. I cannot say, with Shakespeare, 'They were perriwig-pated fellows', for there was not a wig and a half

*(fl. 1745–55) actor known only as a provincial player
†in Colley Cibber's The Careless Husband

throughout the whole company, and, I believe, there were not above two men that could boast of more than an equal quantity of shirts.

Business, they had none; money, so long a stranger to them that they were in poor Sharp's* condition, and had almost forgot the current coin of their own country. With these 'pleasing prospects of despair' I joined their community, and, as my mind was unloaded from the uneasiness I suffered from a fund of impertinent behaviour and everlasting fatigue greatly prejudicial to my health, I sat quietly down, resolving not to repine at the worst that could happen for the short time I intended to stay with them.

A young man at Bath had a mind to indulge himself with a mouthful of tragedy, but, that he might have a bellyful at once, gormandized the part of Othello, which brought us a good house, and was a very seasonable help, for we ate. Our landladies smiled and we could call about us without the usual tremor that had attended our spirits for a fortnight before, with the terrible apprehensions of being answered with a negative or served with reproachful doubts of their being ever paid.

A very few days entirely broke up this disjointed company, and we herded in parties. My friend and I went with another manager, almost as rich and wise as him we left, when, after having starved for two or three towns, we received a very gross affront, on which I went to Devizes, where the above-mentioned notable gentleman, with his wife and a young fellow, besides our two selves, made up the whole totte.

They concluded we should play there but, rather than suffer an insolence from such mortals, even in the greatest severity of fortune, I rather chose to put myself to the utmost inconveniencies I could possibly suffer. As a proof whereof, not having a farthing in the world, I sold a few trifling things for four shillings, and with that scanty sum set out from Devizes in Wiltshire, to Romsey in Hampshire, which, over Salisbury Plain, is full forty miles. But as there are no houses over that long, solitary walk allowed to receive travellers, we went under the Plain, through all the villages, which lengthened our journey full twenty more.

Our night's expenses for lodgings and supper came to nine-pence, so we positively had no more than three shillings and threepence to support us for sixty miles.

* in David Garrick's *The Lying Valet*

My friend, as she had great cause, began, though in a tender manner, to reproach me for having left Bath, and more especially as Miss Ibbott, Mr Falkener, Mr Giffard, and many more, who came to see *The Comical Humours of the Moor of Venice*, at Bradford, used many forcible arguments to make me return, which I should have done, but that I happened to take offence at something said to me on that head by a particular person, who, notwithstanding, I believe, meant well; but being perhaps in a peevish mood, as all the world at different times are more or less, I persisted in my resolution of not going back, and hope it will be no affront to the theatrical community at Bath, to assure them from my heart I never once repented it, but rather pitied my successor for being encumbered with a very fatiguing and unthankful office.

When I set out from Devizes I stood debating near an hour on the road, whether we should march for London or Hampshire, as our finances were equally capable of serving us to either place, but nature asserted her right of empire in my heart and pointed me the road to pay my child a second visit, and after a most deplorable, half-starving journey, through intricate roads and terrible showers of rain, in three days' time we arrived at Romsey, having parted from our last three half-pence to ride five miles in a waggon, to the great relief of our over-tired legs.

It may be scarce believed that two persons should travel so far upon so small a pittance, who had not been from their birth inured to hardships, but we positively did, and, in the extreme heat of the day, were often glad to have recourse to a clear stream to quench our thirst after a tedious, painful march, not only to save our money, but enable us to go through the toil of the day till the friendly inn received us, where our over-wearied spirits were lulled by sleep into a forgetfulness of care.

I was questioned, not long since, whether it was possible for me to have run through the strange vicissitudes of fortune I have given an account of, which I solemnly declare I am ready to make oath of the truth of every circumstance, and if any particular person or persons require it, will refer them to hundreds now living, who have been witnesses of every article contained in my history. Nor would I presume to impose a falsehood, where, as I was desired to give a real account, truth was so absolutely necessary, and I believe the reader will find I have paid so strict a regard to it that I have rather painted my own ridiculous follies in their most glaring lights than debarred the reader the pleasure of laughing at me, or proudly concealed the utmost exigencies of my fate, both which may convince the world that I have been faithful in my declaration either way, for none, I believe, desire through frolic alone to make sport for others, or excite a pity they never stood in need of.

My stay with my daughter was but short as I had made a considerable progress in *Mr Dumont's History*, which, as I had determined not to lead that uncomfortable kind of life any longer, I thought I could easily finish during the weekly publication and frequently declared my intention to my daughter and her husband when I was at Newport in the Isle of Wight, with a positive assurance that I would not go any further with them.

This they either did not, or were not willing, to believe, notwithstanding my frequent repetition of it, and though I promised to make them happy with what might revert to me through my little labours, they injudiciously conceived I was doing them an injury, when, as I shall answer to heaven, I intended it to turn equally to their account as to my own. But a want of understanding and good mind on the one part, and a too implicit regard and obedience on the other, led them both into an error they had better have avoided.

I would not have the world believe, notwithstanding my aversion to the choice of my foolish girl has made, that I would not in all reasonable respects have every action of her life correspondent with the necessary duty of a wife, which I am certain never can or should exempt her from that she owes me, who must, while we both exist, be undoubtedly her mother.

To be short, we parted; and, till I could turn myself about, I went with another of their company (who left them through fears of the smallpox) to Lymington, where my daughter enslaved herself for life. From thence to Fareham, where, under a pretence of bringing over some hands to help us out, we being but six in number, my daughter's spouse came only with a cruel design to take away two of our hands, in pure spite to me, but, against this horrid inclination or knowledge, he did me the greatest piece of service in the world, for I made a firm resolution never more to set my foot on a country stage.

Since the pitiful villainy of strollers could reach one so nearly as one's own blood, I thought it then high time indeed to disclaim them, though I am well assured the girl would not have been guilty of the crime of depriving her mother of the morsel of bread she struggled for had she not been enforced to it by a blind obedience to an inconsiderable fool.

I was monstrously ashamed to see an innocent man, who was the manager where I was then engaged, led into difficulties arising from an impudent revenge on me I did not deserve, which the young gentleman was too sensible of, and was not more concerned for his own than my account.

I prevailed on him to steer his course to London, from whence, if his affairs could have been properly adjusted, I absolutely intended to have returned for a short time into the country with him, from a point of gratitude and honour, to make him in part amends for the injuries he had sustained from my son-in-law; and I shall think he has an everlasting claim on that score, to any act of friendship within my power, whenever he thinks it consistent with his interest to require it.

This good-natured injured person had not only himself, but a wife and child, exclusive of my unfortunate phiz to provide for, without the least prospect of doing it, but as I urged him so strenuously to go to London I was determined to contrive the means, and applied to a friend of his, who very generously complied with the request I made in his behalf, and away we went to Portsmouth, hoping to have been time enough for the waggon which set out that day.

We were unluckily too late, which obliged us to retard our journey two days, and remained at Portsmouth on expenses. This was a terrible disaster, as our finances were at best but slender, but, had they been much worse, I was resolved to see London, by heaven's permission, if I had been obliged to have been passed to it, being worn out with the general plagues of disapointment and ill-usage that are the certain consequentials of a strolling life.

When I set my foot upon London streets, though with only a single penny in my pocket, I was more transported with joy than for all the height of happiness I had in former and at different times possessed.

I hope those who read the description I have given of the inadequacies that all must expect to meet with who come under the impertinent power of travelling managers will make a proper use of it by never forsaking a good trade or calling, or what kind soever, to idle away their lives so unprofitably to themselves, and too often disadvantageously to the inhabitants of many an unsuccessful town.

I won't pretend to say that all heads of companies are without a rule of exception, but I must confess, those I have had to deal with, and that very lately too, are what I have before described, and I doubt but there are numbers of my former fellow-sufferers who are of my opinion.

Thank heaven, I have not, nor ever intend to have, any further commerce with them, but will apply myself closely to my pen, and, if I can obtain the honour and favour of my friends' company at an annual benefit, I will, to the extent of my power, endeavour to entertain them with my own performance, and provide the best I can to fill up the rest of the characters.

I shall very shortly open my oratorical academy, for the instruction of those who have any hopes, from genius and figure, of appearing on either of the London stages, or York, Norwich and Bath,* all which are reputable, but will never advise or encourage any persons to make themselves voluntary vagabonds, for such, not only the laws, but the opinion of every reasonable person deems those itinerant gentry who are daily guilty of the massacre of dramatic poetry. But of them no more, but a lasting and long farewell!

When I first came to town I had no design of giving any account of my life further than a trifling sketch, introduced in the preface to *Mr Dumont's History* (the first number of which will shortly make its appearance, and I hope will be kindly received by my worthy friends, who have favoured me in this work, which I should never have undertaken had I not been positively and strongly urged to it, not conceiving that any action of my life could claim that attention I find it has, by the large demand I have had for my weekly numbers throughout England and Wales, for which I humbly offer my sincerest thanks, and shall ever own myself not only indebted, but highly honoured).

As I propose my pen to be partly my support, I shall always endeavour to render it an amusement to my readers, as far as my capacity extends, and as the world is sensible I have no view of fortune but what I must, by heaven's assistance, strike out for myself, I hope I shall find a continuance of the favour I at present am blessed with, and shall think it my duty most carefully to preserve, not only in regard to my own interest, but from a grateful respect to those who kindly confer it.

I entreat the readers to excuse some faults which were slips of the press, occasioned through a hurry of business that rendered it

* the leading provincial stages

impossible to give time for a proper inspection either by me or the printer, who had been greatly hurried on account of the benefits at both the theatres, which he is indispensably obliged to pay regard to in point of time.

THE FACTS
1753–60

The Major who rented Mrs Charke a 'very handsome house with a large garden' must have been Major William Aldey, an ADC to the Duke of Marlborough, for Aldey was the only property-owning military man in Chepstow in the mid eighteenth century.

Aldey took up his commission as ensign to Captain Cookham in November 1701. In 1704 he was promoted to Lieutenant in the Welch Fusiliers, wounded during the storming of Schellenberg and awarded £28 bounty in the Blenheim Roll. The following year he became a Captain in Colonel Lillington's Regiment of Foot (now the 38th South Staffordshire Regiment of Foot). He was promoted to Major in 1707 and left the regiment in 1710.

The Aldey family of Hardwick, Chepstow, were prosperous property owners, and William Aldey owned several houses in the Chepstow area.

He died without legitimate issue in 1753, and in his will left his property to Elizabeth Harper, who he may or may not have married. Elizabeth Harper had a daughter, Frances (also called Anne), perhaps from a previous match, or maybe an illegitimate daughter of William Aldey. Whichever, the Major adopted Frances (Anne), and left her his coat of arms. She later married Thomas Stokes of Stanshawes near Chepstow.[1]

I believe that Miss Aldey was the lady who favoured Charlotte with 'friendly letters' and who was responsible for renting her the house.

The man who kindly gave Mrs Charke money to furnish the house at Chepstow, Val—ne M—s from P—d, must have been Valentine Morris from Piercefield, a man renowned for his generosity and extravagance.

Born in Antigua in 1727, Morris inherited the house, Piercefield, along with large plantations in the West Indies. He had a huge entourage of servants and slaves, including slaves called Lucy

Locket (a character occasionally played by Mrs Charke in *The Beggar's Opera*), Nero, Scipio and one named after his English country estate, Piercefield.

Piercefield was a large country house worth £50,000, which stood on the site of what is now Chepstow racecourse. It was surrounded by wonderful gardens full of tricks and surprises – alcoves, grottoes, a giant's cave, Chinese seat, druid's temple and lover's leap.

Morris's money helped build 300 miles of turnpike roads in Gloucestershire and Monmouthshire, and his magnaminity went much further. Other local gentry did not approve. *The Gentleman's Magazine* described the welcome he offered: 'At Piercefield the rich were entertained, the poor fed and the naked clothed. Nay, the very ale-wife at Chepstow had the command of Mr Morris's garden and even hot-house to entertain those visitors who were strangers to him.'[2]

But, like Mrs Charke, although Morris began life with a silver spoon firmly in his mouth, he died in poverty. His first expensive escapade was standing for election to Parliament in 1772. He was beaten, but not before he had run up huge debts in the attempt. Humiliated, he left the country for his West Indies plantations.

He was shortly appointed Governor, Captain-General, Commander-in-Chief and Vice-Admiral for the island of St Vincent. Unfortunately, his unpopular methods of dealing with uprisings of the local Caribs, and his poor handling of the vital defence of the island from the French, who actually took the island in 1779, led ultimately to his being gaoled in the King's Bench Prison, in London, for massive debts incurred in that defence.

His wife had gone insane after his parliamentary attempt, and lived in a madhouse in Wimpole Street. She had become too frightened to go out, after being abused during the election campaign, and at one point tried to kill herself by eating the works of her watch.

The sale of all Morris's property (at much less than it was actually worth) could not cover the debts he had run up in his troubles in the West Indies. He died, a broken man, at his sister's home in August 1789. But 'the inhabitants of Chepstow', wrote Archdeacon William Coxe in 1801, 'idolise his memory, and relate numerous instances of his benevolence which borders on enthusiasm'.[3]

Pill, a thriving port on the Bristol estuary, was visited a few years after Mrs Charke's stay by the founder of 'the methodical tribe' (the recently created Methodists), John Wesley. She may not have thought much of his new religion, but, in his *Journal*, he supported her theory about that 'terrible abode of infamy and guilt', Pill: 'I rode over to Pill, a place famous from generation to generation . . . for stupid, brutal, abandoned wickedness.'⁴

To help earn enough money to leave Pill, Charlotte wrote and typeset for a newspaper. At first I thought T—y must be a misprint and the newspaper was the *Postboy*. But further investigation turned up another Bristol newspaper, the *Bristol Weekly Intelligencer*, published by Edward Ward (Mr W—d), from June 1752 at the Stamp Office on the Tolzey (T—y). Unfortunately only a few copies exist for the appropriate years 1752–3, and I have been unable to identify any of her actual writing.

After leaving Mr Ward's employment, Charlotte performed *The London Merchant* at the Black Raven. The Raven in the High Street was 'a noted and well-accustomed public house with a very good brew-house, and plenty of water; also [and this would have interested Mrs Charke] a large arched cellar'. It was advertised to let from June 1750 to January 1752, when it was taken over by John Cogden, who announced that it was now 'in exceeding good repair, and well-stocked with all sorts of the best liquors'.⁵

In the autumn of 1753, after leaving the company in which her daughter acted, Mrs Charke accepted Simpson's offer to be prompter at the new Orchard Street Theatre in Bath.

Defoe had described the attractions of Bath in the mid-1720s: 'it is the resort of the sound, rather than the sick; the bathing is made more a sport and diversion, than a physical prescription for health; and the town is taken up in raffling, gaming, visiting, and in a word, all sorts of gallantry and levity . . . In the afternoon there is generally a play, though the decorations are mean, and the performances accordingly; but it answers, for the company here (not the actors) make the play, to say no more.'⁶

Mr Kennedy, who gave Mrs Charke the money to redeem her waistcoat from her Bath landlady, was an actor-manager. He had played at Goodman's Fields and Covent Garden in 1745–7, and joined the Bath company in 1748. The following year, while playing with Simpson's company, he took on the management of the Exeter theatre. He continued to act and run Exeter while Mrs Charke was prompting for Simpson. Soon afterwards he took over management of companies at Plymouth and Portsmouth.

Mrs Charke singles out two performers from Simpson's com-

pany, Miss Ibbott and Mr Maddox. At this point in her career, the
nearest Sarah Ibbott had played to London was Richmond, in 1752,
where she took on a magnificent array of roles including Indiana,
Ann Lovely, Mrs Sullen, Mrs Marwood, Lady Townly, Alicia, Zara
and Cordelia. A 1753 lampoon, *The Bath Comedians*, praised her:

> I'll censure some and some I'll rally,
> And first begin with charming S–lly,
> I–b–tt, I–b–tt, that's her name,
> And faith she is a lovely dame;
> They say her voice can charm like magic,
> In comic scenes as well as tragic;
> She acts well, and speaks well too,
> What more can any woman do?
> So,Madam, that's enough for you.

She stayed on in Bath until 1760 and, although she seems to have
considered playing Hamlet, did not do so.

Sarah Ibbott made her London début as the Queen in *Essex* in
1760. It was not successful, and she left London to work in Dublin
during the 1761–2 season. She returned to England in 1766, and
from 1774 to 1825 was the proprietress of the Norwich Theatre,
where, as an actress, she moved on to the older duenna roles – Lady
Wishfort, Mrs Heidelberg, etc. At one of her benefits she is said to
have taken a leaf out of Mrs Charke's book and played Falstaff. She
was left a fortune by a relative in 1787, retired from the stage in
1795, and died in 1825.

In 1751, when there was talk that the celebrated equilibrist,
Anthony Maddox, was to perform at Drury Lane, David Garrick
was moved to some pretty strong language. 'I cannot possibly
agree to such a prostitution upon any account; and nothing but
downright starving would induce me to bring such defilement and
abomination into the house of William Shakespeare.'[7]

Maddox performed in Bath in December 1753. According to a
contemporary engraving, his programme often consisted of the
following activities:

1. He tosses 6 balls with such dexterity that he catches them all
alternately without letting one of 'em drop to the ground, and
that with surprising activity.
2. He balanceth his hat upon his chin.
3. He balanceth a sword with its point on the edge of a
wine-glass.

4. He at the same time plays the violin.
5. He lies extended on his back upon a small wire.
6. He balanceth a coach wheel on his chin.
7. He standeth upon his head upon the wire.
8. He balanceth a chair on his chin.
9. He balanceth seven pipes, one in another. And
10. Blows a trumpet on the wire.
11. Balanceth several wine-glasses, full, on the wire.
12. Balanceth two pipes across a hoop on the wire.
13. Tosseth a straw from his foot to his nose.

By the time he was in Bristol in January 1754 he was also discharging a brace of pistols while standing on his head, balancing a straw on his face and shifting it to his foot, kicking it and catching again on his face and dancing a hornpipe.

One wonders what had happened to the taste of the young Charlotte Charke who, in 1735, had been so outraged when Drury Lane stooped to presenting harlequinades.

Mrs Charke describes a three-month fracas at the Orchard Street Theatre, instigated by a certain A—. On 25 March 1754 the theatre was closed down. The *Bristol Journal* gave a fuller account: 'Information was made before our magistrates against the Playhouse in Orchard Street by a gentleman who had been there the night before at the acting of Richard III. And yesterday the company of the said house were summoned to appear at the Guild Hall to answer such information, when they were fined, agreeable to Act of Parliament. Since when the said house has been entirely shut up.'[8]

Simpson, undeterred, brought in the concert formula, and reopened on 15 April. The theatre was henceforth billed as 'The Concert Room near the Parade'.

Charlotte Charke took the bills to the printer Thomas Boddely of the *Bath Journal*. Although she was amusingly disparaging about the Bath actors' demands over billing, her own billing had always been excellent; very often the enviable end-billing: 'and the part of xxxx by Mrs Charke'.

During the rest of 1754 Charlotte Charke toured with small unidentified troupes. It is quite clear from Charlotte's account of her time strolling and prompting that she thought herself, in terms of talent and experience, vastly superior to the actors with whom she was now driven to work. This may have been true, but her attitude undoubtedly led to much of the ill feeling she met from other actors, like her son-in-law. Today it is still an unforgivable sin, in the eyes of their colleagues, for actors who have fallen on hard times (and who now *have* to accept work in lower positions or worse theatre companies, when once they played alongside stars in important companies) to complain in terms of 'Sir Larry would never have allowed this', or 'When I was at the "Shakespeare", they never expected us to. . .'. Charlotte Charke was a theatrical snob. I am sure she had good reason; by this time snobbery was a luxury she could not afford.

She returned to London in December 1754. Shortly afterwards the printer Samuel Whyte and a bookseller friend came to visit her at her lodgings in Islington.

'Her habitation was a wretched thatched hovel, situated on the way to Islington in the purlieus of Clerkenwell Bridewell, not very distant from the New River Head, where at that time it was unusual for the scavengers to leave the cleansings of the streets, and the priests of Cloacina to deposit the offerings from the temples of that all-worshipped Power.

The night preceding a heavy rain had fallen, which rendered this extraordinary seat of the muses nearly inaccessible, so that, in our approach, we got our stockings enveloped with mud up to the very calves, which furnished an appearance much in the present fashionable style of half-boots. We did not attempt to pull the latch-string, but knocked at the door, which was opened by a tall, meagre, ragged figure, with a blue apron, indicating, what otherwise was doubtful, that it was a female before us; a perfect model for the Copper Captain's tattered landlady, that deplorable exhibition of the fair sex in the comedy *Rule a Wife and Have a Wife.* With a torpid voice and hungry smile, she desired us to walk in.

The first object that presented itself was a dresser – clean, it must be confessed, and furnished with three or four coarse delft plates, two brown platters and underneath an earthen pipkin, and a black pitcher with a snip out of it.

To the right we perceived and bowed to the mistress of the mansion, sitting on a maimed chair under the mantelpiece, by a fire merely sufficient to put us in mind of starving. On one hob sat a monkey, which by way of welcome chattered at our going in. On the other a tabby cat of melancholy aspect. At our author's feet, on the flounce of her dingy petticoat, reclined a dog, almost a skeleton.

He raised his shagged head and eagerly staring with his bleared eyes, saluted us with a snarl.

"Have done, Fidele, these are friends!" The tone of her voice was not harsh, it had something in it humbled and disconsolate, a mingled effort of authority and pleasure. Poor soul! Few were her visitors of that description. No wonder the creature barked!

A magpie perched on the top ring of her chair, not an uncomely ornament, and on her lap was placed a mutilated pair of bellows – the pipe was gone, an advantage in their present office. They served as a *succedaneum* for a writing desk, on which lay displayed her hopes and treasure, the manuscript of her novel [*Henry Dumont*]. Her inkstand was a broken teacup, the pen worn to a stump – she had but one, A rough deal board, with three hobbling supporters, was brought for our convenience, on which, without further ceremony, we contrived to sit down and enter upon business.

The work was read, remarks made, alterations agreed to, and thirty guineas demanded for the copy.

The squalid handmaiden, who had been an attentive listener, stretched forward her tawny length of neck with an eye of anxious expectation. The bookseller offered five.

Our authoress did not appear hurt, Disappointments had rendered her mind callous. However, some altercation ensued. This was [this] writer's first initiation into the mysteries of bibliopolism and the state of authorcraft. He, seeing both sides pertinacious, at length interposed, and at his instance the wary haberdasher of literature doubled his first proposal, with this saving proviso – that his friend present would pay a moiety and run one half the risk, what was agreed to. Thus matters were accommodated, seemingly to the satisfaction of all parties, the lady's original stipulation of fifty copies for herself being previously acceded to.'⁹

Although Mr Whyte revelled in Mrs Charke's poverty, he seems not to have encouraged his friend to raise his offer a little higher, and he with H. Slater junior published her novel, *The History of Henry Dumont and Miss Charlotte Evelyn*, in 1755.

The first weekly part of the *Narrative* appeared in April 1755. The instalments sold so well that they were published as a book, which went into two editions before the end of the year. Down in Bristol Edward Ward on the Tolzey advertised the eight numbers (at threepence each), and 'with a last number, a curious copperplate of

Mrs Charlotte Charke, and a general title will be presented to subscribers gratis'.[10]

In September 1755 Mrs Charke was back on stage, with her brother's Haymarket company, giving her promised appearance as Agnes Wilmot in *Fatal Curiosity*. She stayed with Theophilus to play Volscius in *The Rehearsal*. Also in the cast was her sister Elizabeth Marples's daughter Anna Chetwood (she had married the prompter William Rufus Chetwood at St Benet's in 1738).

Another member of the company was 'Mrs Midnight' (a performer generally thought to be Christopher Smart working under a pseudonym, as Smart had already used the name in his journal *The Midwife*; Mrs Midnight is also the name of one of the characters in Farquhar's *The Twin Rivals*, and it is possible that some other performer took the name from her), who produced mad theatrical evenings (or 'impromptu faraglios and medley concerts'), with bills reminiscent of Mrs Charke's and Fielding's. For example her *New Carnival Concert* was 'set for a smoking pipe, a tankard, a bassoon, a pair of tongs, 2 wooden spoons, a salt box, and a pair of slippers; by the best Italian masters, viz signiors Zappino, Sallybotino, Diavolino, Ferantini, Cochinino, Battcrino, Ciavartino and several others just arrived from the Republic of San Marino, With dancing by an extraordinary original who will not touch the ground either with his hands or feet.'[11]

Alongside fictional performers, like Myn Herr Van Poop-Poop Broomstickado, Theophilus Cibber acted and Anthony Maddox and Miss Isabella Wilkinson performed on the slack wire.

Mrs Midnight pops up with uncanny regularity in the later years of Mrs Charke's career, and I feel sure that there was a strong link between the two eccentric, actor-managers.

Another short book by Mrs Charke, *The Mercer: or, the Fatal Extravagance*, came out around early 1756. Its opening lines give the general gist: 'Of all the follies and vices incidental to mankind, none can be deemed more contemptively erroneous than that of living beyond our fortunes, and running into expensive dignities superior to the sphere of life in which providence has placed us.'

In September 1756 she performed at Bartholomew Fair. The bills announced 'Mrs Charke's and King's company of comedians . . . *England Triumphant and the Merry Beggars: or The British General with the comical humours of His Royal consort Queen Tatter* . . . with a variety of singing, dancing, rope-dancing, tumbling by eminent persons lately arrived from Italy.'

Charlotte Charke's daughter and her husband were performing across the yard in Hallam's company (their bill included 'a grand dance of grotesque Lilliputians'). Catherine Charke had married John Harman in Lymington on 6 January 1750 (while Charlotte was still working with the Linnets and Elringtons).

On 18 September Charlotte was a member of Theophilus's Histrionic Academy on Richmond Hill. The 'Academy' was a new device of Cibber's to evade the Licensing Act. There were no 'performances', only 'rehearsals', but to be doubly sure, admission was by 'cephalic snuff'. The plays offered were *The Stratagem* (Mrs Charke was not in this) and *Lethe*, in which she played Mercury. The company played until 25 September, and then moved to Southwark for December. There they were not so lucky, for on 15 December Theophilus announced: 'Some sudden disappointments (as unexpected as unforeseen) compel me to defer opening my Histrionic Academy.'[1][2]

Mrs Charke's father Colley Cibber died peacefully at his London home on 12 December 1757. Mrs Charke's eldest sister, Catherine Brown, rushed Cibber's will through probate. In it their sister Anne Boultby and brother Theophilus were left £50 each; and Theophilus's daughters Jenny and Betty received £1000 each. (In her autobiography the actress George Ann Bellamy claimed that Cibber had left to her care his granddaughter, Betty, as she was 'weak in her intellects'.) Elizabeth Brett/Marples, the daughter who had always stuck by Charlotte, and Charlotte herself both received the insulting amount of 'five pounds and no more'. As Charlotte suspected, her eldest sister Catherine got the rest of Cibber's considerable estate.

Within months Mrs Charke published *The Lover's Treat: or, Unnatural Hatred*, the novel which tackles sibling rivalry.

Charlotte had been shocked that her father and sister were prepared to abandon 'an innocent and hapless child to that rigorous fate my fears suggested' (p. 70). She must have been even more surprised when her father left insulting sums to her sister Elizabeth and herself, but did not even mention in his will their daughters, his grandchildren Catherine Charke/Harman and Anna Brett/Chetwood.

Shortly after her grandfather's death, Elizabeth's daughter Anna, encouraged perhaps by her aunt Charlotte, wrote a pitiful, semi-literate letter to an unnamed member of the nobility.

May it please your Grace, I am an unfortunate grand daughter of the Late Colley Cibber whose unhapines was never to feell for the distress of his own family otherwise then by a Partill Judgement the flictions of his Children was greatly owing to his unfeelingnes my Mother My Lord never Commited She Could Say it on her Death Bed an Act of Disobedeince; to her and my Aunt Charke he Left but five pound Each to there Children nothing but the bulk of his fortune my Aunt Brown had and my uncle Theophilus Daughters had a thousand pound Each Worn down by Affliction and growing in years not brought up to Earn my Bread by Servile Business a wrong Judgement in Parents who flatters us with Hopes we never tast the old Nobility all dead who usd thro pity to Aleavate the Distresses of my family inforces me to plead to your pity in this hope that my Aunt Charke Shard in your Compassion I never and please your grace Intrested your Assistance before but as I am informed your Benevolence at this to be in the Number as my distress is great and all I am Capable to do is with my Needle and there is no imploy all Publick Charity, taking it in that Heaven with its Choisest Blessings may await you Shall ever be the fervent Wish and Prayer of your most Obeadent servant. Ana Cheetwood.[13]

At the end of 1757 Mrs Charke lost her estranged father. During 1758 she also lost her daughter, for Catherine Harman emigrated to America with her husband, never to return. She acted, with her husband, in David Douglass's company at Cruger's Wharf, New York. Also in the company was Lewis Hallam (Adam Hallam's nephew). Over the next fifteen years Mrs Harman played at Philadelphia, Charleston, and John Street Theatre, New York. Her husband, John Harman, died in about 1759. She herself died, aged forty-three, in 1773. She left her money to another actress, Miss Cheer.

According to her mother, Catherine's figure was fitter for low comedy parts. In 1773 her American obituary made the same point: 'she was a just actress, possessed much merit in low comedy, and dressed all her characters with infinite propriety, but her figure prevented her from succeeding in tragedy and genteel comedy.' Her character was remembered as 'sensible, humane and benevolent'.[14]

On 26 August 1758, Mrs Charke arrived in Canterbury 'with a design, next week (for one night only) to entertain the ladies and gentleman here with a comic medley; after which will be a ball'.

During the following week the *Kentish Post* announced that Mrs Charke had been granted 'the liberty of the Town Hall for her dissertation and auction on Wednesday next; after which will be a ball'. A month later the paper declared 'that Mrs Charke's worthy friends of this city have requested her to exhibit her Medley of Entertainments, with additions at the Playhouse in Canterbury on Monday the second of October next'. Her company was followed in by Mrs Midnight's Jubilee Concert and Oratory.[15]

A few weeks later, on 27 October, Theophilus Cibber, along with Anthony Maddox and other performers, set sail for Dublin. The ship, the *Dublin Trader*, was caught in a storm, struck a sand bar and sank the same day. Everyone on board was drowned.

Charlotte Charke's entourage was rapidly diminishing – Job Baker had disappeared from the bills in the 1740s, Mrs Careless died in 1752, her daughter was in America, Maddox and her brother were now dead.

In August 1759, Mrs Charke applied to the Duke of Devonshire for a licence to perform, but the tone of her letter shows that she was a changed woman.

> May it please your Grace,
>   I must confess this liberty may be deemed a piece of presumption which would stand a terrible chance of being rendered inexcusable from many others of an equal rank with your Grace, and might naturally have prevented my making so bold an attempt in intruding on your Grace's retirement, but as your humanity is too well known to admit of a doubt of being forgiven when prompted by necessity I have ventured to earnestly implore your Grace's permission in this vacant season of the year to perform for ten nights only, at the Haymarket Theatre, and humbly hope for the sake of the memory of my late father, Colley Cibber, you will permit the daughter, who was bred on the stage, to take an honest chance for those few nights, of establishing herself in a way of business which will make her happy and greatly add to the numerous blessings heaven has inspired your Grace to bestow on many others. An ill state of health obliges me to decline my profession in the winter, and as the houses are both shut up, it can be no detriment to those whose happier fortunes receive the general advantage of that season of the year, which renders me incapable of striving for a support. If your grace's wonted tendernesses to the distressed

will extend itself to me in this case, I beg you'll give an immediate order to any of your servants to write your pleasure, directed to Mrs Charke at Mrs Hinds' in Leicester Street, near Swallow Street, Piccadilly. If your Grace conceived how happy I may be made by your favourable compliance I dare believe you'd both pity and forgive this trouble from your grace's most devoted obediant servant,

    Charlotte Charke, formerly Cibber

Please, your Grace, in case 'tis necessary I shall call at Devonshire House to know your Grace's commands.[16]

Her request for a performance licence was granted, and in September she announced (on the seventh night of the run), a benefit performance of Mrs Centlivre's *The Busy Body*, in which she took the leading role, Marplot. Mrs Midnight played a supporting role, Patch. Mrs Charke closed her advertisement with a plea – 'As I am entirely dependent on chance for subsistence . . . I humbly hope the town will favour me.'

She did not appear on stage again.

On 16 April 1760 the *British Chronicle* printed her obituary: 'Died, the celebrated Mrs Charlotte Charke, in the Haymarket, daughter of Colley Cibber Esq; the poet laureate; a gentlewoman remarkable for her adventures and misfortunes.'

Her grave has not been found.

1 Army Lists; *Miscellanea Genaelogica et Heraldica*; Bradney, *History of Monmouthshire*.
2 Quoted in Ivor Walsh, *The Unfortunate Valentine Morris*, 1964.
3 *Historical Tour Through Monmouthshire*.
4 3 October 1755.
5 *Bristol Weekly Intelligencer*.
6 Defoe, *A Tour . . . Great Britain*.
7 Letter to Draper, 17 August 1751.
8 30 March 1754.
9 Samuel Whyte, article in *The Monthly Mirror*, 1760.
10 *Bristol Weekly Intelligencer*, March 1755.
11 Haymarket, Friday 13 September 1754.
12 *Public Advertiser*, September 1756; *London Stage* calendar.
13 Harvard Theatre Collection.
14 *Rivington's Gazette*, 3 June 1773.
15 Sybil Rosenfeld, *Strolling Players and Drama in the Provinces 1660–1765*, 1939, pp. 255–6.
16 LC 72/3 no. 79, 7 August 1759.

Postscript

THE NARRATIVE

It is generally the rule to put the summary of books of this kind at the beginning, but as I have, through the whole course of my life, acted in contradiction to all points of regularity, beg to be indulged in a whimsical conclusion of my narrative, by introducing that last, which I will allow should have been first. As for example:

This day, 19 April 1755, is published the eighth and last number of *A Narrative of the Life of Mrs Charlotte Charke*, with a dedication from and to myself: 'the prosperest patroness I could have chosen, as I am most likely to be tenderly partial to my poetical errors, and will be as bounteous in the reward as we may reasonable imagine my merit may claim.'

This work contains, first: A notable promise of entertaining the town with *The History of Henry Dumont, Esq. and Miss Charlotte Evelyn*; but, being universally known to be an odd product of nature, was requested to postpone that, and give an account of myself from my infancy to the present time.

Secondly – My natural propensity to a hat and wig, in which, at the age of four years, I made a very considerable figure in a ditch, with several other succeeding mad pranks. An account of my education at Westminster. Why did not I make a better use of so happy an advantage!

Thirdly – My extraordinary skill in the science of physic, with a recommendation of the necessary use of snails and gooseberry leaves, when drugs and chemical preparations were not come-at-able. My natural aversion to a needle, and profound respect for a curry comb, in the use of which I excelled most young ladies in Great Britain. My extensive knowledge in gardening, not forgetting that necessary accomplishment for a young gentlewoman, judiciously discharging a blunderbuss or a fowling-piece. My own, and the lucky escape of life, when I ran over a child at Uxbridge.

Fourthly – My indiscreetly plumping into the sea of matrimony and becoming a wife before I had the proper understanding of a reasonable child. An account of my coming on the stage. My uncommon success there. My folly in leaving it. My recommendation of my sister Marples to the consideration of every person who chooses to eat an elegant meal or chat away for a few moments with a humorous, good-natured elderly landlady. My turning grocer, with some wise remarks on the rise and fall of sugars and teas. An unfortunate adventure in selling a link. A short account of my father and mother's courtship and marriage.

Fifthly – A faithful promise to prefer a bill in chancery against my uncle's widow, who had artfully deprived his heirs at law of a very considerable fortune. (N.B. The old dame may be assured I will be as good as my word.) My keeping a grand puppet-show and losing as much money by it as it cost me. My becoming a widow and being afterwards privately married, which, as it proved, I had better have let alone. My going into men's clothes, in which I continued many years, the reason of which I beg to be excused, as it concerns no mortal now living but myself. My becoming a second time a widow, which drew on me inexpressible sorrows that lasted upwards of twelve years, and the unforeseen turns of providence by which I was constantly extricated from them. An unfortunate interview with a fair lady, who would have made me master of herself and fortune, if I had been lucky enough to have been in reality what I appeared.

Sixthly – My endeavouring at a reconciliation with my father. His sending back my letter in a blank. His being too much governed by humour, but more so by her, whom age cannot exempt from the being the lively limner of her own face, which she had better neglect a little, and pay part of that regard to what she ought to esteem the nobler part, and must have an existence when her painted frame is reduced to ashes.

Seventhly – My being gentleman to a certain peer. After my dismission becoming only an occasional player, while I was playing at bo-peep with the world. My turning pork merchant. Broke, through the inhuman appetite of a hungry dog. Went a-strolling. Several adventures during my peregrination. My return, and setting up an eating house in Drury Lane. Undone again, by pilfering lodgers. Turning drawer at St Marylebone. An account of my situation there. Going to the Haymarket Theatre with my brother. His leaving it. Many distresses arising on that account. Going a-strolling a second time, and staying near nine years. Several remarkable occurrences while I was abroad; particularly my being sent to G— jail, for being an actor, which, to do most strolling players justice, they ought not to have the laws enforced against them on that score, for a very substantial reason. My settling in Wales, and turning pastry-cook and farmer. Made a small mistake in turning hog merchant. Went to the seat of destruction called Pill. Broke, and came away. Hired myself to a printer at Bristol, to write and correct the press. Made a short stay there. Vagabondized again, and last Christmas returned to London, where I hope to remain as long as I live.

I have now concluded my narrative, from my infancy to the time of my returning to London; and if those who do me the honour to kill time by the perusal will seriously reflect on the manifold distresses I have suffered, they must think me wonderfully favoured by providence, in the surprising turns of fortune which have often redeemed me from the devouring jaws of total destruction when I have least expected it.

I wish the merciful example of the great Creator, who never yet forsook me, had prevailed on the mind of him who, by divine ordination, was the author of my being; and am sorry that he should so overshoot his reason as not to consider, when I only asked for blessing and pardon, he should deny that which from a superior power he will one day find necessary himself to implore; and I hope his prayer will be answered, and that heaven will not be deaf to him, as he has been to me.

I cannot recollect any crime I have been guilty of that is unpardonable which the denial of my request may possibly make the world believe I have, but I dare challenge the most malicious tongue of slander to a proof of that kind, as heaven and my own conscience can equally acquit me of having deserved that dreadful sentence of not being forgiven.

The errors of my youth chiefly consisted in a thoughtless wildness, partly owing to having too much will of my own in infancy, which I allow was occasioned by an over-fondness where I now unhappily find a fixed aversion. But, notwithstanding that unkindness, nature will assert her right and tenderly plead in behalf of him, who I am certain through age and infirmity, rather than a real delight in cruelty, has listened too much to an invidious tongue, which had been more gracefully employed in healing, not widening a breach between a father and a child who wanted only the satisfaction of knowing her name was no longer hateful to him, who, in spite of fortune's utmost rigour, I must think myself bound by all laws, both divine and human, still to cherish in my heart and tenderly revere.

As I have nothing further to entertain my friends with, as to my life, I shall with the humblest submission take my leave of them; and as I design to pass in the catalogue of authors, will endeavour to produce something now and then to make them laugh, if possible, for I think it is pity to draw tears from those who have so generously contributed towards making me smile.

Epilogue

Being a discussion of the life of Mrs Charlotte Charke and her treatment at the hands of biographers

Charlotte Charke worried that the *Narrative* of her own life might 'fall into the hands of people of disproportioned understandings' and hoped 'to prevent an error a weak judgement might have run into, by inconsiderately throwing an odium upon [her, she] could not possibly deserve; for alas,' she cried, 'all cannot judge alike'.

Unluckily for her, practically all her modern biographers have judged alike. When mentioned in passing, she is 'the well-known troublemaker, Charlotte Charke', 'Colley Cibber's queer daughter', or even 'Cibber's unsatisfactory daughter'.[1]

Her *Narrative*, which has supplied the information for these biographers, seems to have led many of them astray: 'This fascinating book is neither literature nor history, but the inconsequent and madly egocentric memories of an ageing and desperate woman, a glimpse into a twisted and distraught human soul. Modern psychoanalysis would, no doubt, neatly label Mrs Charke as a psychopathic lesbian, but we need not here peer too far into the deep well of loneliness from which this unhappy woman drew her inspiration.'[2]

Although it is used to condemn her, the theatrical and historical information it provides is not taken seriously: 'Charlotte herself is not a very reliable authority, and too much importance can easily be attached to her remarks', and 'This work is . . . in many respects untrustworthy'.[3]

I hope I have shown that, on the whole, she is a reliable historian, if anything slightly modest about her own achievements.

In her own lifetime the only personal comments about her which appeared in print were those which dealt with her famous quarrel with her powerful father. Shortly after her death the few obituaries describe her only as a woman famous for her adventures and misfortunes, and Samuel Whyte wrote the vivid description of her accommodation when she had just arrived back in London from nine years in the provinces.

About sixty years later, her *Narrative* was being read and interpreted in a new light: She was 'born in affluence, educated with care and tenderness, ' wrote the author of the 1825 work *Dramatic Table Talk*, but 'though possessing considerable talents terminated her miserable existence on a dunghill'. Within a few years the playwright-theatre manager, Charles Dibden, had come to the conclusion that her 'memoirs' belonged 'in the annals of profligacy . . . in short, [she was] one of those disgraces to the community that ought not to be admitted into society . . .'[4]

Recent studies in specialist theatrical journals have been more sympathetic, but even her champions could not help falling into the pontificating tones of her nineteenth-century critics: 'Her *Narrative*, as revealing as it is, remains but the scattered tesserae of the macabre mosaic that was her life.'[5]

Her reputation as a disgrace and a wastrel grew steadily through the nineteenth and into the twentieth century. But if it comes from the evidence Mrs Charke herself gave us in the *Narrative*, how well does that evidence stand up to close examination?

In order to try to disentangle the real Mrs Charke from the dissolute profligate who now goes by her name, it is important to show how the words of Mrs Charke have been used and abused; how biographers have paraphrased her, altered (albeit slightly) the meaning of her words, and set up chains of Chinese whispers, which have slowly but surely over taken her real story and left quite another in its place.

It is generally agreed that 'the last of Colley and Katherine's children was the oddest'.[6] Charlotte confessed that she was an 'odd mortal' and proudly proclaimed that she needed 'no force of argument, beyond what had been already said, to bring the whole globe terrestrial into that opinion' (p.47), for 'if oddity can please my right to surprise and astonishment', she declared, 'I may positively claim a title to be shown among the wonders of ages past and those to come' (p.4). But with this she also claimed that there was 'no one in the world more fit than myself to be laughed at' (p.47). I would imagine that the only type of oddness she was laying title to was the oddness which could make people laugh at her (just as comics today might claim to be mad, meaning zany, not psychologically unstable).

Further, she promised that she would not 'escape a laugh, even at my own expense, deprive my readers of that pleasing satisfaction, or conceal any error, which I now rather sigh to reflect on; but formerly, through too much vacancy of thought, might be idle enough rather to justify than condemn' (p.4). From this we can deduce that as far as Charlotte was concerned she was exposing her follies *in all their glory*, to give the reader a laugh.

The Victorian theatrical historian Dr Doran was obviously swayed by her plea, for he wrote, sympathetically: 'Cibber's erring and hapless daughter ... published her remarkable autobiography, the details of which make the heart ache.'[7] Indeed, the bitter-sweet tale of her life works because the mad, insuppressible energy of Mrs Charke bubbles away just beneath the surface, even when she is describing the most heartbreaking episodes.

Her education, she boasted, was 'genteel' and 'liberal' and 'such indeed as might have been sufficient for a son instead of a daughter' (p.5). This early eighteenth-century notion of hers has been made much of ever since.

In the following quotes I have italicized the embroidery and additions which transform Mrs Charke's own confessions:

'[She] ... had an education more suitable to a boy than a girl. As she grew up, she accordingly delighted in masculine amusements – shooting, hunting, riding, etc . . . . This *wildness, however, was checked in a measure by her marriage*, when very young, with Mr Richard Charke, an eminent performer on the violin . . .'[8]

'Indeed, by the time she had reached her late teens, *her family began to worry about her masculine pursuits and her total ignorance of female accomplishments, so Charlotte was sent to a physician* named Hales, in the country, *to learn housekeeping*.'[9]

'It must be confessed, that she very early seemed to show a *disposition so wild, so dissipated, and so unsuitable to her sex, as must very naturally be supposed to have given disgust to those of her friends*, whose wishes were even the most favourable towards her. In short, from infancy she owns she had *more of the male than female in her inclinations*, and related two or three droll adventures of her dressing herself up in her father's clothes; her riding out on the back of an ass's foal when not above four or five years old, etc. that seem an evident *foretaste of the like masculine conduct which she pursued through life*.'[10]

Gardening, and all things floral, are now considered most sedate and genteel occupations for women of all ages. When I was a child, a girl who *did not* have a crush on ponies and everything that went with them: tackrooms, mucking out, gymkhanas and Pat Smythe, was considered quite abnormal. In the twentieth century women ride in the Grand National, The Princess Royal rides in National Hunt races, the Queen herself expresses a personal interest in her own string of horses and one of the most popular fiction works for young girls is *National Velvet*, the story of an adolescent girl with Charlotte's proclivities. In the eighteenth century it was not the done thing to be a stable-girl. But that is not quite the point, because her chief purpose in telling these stories is to enhance the *theatricality* of the world she created, alone, in her childhood. She is telling us that she was a born actress, not because her father had spent years drilling her in Shakespearian verse-speaking, but because she was a *natural*, acting ran in her veins, she could not *help* herself acting. And when she describes taking up the role of gardener she never leaves us in any doubt that she is role-playing. She has observed the gardeners at work and has got it off to a tee:

'I thought it always proper to imitate the actions of those persons whose characters I chose to represent, and, indeed was as changeable as Proteus.

When I blended the groom and the gardener, I conceived, after having worked two or three hours in the morning, a broiled rasher of bacon upon a luncheon of bread in one hand, and a pruning knife in the other (walking, instead of sitting to this elegant meal), making seeds and plants the general subject of my discourse was the true characteristic of the gardener, as, at other times, a halter and horse-cloth brought into the house and awkwardly thrown down on a chair were emblems of my stable profession; with now and then a shrug of the shoulders and a scratch of the head, with a hasty demand for small beer, and a "God bless you make haste. I have not a single horse dressed or watered. and here it is almost eight o'clock, the poor cattle will think I have forgot 'em – and tomorrow they go a journey, I am sure I'd need to take care of 'em." Perhaps this great journey was an afternoon's jaunt to Windsor, within seven miles of our house; however it served me to give myself as many airs as if it had been a progress of five hundred miles' (p.17)

As an old codger Charlotte 'rested on my spade and with a significant wink and a nod, asked whether [her mother] imagined any of the rest of her children would have done as much at my age, adding, very shrewdly, "Come, come, madam, let me tell you, a pound saved is a pound got"'.(p.18)

She does not discuss how much she preferred to feel that she *was* a gardener, groom or old codger, but that she *could convince others* by her dressing up and acting: each role was played 'with as significant an air as I could assume' (p.16). When she played the young doctor she put on 'significancy of countenance that rather served to convince them of my incomparable skill and abilities' (p.14). Then as a shopkeeper her friends 'came in turn to see my mercantile face, which carried in it as conceited an air of trade as it had before in physic and I talked of "myself and other dealers", as I was pleased to term it. The rise and fall of sugars was my constant topic, and trading abroad and at home was as frequent in my mouth as my meals' (p.39).

An essential ingredient of this transformation was often the ultimate acting feat: playing the opposite sex. From the age of four she declared she had 'a passionate fondness for a periwig' (p.5) (to any theatre-goers who had seen her as a man this would have been a further proof of her lifelong search for perfection in her roles and not a comment on her sexual predilections). In order to stun the public with her ability, what could be more impressive than that she could not only dupe a paying audience, who were in on the joke, and kept at a reasonable distance to assist the trickery of the art, but could do just as well at close range, with an audience of unsuspecting individuals. When in character she could manage 'not making the least discovery of my sex by my behaviour, ever endeavouring to keep up to the well-bred gentleman' (p.75).

The theatre is a place of illusion and transformation. The word 'player', the more usual word for an actor in those days, indicated the qualities that were (and still are) essential for the transformations required.

In the art of autobiography it is still essential to enhance and exaggerate the public personality. Actresses famous for their sexy roles recount passionate encounters, comedians tell of the funny escapades and narrow scrapes which they survive only by the sharpness of their wit. A general will tell messroom tales from the battlefields rather than discuss his own sexual infidelities. Thus Charlotte Charke told of her success at kidding people she was a man – because she was an actress who specialized in male roles.

The stage tradition of women in male roles only just survives nowadays in the Christmas pantomime, but in the eighteenth century it was a craze. From its beginnings, drama, the literature of theatre, depended on men playing the roles of women. By Shakespeare's time we can see the playwright actively helping the inexperienced boy-players out by giving them scenes in which they can relax, and play boys, or rather girls dressed up as boys. The character of Viola in *Twelfth Night*, for instance, spends only a few scenes as a girl, so for most of the play the young boy would have appeared disguised as Cesario, a male – not too hard when you are one.

When, after the Restoration of the monarchy in 1660, women started playing women, far from dying out, the theatrical illusion of women becoming men in the course of the plot thrived and at the same time took on a whole new depth. For, instead of lessening the art needed by the performer, it increased it. All the major playwrights of the late seventeenth and early eighteenth centuries: Dryden, Shadwell, D'Urfey, Ravenscroft, Southerne, Behn, Pix, Wycherley, later Colley Cibber himself, wrote 'breeches parts', or parts where, within the action of the play, a female character passes herself off as a man. Certain actresses excelled in such roles; not those who were in any way manly, but, rather, those whose reputations had quite titillating heterosexual undertones: Nell Gwyn, Elizabeth Barry, Betty Bowtell, Anne Bracegirdle, Susannah Mountford and Peg Woffington.

The diarist Samuel Pepys witnessed a breeches performance given by Nell Gwynn in *The Maiden Queen*: 'But so great a performance of a comical part was never, I believe, in the world before as Nell doth this, both as a mad girl and then, most and best of all, when she comes in like a young gallant; and hath the motions and carriage of a spark the most that ever I saw any man have.'[11]

But Pepys's analysis of Nell Gwyn's performance only touched the surface, for he did not state something which would have been obvious to him as the spectator: 'in presenting the habits and behaviour of a man, she was still very much a woman. She was presenting a woman's idea of a man, or rather, her attitude to a certain kind of male behaviour to which she was often subjected.'[12]

Apart from the obvious acting challenge, this device presented the audience with a new perspective on the 'male' character being performed, for, 'by having the boy played by a girl, the audience is made continually aware of the Ideas involved in the encounters of the "characters", while any exploration of the emotional basis of these ideas is avoided ... audience and actors have a dialogue, as it were, over the characters' heads.'[13]

By the time of Charlotte Charke's début, the use of dramatic travesty had developed from a literary device (in which a female character dresses as a male character to further the plot of the play), to a much more theatrical or stylistic one.

The Restoration had seen a few novelty productions such as an all-female performance of the pastoral *Pastor Fido*. But the theatrical impact of a bunch of women dressed as nymphs and shepherds would have been very different from that created by a production seen within a month of Mrs Charke's début, when the Haymarket Theatre put on one performance of *The Metamorphosis of the Beggar's Opera*. The prostitutes, Mrs Peachum, and all female roles were taken by men, the male crooks and rogues were played by women. By giving the roles to the opposite sex, without any dramatic or literary explanation, there is a theatrical distancing (what would now be called a Brechtian or alienation effect), through which some of the ideas presented within the text are highlighted, and the audience is forced to *think* rather than just empathize. At the same time the actors are given the opportunity to comment on their roles instead of just hiding behind them.

It is no coincidence that the male roles most frequently played by eighteenth-century actresses were rakes and bullies: Peg Woffington (who had started her career as a child in Dublin playing Macheath in *The Beggar's Opera*) had one of her greatest triumphs as Sir Harry Wildair, a rake. Other 'women's' roles included Alexander the Great, and Macheath, which was tackled by, among others, Ann Catley, Elizabeth Griffith, Margaret Farrell, Miss Fontanelle and Miss Blake. So Mrs Charke's frequent playing of male roles can be seen as quite acceptable within her own time. But her wearing of male clothing off-stage begs an explanation.

In the seventeenth and eighteenth centuries there are many known cases of women who, for one reason or another, spent years in male dress.

The army and navy were popular careers for such women. Hannah Snell, the famous female soldier, was, by the 1750s, presenting herself on stage as a phenomenon. Christian Cavenaugh (known as Mother Ross), despite having three children, followed her husband after he was kidnapped and carried off to Holland. Leaving her children with her brother, she went to Holland, enlisted, and fought at the battle of Landen. Despite a bullet wound in her hip, she was not discovered and went on to fight in the battle of Hochstadt. When she eventually found her husband, he was having an affair with a Dutchwoman. Mother Ross remained in the service and fought at the Battle of Ramillies where her skull was fractured. During the treatment her sex was discovered. She presented a petition to Queen Anne (claiming twelve years' service, with war wounds) and received a bounty of £50 and pension of one shilling per day. After another marriage (to another soldier) she joined his barracks as sutler, and when her husband was admitted to Chelsea Hospital, she joined him and lived with him there until her death in 1739. She was buried at the hospital with military honours.

The women made good soldiers and sailors, and sometimes their sex was never discovered.

One woman spent a year at sea taking all the duties of sailor, before she met and married Mary Parlour in 1766. Her wife pawned her clothes to maintain her 'husband'. As 'Samuel Bundy', she joined the *Prince Frederick* of Chatham, but deserted due to the large number of hands on board. She then joined a merchant ship but left this as she missed her wife.

The handsome and active Negress 'William Brown' became captain of the foretop on HMS *Queen Charlotte*. Another woman in the marines was sentenced to 500 lashes, received 400 before the officers begged her off, but still her sex was not discovered. Another woman was found out by being tied up for 24 lashes.

Some women transvestites took less demanding jobs. Two women lived together in Poplar for thirty-six years, as man and wife. Together they kept the White Horse, a public house. On the death of the wife, the 'man' retired from business. 'He' had served every office in the parish except churchwarden, which she was due to serve the following year.

Another woman took on the behaviour of a man while still wearing a skirt. She succeeded her father as sexton and grave-digger of the parish, dug graves, never spent time in women's company, drank with the men, talked, drank, smoked tobacco and swore. She cut her hair short, wore a man's coat, cape, boots and a woman's skirt.

But some women had more pressing reasons for disguising themselves as men.

In April 1793 a well-known pedlar who had been on the road for many years confessed on her death-bed that her name was Fanny.

She had taken an active part in the 1780 riots and, afraid of arrest, spent the rest of her life dressed as a man.

Charlotte confessed that she was 'for some substantial reasons *en cavalier*'. She was, like many people in those times, frequently pursued by bailiffs for debt. A random sample of the collector's comments from the Westminster rates books for 1737 show the sort of life which many led: 'Poor. Pretty'; 'Don't care a turd at £9.10s'; 'ran a Way'; 'Newgate'; 'Never did, nor never will. Not able'; 'Won't pay. Gone to the alehouse'; 'Won't pay. The husband is run away'; 'Impudent and poor. Ran away'. It should be noted that people in the position of paying rates were among the better off. If by illness, misfortune, or stupidity, a person got themselves into debt there were no safety nets, no welfare payments, but only a system by which bailiffs could have you imprisoned for life without trial.

But a bailiff with a writ against Mrs Charke was not going to be looking out for a young gentleman, a role Charlotte had already proved she could get away with on stage.

She described her worries about being caught: 'being then but ten miles from London, and every hour of my life liable to be seen by some air-taking tradesman to whom it was twenty to one I might be indebted.' (p.96); 'which, as my circumstances stood, was no small comfort to one who proceeded in paralytic order upon every excursion' (p.99). She also expressed her relief when she could cock a snook at the bailiffs: 'I marched every day through the streets with ease and security, having his lordship's protection, and proud to cock my hat in the face of the best of the bailiffs and shake hands with them into the bargain' (p.100), or when she could actually put her creditors out of countenance by paying up: 'The first thing I did was to hasten to my principal creditor, who, by the by, had issued out against a writ against me a month before, but was, through a fruitless search, obliged to drop his action' (p.107).

She also describes looking for work at night, when there would have been few bailiffs on the streets: 'I sometimes used by owl-light to creep out' (p.73); 'As soon as I was capable of speaking to be heard, I took a second owl-light opportunity to seek for business, and happily succeeded in my endeavour' (p.98).

Practically the only women who would have ventured out on to the streets alone at night would have been prostitutes. Wearing men's clothes was as good a method as any of avoiding being taken for a prostitute. It would also have given her some protection against the threat of attack by footpads – eighteenth-century muggers.

Today there is still a belief that an actor has more chance of obtaining a part if he goes to the interview in something resembling the costume of the character he is reading for. Mrs Charke's chances would certainly have been enhanced by her appearance at the theatre in costume, for in those days actors were usually expected to provide their own costumes. She admits this as a cause of her appearance in male dress on one occasion: 'I happening on that day to be in the male habit, on account of playing a part for a poor man, and obliged to find my own clothes (p.113).

For similar reasons, when times were hard, Mrs Charke would have been more likely to pawn her dress than her breeches, not only because a dress was a much more expensive item, but because her breeches were a tool of her trade, and, as there are many more acting parts for men, so it follows that there was more work available for her breeches than her dresses.

When her theatrical opportunities ran out, however, she was driven to earn a living by taking other, non-theatrical, work. But here, too, work opportunities for women were very limited compared to those available for men. Usual jobs for women included working as a maid, shop-keeping and tavern-keeping. Charlotte had a stab at the last two but would have us believe she had more generosity than business sense and, as a result, failed. However, it was not an inconsiderable achievement that both as a shop-keeper and tavern-keeper she was self-employed.

When she was driven to seek employment by others, she donned her breeches, In non-theatrical work it was not simply that there were again more jobs for men, but that those jobs were better paid and had more authority. But I believe she had a more profound reason for boasting of the work she undertook *en cavalier*.

She needed money. She had a child to support, and a husband and father who chose not to support her. Although she had had a good education there was little opportunity to use it, especially if she was to take the kind of jobs which would leave her free to return to her theatrical career if a part should come up. If she took a job as a chambermaid it would have been a humiliating comedown, an inescapable admission of failure (if only to herself); if she dressed as a man and took a job as a *valet de chambre* it was a triumph of her art. 'Acting' the role of *valet de chambre* would have been much less psychologically damaging, for the acting skill required provided a buffer that made the actual reality of the job like a joke, a trick, brilliantly performed by a consummate actress.

Another point that must be considered in an appraisal of Mrs Charke is her tendency to leave a story half told. We become used to the idea of her in male dress, and carry it on into the next episode, although external evidence indicates that she was no longer making any attempt to pass herself off as a man. For instance, the reader can easily infer that she ran her Drury Lane tavern as a man, but newspaper advertisements describe it as 'Mrs Charke's Steak and Soup House'. Similarly when she took the job of prompter for Simpson's company at Bath, the account books have her on the payroll as Mrs Charke.

Unfortunately Charlotte never attempted to give any direct explanation for her wearing of male dress, but she played right into the hands of her detractors by trying to draw a veil of mystery over the whole procedure. This also has provided her biographers with more words to interpret:

'My being in breeches was alleged to me as a very great *error* but the original motive proceeded from a *particular cause*; and I rather chose to undergo the worst imputation that can be laid on me on that account, than unravel the secret.' (p.102)

'Luckily, I met an old gentlewoman whom I had not seen many years, and who knew me when I was a child. She, perceiving sadness in my aspect enquired into the cause of that, and my being in men's clothes; which as far as I thought *proper*, I informed her.' (p.104)

Then, as now, the word 'proper' had many meanings, and in this context could have meant 'fit, apt, suitable; fitting, befitting; *esp.* appropriate to the circumstances or conditions; what it should be, or what is required' rather than the alternative 'becoming, decent, decorous, respectable, genteel, "correct"',[14] which is the interpretation most of her biographers have gone for.

It is only on the evidence of her cross-dressing and her use of words like 'proper' that contemporary historians can write, 'But even in her early years it was rather generally known that she was disreputable – if not indeed, sexually abnormal', and go so far as to call her *Narrative* 'A document in the history of sexual deviance', adding knowingly, 'The probability is that her sexual tastes were exclusively lesbian'.[15] L.R.N. Ashley in the Introduction to his edition of the *Narrative*, writes: 'by 1735 Charlotte had been fired by Fleetwood for recalcitrance and some kind of "immorality"'. Similar statements are to be found elsewhere: 'Fleetwood . . . who had fired her for immorality . . .';[16] 'She was intensely masculine and scorned all pursuits except hunting and shooting, spending most of her time in the company of the stable-boys';[17] 'Charlotte, whose tragedy was that she had failed to be born a man', and 'She felt that she, who had the mind and feelings of a man, had been cheated in being born a woman'.[18]

These writers ignore Charlotte's frequent declarations that her book was intended to be moral: 'As morality is the principal foundation of the work, I venture to recommend it to the perusal of the youthful of both sexes, as each will find a character worthy their observation, and I hope won't blush to make their example' (p.119); 'I have paid all due regard to decency wherever I have introduced the passion of love; and have only suffered it to take its course in its proper and necessary time, without fulsomely inflaming the minds of my young readers, or shamefully offending those of riper years; and here she takes the time to let us know what she thinks of writers who don't obey these rules of decency, 'a fault I have often condemned, when I was myself but a girl, in some female poets. I shall not descant on their imprudence, only wish that their works had been less confined to that theme, which too often led them into errors, reason and modesty equally forbid.' (p.3).

Whenever her reason and modesty have short lapses there is a strong financial reason behind it: surely she dragged in the episode in which Mrs Dorr's niece fell in love with her (out of its chronological place) because the earlier instalment (concerning another young lady who had been in love with her) had sold well on the bookstalls. In the mid eighteenth century nothing was so popular with the reading public as a little soft pornography parading itself as a moral tale. Samuel Richardson's *Pamela* is perhaps the best known example.

In telling her own story (and attempting to write a best-seller at the same time) Mrs Charke introduces slightly titillating tales while protesting her own innocence:

'In the interim somebody happened to come who hinted that I was a woman. Upon which, Madam, to my great surprise, attacked me with insolently presuming to say she was in love with me, which I assured her I never had the least conception of. "No truly, I believe", said she, "I should hardly be enamoured with one of my own sect!" Upon which I burst into a laugh, and took the liberty to ask her if she had understood what she had said. This threw the offended fair into such an absolute rage, and our controversy lasted for some time, but in the end I brought, in vindication of my own character, the maid to disgrace, who had, uncalled-for, trumped up so ridiculous a story. (p.113)

The point of this anecdote, far from demonstrating the miseries of a frustrated lesbian, is surely to prove yet again how impeccable her acting was, but she also shows how ridiculous she thought the girl she had duped. She is not ashamed of introducing these tales, is obviously amused at the girl's mistakes in semantics, and is clearly proud of her own performance. Further, the story of her near-engagement to the heiress is strictly a tale of 'I could have had her money', not 'I could have had her' and she talks of 'the poor lady's misfortune, in placing her affection on an improper object' (p.76).

Her other books, *The Lover's Treat*, *The Mercer*, and *Henry Dumont* are also essentially moral tales. *Henry Dumont* has a complicated plot, featuring Loveman, a homosexual and transvestite, to whom Mrs Charke is totally unsympathetic: 'no punishment was sufficiently severe for such unnatural monsters' (pp.58–68).

Despite this stern morality, Peter Ackroyd believes 'Charlotte Charke's own account suggests the presence of sexual or fetishistic elements in her dressing up.'[19]

Certainly Charlotte admits that she travelled with a woman companion, and that her companion went by the name of Mrs Brown, and although she felt herself 'bound in honour to ask her pardon, as I really was the author of many troubles from my inconsiderate folly, which nothing but a sincere friendship and an uncommon easiness of temper could have inspired her either to have brooked or to have forgiven' (p.150). She never even hints at anything more serious than her own selfishness.

Her faults and errors she declared were known to all. If she thought these faults had been of an active lesbian nature she would have been ill-advised to advertise them in a book, or she could have found herself before a magistrate, like the infamous 'female husband', who was tried by her old employer Henry Fielding (and reported in his book *The Female Husband*):

'At a quarter sessions of the peace, held at Taunton, Somersetshire, Mary Hamilton, otherwise Charles, otherwise George Hamilton, was tried for pretending herself a man, and marrying fourteen wives, the last of which, Mary Price, deposed in court that she was married to the prisoner, and bedded and lived as man and wife a quarter of a year, during which time she thought the prisoner was a man, owing to the prisoner's vile and deceitful practices. After a debate of the nature of the crime, and what to call it, it was agreed that she was an uncommon notorious cheat, and sentenced to be publicly whipped in Taunton, Glastonbury, and Shepton Mallet, to be imprisoned for six months, and to find security for her good behaviour for as long time as the justices at the next quarter sessions shall think fit.'

In her own, unwitting defence, Charlotte gives one tiny indication that when she was travelling with Mrs Brown, the two women slept separately, for she 'consulted my pillow what was best to be done. And communicated my thoughts to my friend' (p.158). If she had slept with her friend she needn't have wasted any time discussing the matter with the pillow first!

One thing that is invariably left out of the equation is the strength of women's friendship. Though companionship has always stood for a lot with women, there are no celebrated couples, no Davids and Jonathans, or Boswells and Johnsons. (Theatrical historians are frequently surprised that actresses leave each other bequests; indeed Charlotte's daughter Catherine left all her money to another actress.)

The sexologist, Havelock Ellis, investigated the case of Charlotte Charke, as presented in her *Narrative*, and came to the same conclusion as I have done: 'Charlotte Charke, a boyish and vivacious woman, who spent much of her life in men's clothes, and ultimately wrote a lively volume of memoirs, appears never to have been attracted to women, though women were often attracted to her, believing her to be a man; it is, indeed, noteworthy that women seem with special frequency, to fall in love with disguised persons of their own sex.'[20]

Unfortunately, contemporary reference works have not gone beyond the simple ambiguities of Mrs Charke's semantics, and have taken her frequent use of words like 'odd', 'unfortunate', 'folly', 'indiscretion' and 'misconduct' and inferred that these amounted to a public confession of 'sexual deviation'. But, in expounding such theories, the Charke biographers have to explain away her two marriages, and this they do with unanimous gusto (and no corroborative evidence):

Married at sixteen to Richard Charke, a violinist at Drury Lane, *in the hope of taming her* . . . [21]

It was hoped that her marriage while still a young girl to Richard Charke, a violinist of some note, *would help sooth her riotous nature* . . . [22]

Mrs Charke (having been married off while young to a flighty violinist . . . in *an optimistic but wholly futile attempt to settle her down*) . . . [23]

This is all very convincing until we remember that Charlotte married Richard Charke when she was only seventeen years old, and that she had, until that year, led a very sheltered life in the country with her mother.

The birth of her daughter has to be treated with a snide air of fun: 'By the time she was four Charlotte manifested a liking for male attire . . . after which she took time off to engage in the *exclusively feminine activity* of having a baby . . .' [24]

But there remains the even more puzzling second marriage: 'When she did act in a play, at one of the various booths or wells, she was announced for Lothario, Macheath, Marplot, or other male roles. [note] *Curiously enough*, she apparently remarried.' [25]

Here again the real mystery is left unexplored. Who was Charlotte's second husband, and what can explain her extraordinary descriptions of their relationship?

'I was addressed by a worthy gentleman (being then a widow) and closely pursued till I confessed to an honourable though very secret alliance, and, in compliance to the person, bound myself by all the vows sincerest friendship could inspire never to confess who he was. Gratitude was my motive to consent to this conjunction, and extreme fondness was his inducement to request it.' (p.48)

Whatever her motive, she married John Sacheverell of St Andrew's, Holborn at St George's, Hanover Square, a church which specialized in quick weddings.

Two weeks later she was proudly announcing herself 'Mrs Sacheverell, late Mrs Charke' in newspaper advertisements and playbills. Yet nine years later in her *Narrative* she was being very precious about giving her second marital surname: 'not even the most inexplicable sorrows I was immersed in ever did, nor shall any motive whatever, make me break that vow I made to the person by a discovery of his name' (p.48). My instinctive conclusion is that no such vow was ever made, but that in this marriage lay some unpleasant mystery which Mrs Charke wanted to forget, and was determined not to jog anyone's memory with a mention of her late husband's name.

Six weeks after the wedding she dropped out of the show she was appearing in (after a four-week run), although the show itself did not close. She was still in London a few weeks later when she visited the Fleet prison and discovered the dead body of her friend John Russell. After this she donned her alias, Mr Brown, and left London for the West of England (six days' journey) and stayed at a similar distance from London for nine years. These strange circumstances indicate that she was (like Fanny, the woman who donned male clothing and became a tramp rather than risk being arrested for her part in the Gordon riots) seeking anonymity after an unpleasant experience.

Two questions are posed: who was John Sacheverell, and what did he do to make his wife proud enough to bear his name in 1746 and desperate to keep it a secret by 1755? There are innumerable possibilities, and we shall probably never know the truth.

It is possible that he was an impostor. Maybe, as he declared himself Sacheverell of St Andrew's, Holborn, he wished to associate himself with the family of the famous and wealthy Dr Sacheverell of St Andrew's, Holborn (who had been the centre of a religio-political scandal at the beginning of the century). Perhaps he actually was related to Dr Sacheverell. Either way, he could have hinted that he was wealthy, and married Charlotte assuming that (as the daughter of one of the richest commoners in England) *she* was loaded with money. An amusing case of two people marrying each other for money that neither had. If Charlotte had (as would have been likely) boasted that she was marrying a rich man, it would explain why, on her husband's death, a woman assumed Charlotte would now come into a fortune.

Maybe Sacheverell was (as were many men in eighteenth-century England) a bigamist, and, rather than allowing herself to be involved in any scandal, Charlotte got out of town quick.

Whatever, this episode in Mrs Charke's life does seem to present the most challenging puzzle, and if she was involved in any scandal, I believe it would be found in this marriage.

*

Her exodus from London and with it the chance of any really decent work, must also be seen in its place in the continual downward slide of her career, and in light of the theatrical conditions of the mid century.

Charlotte Charke made her début when London's theatre was on the brink of turbulent upheaval. During the 1730s Drury Lane was undergoing a frequent turnover of managers (caused in no small part by Charlotte's father's disposal of his share in the royal patent). The new patent-holders were businessmen rather than men of the theatre. For them the demands of their job were biased towards policies which would cram in as many audience members (charging them as much money as they would pay), while spending as little as possible on actors' salaries and production budgets. Consequently, artistic standards fell.

Charlotte was not afraid of letting her voice be heard in opposition to these artistic policies (unlike some other players, for instance, Kitty Clive, who preferred to stay in with the managers and thereby improve her own position, while standards around her tumbled).

After being sacked by Drury Lane as part of a programme of backstage cost cutting, Mrs Charke aired her personal and critical grievances in a play, *The Art of Management*, which looked forward with dread to a theatre in which 'nonsense, noise and spangles shall prevail'.[26] On her apology and reinstatement with the company, she was not given any promotion, but, rather, a steady stream of dull supporting roles. She spent her summers fruitfully, though, presenting amusing and anarchic seasons of classical and stock plays.

Then Henry Fielding appeared on the scene. He had already quarrelled with Charlotte's father, and was the personification of a new theatrical order. He was attracted to young untarnished actors, those whose work was not tainted with 'Cibberisms' or the affected mannerisms of the established theatre. His acting company included the writer Eliza Haywood (who provided him with some adaptations). Alongside his own satirical comedies he presented plays of a new style; plays which point towards the nineteenth-century problem play and Shavian comedy. His theatre was political, ideological, intelligent and youthful. More importantly, it proved a popular theatre. Without stooping to present the harlequinades and variety turns so popular with the patent houses, he managed to fill his theatre and attracted attention from some very important people: the Duchess of Marlborough, the Prince of Wales, the Earl of Egmont, the English royal princesses, and eventually, of course, leading members of the English cabinet.

But it was his success which put an end to his own career in the theatre, and with it the careers of all like-minded playwrights and actors. Walpole's fear of Fielding's theatrical productions was encouraged by the managers of the patent houses, who were jealous of his success, and who were frightened of losing their audience to him. The result was the Stage Licensing Act of 1737.

After the passing of this Act actors had to align themselves with a patent house or remain unemployed. Charlotte Charke had already made such a stand that she had burned her boats. Henry Fielding was in a similar position, and, wisely, retired from the theatre altogether.

Accounts of Charlotte's life imply that because she was a failure she went into trade; the truth was that the theatre had failed her. (Who will say Fielding gave up playwriting because he was a failure?)

After a short spell out of the theatre, Mrs Charke became one of the most active opponents and evaders of the 1737 Act. First she employed her puppets. But, unlike other puppeteers of the time, she did not play harlequinades, but kept up a repertoire of classical drama, and plays from her seasons with Fielding. She also had her puppets cut to resemble famous figures of the day, and thereby created a political puppet theatre, a puppet theatre of ideas. It was a revolution in puppetry, as well as providing her with some decent work at a time when most of her colleagues were forced into retirement. In this her career was developing in a direct and positive line from the work she had done with Fielding.

Due to illness, bad luck and lack of cash, she was, by the mid-1740s, driven back, exhausted, to aspirations of being accepted by the legitimate theatre, By this time it was clear that the Act was there to stay. Evading it needed a lot of effort and provided very little reward, sometimes none at all. But Mrs Charke had been out of the system too long to understand that the style of classical acting had changed.

In her brother's 1744 season she attempted to play in the style of the old bastion of legitimate theatre, Colley Cibber. Presumably this on-stage salute to her father's method was an attempt to reconcile herself with him. He was sure to be in the audience, if only to see his little grand-daughter Jenny. In fact, his only action arising from the season was to forbid Jenny to take part in her aunt Charke's production of *Pope Joan*. Charlotte Charke had, for no gain, compromised her own style, and disgraced herself in the presence of the new theatrical trend-setter, David Garrick.

Garrick had obviously seen her earlier work, or heard enough about it to expect more of her, for he was 'shocked' at her affectation and her Cibberisms.

Almost two years after this unfortunate season, Mrs Charke made her second marriage and then spent her nine years strolling. By the time of her return in 1755 she had done an artistic turn-about, and supported the 'nonsense, noise and spangles' she had decried twenty years earlier.

London theatre was split down the middle by the 1750s. There was a very serious tragi-classical theatre led by Garrick, and an extremely light comic alternative which featured such oddities as hydrostatics, dancing fountains, the Matchless Learned French Dog ('Le Chien Savant'), the learned pig, dwarfs, giants and fire-eaters.

For the last years of her life, Mrs Charke aligned herself with the light theatre. She did manage to hang on to fragments of her old satirical style. She played with Mrs Midnight, for instance, who, while employing the methods of variety theatre, managed to send the whole thing up.

Charlotte Charke's theatrical work did not make her a star, but her lifelong fight with the Licensing Act was a real achievement, and her methods are still in use today.

Unfortunately much more attention is paid to her time strolling than her work in London, and consequent word association (derived from the Queen Anne statute declaring actors rogues and vagabonds) has again worked to the detriment of her character: The nineteenth-century notion that she suffered from a '*constitutional tendency towards vagabondism*, discernible in mere childhood, and resisting, as years increased, all the restraints of education and reason'[27] had developed, by the 1920s, to the opinion that people like Charlotte Charke 'afford interesting matter for study to the observer of human nature aware that such eerie mortals as she was constrained, by a *natural and perverse predisposition towards vagabondising, to careers more wildly bizarre than the conceptions of an opium-smoker or a Bedlamite*'.[28] By 1968 she was accused of what would have been in the eighteenth century a very serious crime: 'In one of her wanderings, picking up jobs at fairs and *laundry from hedgerows.*'[29]

These accusations are made despite her own statement, based on her own miserable experiences, that she would 'never advise or encourage any persons to make themselves voluntary vagabonds, for such, not only the laws, but the opinion of every reasonable person, deems those itinerant gentry, who are daily guilty of the massacre of dramatic poetry' (p.175).

Similar moralizing and misunderstanding has led to some extraordinary and baseless descriptions and some remarkable imaginative leaps:

'She was brought up to the stage, but rarely an ornament to it . . . her behaviour and character were so unpredictable and irresponsible that she was *unable to hold any engagement for any length of time*.'[30]

'After being *disowned by her family as an "alien"*.'[31]

'When she rented a house in Drury Lane and attempted to take in boarders, it turned out to be a *notorious brothel* . . . '

' . . .Gladly she read them her manuscript of Henry Dumont probably in a *voice as croaking as that of the magpie* and much affected by years of busking and *raw gin*; . . . she was to appear in male dress or *undress* as Mercury.'[32]

'It would have been hard to find a less suitable person to raise these little girls than Charlotte, who had matured into a *bellicose and dissolute woman* who supported herself in various *unsavory theatrical enterprises*, dressed in men's clothes, and *strutted and brawled like a caricature of her brother*, who was in turn a caricature of their father.'[33]

The foundation for all these accounts is the *Narrative*. Unfortunately, I wonder whether the authors of the reference books and biographies have strayed from the truth for so long that their version has become in itself another 'truth'. Maybe Charlotte Charke's reputation is as unsavable as Nell Gwyn's, Boadicea's, Lady Macbeth's and Richard III's. These four have passed from history into folklore and legend, and probably in the popular imagination they will always be stuck with their image. But historians know better. Charlotte Charke has not passed into folklore, but, for her, the historians are the ones who have created a mythical virago and who keep the snowball rolling. Charlotte, with unconscious foresight, declared 'It is certain, there never was known a more unfortunate devil than I have been' (p.46).

But a description in another account of the strolling life (published almost fifty years after Mrs Charke's death) hits the mark, and although not actually describing Mrs Charke, expresses what I believe to be the truth behind her life:

'We players are a set of merry, undone dogs, and though we often want the means of life, we are seldom without the means of mirth. We are philosophers and laugh at misfortune; even the ridiculous situations we are sometimes placed in, are more generally the cause of mirth than misery.'[34]

At the opening of the *Narrative* Charlotte claimed to 'tremble for the terrible hazard it must run in venturing into the world, as it may very possibly suffer, in many opinions, without perusing it' (p.3). Sadly she was right to worry, for Charlotte Charke, 'one of those reckless and anomalous individuals whose existence forms part of the romance of *real* life',[35] unwittingly set herself up as a perfect foil by which her father's biographers could, at the expense of her good character, win sympathy for him, when all she had intended to do was to earn a little money from the public, and by employing 'her utmost endeavours to entertain them' (p.4).

1 Arthur H. Scouten, *The London Stage 1729–47*, 1968, p. iii; W. McQueen Pope, *Theatre Royal, Drury Lane*, p. 163; Robert Gore-Brown, *Gay Was the Pit*, p. 183.
2 George Speaight, *The History of the English Puppet Theatre*, 1955, pp. 107–8
3 R. H. Barker, *Mr Cibber of Drury Lane*, p. 19; *Dictionary of National Biography*.
4 Quoted in W. Clark Russell, *Representative Actors*.
5 Charles D. Peavy, 'The Chimerical Career of Charlotte Charke', in *Restoration and Eighteenth-Century Theatre Research*, VIII, May 1969.
6 P. Highfill, *Biographical Dictionary*, III, p. 239
7 Dr Doran, *Their Majesties' Servants*, ch. XXIX.
8 Hurst, *Biography of Female Character*, 1803.
9 L. R. B. Ashley, Introduction to facsimile reprint of *Narrative*, 1968.
10 Baker, Reed, Jones, *Biographia Dramatica*, p. 103.
11 *Diary*, 2 March 1667.
12 Jocelyn Powell, *Restoration Theatre Production*, p. 105.
13 Powell, ibid., p. 72.
14 *Oxford English Dictionary*.
15 R. H. Barker, *Mr Cibber of Drury Lane*, p. 178; *Everyman Companion to the Theatre*, ed. Peter Thomson and Gamini Salgado, 1987.
16 L. R. N. Ashley, *Colley Cibber*, p. 157.
17 Phillis Hartnoll, *Oxford Companion to the Theatre*, third edition, p. 178.

18 W. McQueen Pope, *Ladies First*, 1953, pp. 241, 247.
19 *Dressing Up*, 1979, p. 76.
20 *Studies in the Psychology of Sex*, vol. 1, pt 4, p. 245.
21 Phillis Hartnoll, *Oxford Companion to the Theatre*, third edition, p. 178.
22 Charles D. Peavy (previously cited article).
23 L. R. N. Ashley, Introduction to facsimile edition of the *Narrative*, 1968.
24 P. Highfill, *Biographical Dictionary*, p. 167.
25 Arthur H. Scouten, *The London Stage 1729–47*, CXXXII.
26 *The Art of Management*, p. 17.
27 Introduction to Hunt and Clarke's edition of the *Narrative*, 1825: 'The Most Instructive and Amusing Lives Ever Published'.
28 F. Dorothy Senior, *The Life and Times of Colley Cibber*, 1928, p. 63.
29 L. R. N. Ashley, Introduction to *Narrative*, 1968
30 *The Europa Biographical Dictionary of British Women*, 1983
31 Peter Ackroyd, *Dressing Up*.
32 L. R. N. Ashley, Introduction to *Narrative*, 1968
33 Mary Nash, *The Provok'd Wife*, 1977, p. 123.
34 S. W. Ryley, *The Itinerant*, 1808.
35 Introduction to Hunt and Clarke's edition of the *Narrative*, 1825.

Chronology

Note: new information or dates discovered by the author are shown in **bold** type.

1712		Last witchcraft execution in England
1713	Born 13 January; christened 8 February; parents' twentieth wedding anniversary 6 May; Aunt Rose Shore dies August	Treaty of Utrecht ends war of Spanish succession
1714		Queen Anne dies; George I succeeds; Centlivre's *The Wonder*; Rowe's *Jane Shore*
1715		Jacobite rebellion. Rowe becomes Poet Laureate; Wycherley dies
1716	Sister Catherine 21 in December	
1717		David Garrick born
1718	Aged 5; Colley Cibber and Drury Lane company at Hampton Court September	Death of Rowe
1719	Letter to original weekly journal states daughter 'very bare in clothes'	Defoe's *Robinson Crusoe*
1720	Sister Catherine marries Colonel Brown February; sister Anne 21 in October	South Sea Bubble
1721	Sister Elizabeth 21 in March	Walpole becomes first prime minister
1722		Steele's *The Conscious Lovers*
1723		Death of Mrs Centlivre
1724	Aged 11; Brother Theophilus 21 in November; **stay with Dr Hales**	
1725	**Still with Dr Hales**	
1726	**Dr Hales wife dies; Charlotte returns to mother**	Death of Vanbrugh; Swift's *Gulliver's Travels*
1727		Death of George I; Accession of George II
1728		Pope's *Dunciad*; Gay's *The Beggar's Opera*
1729		Death of Congreve
1730	Aged 17; marries Richard Charke in February; two performances as Mademoiselle in *The Provok'd Wife*	Goldsmith born; Wesley founded Methodist group; start of agrarian revolution

1730	April; father made Poet Laureate; daughter Catherine born December
1731	Performances with Drury Lane company January, February, April–December
1732	Performances with Drury Lane company February–December and Bartholomew fair August
1733	Aged 20; few roles at Drury Lane January–May; father sells share in patent – results in actors' barricade and mutiny in May; performs Haymarket October–December
1734	Aged 21; her mother dies January; acting at Haymarket January–February and Drury Lane February–March; brother marries Susannah Arne April; own company plays 'mad' season at Haymarket May–August; acts Drury Lane September–November
1735	Acts Drury Lane January–February, April–May; **takes over as Cleopatra in May;** acts Lincoln's Inn Fields June–November; puts on *The Art of Management* at York Buildings September–October; acts Drury Lane November–December
1736	Joins Fielding's 'Mogul's Company' March–June: Bartholomew Fair August; Southwark Fair September; acts Lincoln's Inn Fields October–December; ?Richard Charke leaves for Jamaica?
1737	Aged 24; acts Lincoln's Inn Fields January–February; acts Fielding's Haymarket company March–May; ?worked for Mrs Dorr at Marylebone?
1738	?Maybe ran oil shop now?; manages puppet show at James Street tennis court March–May; sister Elizabeth's husband Brett dies November; niece Anne marries Chetwood; brother involved in Sloper scandal
1739	?Trip to Tunbridge Wells?

Right column events:

- 1731 — Death of Defoe; Lillo's *London Merchant*; Fielding's *Grub Street Opera*; 10 Downing Street built
- 1732 — Death of Gay
- 1737 — THE STAGE LICENSING ACT
- 1739 — Death of Lillo; war with Spain

1740	Father's *Apology* published	War of Austrian succession begins; Richardson's *Pamela*
1741	Aged 28; **takes over as Plume in** *Recruiting Officer*, **James Street tennis court September**; ?taken by bailiffs, but bailed out before imprisonment for debt?; ?*valet de chambre* to Lord Anglesey	Garrick's first performances; Fielding's *Shamela*; Handel's *Messiah*
1742	?Acts New Wells summer?; Bartholomew Fair August; plays James Street November	Walpole resigns from office; Fielding's *Joseph Andrews*; centigrade thermometer invented
1743	Aged 30; plays? and puppets James Street, including her own *Tit for Tat* February–March	Cibber becomes central dunce in Pope's revised *Dunciad*
1744	Running steak and soup house at **Princes Court**; benefit under concert formula James Street March; plays May Fair May; uses licence evasion tactic – entrance by pint of ale; acts in brother's company Haymarket September–November; her own Queen of Hungary's Company Haymarket December;	Death of Pope
1745	Pope Joan performance advertised for Haymarket in March; joins Hallam's company at Goodman's Fields November; ?works puppets for John Russell?	Jacobite rebellion; death of Swift
1746	**Russell imprisoned January; plays in** *Recruiting Officer*, **with her own prologue, benefit Scudamore, April**; marries John Sacheverell May; plays New Wells May–June; **Russell dies July**; ?leaves London for nine years provincial work?	Battle of Culloden
1747	?Acts with Linnets?	Garrick goes into management at Drury Lane
1748	?Acts with Linnets?	End of War of Austrian Succession
1749	In Chippenham with Linnets February; ?acts with Elringtons?	Handel's music for Royal Fireworks; Fielding's *Tom Jones*
1750	Aged 37; daughter marries John Harman January; manages Elringtons' company while they play in London	
1751	Manages Elringtons' company while Mr E acts in Bath November	Gin act passed; Sheridan born
1752	?Takes house in Chepstow? ?short stay at Pill?; Uncle John Shore dies	Gregorian calendar adopted in Britain

1752	November; Betty Careless dies April; **working for Ward on** *The Bristol Weekly Intelligencer*	
1753	Aged 40; Prompter at Bath September–December	Mrs Inchbald born
1754	Prompter at Bath January; tours with small troupes; returns to London December	Death of Fielding
1755	First weekly part of *Narrative* published April; *Henry Dumont* published; acts with brother's company at Haymarket September	Johnson's *Dictionary*
1756	*The Mercer* published; her company plays at Bartholomew Fair September; acts with brother's academy at Richmond September	Black hole of Calcutta; Seven Years War begins
1757	Her father dies December	Blake born
1758	Aged 45; published *The Lover's Treat*; plays in Kent August–October; daughter leaves for America; brother and friends drowned *en route* to Dublin October	Halley's comet
1759	Applies for licence August; plays a week at Haymarket September	
1760	Aged 47; dies April	George II dies; George III succeeds

Further reading

Ackroyd, Peter, *Dressing Up*, 1979
Ashley, L. R. N., *Colley Cibber*, 1965
– Facsimile reprint of Charke's *Narrative*, 1968
Baker, Reed and Jones, *Biographica Dramatica*, 1812
Barker, Richard Hindrey, *Mr Cibber of Drury Lane*, 1939
Burney Newspaper Collection
Charke, Charlotte, *A Narrative of the Life of Mrs Charlotte Charke*, 1755
– *The Art of Management; or, Tragedy Expell'd*, 1753
– *The History of Henry Dumont Esq; and Miss Charlotte Evelyn*, 1756
– *The Lover's Treat; or, Unnatural Hatred*, 1758
– *The Mercer; or, Fatal Extravagance*, 1758
Cibber, Colley, *An Apology for the Life of Colley Cibber*, 1740
– Dramatic Works
Dictionary of National Biography
Ellis, Havelock, *Studies in the Psychology of Sex*, 1942
Europa Biographical Dictionary of British Women, 1983
Everyman Companion to the Theatre, ed. Peter Thomson and Gamini Salgado, 1987
Fielding, Henry, *Complete Works;* 1967
Fiske, Roger, *English Theatre Music in the Eighteenth Century* 1973
G. E. C., *The Complete Peerage*, 1982
Garrick, David, Dramatic Works
– *Letters*, ed. David M. Little and George M. Kahrl, 1963
Gentleman's Magazine
George, M. Dorothy, *London Life in the Eighteenth Century*, 1925
Grove, Sir George, *Dictionary of Music and Musicians*, 1981
Hartnoll, Phillis, *Oxford Companion to the Theatre*, 3rd edn, 1967
Highfill, Philip H. Jr. *et al.*, *Biographical Dictionary of Actors, Actresses, etc. 1660–1800*, 1971–
Hill, Aaron, *The Prompter*
Hogarth, William; *Complete Engravings*, 1981
Jarrett, Derek, *England in the Age of Hogarth*, 1974
Lillo, George, Dramatic Works
McQueen Pope, W., *Ladies First*, 1952
– *Theatre Royal, Drury Lane*, 1945
Nash, Mary, *The Provok'd Wife*, 1977
North, Roger, *On Music*, ed. John Wilson, 1959
Parish registers and rates books

Peavy, Charles D, 'The Chimerical Career of Charlotte Charke', in *Restoration and Eighteenth-century Theatre Research*, VIII, May 1969, p. 1–12

Plumb, J. H. *England in the Eighteenth Century*, 1969

Porter, Roy, *English Society in the Eighteenth Century*, 1982

Powell, Jocelyn, *Restoration Theatre Production*, 1984

Rosenfeld, Sybil, *Strolling Players and Drama in the Provinces 1660–1775*, 1939

– *Theatre of the London Fairs*, 1960

Rowe, Nicholas, Dramatic Works

Scouten, Arthur H., *The London Stage 1729–1747*, 1968

Senior, F. Dorothy, *The Life and Times of Colley Cibber*, 1928

Speaight, George, *The History of The English Puppet Theatre*, 1955

Strange, Sally Minter, 'Charlotte Charke: Transvestite or Conjuror?', in *Restoration and Eighteenth-century Theatre Research*, XV, No. 2. November 1976, p. 54–60

Survey of London

Vanbrugh, John, Dramatic Works

Victoria History of the Counties of England,

Water, Ivor, *The Unfortunate Valentine Morris*, 1964

THE PLATES

householder), and to his left, Mary Heron (the actress who broke her knee-pans, and whose mother stayed with the Cibbers when Charlotte was a child). A monkey on a tightrope carries Highmore's motto 'I am a gentleman'. On the right stand Highmore and his group: Highmore himself clutches a bill 'it cost £6000' (£2500 paid to Barton Booth for his share, 3000 guineas to Colley Cibber for his). Beside him is the painter John Ellys, who had bought half of Mary Wilks' share. Behind them the two female shareholders, Mary Wilks and Hester Booth, widows of the actors Robert Wilks and Barton Booth. (Or possibly it is Wilks' widow and their daughter). One of the women waves a banner 'We'll starve 'em out'.

In the corner, wearing the bays of poet laureate and counting his money, sits Charlotte's and Theophilus's father, Colley Cibber. At the start of the rumpus following the sale of Cibber senior's share, a letter appeared in the St James's *Evening Post* which explained the 'reason which he gave for such conduct was, that he might make a proportionable division of what fortune he may happen to have among all his children.' The true outcome was that two of them – Theophilus and Charlotte – were put out of work and in all probability never saw a penny of that 3000 guineas.

PLATE IV

Southwark Fair

Hogarth's 1733 engraving depicts that year's events at Southwark Fair. The fair was held annually in the first week of September, shortly after Bartholomew Fair, and featured much the same programme.

Theophilus Cibber's production of Nicholas Rowe's *Tamerlane; or, the Fall of Bajazeth* was announced in the *Daily Post* during the Bartholomew Fair:

A booth is building in Smithfield for the use of Mr Cibber, Mr Griffin, Mr Bullock, and Mr H. Hallam, where they are to perform the tragedy of Tamerlane, with the fall of Bajazet; intermix'd with the comedy of the Miser; the entertainment is to conclude with the Ridotto al Fresco. The scenes, habits, and all the decorations, are very magnificent, and entirely new; the boxes are to be gilt, and adorn'd in the handsomest manner, for the reception of the quality, and the whole will be illuminated with a number of glass lusters.

The cast at Bartholomew Fair was:
TAMERLANE   Adam Hallam
BAJAZETH   Theophilus Cibber
AXALLA   Mr Cross
OMAR   Mr Berry
DERVICE   William Hallam
MIRVAN   Henry Tench
HALY   Mrs Charlotte Charke
SELIMA   Mrs Grace

and probably remained the same for the Southwark showing.

Hogarth's illustration shows many relevant details: the banner in the top left corner is taken from Laguerre's engraving *The Stage Mutiny* (adding a comment beneath Colley Cibber – 'quiet & snug'). The poster on the tumbling left-hand booth reads 'Ciber and Bullock – The Fall of Bajazet'. Mary Heron, in the middle of the crowd, is beating a drum for the Cibber company. Behind her, being approached by bailiffs, is a person in a feathered helmet. This character also appears in the Laguerre print, lurking behind Mrs Heron and Theophilus.

I suggest that this figure is a caricature of Charlotte Charke. She was one of the leaders of the stage mutiny, and apart from this would have been a suitable candidate for inclusion in Laguerre's and Hogarth's print if only because she was a Cibber. (The mutiny was notorious because it split not only a theatre company, but also the Cibber family.) By the time of Hogarth's *Southwark Fair*, Charlotte had established herself in a few male roles, and indeed her role at Bartholomew Fair, (and therefore Southwark) was a man – Haly. The costume seems exaggerated compared to other similar ones in the same scene, and would certainly appear to include enough of the necessary theatricality of the costume of a woman playing a man's role. The helmet, too, is a little over-feathered; Charlotte was later easily recognizable by her own 'handsome laced hat'. The poor gentleman is also undergoing the public humiliation of being caught by the bailiffs, something Charlotte was to spend the whole of her life trying to avoid.

Hogarth's Morning (1783)

The lady with fan to mouth and lappets flying in the wind is thought to be Charlotte's friend Mrs Betty Careless, followed by her link-boy, Little Cazey.

She features, in name only, in another Hogarth engraving, for scratched on the banisters in Hogarth's plate VIII, 'Bedlam', in *The Rake's Progress*, is the name 'charming Betty Careless'. This print has another link with Charlotte as two of the figures in it are based on *Melancholy* and *Raving Madness*, sculptures by her grandfather Caius Gabriel Cibber.

PLATE I

PLATE II

PLATE III

PLATE IV

PLATE V

Index